THE NERD AND THE BULLY

TIFFANY RANSIER

INDIGO HEARTS PRESS LLC

Ebook ISBN: 978-1-949079-19-7

Paperback ISBN: 978-1-949079-26-5

Hardback ISBN: 978-1-949079-27-2

Published by: Indigo Hearts Press LLC

Editing: Pretty Little Book Editing

Cover design: Indigo Hearts Designs

For anyone who thinks it's too late.
It never is.

BLURB AND WARNING

Please be advised that this story is a dark romance with triggers including dubious/non consent and the use of drugs. If you believe this book isn't for you, please don't read it.

I'm a nerd, former orphan, and plus-sized nobody.

All of that changed when Collette Goldsworthy decided I was somebody she needed. Because of her, I have people in my life I can count on.
I can't say the same for my aunt, the woman who raised me after my parents went missing years ago.
Her words have torn me down over the years, but this time she's done something worse. She sold my parent's house along with everything inside it to pay off her debt and there was nothing I could do about it besides buy it back.
Except I'm just as poor as she is.
Any of my friends could've easily bought it, and they offered to, but before they got the chance to, Noel Hardington, Callan's rich playboy best friend does.

Now I owe him and there's only one thing he wants…

Me.

The only girl who's ever told him no.

To get my parent's house back, he's only taking two forms of repayment, working in the place that ruined my life or my body.

But he doesn't remember the dark secrets of our childhood and he doesn't remember me.

He'll come to find out that some things are better left buried.

CONTENTS

PROLOGUE

Eight Years Ago

Gemma

I n the dark, everything seems to vanish.
I can't see a thing. Not my hands, not my feet, and
certainly nothing in front of me.

It's like an endless black hole swallowing me whole.

At home, the dark is nothing like this. It's always accompanied by the light.

There's still the smallest amount of light that streams beneath my door from the hallway light, or the moonlight peeking through the blinds in my room.

Even the tiny amounts of light coming from the digital

clock on my nightstand and the glow in the dark star stickers on my ceiling.

But this, this is different.

If I try hard enough, I can imagine that I'm not stuck in the dark.

That I'm out on the street, walking under the bright sun with my parents. That I'm at school under the relentless fluorescent lights.

I can't allow myself to be afraid, because he's plenty afraid for both of us.

If only there was light coming under the door from the room outside. They aren't nice enough to do that, no. And especially not when something is supposed to be a punishment.

His deep sobs fill the air and I reach my hand out, abruptly reaching his shoulder and letting my hand rest there.

"It's going to be okay," I soothe.

"No, Jewel, it's not. They're really angry at me this time."

"Close your eyes and pretend to be somewhere else. Somewhere warm and bright."

"I can't," he cries. "Do you know how many times I've tried? I did my best, but it's never enough for them. How are you so okay with this? With being here?"

I circle my hand on his shoulder. My parents do this for me when I'm upset and it helps me feel better. I hope this has the same effect for him.

"Because I came of my own free will. For you. It's my fault isn't it?"

His crying stops and he hiccups. "You can't blame yourself. But...thank you for being here with me. You're the best, Jewel. Don't tell anyone, but sometimes I prefer your company to Callan and Vincent's. I don't think they'd understand." He sighs heavily and goes quiet. "I can barely breathe. I just want to leave."

"I know. I want to leave too. Breathe slowly and close your eyes." I pull my hand away and let it rest on my leg.

"I can't," his voice shakes and I sigh.

If only it was as easy for him as it is for me. Maybe if I had gone through this as many times as him, it wouldn't be so easy. I feel so bad for him.

Stretching my hand out, I find his hands covering his face and take the one closest to me. I place his hand on top of my nose and mouth, breathing slowly to show him how.

"In and out, just like me. Slow and steady. Picture yourself outside. You're having a good time with your other friends. Outside in the sunshine."

His hand shakes on top of my face, until it slows to a stop.

"I'm having a good time outside in the sunshine," he murmurs.

"You're laughing and nothing is wrong."

"Nothing is wrong," he whispers. "Except you aren't there."

"Then I'm there too," I tell him in a soft tone, lifting his hand off my face and holding it in mine.

He whispers something too soft for me to hear and his hand goes slack.

I wait, holding my breath as I hear the sounds of steady breathing that happen only when someone has fallen asleep.

"Sweet dreams, Noel."

And just like that, I'm alone in the dark, facing the door and hoping it'll open in the next few hours.

But how would I know how much time passes when there's no way to tell?

There's no clock on a night stand with an alarm set to go off.

There's nothing in this dark closet.

CHAPTER ONE

The Night Before Orientation

Gemma

The day is almost over. Tomorrow, is the day I get to see it. Everything I've worked so hard for.

I was lucky enough to win a scholarship to SGU. It's incredibly rare and hard to get.

It's the college both of my parents dreamed about attending at my age. Neither of them were able to win scholarships so they couldn't go. They ended up at a CSU and then at UC for their masters.

Ever since they told me it was their dream, I made it my goal to go there. It hurts that they won't be here to see it coming to fruition.

For so many students it's the dream to be among the rich and elite. To make friends with them and be a part of their world.

But that's not why I want to attend SGU. What a lot of people seem to overlook is the excellent staff and classes.

SGU is ranked number two in the best colleges in California to go to. Not the best, but close enough. Someday, I'm sure it'll steal the number one spot from Stanford.

I pull my hair into a ponytail and arrange the orientation papers together in a neat stack. Organization is everything and I want to make sure I'm fully prepared for tomorrow.

A loud ding-dong echoes through the house. Lifting my head up, I sigh heavily. I hate being interrupted when there's stuff to do.

"Get off your ass and get the door, Gemma!" Aunt Cindy yells through the other side of the closed door.

I push my glasses up the bridge of my nose. Ridiculous. She's closer to the door, she should get it.

Pulling the door open, I stomp down the hall to the living room and turn to the front door. When I reach it, I peek through the peephole just in time to watch a girl with huge round glasses and a ballerina outfit knock.

"The door, Gemma. Get the door!" Aunt Cindy yells.

"I got it," I mutter.

Unlocking it quickly, I pull it open and ask, "Can I help you?"

She smiles smoothly. "Hi. Do I look familiar to you?"

"Honestly, no," I say bluntly.

She frowns. "Well, I'm Collette Goldsworthy, but you can call me Coll. My dad is the Dean."

Goldsworthy as in Southern Goldsworthy University? I know the Dean is Antoure Goldsworthy, youngest son of the founder of all three Goldsworthy Universities. I never cared enough to find out about his family.

But what's she doing here at my house?

My eyes widen and she laughs. "Yes, that's the look I was hoping to get when you opened the door, but whatever. I think we should be friends, Gemma."

"Why me?"

She tilts her glasses down and looks me up and down. "I need a treasurer for my sorority and I think you'd be perfect." She pushes the sunglasses back on her face. "There's a lot of backstabbing bitches around, you know? Money is important and I need someone capable of handling the job. So, how about it?"

"Absolutely," I breathe. This is the opportunity of a lifetime. Of course, I was hoping I'd be able to get into a sorority, but to have it handed to me on a silver, no, gold platter like this. This is insane. How could I even think of turning it down?

"Awesome. My two best friends Ashlynn and Luella are also helping me with Zeta Delta Beta. You can meet them tomorrow. Still looking for our advisor, but hopefully I'll find her by the first day. I'll come pick you up tomorrow at seven so be ready."

My throat tightens at the mention of her friends Ashlynn and Luella. Collette might be fine with me, but what about them? Ever since I started gaining weight, friends have always been harder to make. In fact, the last time I had a really good friend was...

I nod. "Thank you. I'll be ready and waiting."

Collette swivels around with a satisfied smile and takes off down the overgrown path from the door to the driveway.

"Who was that?" A voice snottily asks behind me as I close the door.

I turn around, facing my aunt with as neutral a face as I can manage. "Just someone from the college."

"You sounded awfully happy," she says, narrowing her eyes.

As if me being happy bothers her so much. "I was invited to join a sorority." I need to downplay my role as much as possible and hope that she'll never find out. If I even breathe a word having to do with my actual role, I know she'll try to force me to embezzle money from the sorority.

A smile lights up her face. "Oh you were invited, that's great! Congratulations. You'll probably have a bunch of rich friends. Make some good ones. Some *nice* ones that don't mind giving to the less fortunate."

"Of course, Aunt Cindy," I reply, ducking past her to head to my room.

"I'm fucking starving Cindy, when will dinner be ready?" Chad yells from the kitchen.

Guess I'm not going to my room. I glance at the wall to find it's 4:45 P.M.

Usually she doesn't like me to start making dinner until 5:30. I guess with her newest boyfriend Chad the rules are different.

Turning around, I walk through the living room, turn the corner and pass Chad at the kitchen table.

I throw some already made burger patties in the pan and cook them while the fries cook in the oven.

"Next time, start dinner at four," he grunts.

"Will do," I respond even though I don't want to.

While cooking, I go off into my own world, thinking about tomorrow. It makes the cooking go by quicker. I plate their food and bring it over to them.

As soon as I do, I rush back to the refrigerator and grab

every condiment I can think of and place it in front of them. Walking back into the kitchen, I stare down at my own plate.

"Come and eat, Gemma."

"Coming," I respond in a light tone.

Gritting my teeth, I grab the edges of my plate and walk back to the table. I sit on the opposite side of my aunt and her boyfriend.

The moment I sit down, I can feel my aunt's eyes on me. Her boyfriend is completely focused on stuffing his face.

I've always enjoyed ketchup with my fries. On nights like these, I disregard the ketchup completely in favor of finishing my food as quickly as possible.

Grabbing fries in bunches, I shove them in my mouth and chew them slightly before swallowing. My burger is gone with four bites. I know it tastes good, but I can't be bothered to enjoy it. This is how it is every meal with my aunt.

"You sure enjoyed your food, didn't you, little piggy? With every day that goes by, you look like your mother," she says with a smirk, dipping a fry in mayo.

I ignore her comment, instead choosing to keep the peace. "Thank you for the food," I say with a hint of a smile as I rise from the table.

These past few years, I've stopped fighting back. I've come to accept whatever she says. It's only embarrassing when she says these things in front of other people other than her boyfriends. In fact, I've gotten so used to it that I try my best to beat people to the punch. I'm fat and ugly, just as she says.

I used to wish my parents would walk through the front door and kick her out on the street, but it's been eight years. They'll never come back. She's been living off the money my parents left since the day she moved in. So technically, it's my money she's been using.

Her boyfriend belches and hands the plate to me as I go to move past them.

Gripping the edge, I bring it with me to the sink, starting on the dishes.

By the time I'm almost done, Aunt Cindy places her plate on the counter. "Thanks, Gemma. Go to bed and don't touch my shit. Let's go, Chad!"

"I will," I reply in a robotic tone, grabbing her plate. As if anyone would want her trash. Her room, originally our guest bedroom, is full of everything you can imagine. There's even a deflated kiddie pool in her closet. She'll buy anything just to have it and never use it.

When the front door slams, a smile forms on my face. After drying the dishes and putting them away, I walk back to my room happily and go back to staring at the orientation papers.

Soon I won't have to deal with her anymore. Even if I have to go through some kind of hazing, it'll be worth it to escape from here.

Hazing Night

He's here. I've managed to avoid his attention up until now. I knew I'd end up being one of the last girls here. No one wants to carry the fat chick. It doesn't matter to me because I get to be treasurer no matter what.

Mera, Lisa, Luella and I are the only girls left. Collette's twin brother Callan, Noel, Tyrell and two other guys are left.

Callan is clinging to Mera hard. I feel really bad for her

since she looks so uncomfortable. As much as I hate to say it, she has no choice but to go with Callan. He looks like he'll wring the neck of any guy that goes near her.

Noel and the other two guys are hanging on to Lisa's every word. I can't blame them. She's beautiful.

Tyrell is the only question mark. His eyes are trained on Luella and I.

In a flash, he stalks over and picks her up.

Cringing, I turn away as she has words with him. Poor Luella. He's definitely not the guy she's been writing her poetry about lately.

This narrows it down further. Any minute now, Noel and the two other guys will walk off each touching a part of Lisa's body. Noel won't look my direction at all.

"Noel, carry Gemma back," Callan orders.

I freeze and my blood runs cold. Gritting my teeth, I watch Noel's eyes flit to me. My skin warms as I feel his eyes studying my body. Yeah, I'm fat. Now tell your friend that you don't want to be bothered by being seen with the fat girl.

His eyes fly to Callan as he yells back, "Are you serious? I was just about to carry Lisa."

"Don't take another step this way, and just do it," Callan responds flatly.

There's no flying under the radar then. This is what it's come to.

Noel sighs. "Right. You owe me then."

Fuck. I'll just act normal as if I don't know him at all. He's just a stranger.

Noel stops in front of me and I stare up at him. "You collected a bunch of numbers right, so you don't need mine?"

He blinks slowly. "Well, yes."

"Good." I don't want him to have my number. "And you're strong enough to carry an ugly fat girl like me?"

His eyebrows draw together as if he's irritated. He stares at my face for a long time. Way too long for my comfort. Even with my weight gain, my face hasn't changed much. My cheeks are a little bit chubbier.

Please, don't let him recognize me.

Suddenly, he bends, hooking an arm around my leg and putting the other around my back. My breath rushes out of my chest, flabbergasted as he lifts me off the ground, pulling me to his chest.

His hands are warmer than I expected, a sharp contrast to my cold skin from the breeze in the air.

In shock, I watch his face looking for the smallest indication that he's struggling. There is none. Turning, he starts to carry me away back toward the sorority.

"Gemma! You're beautiful and don't let anyone tell you that you aren't," Mera says in a high pitched tone.

Her words bring a small smile to my face immediately. Mera's nice for trying to put something positive out there even if it's a lie. I have to thank her for that even if it means touching him.

I place a hand on each of his shoulders and pull myself up enough to see her. "Thanks, Mera. Good luck."

She smiles at me for a few seconds more before turning her attention to Callan. I hope that she'll be okay.

Dropping my hands off, I let them both rest on top of my body. My side is pressed right into his chest and six pack.

As we get further away, I start to feel comfortable in the silence. Of course, he has no words to say to someone who looks like me.

"Why do you talk about yourself like that?" he asks in a gruff tone.

The abruptness of his question startles me and I grit my teeth. So he does plan on talking to me. "Does it matter?"

My question hangs in the air.

"So you're one of Collette's minions?"

He completely ignored my question. That's irritating. And so is the word minion. A servile dependent, follower, or underling. Collette is genuinely my friend. Sometimes she can be harsh, but that's just who she is and she sees me as a friend.

"I help Collette, yes, but I don't do everything she tells me to. I have my own mind."

I face the sidewalk in front of us.

No. We're still really far from Sorority Row.

"Good to know. I think you should go out with me."

My mouth drops open in shock and I gulp. Wait, what? This isn't going in the direction it should be at all. "No."

He tilts his head down, staring at me with a confused look. "You know a lot of girls would be happy to go out with Noel Hardington. You're really turning me down?"

"I have no interest in guys," I respond, glancing away. "Besides, I don't even know you."

A partial lie. I do know him, just not the person he is now.

Seeing him on campus for the first time, at Callan's side, made my heart drop. I won't deny that after all this time, part of me wanted to go up to him and ask him if he's okay. But immediately, I could tell there was no hint of the boy that was my friend once upon a time. He's so cocky. So sure of himself. And he has a different girl on his arm every time I see him.

This makes everything easier.

"We could get to know each other right now."

"No," I slowly respond.

He turns off to the right, following a path leading to the

one building on campus that's unfinished. We're basically backtracking. What a waste of time.

"Put me down, right now," I say, my voice rising as I push at his chest. He's completely unbothered. With a smirk, he walks around the corner of the building to the shadowed side. The only people who could see this part of the building are anyone who parks in the parking lot and since this parking lot is away from everything but this building, no one parks here unless they're desperate.

He lets my feet down, dropping me onto the cold concrete.

"Why are we–"

Noel steps close all of a sudden, backing me right into the wall. He places a hand above my head and stares down at me. "So let's get to know each other better so you can say yes to me. Are you ready?"

"No," I snap, looking away from his intense gaze. "I'd like to go back to the sorority. In fact, why don't you just grip one of my fat rolls and we can be on our way? You don't even have to carry me again."

He grabs my chin with his other hand, forcing me to look him in the eye. His mouth forms a thin line and he leans in close, pushing his body close to mine. "No. I want to know why you turned me down. What is it about me that you don't like? It can't be my face." Smirking, he lets go of my chin and grabs my wrist, using it to place my hand on his chest.

His grip is tight as he forces my wrist down, guiding my hand down his chest to his six pack and stopping right above his dick.

I let my eyes follow my hand on instinct and I really shouldn't have. He's way too fucking bold.

And...I don't think his dick should be that big. He isn't even hard and it's *that* big.

My glasses start to slip down the bridge of my nose. I turn my face to the side to avoid looking at his body and use my other hand to try and peel his fingers off.

"It's certainly not my body that made you say no. So, what is it?"

"None of your business," I reply matter of factly.

He lets my wrist go and leans in so close, his breath mingles with mine. "Your face...there's something familiar about it."

Oh crap.

I push my glasses up my face and his hands shoot out, pulling them off.

My vision of everything behind him is blurrier, but I can still see him perfectly clear.

Does he...recognize me?

Please, please don't.

"Gem..."

"Gemma," I correct him. I don't want him to form any attachments to me.

He shakes his head and looks down, studying my body. "No, I got it right the first time." He closes the gap between us so suddenly, letting his lips come down on mine. They're so warm. Not cold like they were the first time.

His lips are insistent, moving over mine and pushing for a response. One that I refuse to give.

He pulls away with a disappointed look. "Well you look like you didn't completely hate it."

I cross my arms over my chest. "I just want to go back. I'm not interested in you or any other guy."

He puts my glasses back on and picks me up again in a flash, bridal style. "It's fine, Gem. I'll let tonight sink in. Tomorrow, I think you'll have a different answer."

Tomorrow at the party? No. My answer to him will stay

the same. For my own safety, I need to stay as far away from him as I can. Somehow, I need to make it clearer.

Present

I hate that I'm poor and have to rely on my friends for things. I'm going on vacation for technically the second time. My first time we went to Kardenia and it wasn't too big of a deal since we all stayed for free at Mera's palace.

This is a different story. They're all paying for their own hotel rooms during our week there except for me.

I'm the outlier and it makes me feel horrible.

I offered to share a room with someone, even just sleeping on the floor would be fine, but they insisted that I get my own room.

"You're thinking too hard again, Gemma," Luella says gently. "Don't worry about anything."

"I just hate that you, Ashlynn, and Collette chipped in for me. If I had a job I could've paid my own way, but then I guess if I had a job I wouldn't be able to go with you anyway."

I open my mouth to respond when my phone goes off in my pocket. Sighing, I pull my phone out, expecting to see my Aunt Cindy on the screen, but it's an unknown number.

Is this another scam caller?

After pressing accept, I hold the phone against my ear to listen.

There's heavy breathing on the end only. I'm about to hang up when the person, a man, asks, "Is this Gemma Brighton? We're contacting you about your loan repayment."

"My what?" I ask.

"You took out a loan in January and it's time for it to be paid back. You verbally agreed to–"

I hang up the phone immediately as my stomach sinks. Either that was a scam or more likely, my aunt took out a loan in my name.

But that didn't sound professional like they belonged to a company. They didn't even say a company when they started talking.

"Is everything okay?" Luella asks, worry in her voice.

"I need to go inside," I mutter, staring at the front door.

Aunt Cindy has done a lot these past few years, but now she's messing with my financial future. Whatever money she borrowed, she needs to pay back and right away.

I pull upon the latch and get out, stomping up the driveway all the way to the door. Glancing over my shoulder, I find Luella right behind me with a nervous expression.

"You didn't have to come," I say, pulling the key out of my pocket.

Especially because this is going to get ugly.

She nods. "I know. Thing is, you've told us many times how your aunt is a horrible person. Maybe if there's someone with you, it won't be so bad?"

I smile at her optimism. Luella always has a way of making anyone feel better. It's too bad my aunt won't care. I unlock the door and push it open.

The smell of coffee hits my nose and I spot my aunt in the old recliner in the living room with the TV going. She turns around looking at the door. When she sees it's me, she deflates.

"Still hoping Chad will come back?" I ask.

She frowns. "He will be back. Anyway..." Aunt Cindy

stands up. "It's good that you're here. I have some news for you."

"News?" I ask. I study her face as a broad smile forms and she nods happily. "I'm selling the place."

My stomach drops and I clutch the house keys in my hand hard, letting the ridges dig in. "You're what?"

"I'm selling the house," she enunciates. "It's way past time. You're in college now. You barely come home." She lets out a hideous laugh. "What's the use of keeping the house?"

"Because it's my parents' house," I say in a low tone. My hands shake as I fight to keep my anger inside.

"Your parents are *never* coming back. You're smart enough to know they're dead." she says it as if her own sister isn't missing. That this is just my problem.

"You have no right to sell this house," I respond.

"Technically, I do. This house was awarded to me along with the rest of their fucking junk. They suggested I give it to you when you come of age, but I've decided to keep it."

"That can't be right," I say, on the verge of tears. All of my parents things. I need to get them all before this house is gone. But I don't even have the money to get a storage unit to store all of this stuff. What am I going to do?

"It *is* right." Smiling she touches her finger to her chin. "So listen, you might be getting a few calls, but it's best just to ignore them. If you want to answer, you can. Just tell them once your house is sold, you'll give them back their $50k."

I choke and Luella gasps behind me. "You got a loan in my name for $50k."

"Well, yeah," she says with a shrug. "I needed it."

"For what?" I yell. "To go on a cruise again? Bora Bora for a month? Or was it Hawaii?"

She stalks over to me and slaps me across the face.

"Gemma, you know better than to yell. Lower your fucking voice when you speak to me."

I clench my jaw and stare up at her. The sting from that slap is nothing compared to the hurt in my heart at this house being gone. This house holds so many memories between my parents and I. All of their things are still here. Their room has been left as is. All of this furniture is theirs.

"I already have a few buyers. It looks like there's going to be a bidding war for this place. This is a prime area you know?" She laughs gleefully.

Talking to her is going to do nothing for me. No matter what I say, she won't change her mind. That's a hefty sum she has to pay back. She works when she feels like it and she hasn't worked in years.

I stalk past her, hitting her arm as I start down the hallway to my room.

She exclaims, "You should be glad. You'll be able to finally be free and move on with your life. I took the liberty of packing the rest of your things in trash bags. You should thank me."

When I get in my room, I eye my bare bed, dresser, nightstand, and desk with the small bookcase over it. Three trash bags are in the center of the room.

"I can help," Luella says behind me.

Nodding, I wipe the tears from under my glasses and grab one bag and hand it to her. "Thank you," I say in a small voice.

I grab the other two bags myself and tell her, "Let's go."

Turning around, I take what could be my last look at my room with my heart in my throat. It's not fair. I haul the two bags with me down the hall, and follow Luella outside as my aunt watches on, sipping her coffee happily.

I slam the door behind me and continue to Luella's baby

blue Prius. She opens the trunk and we fit all three bags in just barely.

When we get back inside her car, she puts her hand over mine. "Gemma, whatever you need, I'll help you."

"I can't take advantage of you, Lu. You've done plenty for me."

She shakes her head and starts the car. "No. We can't let her get away with doing this. Sorry, I didn't know she was that awful. I'm sure Ashlynn and Collette will have an idea."

I cover my mouth with my hand, letting my elbow rest on the car door as I watch us drive away. "Thank you," I say, between my fingers.

If only my parents were still around. But they aren't, and it's all my fault and Noel's.

I take the steps up the plane slowly, with Luella and Ashlynn ahead of me. As soon as I get inside the cabin, I spot Mera who waves at me. Two men wearing all black and earpieces are seated in the first two seats.

Bodyguards? They must be Mera's.

Did her parents make her come back just to tell her that from now on she'll have to have security with her.

She waves us over and I sit in one of the empty seats across from her and Callan. Luella and Ashlynn sit in the seats in front of me and Collette slides into the seat next to me.

Noel, Tyrell, and Vincent sit in the seats in front of Callan and Mera.

Noel is seated in the aisle seat, so when he turns, his eyes meet mine for a second before turning back to look at Callan directly behind him.

"So what was the big hurry?" Noel asks Callan.

Mera sighs. "Mary Catherine is missing."

Luella gasps and Ashlynn says, "I'm so sorry."

"Her security weren't with her?" I ask. Cringing, I cover my mouth. This is the wrong time to criticize them, but I can't help it.

Mera sighs. "She ditched them in the same manner I used to ditch mine when I had them. She traded outfits with a friend and by the time her bodyguards realized it, she was gone. They gave her more wiggle room than me since she never tried to get away from them. Even hearing it, it sounds wrong."

Callan continues, "But the strangest fucking thing is according to her phone, the last place they can place her is on campus."

"What was she doing here?" I ask.

"It was for me," Mera states. "Because of this jerk." Mera elbows Callan and he catches her arm and brings her hand in to kiss.

"I'm sorry, princess."

Mera sighs as he holds on to her hand. "She had to sneak here because she wasn't allowed to come. My parents wanted my punishment here to be as severe as possible."

Collette clears her throat. "So do I have to bow to you or something now that you're going to be Queen?"

Luella turns around, peeking through the seat. "Collette!"

"It's fine," Mera says softly. "If my sister isn't found, it'll be true. My punishment is basically over. They gave me back all my cards and there's plenty of money on them. And now, I have Cate's bodyguards, Barnaby and Edmund. By the way, both pairs of my grandparents are pissed at my parents for not giving me bodyguards here and think it was ridiculous including it as part of my punishment."

"Excuse me, everyone," one of the pilots interrupt. "We'll be taking off now so please put your seatbelts on."

I buckle my seatbelt and Ashlynn says, "Well since you weren't here, there's a bit of a situation with Gemma."

I feel Noel's eyes on me as I push my glasses up the bridge of my nose. I was hoping to talk to Mera about it when he isn't around.

Mera leans forward, looking at me past Callan. "What's going on, Gemma?"

I take a deep breath. "My aunt is selling my parents' house. There are already buyers lined up to buy it. I don't have any say in it."

"Oh my God," Mera says and covers her mouth. She looks at Callan and then everyone else. "We have to give her the money to buy it, as soon as possible."

"Unfortunately, my aunt is a spiteful person and I believe if I myself were to try and buy it, she'd decline the offer."

Mera scoffs. "What a bitch."

"I have my agent on it already," Collette says as she puts her sleep mask on. "By the time we land in Cancun, she'll have accepted my offer of two mil. That's $500k over asking and honestly, it shouldn't have even been listed for that much. That house is a shack and worth way less, no offense Gemma."

I guess compared to what she's used to it's a shack.

My aunt is greedy and Collette's offer is way above asking. There's no way anyone else submitted a higher offer than her.

"Do Mom and Dad know what you're doing?" Callan asks.

Collette scoffs. "I don't give a flying fuck what either of them think. Especially Mom."

Callan chuckles. "That's the spirit."

Everyone around me starts talking amongst themselves and I breathe a sigh of relief. Everything is going to work out fine. I've thought of everything.

As the plane roars to life, I relax into the seat. That's when I feel that intense stare again.

I glance up to find Noel smirking at me.

Why won't he just give up?

Suddenly he turns away, chuckling.

I can't help but feel a flare of annoyance. Is he laughing at me? It's nothing that I'm not used to, so it doesn't hurt, but I'd like to know why? What's so funny?

A knot slowly forms in the pit of my stomach.

CHAPTER TWO

Noel

Finally, I have her. There's finally a way to make Gemma Brighton do what I want, and I'm ready to exploit it as much as I can.

Never have I ever met someone who didn't want to go on at least one date with me. I mean, how could someone turn me down? A model would kill for my thick eyelashes, facial structure and naturally straight teeth. Brown eyes to suck you in for days.

At least that's what they tell me.

But it's always my smile that seems to do it. I smile once at them and they melt.

Everyone except for her. First party of the year and she turns me down in front of everyone. I hate how ridiculous I looked. But I was determined to change things around. Give her a chance to get to know me better before accepting.

But every attempt is turned down. The Dining Hall, she ignores me. The trip to Kardenia, she ignored me.

All of my so-called friends except Callan, Tyrell, and Vincent call me Strikeout Noel. I'm fucking sick of it.

After today, she'll have no choice but to do whatever I want her to do. We'll go out on dates and fuck. When I'm tired of her, I'll be able to go back to having a 0% fail rate. All of this is contingent on if she loves her home as much as she's made it seem. If not the home, she has to at least want her parents' belongings.

Luckily, I've been wanting to move out of my parents' house since the beginning of last semester and I finally found a real estate agent I can count on. I haven't found a house to my liking yet, but he can finally do something for me.

Grinning, I pull out my phone and go looking for the most recently listed houses in the county for $1.5 mil. Only one house is listed for that exact amount, and it was listed last night.

This is it.

I send my agent the link and tell him to write up an offer that I can DocuSign.

And not just any offer. Five million.

Is it aggressive? Of course. Who in their right mind would offer five million on a house worth one million?

But I refuse to let this opportunity slip through my fingers.

I'll blink and Gemma will be at my feet, sucking on my cock like no tomorrow.

Her aunt would be insane to not accept it immediately while she thinks about other offers.

I cruise through my socials, responding to all my messages, which takes a while when finally, a new email from my agent pops up at the top.

Smiling widely, I click on the link and watch as the DocuSign page loads in.

Just a few signatures and a few initials and it'll be done.

"What are you so happy about?" Vincent asks curiously.

"You'll see," I respond cheerily, clicking on each blank space to sign.

"Is it a new girl?" he asks, a smirk in his tone.

"You could say that."

He chuckles and sighs. "Of course. You have all the luck."

"Hey, you'd have plenty of luck too if you weren't blinded by your lust for your stepsister."

He doesn't respond and I glance to my right at him to find him glowering at me.

I shrug and put my empty hand in the air. "It's true. Aren't I right, Ty?"

Ty grunts from the seat in front of me.

"See?" I gesture toward his seat and put my hand back down. "You're *almost* as attractive as I am. Try and you might surprise yourself."

"Just shut up." He gets out of his seat, moving past me and goes up to sit in the empty seat next to Tyrell.

Guess that rubbed him the wrong way. Oh well. Someone has to say it and keep saying it.

But I need to focus on the precious jewel I'll receive when I get this done and the offer is accepted. She'll probably think this is the worst thing to happen to her, but I guarantee once she accepts, she'll enjoy it all so much she'll beg me to stick around.

She'll have to stay strong and resilient and above all, not shatter as so many women have before her.

We'll have to talk about that.

Clicking the submit button causes a rush of excitement to hit me.

It's still early in the day. In a few hours, I should have my victory.

There's a huge fucking crowd when we approach the desk to sign in. Not every voice that rises is friendly.

"What the fuck is going on?" Callan mutters behind me.

Mera groans. "I thought we'd be able to go for a swim before dinner."

"Nothing we can do except wait," Gemma says from next to her.

She wrinkles her nose and adjusts her glasses.

While we wait, I check my phone for an email back. Nothing new comes up. I refresh my inbox over and over, hoping for a response.

"It's been thirty minutes. This line hasn't moved an inch. I'm not waiting another fucking second. I'm getting up there to see what the hold up is," Callan says, going around the crowd of people.

Being curious myself, I follow him.

All five employees at the desk are frantic as they go from person to person lined up at the counter, trying to explain something that's obviously upsetting each person.

The word "room" and "mix-up" are the words they say most frequently.

"What's going on?" Callan barks at the closest employee to us.

The middle-aged man with a forced smile looks between Callan and I. "We apologize for the wait. Please, be patient and we'll be with you soon. We're trying to solve this problem as quickly as possible."

Sighing, I take my sunglasses off and put the temple in

my shirt. Leaning forward, I whisper, "I will pay you right now if you just check us in so we can get on with our vacation."

He smiles. "Well, of course sir."

Callan and I exchange an annoyed look.

Both of us pull out our wallets and each throw $100 USD to him in pesos.

His eyes grow wide as he grabs it quickly and shoves it into his pocket. "What's the name under?" he asks looking at us.

"Callan Goldsworthy," Callan responds.

He types something in quickly and after a few moments, winces. "I was afraid of this."

"Afraid of what?" I ask, looking from him to his computer.

"There was a bug in our system and a few rooms were overbooked. It seems that a few of your rooms were booked by someone else."

"Son of a bitch," Callan mutters, rubbing a hand over his chin. "Fine. I'll pay for more rooms."

The man laughs nervously, looking between us. "I'm sorry, but we're completely booked. We'll only charge you for the rooms that were successfully booked."

"And how many is that? There were supposed to be eight rooms," I bark. Every single room Callan booked had a king bed.

This is supposed to be the best resort to stay at and something like this happens? I knew I should've just bought a house down here.

"I'm so sorry, there's only four rooms."

"Four?" Callan echoes. He glances at me and we both do the math.

Him and Mera were supposed to share a room, but

everyone else had their own room so everyone can double up except for one person.

From behind me, I feel someone squeezing in between Callan and I, and Callan looks furious at being interrupted while I feel annoyed.

I'm about to tell them to wait their fucking turn when I notice the black hair and gray eyes. "Hey, this is taking too long and I want to check in right now so I can start my vacation."

"What the fuck are you doing here, Kane?" Callan asks with a glare.

Kane turns to him. "I'm on vacation, same as you."

I cross my arms together and lean against the counter. "Out of all the resorts, you chose this one?"

The man in front of us clears his throat. "What is the name under?"

"Wait a damn minute," I say, turning to him. "We haven't finished getting our situation straight."

"Kane Silverstone."

After typing his name in and staring at the screen, he nods. "Room 410, sir. Let me get—"

Callan laughs in a tone that makes my hairs raise. "Wait a second, you're telling me that this asshole was able to get his room, but ours got fucked up?"

The man looks at Callan nervously, mumbling and glancing around, looking for help.

Kane chuckles and gazes at Callan. "It's called karma, asshole."

Callan looks about ready to punch the living daylights out of Kane so I push Kane back and step in between them. The last thing we need is for the police to be called our first day of vacation.

"Just get your room key and get the hell out of here," I tell him.

He smirks. "Actually, I was thinking that maybe, I could be of service. I couldn't help but overhear you have only four rooms and nine people. There's enough room for one more person in my king bed."

"Not Mera," Callan snaps.

Kane shakes his head and before I realize it, I'm saying, "Not Gemma either. We can talk to Vincent or Tyrell and see if one of them would be willing to share with you."

Kane chuckles. "Nah. That invitation is good for one person only."

It isn't too hard to figure out who that person is. Of the three girls left, there's only one he's shown interest in. I remember hazing night very well.

"No," Callan says in a low tone.

"Okay, well. Can't say I didn't offer," Kane says with a shrug.

As I turn back to Callan to ask him what we're going to do, I hear a chorus of familiar voices coming from behind us that are steadily getting louder.

The loudest one ironically comes from the person that Kane wants to share his room with.

"What is *he* doing here?" Collette says with a scowl.

"Spring break," Kane responds. He tilts his head, glancing behind her. "Hey, Mera."

"Kane," Mera says flatly, crossing her arms.

"Listen," I say, raising my voice. "Something went wrong in their system and there are only four rooms. We're going to have to share."

There's an immediate mixed reaction as everyone murmurs.

"But that means one person will have to room with two other people," Gemma points out.

"That's right. Unless," I cough and clear my throat. This next part coming out of my mouth is such bullshit. "Out of the kindness of his not-at-all black heart, Kane has offered to let one of us room with him."

"I'd rather sleep on the floor of someone else's room. I'm the odd one out so–" Gemma starts.

I interrupt her by holding up my hand. "His invitation is only good for our resident ballerina."

Everyone turns to look at Collette whose mouth is wide open. "Absolutely not. Sorry Gemma, I guess you're just going to sleep on the floor of a room."

Kane chuckles.

I can only see things happening two ways, and if I'm correct, I'm about to win out big time.

Callan clears his throat. "The only person I'm rooming with is Mera." He glances at Tyrell, Vincent, and I. "No offense guys."

Fuck. Yes.

Tyrell nods and Vincent looks my way. "Sorry, man. Tyrell and I think we should share a room."

So I'm the only guy left. Either I have the room to myself or I have to sleep in the room with one girl.

And there's only one girl I want to share a room with. I look at Gemma pointedly while she looks everywhere but at me.

Ashlynn looks at me. "I'm not sharing a room with you, and neither will Luella." She looks at Collette and Gemma. "I guess you two can sleep on the floor or something."

Collette gasps. "Me? On the floor? Ashlynn! You have to be kidding."

Nice. It's always good to see someone stand up to Collette.

"Sorry Coll, but I paid to come here too just like you. You have an offer to sleep on a bed. You should. After all, it's only for a week."

Collette huffs and crosses her arms.

There really is only one option for her.

"The offer is still open," Kane says smoothly.

"Fine." Collette tosses her hair over her shoulder. "Don't be surprised if I murder you in your sleep."

"I'd love to see you try," he responds.

Ashlynn turns to Gemma. "And I hate to say it, I'm sorry, but you should sleep in Noel's room. It's only for a week. If he tries to pull something, knee him in the balls."

"Don't give her ideas, Ashlynn."

Gemma stares at me. "Let's just get this over with."

Callan and I turn back to the man, only to find him with other people.

Sighing, I take my wallet out and wave more money. Instantly, he comes back. Before he can grab it, I shove it back in my pocket.

"All ready for your room keys?" he asks with an air of disappointment.

"Yes," Callan replies in an irritated tone.

Mera's two bodyguards suddenly materialize out of nowhere. "And our room too. Under Barnaby."

The man behind the counter looks intimidated by his gaze and he nods quickly.

Turning around, I find Gemma staring at me with an annoyed expression.

This is going to be a fun week.

If only that email would come through.

After figuring out who gets which room and dinner, Gemma and I are finally alone. Well, I'm alone in the room while she's taking a shower.

Still no response from my agent.

The door to the bathroom opens and Gemma comes out, holding a towel around the end of her hair. My eyes are immediately drawn to her pajamas with foxes on them. She completely ignores me, sitting on the opposite side of the bed.

"You done in there?" I ask.

"Yeah," she responds dismissively.

As I reach for my shorts, my phone vibrates in my pants.

This better be my agent calling with good news.

I slide the phone out of my pocket and glance down to find my father's name on the screen.

If I answer this call, maybe I can get him off my back quickly. If I don't, he'll fly down here to talk to me in person. With my mother too.

"I have a call to take," I mutter to Gemma, letting my finger hover over the answer button.

She doesn't respond, so I grit my teeth, and answer. "Hello? How may I help you today?"

Just a few minutes. It'll only be a few minutes.

"Noel. Is there something you forgot to tell us?" Dad asks in his usual smart-aleck tone.

I glance around the room. "Hmm, no. Nothing's coming to mind."

He sighs and there's the sound of shuffling and then a softer voice comes on. "Noel, sweetie, you know you need to tell us when you're leaving the country. We shouldn't have had to find out from Marguerite."

Of course it was Callan's mom. She never knows how to keep her fucking trap shut.

"I'm sorry I didn't tell you, but listen, my friends are calling me so I have to go." I pull the phone away and shout, "Yeah I'm coming" to my nonexistent friends in the room.

She sighs. "We'll talk when you get back. Make smart choices."

"I always do." I end the call quickly before she keeps me on even longer.

Breathing a sigh of relief, I stand up with my shorts in my hand and let my phone drop to the bed.

"Sorry about that," I say to Gemma.

Her hair is tied in a loose bun and her hair is curled as the water drips down from the curls around her face. I've never seen her hair this way before. She should leave it like this instead of straightening it.

That curly hair would look sexy pulled back in my fist.

She looks from her phone to me. "It's none of my business. Talk to whoever you need to talk to."

Complete disinterest now, but I'm sure that'll change tomorrow.

After taking a quick shower, I come out to Gemma facing away from me and the lamp on her nightstand being off.

Is she asleep already? I watch her form

Before doing anything else, I cross over to the bed and grab my phone to check my emails. Bingo, there it is.

Smiling, I click on the email to find my offer has been accepted. We'll go into escrow and that house will be mine in two weeks. And Gemma will be mine for however long I decide starting tomorrow.

Tomorrow is going to be a great day for her.

Smirking, I set my phone down and turn the light off, lying down with my back to her.

The instant my head hits the pillow, I feel out of sorts. Elbowing the bed, I feel for any semblance of support, but there is none.

How the fuck am I supposed to sleep on this mattress?

"I can't sleep if you keep squirming around like that," she says in an irritated tone.

"Why don't you help put me to sleep then?" I suggest.

She makes a disgusted sound and I chuckle.

Should I tell her tonight?

Nah. I'd rather start our arrangement in the morning.

It takes forever, but I finally find a position I'm comfortable in. Closing my eyes, I start to drift off when I hear the sound of a thump.

I pop my eyes open and look around the dark room.

Where the hell did that come from?

I open my mouth to ask Gemma if she did something when I hear that same thump, except this time it's louder. And another one, and another.

Right against the wall where the headboard of our bed is.

That's when I remember. I chose to have the room next to Callan and Mera's.

Whistling, I glance over at Gemma's form. "They're really going at it."

Gemma groans and puts her hand over her ears.

The knocking against the wall continues over the next hour, and just when I'm almost asleep, it continues. Turning over to my back, I face the ceiling.

"They should've stopped by now. It can't be that good," Gemma mutters as she turns over to face the ceiling.

"Oh, but it can be. I'm even better than Callan at it." I turn to gaze at her as she turns to me. In the dark, I can see the whites of her eyes, so I watch as she rolls her eyes and turns back over.

"Too much information," she states.

For now. But she'll find out soon enough.

Bright and early at breakfast the next morning, we're all crowded around three tables.

"How did everyone sleep last night?" I ask, opening a water bottle and taking a swig.

"Like a log," Vincent responds.

"Fine," Tyrell says.

"Horrible," Collette snaps, glaring at Kane.

"I slept great," Kane says with a shrug.

Mera sighs. "I slept okay but I really miss Scarlett and Peyton. I wish they could've come."

"When did you have time to miss them during that marathon of yours?" I ask.

"Marathon?" Her face turns red. "Oh."

"Stop being so nosy, Noel," Callan says.

Scoffing, I set my bottle down. "No. This was not Nosy Noel this time. Your headboard was fucking banging against the same wall my headboard is against."

Ashlynn looks up from her plate of food. Her eyes look dead tired. "Yeah, and that's not all. We were able to hear the thumping from our room. Lu and I heard it all night long."

Luella's face turns pink as she twiddles her fingers. "It didn't bother me that much. When passion and love call... you have to answer. I'm so happy for you guys."

Mera groans and hides her face in her hands. "Ugh, this is *so* embarrassing. Gemma, please tell me you were able to sleep?"

I'm pretty positive she slept less than I did since she was already awake when I woke up.

Gemma shakes her head slowly. "Not the whole night. I do appreciate those pauses you guys took though."

"Wait, everybody shut up for a second," Collette says, her eyebrows furrowing as she glares at her phone. "This can't be right."

"What's wrong?" Gemma asks.

I can't hide the smirk that forms on my face. I take a nice big gulp of water. Collette must be getting the bad news right about now.

"That bitch didn't take my offer. She's accepted another offer."

"No," Gemma says, in a low tone. I glance across the table at her as she raises a trembling hand to her mouth. "That makes no sense. I did the math. No one in their right mind would offer above what you did. Any higher offer would be a huge loss to the buyer."

"It's not a loss at all," I say with a grin.

Gemma's eyes slide to me. All color floods out of her face. "What?"

"No fucking way," Collette breathes, staring daggers at me.

"Yeah, I bought the house."

Everyone looks shocked, except for Gemma and Collette. Collette looks more furious by the second and Gemma looks horrified.

She scoots her chair back and rushes off. I watch as she disappears into the hallway, in the direction of the elevator to our room.

Callan nudges me. "I know you have something up your sleeve, and you don't have to tell me. But how much did you offer to make this happen?"

"Five mil," I say without blinking.

He laughs and Mera elbows him. "Callan!"

Callan shakes his head. "So that's how far you were willing to go."

"No," I say simply. "I would've spent ten, twenty, thirty, whatever it took to make sure that house became mine."

"I admire the determination," Kane says with a chuckle.

I move my chair back and stand up with a wide smile. "Actually, I'd like to think something like this was inevitable."

Leaving my plate uneaten at the table, I head back to our room.

After unlocking the door, I open it carefully, expecting to get a pillow or two thrown at my face.

But there is none. Opening the door fully, I walk inside and close it behind me.

Gemma is sitting at the edge of the bed, facing the mirror.

"So this is your revenge?" she asks, her tone flat.

I walk over to the bed and sit down next to her. "I wouldn't say revenge. I'd say this is an opportunity. Something good will come out this for you too. I'd like to make a deal."

She slides over to the edge of the bed, as far away from me as possible without standing up. "What good could come out of making a deal with you?"

"I'll give you the house," I say, glancing at her from the side to watch her reaction.

Her jaw clenches. "For what? Sex?" She makes a disgusted sound.

I don't take offense because she doesn't know yet how good I am.

"That's part of it. But I'm not a complete asshole. I'd take you out on dates. Wherever you'd like to go, you name it. And you can work some of the money off by working for my parents."

Her eyes widen and her face turns pale. "I'll do everything else except go there."

"It'll only be part time. What's the big deal? It's not like I'll have you do hard labor."

"How long?" she asks tersely.

"As long as I say."

She shakes her head. "No. I won't stay your sex toy or work there for years of my life."

I burst out laughing. "For years? No. I've never been with just one person for even a single year. Three months has been the longest I've gone with just one person and even that was boring. Does that help?"

She moves her glasses up her nose. "No. I don't like the uncertainty of this arrangement. I need a hard deadline. Something to look forward to so I know when I'll be free."

With a sigh, I lean back on my hand. "Fine. No longer than eight months." That should be long enough. That's an insane amount of time, there's no way it'll last that long.

"Five," she counters.

"Eight," I say firmly. "Or I'll just tear down the house and build a brand new one in its spot."

Her lips flatten and she turns to me with rage in her eyes. "Fine." She runs a hand through her curly hair. "No more than eight months. I'll work the stupid job and then give you the money. But there's one thing you don't seem to get. Look at me. Look at the girls you're usually around. You aren't attracted to me one bit. How do I know you'll actually give me the house if I'm unable to satisfy you?"

Here we go again. I hate when she brings this up because I don't see how she'd think she isn't sexy. Her full lips, bright eyes, heart shaped face, and plump tits and a well-rounded ass. She's got it all. So what if her stomach hangs down and that includes a fat roll or two?

THE NERD AND THE BULLY

"I'll prove it to you," I say in a soft tone, scooting over to close the distance between us.

"How?" she asks, with a skeptical look.

I grab a strand of her curly hair and twist it around my finger. When I let it go, it bounces and settles back with her other hair. "Get on your knees."

CHAPTER THREE

Gemma

Either he's really dumb or this is a test.
Does he truly think I'll just give in and do
whatever he says? I want to save my childhood
home. I don't want to be his sex slave.

I never wanted to be anywhere near him and now, for
what could be the next eight months, we'll be spending a lot
of time with each other.

At any point in time his memory might come back. He'll
remember and...

Things between us will really change.

Do I pretend like I don't remember?

No, that isn't me.

I'll never be able to forgive him, and I'll have to tell him
that.

There were two things my parents made me promise

them before they walked out the door for the last time. The first, go to school and succeed. Don't get sucked into the wrong crowd and lose sight of my goal. And second, stay as far away from the Hardingtons as possible. The more time that passed the more important those promises became. And I've now broken one of them.

The Hardingtons. The husband-wife duo of ultra smart scientists and their one and only brilliant son, Noel.

I hate that he made me agree to go back to that place. Their cursed pharmaceutical company where all of this started. Of course he doesn't know that I know that building very well.

That part of the deal is the worst part.

I don't care that I've basically signed over my virginity to him. It never meant much to me to begin with.

But I don't plan on making any of this easy on him. I think it should be super clear with this.

"So I need to suck you off to prove you're attracted to me? How does that make sense?" I ask, eyeing his crotch. "I think I'll pass. All you need to do is assure me that even if I don't satisfy you, you'll still give me the house."

"I like where your mind is going, but no, you don't have to suck me off…yet. I'd rather show you proof."

I glance up to find him looking intensely at me with a hint of something I've only seen once. The night of the hazing he looked at me the same way.

Desire. That's it.

But I don't understand why, when I look like this.

"I'm still not kneeling in front of you," I mutter.

He chuckles. "Fine. I'll let you have it your way this time. I should've known you wouldn't just do whatever I say."

"Got that right," I retort.

He leans in close to my ear. "Stand in front of me then."
His mouth is way too close and I shiver involuntarily.

I stand immediately, anxious to get away from him. My
heels are touching the bottom of the dresser. I can't get any
further away than this. "What now?" I ask.

His mouth tightens. "You're so far away. Why don't you
come closer?"

"I'm fine where I am," I say closing my arms.

In a flash, he's off the bed and right in front of me,
dragging me back to the bed with him. He holds my arm in a
bruising grip and stares at me with a warning in his eyes.
"I'm starving. And I'm sure you are too, so why don't we
make this quick? Don't run. Just stand and look at me."

So just this one thing and I'll be free until it's time for
bed? "Fine."

He pulls down his swim trunks, exposing himself to the
air. I keep my eyes trained on him. To my utter shame, I still
remember what it looks like from the night of the hazing.

He leans back on his elbows and stares at me.

How is this going to–?

Suddenly, in my peripheral vision I notice movement.

A small smile forms on his face and I want to look away
more than anything.

"Is that a blush on your cheeks, Gemma?"

I flatten my lips, refusing to respond to that.

The movement continues and suddenly, I'm able to see it
without meaning to.

His hard dick.

He got hard just seeing me like this? That's impossible.

And its size is even more ridiculous now that he's hard.

"Which girl did you think about to get like that?"

"No one but you, precious. I'm looking at your face, but
that's not all I see. You may be wearing that ugly baggy shirt

and shorts right now, but I remember how you look without them. So, is this evidence enough that I'm attracted to you?"

I bite my lip and glance away. It's still hard to believe. "So I'll get my house?"

"You'll get it," he reassures me.

I hear the crinkling of his shorts as I walk over to the door. A few seconds later, I hear footsteps and reach for the doorknob.

Before I can turn it, he reaches past me, putting his larger hand over mine. "Do we have a deal, Gem?"

"Yes."

"Good," his deep voice rumbles. I can hear the satisfaction in his voice and it's annoying.

My parents would never want me to make a deal like this for their things. I just can't let go of them yet.

He moves his hand away. "Be ready tonight."

I twist the doorknob, pulling the door open and stalking outside. Instantly, I feel more free and less suffocated.

I'll worry about tonight when I get there. For now, I want to spend the rest of my day relaxing with my friends.

The elevator ride down is quiet, and when we get back to the table where our friends are, all of them stop talking as soon as they see us.

The only plates left are mine and Noel's and I know mine is cold.

"Don't worry, everyone, we talked and…" I feel his eyes on me as I sit back in my chair. "We talked it out and out of the kindness of my heart, I'm going to give her the house back."

Everyone starts chattering and I clear my throat. "I think you forgot the whole being your girlfriend for up to eight months part of it, Noel."

Collette gasps and the table erupts into chaos.

Noel eyes me and shrugs. He mouths "tonight."

I shove a hard piece of bacon in my mouth, crunching down hard.

Eight months of misery here I come.

After the initial chaos of that bombshell, everyone decided to let us sort it out ourselves. Out of everyone, Collette is the most disgusted and to Noel's annoyance, rallied the other girls into getting them to stay in the room with Noel and I. The moment they were out of earshot, he whispered that we'd do what he had planned whether they're in the room with us or not.

That is a huge no. I already don't want to do this. I don't want anyone else to hear my embarrassment. Reluctantly, she's backed off for now.

Mera's last ditch effort for me was to get Callan to talk to Noel, but all Noel did was tell him that he didn't try to stop Callan on Halloween. Whatever that means.

The rest of the day was fun by the pool. Everyone except me got in the water, but it's okay. It's hard to shake off the feeling that everyone's staring at me. I'd feel even worse if I was only in my one-piece.

Dinner flew by too quickly, and now, Noel and I are outside our room.

Without pause, I stick the key in and open the door. I walk over to my side of the bed while the smallest ray of light from the hallway streams in. When he closes the door, the room is left to complete darkness until I turn the lamp on. I slide my flip flops off and sit at the edge of the bed.

Tapping my fingers on the edge of the bed, I think about how uncomfortable this is going to be. Wave after wave of dread hit me, until he says, "Hey. Why don't you take a shower first?"

Happily, I grab my pajamas from my suitcase and walk into the bathroom. The shower helps the tension in my limbs fade away. By the time I get out, I'm ready for him to do what he wants so I can stop dreading it.

He takes a shower after me, and when he comes out, he's shirtless again, like last night with a different pair of shorts.

Immediately, I turn the light off and lay down.

I pull the glasses off my face, setting them on the nightstand, and listen to the shuffling on his side of the room. Eventually, I feel the bed dipping as he gets in.

"You know, this would be more fun with the lights on," he notes.

My eyes haven't adjusted to the dark yet, but I know even when they do, it won't feel as embarrassing as it would if the lights were on.

"You can relax a little, you know. I'm not going to fuck you tonight."

Relief floods through me and I sigh out loud accidentally.

There's a smile in his voice as he says, "Make no mistake, it'll happen one day. Tonight, I'd rather you do something else for me."

Grimacing, I think about how unbearable it's going to be.

"What?" I ask, turning onto my side to face him.

"Put your hand between your legs. Have you done it before?"

I open my mouth and close it. That wasn't what I was expecting. In fact it's a lot better than what I was expecting. He wants to watch me while I touch myself?

It's dark so he won't be able to see everything.

"No, I haven't done it before." I've had tons of other things to worry about and do, including dealing with my aunt. There was never any time for that. And I didn't care enough to make time.

"I guess tonight will be your first learning experience. By Saturday night, you should have the hang of things," he says nonchalantly.

"By Saturday? As in I'll be doing this multiple times?"

I can't show how excited I am that he won't be touching me. If I do, he might change his mind.

Five nights of touching myself.

I could probably get away with being sick one night.

"This way once you experience what I do to you it won't come as such a shock. So go ahead. Tonight will be the only time I'll let you keep your pajamas and panties on."

As my eyes adjust to the darkness, I'm able to see his eyes are glued to the juncture of my thighs.

I slip my hand between my pajama shorts and underwear. "I'm not doing this all night," I tell him.

"True, but you won't be stopping until I feel satisfied."

As I part my folds and find my clit, I open my mouth to ask him how I'll know, when I watch him pull his shorts down slightly, exposing his hard dick.

He's hard already?

I rub my finger around my clit and jump slightly at the unfamiliar feeling.

Do I close my eyes? Do I keep them open? God, this is embarrassing.

His hand curls around his dick and he tugs it, once and smooths a finger over the head.

Wait, I can't watch that. Anything but that.

I lift my head to the ceiling and focus on that.

"Circle your finger around your clit," he says in a low tone. "Flick it a few times, then pinch it, hard, precious."

His voice is silky smooth. It almost makes me want to

listen to him, but I don't. I just keep rubbing it and feeling the small jolts of electricity that goes to my toes.

"Pinch it," he growls, "or I will."

"Fine," I snap and tug at my clit before pinching it.

My body twitches and I gasp. That small bit of pain shouldn't feel good. It really shouldn't.

"That's it, be a good girl and just listen to me, precious," he says with a groan.

His words cause me to shiver. No. That shouldn't affect me. I tilt my head down to find him furiously jacking off.

"Dip your fingers lower, try and get a finger in," he orders.

I let my fingers rest at my entrance and bite my lip. I've already gone so far out of my comfort zone tonight.

"Finger in, Gem. Now," he says, his hand slowing down.

Gently, I push a finger in at my entrance, I don't go far but he doesn't need to know that. "There," I say breathlessly.

"Good," he murmurs. "I bet your pussy is really tight, isn't it?"

The sound of him jacking off is all I can hear.

"Yes," I say in a barely audible tone.

"And you're really wet, aren't you?"

"I am."

"Someday soon I'll claim it," he says in a heated tone and my eyes widen as he turns onto his back quickly and cum shoots out onto his six pack. He glides his hand from the shaft to the tip a few times with a groan. "Fuck."

"So are we done now?" I ask, pulling my finger out of myself, but keeping my hand in my panties.

"For now," he responds.

Thank God.

A wave of self loathing goes through me as I pull my hand out, slide off the bed and head to the bathroom.

As I'm washing my hand, I watch his hand shoot out to the new toilet paper roll on the counter. He tears a few pieces off and wipes the cum off his chest.

Our eyes accidentally meet in the mirror and I grimace.

I can't believe I did that.

And I can't believe I have to do it the next four nights.

"Maybe if you explore yourself some more, you'll be able to orgasm," he says with a smirk.

"Not interested in orgasming," I say flatly. I dry my hand on a towel and go back to bed.

The shame coupled with the loathing I feel toward Noel are fighting for dominance until I finally let sleep take me under.

Every night after we're done, I hate myself a little more and Noel a lot more. But tonight, it's the last night.

When we get back home I'll be able to make more genuine excuses.

The minute I said I was sick last night, he offered to take me to the hospital. Hospitals always make me uncomfortable. I always feel ten times bigger there because people are always staring in the waiting room with nothing else to do.

So here I am, the last night. A pro at touching myself.

Well, no. Not really. I haven't made myself orgasm once, thankfully. I haven't tried to. And for some reason, Noel hasn't been upset about it. I do the exact same thing every night and he's come every night while watching me.

Tonight is no different.

I slip one finger inside myself and bite my lip as my thumb brushes against my clit.

"It's our last night here, Gem. Let's do something special this time, hm?" Noel murmurs.

I glance up, locking eyes with him. "Like what?" I hold my breath, waiting and hoping it doesn't involve him touching me.

"Touch me with your free hand," he says in a low tone.

"No," flies out of my mouth quickly.

"Okay," he says slowly. "Then I'll touch you with *my* free hand. Choose."

I move my arm from underneath my body and reach for his dick. God, I don't want to do this. I'll close my eyes and do it.

The moment my hand brushes against it, I cringe. It feels so smooth. I move my palm over his head. My hand encounters a small amount of wetness. Oh God, is his precum on my hand? "Down, precious. Put your hand around it and go up and down. And don't neglect yourself."

I clench my jaw and glide my hand, up and down, and move my hand around in my underwear like I'm pushing my fingers in myself.

"Why are you so fucking good at this?" he asks with a groan.

Am I?

The thought sends a weird wave through me and I push it away. Suddenly, his hand grabs my wrist and he holds it so my hand is cupping around the softness of his head.

What is he–?

I open my eyes just in time to watch him pumping his hips, rubbing the underside of his head against my hand as his cum shoots out into my hand.

"Oh my God," I murmur.

He smirks. "Thanks for the assistance. Do me one more favor, though."

My stomach sinks as I can already guess where his mind is going.

"Lick your hand clean."

"That's nasty, Noel."

He laughs. "Maybe it's just nasty because you've never tried it. But you should be happy. I've been drinking pineapple juice all week just for you."

"That's why everyone keeps side-eying me when you guzzle that stuff," I say, my voice rising.

"Just do it before it goes on the bed."

"No," I snap and rub it over his chest instead.

His mouth flattens and a look of annoyance flashes on his face. "Maybe, I should do it again, except fuck your mouth this time, precious."

My body goes cold. "Let's just go to sleep. Travel days are tiring," I suggest, attempting to maneuver without letting my hand with his drops of cum touch the sheets. As I pull my wet hand out of my shorts, his hand shoots out, grabbing my wrist and pulling it to him. My body twists and I try to pull my hand free out of his grasp. But he's too strong.

Before I can even blink he pushes my index finger into his mouth, licking it clean. I shudder at the feeling of his tongue on my skin. His licks my whole hand clean, finishing with my thumb. When he's done, he lets my hand go and I let it fall to the bed, completely shocked.

He licks his lips. "Not so hard is it?" His eyes travel down to my thighs. "You taste pretty good, but I'm sure if I got it direct from the source it'd taste better."

He wants to do *that*.

It's better than the alternative, but still. Why?

I slide off the bed quickly and rush off to the bathroom to wash both of my hands.

Ugh, I can't wait to get back home.

I turn the water off and glance up in the mirror to find him staring at me from the bed.

And I wish he'd stop looking at me like that.

"I hope you enjoyed this week," he says in a low tone. "Because it's just the beginning."

I did *not* enjoy it.

I *hate* that I had to do it.

I don't tell him that though. Instead, I dry my hands and stalk back over to my side of the bed. I turn my back to him and eventually, I feel and hear him get off the bed as it creaks.

With a tired sigh, I lay my head on my pillow and start to drift off.

The water from the sink is still running and putting me to sleep.

Suddenly, a thump sounds against the wall.

No. Don't tell me.

The thump happens again. And again. Over and over.

The water turns off and he comes back to bed a few seconds later, lying next to me.

Noel chuckles. "Good night, Gem."

I put the pillow over my head and groan.

The sun is going down as we step off the plane and get into the waiting SUV.

Being away from Noel is a breath of fresh air.

Collette is sitting up front with the driver while I sit next to Mera and Ashlynn and Luella are in the third row.

"For the love of God, please tell me there's no way you're actually going to fall for a womanizer like him? Promise me, Gemma, that this is only about the house."

"Does it seem like I'm falling for him? I don't want to be anywhere near him," I reply, crossing my arms.

"I'm telling you, if you do, it'll be your biggest mistake. He's charming, I'll admit, but one woman could never make him happy." Collette says loftily.

"I promise I won't." I could never betray my parents like that. I might be playing along with him for this deal, but it's only temporary. Falling for him is something completely different.

I glance over at Mera and she looks at me sympathetically. "Hey, I know it'd be a low blow, but his parents don't know you right? If things get too difficult, you could always tell his parents and maybe they could make him give you your house."

A knot forms in my stomach at the thought of talking to his parents. I shake my head.

Mera touches my shoulder. "Just don't let him walk all over you. You're actually well-liked on campus and a regular student. If he tries something on school grounds, tell the new Dean. Be stronger than me, okay?"

"I will," I affirm.

Luella leans forward, putting her head between us. "But Mera, aren't you in love?"

"I am," Mera says softly, "I just hate the path it took to get here. Some things you can't forget, but you can forgive. Just don't fall in love, Luella. It's easier."

Luella hides her mouth in her arm, nodding.

I relax back into the seat, letting the tension fade away. Tomorrow, it's back to school.

Suddenly, a chorus of beeps and vibrations are heard. I slide my phone out of my pocket and click on the Emergency notification from the school. *Students are missing?*

"Holy shit, Ginger is missing," Mera mutters, "along with

a bunch of other people. That's weird."

Right, Callan's stalker that almost killed her. I'm still surprised the charges were dropped against her.

The message ends with them asking the students if they have any information on their whereabouts to come forward.

"They can't blame this on me," Mera says. "Nope. Not this time. But I do wonder, why ten students and why during spring break?"

The next morning, I walk outside the sorority late after everyone else has already gone to the Dining Hall.

As soon as I close the door, I stop in my tracks when I note a crowd of girls surrounding something, no, someone.

I go to walk by when something grabs my wrist. Following the hand, I look into Noel's eyes. In the morning light they're a russet brown.

I should've known the crowd was for him. These are his fangirls.

"Morning, Gem. Give me one sec, okay?" he asks, grabbing my hand.

I grit my teeth and stare down at our hands touching.

"Ladies, please, I have to go walk my girlfriend to class."

A chorus of disappointed awws, followed by a few giggles fill the air.

"Really? Her? Noel, come on, baby, you can do better than that," a sultry voice says.

I can't say I wasn't expecting that. I know how I look.

"I don't think I can, Jessica. She shines brighter than any of my exes. Sorry that you've suddenly become blind."

Oh God. Now I can feel invisible daggers hitting me like

one of those throwing targets.

Can he just let me go? I walk to class by myself all the time.

I glance toward them to confirm it, and sure enough, they're all glaring in my direction. Noel waves. "See you guys around." He takes a step forward. "Let's go, my precious jewel."

That last word makes all the air in my throat still. Jewel? He hasn't called me that since...

I glance up at him next to me, watching his expression carefully. He smirks. "Now to show you off to all those guys so they can stop fucking calling me Strikeout Noel."

It must just be a coincidence.

The walk to class through campus takes so long, I'm almost late to class. Every guy he talked to laughed at me. I don't know if Noel realized it or not and they've all taken back that nickname he hates so much.

When we reach my classroom door, I heave a massive sigh of relief. No more embarrassment. I just get to focus on class.

"Hey, give me a kiss before you go?" Noel asks, letting go of my hand.

"Not a chance," I reply, and go inside.

I walk over to my usual seat. No one sits next to me in this class, thankfully. Before the professor starts class, I wipe my glasses quickly.

After sliding them back on my face, I get my notebook out.

"Welcome back," Professor Marticien says excitedly. "I hope spring break was fun for all of you. We're going to have a group project and it's going to be a fun one. Pair up first and then I'll tell you all the fun details."

No way! Ugh. Well there's nothing I can do about it. I

always end up doing all the work for things like this.

Glancing around the room, I watch as everyone else goes off, knowing exactly where they're going to find their partner.

I've never had to partner up for a project in this class before and I don't know a single soul.

I suck at approaching people. *Can't I just do this project alone?*

I let my head hit the desk with a groan.

Suddenly, I hear a throat clear.

I sit up to find the palest guy I've ever seen staring at me with a curious expression on his face. "Are you okay?"

"Just fine," I say with a small smile.

He smiles widely and holds out his hand. "I'm Brad. I don't think we've met before."

"Gemma," I say, shaking his hand.

"Gemma," he says slowly. "Want to be partners?"

His golden hazel eyes with tiny flicks of green look friendly and I'm not getting any other offers. "Sure, why not?"

"Awesome." Brad moves around the table, taking the empty seat next to me. "Why don't we exchange numbers?" He takes his phone out and places it on the table.

I grab it quickly and enter my number and then give him my phone so he can return the favor.

As he finishes, the professor clears her throat. "I see everyone found someone. Good. Now let's talk about the project..."

Brad leans over. "Hey, Gemma, let's meet up on the weekend to get this project started."

Initiative? That's a plus. "Sounds great," I whisper back.

What else would I be doing on a weekend but school work?

CHAPTER FOUR

Noel

J ust before noon, I'm waiting outside the doors of the main building of my family's pharmaceutical company for Gemma. It's one of the biggest buildings in the business district of the city. Only a few years ago it was remodeled to be all glass. Their offices are on the top floor, but they spend all of their time on the ground floor working in their lab.

They have over a hundred employees working here. One more won't be a big deal. They always need more people for simple tasks. I'd never force Gemma to do anything super complicated.

And this is less about getting some of my money back than it is about spending more time with her and trying to figure out why she's so uptight and strict.

Over the vacation at Kardenia and the one in Cancun, I

realized something else. Every time Vincent talked to her she'd respond and smile. She even talked to Tyrell for a little bit, though he didn't say much back.

With me, she's always acted differently. I didn't know her before hazing night, yet she immediately didn't like me. At first I thought it was because she was uncomfortable, but she didn't even let me down nicely that night in front of everyone.

There's something more there, and I have to find out what it is.

I glance at my phone and find it's ten minutes before she's supposed to be meeting her supervisor.

She should've just let me drive her.

Suddenly, the screeching of a car echoes through the parking lot and a beat up car stops in front of the sidewalk in front of the building.

Gemma hops out of the passenger door quickly and I spot Mera in the backseat with her friend Scarlett in the driver's seat.

Gemma waves to them and smooths her hair down. I got so used to seeing it curly while we were on vacation, it looks different since she straightened it before school this morning.

She strides over quickly. "Hurry and take me to where I need to go. I don't want to look bad on my first day."

"Margie is a stickler, but it's fine," I say looking her over.

She's wearing pants and a button down shirt. The shirt is a little tighter than the usual clothes she wears so her form is a little easier to make out. I wonder if her pants are doing the same thing for her ass. Pulling the glass door open, I gesture for her to go inside first.

She steps inside, and I glance down to find that they do. That little jiggle it does is hot.

My hand burns with the need to touch it.

I follow her inside, closing the door behind me as she stops in the middle of the foyer. Straight ahead is the reception desk where two ladies sit. There's two elevators on one side and a staircase on the other.

"Where to?" she asks, turning to me.

"Follow me," I respond, sticking my hands in my pockets.

I stride to the reception desk and take a right down the hallway and walk to the first room. Opening the door quickly, I poke my head in to find Margie furiously typing something on her computer.

"What is it?" she asks with a sigh.

I clear my throat and she looks up with a small smile. "Look what the cat dragged in. I'm assuming my new recruit is here?"

"Nice to see you, Margie," I say smoothly with a wide smile. "Thanks for doing this for me."

She waves her hand. "None of that suave stuff. You're basically my boss too. Go ahead then, let her in."

I step back and push the door open and step aside so Gemma can go in. When she's inside, I close the door and lean against the wall, waiting for her to come out. I already told Margie when she was done signing paperwork and explaining her duties that I'd show her to her workstation.

The room she's going to spend most of her time in is right next to my office. I'm clearing away a few messages from my fanclub when the door pops open and I glance up as Gemma starts walking past me.

She wastes no time in walking down the hallway. "She said take a right at the door, then at the end of the hallway make a left and the last door on the right is the room."

Damn. Margie ruins all my fun. I was hoping to walk

slowly there and point out the rooms on the way even though they have nothing to do with her job.

As we make that left, her posture changes. She straightens and shivers as we walk past a room. Is it cold in here or something?

I don't feel a chill.

We approach the end of the hallway, and she stops right in front of the glass door with my name on it.

She turns her head to the right and then back to the door. "I should've known. Do me a favor, don't distract me. I don't want to be reprimanded for wasting time." Pushing her glasses up her nose, she opens the door to her work area with a tiny desk fit for one and the chair, surrounded by printers and filing cabinets.

She'll be here doing filing, copying, and handling the mail as well as fetching coffee and snacks from the break room if asked to.

"I wouldn't waste your time," I say innocently, "in fact, you'd be enjoying your time more with me. I'll be right here. You can come into my office anytime. There's an interesting fact about my office."

She raises an eyebrow. "And that is?"

I lean down to her ear and whisper, "It's one-way glass. You notice you can't see in right? I can see out though. We can do whatever we want in there without getting busted."

She frowns and steps past the threshold. "Work is meant for work."

"Then what'll you be doing on your breaks?" I ask as she steps over to the pile of paper on the desk.

"Using the bathroom," she says firmly. "And don't worry, I already know where it is." She points past me to the two doors across from each other with the man and woman signs over them.

"Of course, you did. By the way, I'm sure Margie already told you, but I just want to reiterate, you can go everywhere except for the ground and top floors."

"No, she didn't tell me," Gemma says slowly, "but I understand."

I don't want her to run into my parents before I get the chance to plan out the exact moment myself.

"I'll leave you to it then."

She looks all too happy for me to go so I pivot to the left and step over to my office door.

I'd like nothing more than to sit beside her and watch her work, and follow her around but I actually have work to do myself. This new software I'm creating will make things easier for them to keep track of their formulas and maybe it'll distract them enough for a while so they don't pay such close attention to me.

The past month and a half I've been so busy trying to juggle schoolwork while fixing the stupid software that's still finicky. More importantly, I haven't had any time with Gemma besides seeing her at work and eating breakfast, lunch, or dinner with her.

My grades last semester were barely passing. Last semester and the beginning of this semester were a lot, and my grades have taken a nose-dive so far, it'll be a miracle for me to pull them back up decently.

Guilt is a heavy burden to bear.

There's only a few weeks left and it'll finally be summer. This year, I refuse to take any summer classes.

I flop down on my bed and sigh. "Ty, what are you doing tonight?"

He clears his throat. "Nothing, I guess. Do you want to go out somewhere?"

It's Friday night. Callan and Mera are on a date. Vincent and Ashlynn had some kind of company dinner with their parents. Wherever we go, it'd just be Ty and me. Sometimes I wish he'd open up to me more. Five years and I still feel like I barely know anything about him. "Sort of. I'd like to take a walk to ZDB."

"For Gemma?" he asks.

"Of course, for Gemma. Time is ticking. There's almost only six months left and we haven't fucked yet."

He sighs. "Why do you want her so bad anyway? Just to prove you can have any girl you want?"

"Precisely," I reply smugly, putting my hands behind my head.

A knock sounds on the door followed by a few giggles.

Tyrell immediately slides off his bed with an irritated expression. "That's my cue to leave."

"But wait, Ty," I say, sitting up.

I didn't actually want to let them in. I would've rather lied and said I was sick.

But he opens the door and they come inside while he walks out.

It's been uncomfortable being around them ever since the first day back. Every chance my fan club gets, they get they ask me if I've broken up with Gemma yet. Am I ready for someone else?

My answer remains the same. No.

I understand their irritation because they all want to be with me. How could they not? But they've never bad mouthed any of my exes like this. They've just patiently waited their turn.

Why pick on Gemma?

It's driving me up the fucking wall. I already saw them earlier today and here they are again.

Jessica and Mindy sit on opposite sides of my bed, staring at me with hungry faces. "How was your class today?"

"Fine," I respond. The other girls crowd around my bed and I smile halfheartedly.

Mindy looks at the other girls, who giggle, and then she looks back to me. "So real talk Noel, no one else is in the room so you can be honest with us. What's the deal with you and Gemma? Does she have something on you or what?"

"Well, hold on Mindy, she also turned him down last year," Jessica says, turning to her and then back to me.

"Guys, I'd really appreciate it if you'd stop bringing her up."

"So she does have something on you," Mindy says with a gasp. "What a treacherous cow. Don't worry, the girls and I can talk to her and get her away from you."

I blink slowly and feel my jaw tic.

Actually, I'm the one with something on her.

More than that, I'm not a violent person. I've only gotten in one fight in high school compared to the many that Callan and Vincent have gotten themselves in.

But I've never wanted to hit a woman as much as I do now.

"Get out of my room," I say in a low, warning tone, gazing around the circle.

"What?" Jessica asks with a puzzled look. She shakes her head. "Why? Are you sick or..?"

"Get out. Right now. And the next time you see me, don't bring up my relationship. Talk about the weather. The next party coming up, anything. I don't give a fuck. Just don't let me hear her name come out of your mouth again. And don't go anywhere near her either."

All of them stay standing with shocked expressions.

I don't think I've ever had to use a tone like that with them.

They might decide to leave my fan club after this, but I don't really care. It'll build back up in no time at all.

Jessica whirls around and leaves, followed by Mindy, and the rest trail right along after her.

After they're gone, I let the anger go instead of holding on to it. Grabbing my phone to call Tyrell to let him know he can come back.

A few minutes go by and he doesn't respond.

Usually he answers right away and comes back.

When I look over to his side of the room, I discover why. His phone is on his nightstand. In his haste to escape my fan club, he must've forgotten it.

I don't want to finish up my homework too quick since the guys are coming over to my parents' house to study on Sunday.

I guess I could play video games, but I'm not really feeling it.

A better idea hits me. It's been a while since I've been able to finish.

After pulling my phone out I go to the internet and type in my favorite porn site. I head straight for the categories, eyeing them, until I click amateur.

I'm halfway through the video, watching the man fucking her against the kitchen counter when I realize I don't even know what I watched. Is this one too boring?

I palm my cock and realize I didn't even get semi-hard.

Frowning, I scroll to related videos and find another one of a woman sucking a man off in a car.

Eventually he drags her off and sits her in her lap. Her moans are so loud and jarring, I have to pause it.

This time, I go back to the categories. This time, something that I don't usually watch catches my eye. BBW.

I bite my lip and click on the first video. This one is short and wastes no time in having her ride him on the bed.

I reach my hand down and palm my cock, feeling it finally coming to life. But even when the video ends, that's as far as it gets. Semi-hard.

Fuck.

Frustrated, I drop my phone onto the bed next to me and sigh. I've never had a problem like this before. Maybe I'm thinking too hard about it.

I close my eyes and imagine myself on the bed as a familiar body joins me, climbing over my legs and settling herself on my lap. Gemma.

Her eyes aren't angry or annoyed, but lustful.

And...

I tilt my head down to find myself at full mast.

Oh fuck. Now this...this is a problem.

I haven't even had the chance to fuck her yet. It's what my cock wants, though. And bad.

I slide my hand down it when the door pops open and I hear, "Forgot my phone...what the fuck, man?"

Ty closes the door quickly. I pull my boxers over myself and shout, "Sorry! My bad, man!" But I know the damage has already been done.

He opens the door slightly, and then opens it fully. "Couldn't you have put a sock over the door or something?"

"Sorry," I say quickly.

He sighs and sits at the edge of his bed. "I kind of need to wash my eyes with bleach now. But since they're gone, which I wasn't expecting, I'll just stay here."

Since I won't be getting to finish, I scoot up against the headboard. "Hey, can I ask you something?"

"Sure. As long as it doesn't involve your dick," he says, scrolling through his phone.

I snort. "No, man. What do you think about Gemma?"

He's quiet for a long time until he moves his phone off to the side. "I think she's nice and smart. Very pretty."

"So you see it too?" I ask. I still don't understand how anyone could think she isn't.

"She is almost as gorgeous a-as..." Ty says and pauses with an anxious expression.

"As...?" I ask, raising an eyebrow.

"Not important," he murmurs, picking up his phone again.

Does Ty have a thing for someone?

I've never seen him have a girlfriend before.

But I won't push him about it.

"It's not important because she'll never look at me like that anyway."

"Sorry, man." For once, I'm at a loss for words.

Heartbreak is hard, which is why I'll never give my heart away. Women are welcome to give theirs to me but I'd rather keep mine locked away.

Sunday afternoon, I pull through the gate to my parents' house and travel up the driveway.

I park behind my Mom's Escalade and hop out with my schoolbag in tow. The guys will be here in a few minutes so I left the gate wide open.

Sliding my hand into my pocket, I go to grab a key when I remember the maids. One of them will probably open the door.

Five minutes later, the door opens and I look up to meet eyes exactly like my own, only sharper.

She smiles slightly, in a way that makes my stomach form a knot. "Noel, great timing. We were just talking about you."

I glance back at her Escalade. They never take it to work. They'd rather take my Dad's Tesla, but it isn't in the driveway. They shouldn't be home.

"Your Dad's Tesla is in the shop, dear. Come inside," she says in a cheery tone. She turns and walks back inside, and I reluctantly follow.

If I knew they were going to be home, I wouldn't have invited the guys over.

There's more room here than in the fraternity and the library is always packed on the weekends.

Instead of following her past the foyer to the living room, I take a right to go up the stairs.

"Noel," she barks. "The living room."

I drop my bag, letting it fall onto the first stair and backtrack. She leads the way past the dining room to the living room where my dad is waiting on one sofa.

Mom sits right next to him, crossing one leg over the other.

Dad clears his throat. "We'll just say this quickly since we're busy as usual. Your grades, son. What's going on?"

"I've been trying to get them up. I realize that I almost failed first semester, but I'm doing better this semester."

"Barely," Mom snaps. "Are you trying to make us look bad? All your other friends are doing just fine."

"You've been looking at my friends' grades?"

Mom scoffs. "Of course. We need to see you at the top where you belong. Don't let us down."

I clench my jaw and nod. "Understood."

"If you don't at least get B's in every class, we won't allow you to attend school there anymore."

"I said I understood!" I exclaim, my irritation rising.

For as long as I can remember, they've been anal about my grades. I don't remember if they were the same when I was in the lower grades. I can only remember starting middle school and getting in trouble for getting a C+ on an assignment. They acted like it was the end of the world.

For a long time, I did the best that I could. The pressure eventually wore me down and I cracked. I locked myself in my room for a week and after that, they went easier, but it never lasts. Now that I'm in college, they really want me to be #1. And so far, I'm failing at it.

"Don't raise your voice at me, Noel," Dad says. "You know you're capable of much more than those lackluster grades. Don't embarrass the Hardington name. And if we discover that that stupid fan club of yours is the one causing you to do worse, or a girlfriend, I'll have to make it so they can't bother you anymore."

My eyes widen. "As in what exactly?"

Dad adjusts his glasses, standing up in a hurry. "We don't want to find out, do we?"

Mom nods, with a satisfied expression. She pats me on the head on her way out. "Love you. Study hard."

When the front door opens and closes behind them, I breathe in deeply and shakily stand up.

I can't let them find out about Gemma so I'll have to work hard.

Walking back out to the foyer, I spot a maid dusting the wooden railing. After grabbing my bag, I head up the steps, happy to get to my room. Before turning down the hallway, I ask her to get the door when my friends come.

My door is the second one in the hallway, and the minute

I open the door, I remember how freeing it is to be away from the toxicity of the rest of this house.

But this room is nothing like the one at the fraternity. There's no personality to it. Nothing that says me. It's too clean and tidy and there's nothing on the walls. It's just a bed and furniture. I don't even keep clothes in this closet anymore.

There were many nights in high school that they slept over, only to wake up to my parents kicking them out so I could study.

I don't miss this at all.

Digging through my bag quickly I search for my deadline paper. The paper I use to keep track of when all my assignments are due. Whether I actually do them is another story.

My hand is at the bottom of my bag when I feel it folded and pull it out.

As I tug it out, something else comes out with it, tumbling to the floor at my feet.

Bending down, my stomach drops as I stare at *it*.

The last reminder of that night.

I forgot this was here.

Fuck. I rake my hand through my hair and stare at it.

Every day, the memory of that night stays present in the back of my head. I've done so many stupid things over the years, but that was the stupidest thing I could ever have done.

The sound of voices outside my door jerks me out of my own head. Frantically, I look down at it and grab it, shoving it in my pocket as the door opens.

"Hey, guys," I say nervously, pulling my hand out of my pocket.

"You're actually ready to get started for once? That's a

shock," Vincent notes, plopping down on the bean bag chair next to the window.

"I'm not ready though," Callan says, sitting in the chair by my desk. "Those kids that went missing showed up at their homes today and they're completely fine. I heard the news from my grandfather."

Right. His grandfather is temporarily Dean while his dad recovers.

"That's weird."

Tyrell nods and Vincent shakes his head. "People just don't disappear like that and come back perfectly fine."

"Honestly," Callan begins with a sigh, "it's great for them and their families. Some nights I can't sleep because I keep thinking about Heath's body rotting somewhere."

My blood runs cold and my fingers twitch as I shakily run my hand through my hair. "Guess you should talk to your therapist about that."

He laughs wryly. "You know I hate therapy, Noel. You and Mera are right though."

"Why don't we get to work?" I ask, holding up my notebook.

"Yeah, I've got a lot to do," Vincent mutters.

Tyrell grunts.

As I stare down at my notebook, my pulse accelerates.

I need to stop thinking about it and just focus on schoolwork.

I can't change what I did that night.

Four hours later, we're all finished for the night.

"Why don't we order some dinner?" I suggest. "On me."

I pull out my phone as they start discussing where to go. Before going on Safari, I glance through my notifications, getting rid of a few before I spot two news articles.

One about the missing students at SGU coming back and

the other, an article about something sweeping the SoCal area amongst teens and college students. Something called Space Dust?

"What the hell is Space Dust?" I ask out loud with a laugh.

"A drug," Vincent says. "I saw that article earlier. Apparently it makes you feel good. Like you're out of this world...hence Space Dust. It's brand new and apparently, it's better than anything out there."

"Really?" I ask, scrolling through the article.

I might drink a lot, but I've never taken anything and I don't plan on it, but something about this drug is nagging at me. Somehow, I need to acquire some.

At the bottom of the article, there's a note about not actively seeking it out because the effects aren't wide known yet and they still know very little about how dangerous it is.

I understand why they put this article out. However, I can only imagine the alarming amount of people who are going to seek out dealers for this one.

And I guess I'll be one of those people because it doesn't sit right with me.

CHAPTER FIVE

Gemma

I don't think I've felt more at ease with a guy in so long. Every weekend we've been meeting up at the closest coffee shop to campus to get this project done. We could've gone to the one on campus, but he suggested the mood of this one is calmer and there's less chaotic energy here.

I don't know if it's done anything, but I do know this project is done. Cultural Anthropology was an elective I took on, spur of the moment. Surprisingly, this class is going to give me my easiest A by far.

"All we have left is the presentation," Brad says, putting his folder away in his bag. The written report is inside his folder. He gestures to the poster near my legs. "Want me to take that home with me or do you want to keep it?"

Smiling, I shrug. "I'll take it. That way the responsibility isn't all on your shoulders."

He leans forward on his elbows. "You're so generous, Gemma. I'm glad we got to be partners."

"Me too," I say with a small smile, sipping at my barely touched green tea.

He smiles, and glances down for a moment before locking eyes with me. "I know we finished the project, but do you want to hang around and talk for a while?"

I tap the screen of my phone to see the time. "Sure, why not?"

"Awesome." He grins and sits back in his chair. "So tell me what you like to do, where you like to go."

His questions catch me off guard and I scramble to find an answer.

"Well I mean…besides schoolwork?"

He blinks and bursts out laughing. "Of course, no one likes schoolwork."

My cheeks heat up. I know I'm not normal, but now I feel a little embarrassed about being honest. But I refuse to lie. "I like learning new things. I find it fun. But if you're talking about something other than school, I like to read."

He looks surprised by my answer. "What kind of books?"

I scratch my head. "Well, romance and fantasy are great."

"Oh, so the lovey dovey stuff, okay. That's cool. I'm a gaming kind of guy. And where do you like to go?"

I don't know how to answer this one since it's been so long since I've gone anywhere. My aunt never brought me anywhere because it was extra money that she had to pay. When I was little, I vaguely remember going to Knott's Berry Farm.

Recently, I was able to go to Kardenia and Cancun, but are those even good answers?

My palms start to sweat and his hand stretches across the table, touching mine.

The contact shocks me and I exclaim, "Anywhere! I like to go anywhere and everywhere." God, I sound like I'm on a game show.

He moves his thumb over my hand. "Hey, no biggie. These questions weren't meant to make you anxious. I just wanted us to hang out sometime this summer somewhere. What do you think about that?"

"That sounds fun," I respond and glance down at his hand, still resting on mine. I open my mouth to ask him to remove his hand when I feel a presence to my right, hanging over our table.

I glance up, locking eyes with Noel who's staring not at me, but at the hand on top of mine.

"So is *this* where you are on the weekends, Gem?"

"We're finishing a project, Noel."

Brad moves his hand off mine and holds his hand out in front of Noel. "I'm Bradley, pleased to meet you."

"Not interested," Noel answers flatly, staring at my hand. His gaze is starting to burn a hole in my hand.

I hide my hand under the table and look straight ahead at Brad. "Sorry about his rudeness. Why don't you come to Noel's party next weekend in celebration of the semester being over?"

Brad smiles. "I'd love to. Just text me and let me know where to go." He leans down, grabbing his bag and stands up. "Nice meeting you Noel."

Noel finally glances away from the spot my hand was to watch him leave.

"So, he gets your phone number, but I don't?"

"You never asked," I say getting out of my chair. After I

scoot the chair in, he grabs the hand Brad touched, pulling me out of the shop.

When we get outside, he pulls me over to the side and tilts my chin up with his free hand. "Let's get one thing straight right now, precious. You don't let anyone touch what's mine."

I blink quickly. "But I'm not yours, Noel. Brad is just a friend anyway."

A slow smile spreads across his face. "But you are. For six more months. So Brad," he says his name venomously, "doesn't get to touch you. Friend or not."

I move my chin away and he drops his hand. Whatever. As long as he doesn't see, it'll be fine.

"How do you know that guy?"

"He's in my Cultural Anthropology class. Why?" I ask curiously.

He shrugs. "I feel like I've seen him somewhere before."

"He does go to class on the same campus as us," I point out.

Noel shakes his head, looking off to the parking lot. "That's not it. Oh well, it'll come to me at some point. Make sure you tell your *friend* not to invite too many people. I'm too lazy to clean and the maids don't clean on the weekends."

I cross my arms and shake my head indignantly. "No, he wouldn't do that."

"Fine." He turns around and walks off, heading to the parking lot. "Are you coming?"

"No, the walk back to campus isn't far," I say, raising my voice to make sure he hears.

Noel keeps walking so I guess he heard me. I walk the other direction to the street and start down the sidewalk.

It's such a warm day out. Typical spring weather in

SoCal. The sweat is starting to pool under my breasts. Ugh, what a pain.

A mile and a quarter until I'll be back at school.

The honking of a car startles me and I glance to my left to find Noel in his car with his window down.

"What are you doing?" I ask.

"We're going in the same direction aren't we?"

A car honks behind him and he waves them ahead.

"So why don't you just drive there at a normal speed?" I ask, glancing at the road ahead.

"Just get in the car, Gem."

"Not until you tell me why you're doing this," I insist, stopping in place.

"Fine. Those people that went missing...I'm not so sure it wouldn't happen again. I know they eventually came back from wherever they were, but I'd rather not jinx it. I want to have someone to give that dinky house to when these eight months are up."

The car behind him blares on the horn and Noel sticks his hand out and flips them off. He gazes toward me. "Are you getting in or what?"

Sighing, I dash forward, open the door and slide in. The door locks click and he speeds off in his Porsche.

"That wasn't so hard, was it?" he asks, looking from the road to me.

"Eyes on the road," I respond, looking out the window.

We make it back to campus in no time at all. He stops in front of ZDB and I pull on the handle, but it's locked. Right. I hit the unlock button, only for it to click again.

I swivel my head around to Noel, who's staring at me with a waiting expression. "Your phone number," he says holding his phone out.

Guess there's no getting around this one. I type my

number in and hand it back to him. He holds my gaze for a moment, until his eyes flit down to my lips. "Now we can talk about all the fun things we're going to do this summer in bed."

That's the last straw! I need to get out of here before he thinks about doing something now in front of the sorority house.

I hit the unlock and get out as quickly as I can. "Thanks for the ride!" I yell, and rush to the porch before he decides to park his car and get out to follow me.

How does he plan on finding time to do that when I'm working for his parents' company and doing summer classes? It doesn't surprise me one bit that he wants to take it easy, but I'd rather get ahead if I can.

As I get inside, I hear the roar of his Porsche as he leaves. I breathe a sigh of relief.

He's being generous now because he's distracted by school, but this summer is going to be my biggest problem.

Everyone says Noel throws the best parties. Mera told me we'd probably be jamming out to music drinking a few beers. So why are we sitting in a circle playing spin the bottle for seven minutes in heaven?

Maybe if I scoot out of the circle slowly, no one will notice.

No, two people would notice.

Tonight, I brought a special little tool I'll use if Noel tries to force me into something I don't want to do. Hopefully, I won't have to use them

Brad grins at me, nudging my right shoulder. "Don't worry. You don't actually have to do anything."

The smile on Noel's face lessens as he eyes us. Even a small nudge like that is enough to almost set him off? "Let's get this started, shall we?" He looks so psyched, I almost expect him to grab the bottle. Instead he sits down in an open spot opposite of us.

There's twenty of us sitting in a circle in Noel's parents' foyer.

Not everyone wanted to join so some people are outside in his backyard in the pool and jacuzzi.

Why couldn't I have been one of those people?

Mera is sitting right next to me with Callan next to her.

Luella quietly slipped away when I tried to rope her in to join us.

But Ashlynn is sitting next to Callan and looking very ready and excited to go into the closet.

There's one thing I can't help thinking about. What happens if Noel spins the bottle and goes in that closet?

Will this closet affect him or not?

I recognize a few of the girls in this circle as the girls in his fan club. The other guys I recognize as the ones who kept calling him Strikeout Noel. Since that first day back, they high five him and insist that he's "the man" while his fan club tries to kill me with their eyes.

Such a sharp contrast to each other.

"Who wants to go first?" he asks, looking around the circle.

One of the girls crawls forward and spins the bottle, sliding back into her spot to wait for the bottle to stop.

It takes a few revolutions until it slows to a stop on one of Noel's friends.

They both stand up and rush around the circle, hand in hand to get to the closet behind my side of the circle.

While waiting for them to get out, everyone starts talking

to each other loud enough to drown out whatever's going on in the closet.

"Any plans this week, Gemma?" Brad asks.

"Work," I say simply. "And school. I'm only taking one summer class. Thought I could fit another one in, but I won't be able to with this job."

"Bummer," he says with a disappointed look.

"Most of my weekends should be free, so if you ever want to hang out on one just let me know a few days in advance."

He smiles, "I will. I know a lot of fun things we can do."

Mera nudges me and I turn my head to look at her.

She whispers, "Why is Noel staring over here like he wants to murder someone?"

"Just ignore it," I whisper back.

No matter what he thinks, I still want to be able to hang out with a friend, even if it is a guy.

"Hey, not that it matters, but how is Callan so okay with you hanging out with Peyton so much?" I ask.

She giggles. "I don't think he sees Peyton as a threat. Besides, I have this running theory that Peyton has a thing for Scarlett. Both of them sat out this game when it seems like something they'd like, you know?"

I nod and abruptly, the closet door flies open. Both participants sit back in the circle in their respective spots, but they can't stop staring at each other. The guy has her red lipstick stain on his cheek and neck.

They definitely had a lot of fun in that closet.

"I'll go next," I hear. I glance up in horror as Noel rolls forward to reach the bottle on knees and spins it.

I breathe a sigh of relief. Good. He didn't cheat. My mistake, I thought he would grab the bottle and just point it in my direction and drag me to the closet.

There's no way that bottle will land on me like I assume he wants it to.

It slows to a stop, pointing at one of the girls in his fan club.

Her eyes brighten and she stands up anxiously, practically falling in the process.

Great, she can have him.

Noel stands up and crosses over to her. "Sorry, but this bottle is slightly defective." He leans down over the bottle, grabbing it by the bottom and points it right at me.

My jaw drops as he straightens, looking quite pleased with himself.

"Now it's correct."

She makes an angry noise in her throat, stomping her foot against the travertine tile as he moves over to me.

I spoke too soon.

He holds his hand down for me to grab, and I ignore it, getting up on my own.

His guy friends whistle and shout words of encouragement.

It makes my face burn with embarrassment. They didn't do this for the first guy.

For seven minutes, we'll be alone in this closet. I cross over the threshold, going right past the parted row of jackets and sweaters hanging to the back of the closet.

He steps in, closing the door behind him.

I clench my jaw as my pulse starts to race. It's not the same closet, but it's giving me the exact same vibes.

What will it do to Noel?

Will it even do anything at all?

In the dark, I feel a hand touch my wrist.

"You're disappointing your fan club Noel," I murmur to distract him.

"Who cares? I'm not playing that game for them, I'm playing it for you."

I feel his hand glide up my arm, eventually reaching my neck.

"You know, you…"

His hand stills.

"You what?" I ask, waiting for him to continue.

He doesn't respond.

"Noel?"

"Why?" he rasps.

"Why what?"

"Why is it so hard to breathe all of a sudden?"

He moves his hand off and my breath stills in my throat.

This is it. I knew it would happen.

He doesn't remember but that anxiety and fear is instilled in the deep recesses of his mind.

So many times he suffered alone, but there were times I'd join him.

He breathes shakily, and as my eyes adjust to the dark, I watch as he leans against the wall.

"Fuck. This isn't supposed to happen. I'm supposed to be kissing you right now," he says, his voice getting lower with each word.

"First of all, no." I close my mouth, hesitating. I could do what I used to do and help him the rest of our few minutes in here, but why should I when he did what he did back then?

And now he's holding my parents' house hostage?

"Gemma," he croaks, sliding to the floor.

My heart sinks a little. Seeing this happening again after all these years takes me back. I'm not a horrible person and my parents raised me to be kind above everything else.

"Just think about how it'll only be a few minutes more.

That tight feeling in your chest will go away in a few minutes."

He gasps, "No."

"Noel. Listen to my voice," I say gently. "This isn't that bad. Look, there's even a tiny bit of light streaming under the door. Obviously your parents didn't want this door to scratch up their nice travertine tile."

He clutches at his chest. "How much longer?"

"I don't know. Three minutes maybe?"

"It's too long," he says, holding his hands parallel to the wall, suddenly his fingers scrape down.

My eyes widen and I stretch forward, grabbing his hands. "Don't...do that. If you come out with bloody fingers, people will have questions."

"It's too much," he murmurs, his voice breaking.

If he comes out looking like he's cried, people will have questions too.

"I keep telling you to focus on my voice. Focus on me," I say insistently.

"Trying," he says, his hands shaking in mine.

Sighing, I close my eyes. If this keeps going the rest of our time here, he might remember. I need him to stop thinking.

I grab his chin, turning him to face me and place my lips on top of his. He freezes.

God, I don't know what I'm doing.

I move my lips over his, and he starts to respond, licking the seam of my lips. Two hands grab my waist as he pulls me closer, making my body flush with his. He pulls me onto his lap, reaching under my shirt as his tongue dives into my mouth.

Wait, I was only going to kiss him.

An involuntary shiver goes down my spine as I feel his hand go up my shirt, cupping my bra-covered breast.

His finger starts to pull my bra down when I hear the loud ringing of a timer.

I jump back, as it shocks my brain into becoming clear again.

I get to my feet first, opening the door and striding out.

I've had enough of this game.

I start to turn away but Noel grabs my hand.

The guys hoot and holler. "Go, Noel!"

Collette looks completely disgusted with me.

"You guys should've kept the timer going for another seven minutes. I was so close to scoring," he says smoothly.

That only causes them to get louder.

Collette stares at me with disgust etched on her face.

My cheeks heat up and I wrench my hand away. So much for trying to be a good person.

That was a mistake.

Maybe I should tell all of his little friends how he had a panic attack in the closet just now. But I won't, because I'm not a jerk and it's his business.

I turn on my heel and start down the hallway before I humiliate myself any further.

"Gemma, wait!" Noel calls.

Asshole.

He'll never change. Never stop embarrassing me in front of my friends.

What does Brad think of me?

He makes me sound like I'm one of his desperate fangirls.

My cheeks are still burning as I open the sliding glass door to the cool air.

The music outside is at a respectable level.

I glance around the yard for an empty seat, finding one at a table with Luella sitting alone at it.

I sit across from her, crossing my arms and leaning back.

She's moving her fingers swiftly on her phone and she looks completely entranced by it.

"Are you writing right now?"

Her eyes flit up to me and she sets her phone down with a small smile. "I was just getting an idea down for the next issue. What's wrong? You look pissed."

"Just the usual Noel crap. I'd rather hear about your poem."

A voice rings out from behind me. "And I'd rather hear about what happened in that closet."

The chair beside me scrapes against the concrete as it's pulled back. It makes a chill go up my spine. Collette sits gracefully. "Well?"

"Nothing happened," I blurt, pushing my glasses up my nose.

"I figured. I mean a closet? I know you wouldn't let him force you to do anything in a fucking *closet.*"

"Of course."

"Don't worry, dear. Only a little longer and you'll be last week's news. One of those girls in his fan club will get their shot and he'll forget all about you."

"I hope so," I respond.

I breathe a sigh of relief when Coll changes the subject, talking to Lu about something.

There's no way I'd force Mera to leave since she's my ride, but I wish I didn't have to stay a moment longer. I let myself daydream, staring off into the distance, when the sound of the sliding glass door shocks me out of it.

Turning around, I watch everyone from the circle pour out of his house, with him bringing up the rear. His eyes catch me as soon as they look in my direction. He waves me over.

I flatten my lips and turn away.

"Don't be like that, Gemma!" he yells.

"Is he coming over here?" I ask Coll and Lu.

Lu shakes her head.

"No, he's going over to the jacuzzi. No one's in it right now, but I'd bet it's about to be packed."

I don't know what possesses me to look, but I do.

He takes his shirt off, exposing his toned chest and he gets in the water using the rail.

Ten girls follow him in, not even taking the time to go down the steps he did.

None of them have bathing suits on, just their underwear.

All of them start giggling as they eye him and a few sidle up to him, putting their hands on his chest.

Coll mutters, "Yuck."

"Sorry, Gemma," Lu says in a small voice.

I turn around, facing back toward the table. "It's fine. I'm glad his attention is elsewhere."

She picks her phone off the table and hands it over to me. "You know I value your opinion. It's been a little slow since last year but I'm finally feeling great about my work again. In a few days, I should be able to put it all together."

I scan over her tiny notes and my heart clenches at some of the darker parts. "This one is going to be a tearjerker."

Suddenly, her phone starts ringing. The caller ID name is a skull emoji.

"Um, Lu, death is calling?"

She snatches her phone away in a flash, her face pale. "I'll be back." Scooting her chair back, she runs over to the sliding glass door and disappears inside.

Collette turns to me. "So, I was thinking. We should go to the beach. Which beach is your favorite?"

I shrug. "I've never been. The only beach I've been to was

the one in Cancun." I didn't even stay long, going back to the hotel alone to read instead.

"Well, you have to experience it so we're going. I'll figure out the day." She smiles happily, typing away on her phone so I grab mine.

I go back to the book I was reading a few weeks ago.

Sometime later, a hand touches my shoulder and I glance up to find Mera. "Hey, we're getting ready to go. You're coming with us, right?"

Callan is standing directly behind her. I glance at the other chairs at the table and notice Coll vacated hers and Lu never came back?

"Yeah, I'm ready to go." Getting out of the chair, I immediately feel how stiff my legs are.

What time is it?

I tap my phone and see 1:30 AM.

Could be worse.

Mera walks off with Callan's arm around her shoulder and as I start to follow them, I hear, "Hey, don't leave yet" from across the yard.

Noel.

I'm not interested in hearing anything he has to say the rest of the night.

I pause at the gate behind them as I feel my pocket.

This would be a good opportunity to get some payback.

Whirling around, I glance around the yard to find there's no one else around and he's alone in the jacuzzi.

Smiling, I say in a low tone, "You guys go ahead. I'll be at the car in a few minutes."

Mera turns her head slightly. "Okay."

Callan looks at me curiously, but they both continue on, walking past the gate.

Backtracking quickly, I walk past the olympic sized pool

to the jacuzzi on the far side of the yard. Steam is still rising from it and the bubbles are going. Perfect.

His eyes are locked on me as I slip my flats off and step into the jacuzzi fully clothed.

"I can't believe you're actually getting in with me without a fight," he says, smirking. "You must've realized you enjoyed the closet more than you thought."

I smile and swim over to him near the stairs. It takes a lot of nerve for me to do this, but the end result is what's keeping me going. I maneuver my legs on each side of him. His eyes heat up as I place my hands on his shoulders and lower my head until our lips are about to touch. "Maybe, I did."

His eyes move over my clothes sticking to my wet body. "You don't have to keep those on, you know. There's no one here but me."

"I know," I say in my best sultry voice.

It sounds so weird coming out of my mouth.

I just need to act a little bit longer.

I lower my mouth onto his, kissing him for the second time tonight. His mouth wastes no time in moving against mine, taking over to control the kiss.

His hands come closer to the surface of the water, touching my waist to pull me even closer, as I carefully pull it out of my pants pocket.

I only have one shot to do this.

He has to keep his attention on everything else but my arm.

I grind myself down onto his lap, trying not to lose my nerve as I feel his dick hardening beneath me.

He groans low in his throat, and at the same time, I slide it out of my pocket, put it around his wrist and put the other side around the rail.

Noel's eyes shoot open as he glances at his wrist, tugging at it. "What did you do, precious?"

Using the steps, I propel myself away, but his uncuffed hand shoots out and grabs one of my feet underwater.

I kick frantically trying to get his grip to loosen enough for me to get away.

He chuckles. "You know you really had me. I guess I was too hopeful. Can you uncuff me now?"

I glance down at his hand underwater. "No."

The laughter fades from his face. "Gem."

"No," I answer, my voice rising. "There's no good reason why I should." I use my other foot to kick at his arm, surprising him enough to let my foot go.

"Fuck," he says with a wince.

I swim over to the other edge of the jacuzzi, place my hands on the concrete and pull my soaked self out of the water.

"Don't worry," I say, smoothing my now curly hair back. "One of your fan club members will drop by in the morning I'm sure."

One at a time, I slide my feet into my flats and start walking in the direction of the gate.

"You're going to regret this precious!" he yells. "You're going to regret doing this."

I close the gate behind me, and walk over the grassy area. My hands touch the lock of the second gate when I distantly hear him yell, "Jewel."

Freezing I clench my hands into fists.

That nickname again. Jewel.

The person that used to call me Jewel is long gone. I wish he'd stop using that. It's only a sad reminder of what could've been if everything had happened differently.

I unlock the gate and slam it closed behind me.

CHAPTER SIX

Noel

Like a colossal idiot, I thought she'd come back. When the timer ran out for the bubbles, I knew how much time had passed, but after that I had no clue.

When the sun came up, I realized I was too optimistic. She wouldn't be coming back to free me.

She really left me out here all fucking night long.

Luckily, I didn't drink all night like I normally would have so I don't have to piss badly, but come on, I'm sick of my skin being all wrinkly and shit.

I guess I should be glad I live in Southern California where late spring nights are warm.

I've been alternating between sitting on the steps in the water and sitting on the concrete near the pole. I've always loved this jacuzzi. It was a nice escape from being in the house all day. Now, I'm sick of looking at it and all I want is sleep.

When I close my eyes and start to drift off, I can only see her, crawling onto my lap. And every time, I start getting hard.

What happened in the closet made me too hopeful. I still don't understand why I reacted that way, but right now I can't even think too hard about it.

The only thing I want to do is go to Gem's room at the sorority and punish her all weekend. Lock her door and force her sorority sisters to hear me fucking her and wrenching orgasm after orgasm out of her. She probably has plans with that asshole Brad.

Something about that guy is off.

Even after Gem ran out on the circle, he didn't make one move to follow her out. Does she really think that guy is her friend?

The creaking of the gate makes me look over at the side of the house.

Has someone come to rob me? Just my fucking luck.

"If you're wondering, I'm not rich!" I yell.

I watch a hand reach over to unlock the second gate, holding my breath.

I release it when I see it's Callan.

"Oh it's you, man. Don't scare me like that."

He strides over, dangling a key from his hand. "Nice try with the whole I'm not rich thing. Only a dumbass would look at this mansion and think no, the people who live here aren't rich at all."

I snort as he leans down, putting the key in the lock and turning it.

The cuff comes off, and I put my other hand around my

wrist, rubbing the part that was cuffed all night long. I let the cuffs stay on the ground.

"I'm guessing she gave you the key this morning," I say, glancing up at him as he straightens.

"Yep. She said something last night about karma on the way home. Mera and I were both trying to ask her what she meant, but she said she'd tell us in the morning." He smirks. "How was your night under the stars?"

"Horrible," I reply, standing up and stretching my arms out.

My appendages are so stiff and now that I'm free, there's only one thing I want to do, and that's go back to school with Callan and have him drop me off in front of ZDB.

Callan sighs. "I know I have no right to really say this, but for your own sake, don't take this thing too far."

I scoff. "I think I know when something goes too far. I have no plans to choke her until she passes out, Callan."

His jaw tics and his voice rises, "I'm just trying to stop you from doing something that will affect your relationship with her forever. She already doesn't like you much, but maybe once you give her the house back at the end of the year, you could be friends. Push her too far and she may hate you forever."

I chuckle and pat him on the shoulder. "Nice of you to worry, buddy, but I'm mostly just giving her a taste of her own medicine. For eight months I heard that stupid fucking nickname. Now she can be embarrassed for that same amount of time."

"Fair enough," he says quietly, staring at the key in his hand.

"And I'm sorry about bringing up the choking thing."

His mouth flattens. "It's fine. Not even the worst thing I did, anyway."

I give him a questioning look but he thumbs his finger behind him. "I'm going back. You should get some shut-eye because you look wrecked." He tosses the key to me and I catch it.

All of a sudden, my eyes are starting to feel heavy. I shake my head, yawning involuntarily. "No, I need to go to ZDB."

He rolls his eyes. "That can wait. Besides, Gemma isn't even there. Mera said she was going for a spa day with the girls and she forced Gemma to come along so she can be ready for class on Monday."

A spa day? Class? Suddenly, I feel wide awake. "As in someone is going to massage her beautiful back? Put their hands all over what's mine?"

He nods, looking slightly amused. "I'm not that enthused about it either, but I know when Mera comes back she'll be relaxed and that's all that matters. I'll put my hands all over her anyway, later. Get some sleep, man." Turning, he walks around the jacuzzi and around the pool.

"Wait, Callan, what class is she taking during the summer? And you can't leave without telling me the address of that place."

He laughs and waves, his back to me. "I'll see if I can find out. As for the spa, for your own safety, no. Ashlynn, Scarlett and Coll will wreck you if you ruin their spa day. Sleep well."

Damn it.

I bend down and pick the handcuffs up off the ground, studying them.

A devious tool. Smiling, I grip them in my hand. I'll pull these out when she least expects it.

Summer classes are a pain in the ass. It's the same amount of class time per day but it's fewer weeks of school and the same amount of work to cover.

My parents pushed me every single year of high school to take summer classes. It made it so during the regular semesters of school I'd have one free period. Technically I could've left school to go home, but I'd hang around to wait for my friends to get done and do homework during that free period.

I told myself when this school year started I wanted to actually spend this summer with my friends so there'd be no classes, much to my parents' disappointment.

But if taking a class during the summer means spending more time with Gemma, it'll be worth it.

I only wish she wasn't taking such a hefty class. I didn't plan on taking this until next year.

Opening the door to the class, my eyes immediately find Gemma at the last table in the back corner, digging in her backpack with one arm holding it and the other rifling through it.

With an innocent look, I walk around the back of the class and sit on the stool next to hers.

"Good morning, precious."

She drops her bag in shock to the floor, cursing under her breath.

"Noel, what are you doing here?" she asks in a frustrated tone. She's folded in half, reaching for her bag.

When she brings it back up, she looks incredibly annoyed.

"That doesn't sound like good morning to me."

She sighs, pushing her glasses up her nose. "Because it isn't a good morning, obviously."

I open my mouth to respond when the door opens and heels start clacking on the tile.

"Almost late, but I made it," the professor says with a smile.

Her lips are a bright red and her eyes are bright and excited. Most of the professors here are getting up there in years, but she looks relatively young. She isn't dressed in the usual ugly white shirt and pants the other professors wear, but brighter colors.

They must have hired someone new.

She clears her throat as she reaches the front of the class, brushing her red hair back. "I know this is the part where I'm supposed to say I'm Professor Michaels and this is going to be a tough class yada yada yada. But I'd like to keep this atmosphere relaxed. You can call me Ruby."

Her eyes gaze around the classroom. "Anatomy is one of my favorite areas of science. The body is an amazing thing and I hope that this class helps you discover that fact for yourself. I wish we had time to talk and get to know each other before starting off, but I want you all to have your best chance of passing this class. Please read the syllabus when class is over. We'll do lecture for the first three hours and lab the last two." She grabs a remote from the desk and hits the button for the projector.

Glancing over at Gemma, I watch as she clicks the top of her pen, pointing it over the paper as she prepares to jot down notes.

She has highlighters of every color lined up in front of her notebook and a whiteout pen.

I stare down at the empty spot on the table in front of me. Sometimes, I can't even be bothered to take notes.

This is probably a class where I shouldn't skip out on notes.

I guess it doesn't help that sometimes I'm unable to read my own writing. Unzipping my backpack, I pull out a notebook and flip to some unused pages and pull a pencil out from the front pocket.

"Does anyone here know the organ systems?" Professor Michaels asks.

I shoot my hand up and watch as Gemma raises hers along with several others.

The professor points in our corner. "You, the guy with your backpack on your desk. What's your name?" She glances around the class. "I hope to know all of your names by the end of our class together." Her eyes come back to me.

"Noel," I respond with a smirk.

She smiles. "Well, Noel, please do tell us."

I give her all 11 systems and she nods. "Awesome, you know your stuff. Does anyone know what each system does?"

Gemma shoots her hand up, beating me.

This time, no one else raises their hand but us.

She points over at us. "Girl next to Noel."

"Gemma," Gem quickly responds, and starts prattling off what each system is meant for.

When she's done, Professor Michaels claps. "Amazing, Gemma."

Gemma flushes happily with a giant smile on her face.

She glances from Gemma to I. "You two are going to be a great pair for labs." Her back turns to us and I hear Gemma sigh heavily.

Usually in science classes they let us pick our own partners. I guess Professor Michaels prefers to make it easy and let us do it with the person we're sitting next to.

"Can't wait for lab, partner," I whisper.

She doesn't respond, and I don't expect her to, as she focuses on the slideshow on the screen.

But I know she heard me.

Eight whole weeks for five hours a day. Monday and Wednesday have now become my two favorite days of the week. Not only do I get her in the mornings, but until the evenings too when she comes to work. And when she comes to work today, I'll have her punishment ready.

I scoot my stool over, being careful not to scrape it against the floor. I trail my finger over her smooth pantsed leg. She wastes no time in pinching me hard.

"Ouch," I mutter.

"If we weren't in class I would've slapped it," she hisses. "The worst thing you could do is distract me from school. Save it for later. And focus if you want to pass this class."

"Fine," I whisper back.

She seems surprised at my response. To her, I look like I gave in easily. If she only knew what I have in store for her at work.

Yesterday, I called Margie to let her know ahead of time that Gemma wouldn't be able to do her usual duties in the office today. Though she wasn't happy to hear it, Margie relented. I took a quick trip to my office and completely trashed it. Papers all over, food caked on the nice glass doors, and trash all over the place. No to mention the bits of shredded paper dotting the floors.

I made sure every wall and crevice needed some sort of cleaning.

We have a cleaning company that comes to clean the

office every night when the office closes and I specifically told them not to touch mine.

I get to watch her squat, bend, and stretch her beautiful body all over my office.

Gemma seems to know that something is up as she leaves Margie's office, following right behind me.

"Why aren't you letting me do my job, Noel?"

"Did you think I forgot about what you did Saturday night?"

I open my office door, and the immediate smell that leaks out is a mixture of old cheese and sour milk.

Stepping to the side, I allow Gemma to go inside first.

"Oh my God," Gemma murmurs behind me, covering her nose and gagging. "You did all of this just because of that? This is so unsanitary."

"Make it sanitary then," I say with a grin, moving past her to my desk.

My leather rolling chair is the only thing I didn't touch because I want to be comfortable while I watch her work.

Her eyes narrow. "Don't you have a cleaning lady or something who's more qualified to do this?"

"We do, but for today, that person will be you. Get to work precious." With a smirk, I lean back in my chair, putting my hands behind my head as I let the chair press against the wall behind me.

"Where are the cleaning supplies then?" she says, gritting her teeth.

I point to the cabinet against the wall that's mostly empty except for a few cleaning things I bought for myself in case something needed to be cleaned immediately. I'm glad I bought them.

Anything of importance I keep locked in my desk.

She grabs a mask and puts it on her face, along with a pair of yellow stretchy gloves.

I watch her carefully as she gathers every paper on the floor and tosses it onto my desk. She grabs the battery operated vacuum and cleans every inch of the spotty floor, then starts on the walls. As she stretches up, her shirt comes out from being tucked into her pants and I get a nice view of her lower back.

My phone vibrates in my pocket and I check to find the notification I set for her first break. "You can take your five minute break," I offer as she moves to the second wall.

"I'll pass," she says, wiping her forehead. The wisps of hair near her temples are starting to curl with the sweat.

"Gem, I'm legally required to give you two breaks."

She laughs. "Now you're trying to follow the rules? Don't act like you care about the rules when you trashed your own office like a child so I'd clean it for you when this is nowhere near my job description. I should report this to my real employers, your parents."

My blood runs cold and I shake my head quickly. "Don't. Don't do that."

"I said I should, not that I was going to," she replies with a sigh.

An hour and a half later, she's halfway finished with the last wall of my office when my phone vibrates again.

"Half an hour for your lunch break. And don't say you're not going."

She looks utterly exhausted as she takes her gloves and mask off, throwing them on top of a stand in the corner. "I'm not. I'm hungry." Without a second glance in my direction, she leaves for the lunch room.

I rush around my desk, leaving the door open to let some fresh air in. Gem gets to the room before I do. The fridge is already open and she's looking through it. The few times I've had lunch with her at work I've seen her come with a paper bag lunch.

There's only one other guy in here. Everyone on this floor has usually taken their lunch by now with it being right in the middle of lunch and dinner.

I've learned to watch and see where she sits before sitting somewhere myself. Every single time, she'll sit anywhere but with me.

This time, she sits across from the other guy in the room.

"Hey, Jude," she says, a smile in her voice.

"Turkey sandwich and chips again Gemma?"

"You got it."

Wait. She knows someone else who works here?

I stick my hands in my pockets and stride over, sitting in the seat closest to Gem.

She doesn't even blink at my presence as she takes a bite of her sandwich.

Jude smiles in my direction. "Hey, Boss." He takes a bite of his drenched salad.

I don't even know what this guy does here. Jude looks to be around five years older than us.

My stomach grumbles as her and the Jude guy eat and I have nothing.

"Would you like some carrots, Boss?" Jude asks, holding up a baggie.

"I'm good, thanks," I reply.

"If you're sure," he says, opening the bag. He digs a carrot out and pops it in his mouth. After he swallows, he looks up at Gemma with hesitation in his eyes.

"So, have you seen anything good at the movies lately?"

She stops chewing to say, "No" covering her mouth as she does.

I don't like where this is going.

"That zombie movie is coming out next weekend and I was wondering-"

"Sorry Jude," Gemma interjects, "next weekend is busy for me. Rain check?"

Jude's eyes fall but he smiles all the same. "No problem."

Is she actually busy or did she say that just because I'm here? And how long have they known each other?

"Your boyfriend probably wouldn't like you going out on a date, Gem," I comment offhandedly.

Jude's face turns red. "Oh, I'm sorry, I didn't know you were seeing someone, Gem."

She wipes her mouth. "No need to be sorry. I'm so sorry I didn't mention it."

Jude nods, standing up at the same time. "See you around." he says it so low I can barely hear him.

Poor guy.

Though I get the vibe that he doesn't know her boyfriend is me.

I almost feel bad, but the alternative is him having what's mine. I haven't even been to the movies with her. I'd rather no one have an ounce of hope about going out with Gemma, no matter how minute it is. There's no sound of him tossing his trash out, just the door opening and closing.

Gemma shoves her chips in her mouth and grimaces at me as she stands.

She tosses her empty bag out and goes to leave. I scramble to get up, following her as she stomps back down the hallway.

When we get inside my office, she immediately dons her gear again and grabs the spray bottle, getting immediately back to work. "I don't see how hurting Jude's feelings was necessary."

"It was very necessary," I say, crossing my arms over my chest and sitting back in my chair. "You gave that guy hope when you're still contracted to me for *months*, Gem. No guy would ever wait that long for someone."

She doesn't respond, giving me the silent treatment as she did the first three hours of her shift.

An hour and a half later, I remind her about her break. As if I said nothing at all, she continues cleaning the furniture in the room then polishing it with the furniture spray.

There's only one thing left for her to do, and that's to get the papers off my otherwise clean desk.

Her eyes flit over to me as she holds the spray and a rag in each of her hands.

She walks over to the cabinet, setting them down, and grabs both full trash bags off the ground. "Where do you want me to put these?"

"Just outside the door is fine."

Whirling around, she sets one bag down to open the door and then places both of them on the right side just outside my office.

When she comes back in, she stacks the papers on my desk nicely. "Where would you like me to put these?"

"In my desk drawer," I say, scooting back, gesturing to the thin drawer at the dead center of my desk.

Her lips flatten. "Could you scoot back then?"

I look as if I'm honestly contemplating her question for a moment then shake my head. "No, I don't think I will."

With a sigh of resignation, she grabs the stack with both hands and moves around the edge of the desk. There's only a small amount of space between me and the drawer she needs. It's the thinnest and longest drawer, stretching almost the full length of my desk.

She squeezes in, the backs of her legs touching mine all

the way to my knees. Her body tilts back slightly so she can open the drawer and that's when I make my move. Grabbing them out of my pocket, I lean forward slightly and cuff her left wrist as she starts to pull the drawer open.

She makes an angry sound in the back of her throat.

"Noel." Gem's voice is a lot calmer than I expected. Is she worried because we're at work?

I place the other cuff on my own left wrist, trapping her with me. Tugging my arm back forces her at an awkward angle and I slide the chair forward until she has no choice but to sit back on my lap.

"What are you doing?" she asks, wiggling the wrist with the cuff.

"I'm sure you know that doing that won't help you any. After all, I was outside for hours trying to get this thing off. *This* is your punishment."

Reaching around her body, I grab the top button on her shirt.

She grabs my hand, trying to force it away from her shirt, but all the strength she can manage is nothing compared to mine. "You're really doing this here?"

I maneuver the first button out of the hole. The moment I do she stomps on my foot.

Wincing, I continue down, until her shirt is completely open.

Damn. I should've made it so she was sitting facing me. I'll have to settle for a view from above for now.

Today, her tits are covered by a teal lacy bra. I move her shirt aside and grab her bra, yanking it down to grab her bare tit in my hand.

She squirms slightly at my touch, "Don't do that."

"I am and I will," I murmur into her ear.

I use my index finger and thumb to grab her pink nipple

in my fingers. "If you were a good girl, I wouldn't have had to use the cuffs."

She shudders.

"I could've positioned you facing me and had your nipple in my mouth instead." I twist her nipple slightly and she gasps.

"Don't do that!" she exclaims.

I chuckle darkly. "Precious, I've been a starving man these past few months. You're lucky I don't bend you over this desk right now and fuck you. I know you can feel how hard I am right now."

"You'd really make me have my first time on a *desk?*" she asks, trembling.

With my cuffed hand, I put my arm over hers and pull her other tit out.

She stomps on my other foot, digging her heel into my toes. "The fucking door is unlocked," she explodes. "Anyone can walk in at any minute."

"Can you stop stomping on my goddamn foot?" I hiss, twisting both nipples at the same time.

She takes a sharp intake of breath.

"Are your panties teal like this sexy bra?" I ask, popping the strap on her shoulder.

"No, they're off-white and completely plain. Granny panties."

I chuckle. "Okay. Whatever you choose to wear. Either way, I want them. Take them off," I order.

"No! There's no way I'm walking out of here without my underwear," she exclaims angrily.

Rolling my chair all the way back, I allow her to move off my lap. "You have thirty seconds to get them off before I call Margie in here because I have an urgent question for her. She'll get to see this lovely pair of handcuffs on us and she'll see you on my lap with your tits hanging out."

"Enough," Gem demands.

She slides off my lap and unbuttons her pants, shimmying them off of her.

Right away, I'm able to see that she lied. Pretty teal lacy panties to match her bra.

"I'm wounded, you lied to me, precious," I say, slightly amused.

That damn shirt is covering her ass from my view.

She peels her underwear off, letting them slide down her legs. After taking one step out of them, she bends down to grab her panties, yanking me with her and I choke as I get an eyeful of her pussy in broad daylight. A close eyeful.

Holy fuck.

A painful ache starts in my crotch and I grit my teeth. I was hard before but now, I'm starting to reach my limit. My cock is pressing against the zipper of my pants, aching to be free from its confines.

When she turns to me with her panties in her hand, she looks at me curiously. "Why do you have that look on your face? Here, take them." Her panties go flying as she tosses them in my general direction. I only just manage to catch them.

My cock only gets harder as I hold them in my hand.

"Now I just need my pants," she mutters. Sighing, she steps into the legs of her pants, bending down again to grab the sides, pulling me in once again and giving me another look at her pussy.

My mouth waters with hunger. I already know how good she tastes.

Fuck, she doesn't even realize what she's doing to me.

When she straightens, I'm able to sit back in my chair

properly. I fight the urge to undo my zipper and let my cock free.

After a few minutes, her pants are back on and she starts buttoning her shirt. My eyes stay locked on her form the entire time as I picture her body without them. When she's done, she turns her body to the left, shaking the cuffs. "Can you please get the key now so we can be done?"

I chuckle and yank her over, pulling her back on my lap. "After teasing me like that?"

Immediately, she tries to stand. "What are you talking about?" she asks slowly, turning to face me halfway.

"That great view I got of your pussy. Twice."

Her eyes widen and she looks speechless as her face flushes. "I didn't–"

"I know, but now I need this." Gripping her hips in my hands, I press her down onto my clothed cock and grind against her.

"You're so lucky I don't have condoms right now. But from now on, I'm carrying them with me wherever I go with you," I grit.

She grips my right arm with her right hand, digging her fingernails in. "Stop."

I move my hips up, gridding myself into her and groaning at the friction. "No."

Her nails dig in more as she lets out a small moan. Immediately, she covers her own mouth, letting out a muffled, "No."

"Yes," I declare, feeling a shiver go through her.

I grind myself against her, picturing myself thrusting into her pussy. It's too fucking good. I've gone too long without coming.

I thrust my hips up, holding her hips flush against me as I

come with a groan. My head falls back against my chair with satisfaction.

"Noel," she says, in a high-pitched tone.

"Yes, I'm letting you go in a second, precious. You can get off early."

"Noel, Margie!" she shrieks.

I tilt my head up just in time to watch Margie knock. Gemma scrambles to get off my lap but before she can, the door opens and Margie covers her mouth. "Oh my God. I'm so sorry, Noel. I thought that..." she stares at us with her mouth hanging open, obviously eyeing the handcuffs.

"No worries Margie," I tell her smoothly with an unbothered look.

She nods, her face turning a bright red. "I'll just email you about it later. Bye!" Pulling the door closed, I watch through the glass as she turns around, and dashes back down the hall to her office.

I'll have to talk to her later to make sure she doesn't talk to my parents about it. She's not the kind of person who would, but I'd rather be absolutely sure.

"That was humiliating, Noel. What is she going to think about me now?" Gemma cries, shaking her head in dismay.

"That you have a hot, rich boyfriend who couldn't keep his hands off of you. It's no big deal," I reassure her, pulling the key out of my pocket and handing it to her.

In a flash, she unlocks the cuffs and twists my chair slightly to the left so she can get off my lap.

She strides to the door and throws it open without saying another word to me.

A smirk plays at my lips as I pull her underwear out.

I'll give these back to her after they've served their purpose.

CHAPTER SEVEN

Gemma

All night long, it kept replaying in my head. Margie opening the door and seeing me on Noel's lap handcuffed to him.

Most of my time at work today I spent going to other floors so I successfully evaded Noel. Margie couldn't look me in the face all day. My professionalism has been completely ruined.

But that's not the only thing. No. I keep thinking about my reaction to him yesterday. I hate that there's a small, extremely tiny part of me that secretly enjoyed it. That part of me is definitely nowhere in my brain.

My brain knows better. My heart knows better.

That part of me I need to have a better handle on, starting today.

As soon as it hits two, I sign out and rush out of work.

Scarlett's car is parked on the far right side of the parking lot. On a scorching day like this, it's hell walking on the pavement, but as I power-walk over, the only thing I can think about is how glad I am to be away from Noel.

I hop in the passenger seat and put my seatbelt on. "Thanks again, Scarlett."

She laughs. "Girl, you don't have to thank me every time. It's simple. You don't have a car, I have one, end of story." Scar gets out of the parking lot in a flash and heads back toward campus.

"I just hate to ruin your summer," I say, enjoying the blast of cold air against my face from the vents.

She side-eyes me. "Of course not. I'm not doing anything special. Just the usual running around for my mom. Really wish I could get a summer job and take a class like you, I'm jealous."

Whenever I talk to her, she always mentions her mom, but never her dad.

"Does your dad work with your mom?" I ask, hoping I don't step on a landmine.

She blinks several times before answering. "Yeah. It's a family thing that we do. He's not as uptight as she is, so I'm thankful for that. I know she just means well and she wants the best for me though." Scar pauses, glancing at me. "Oh I'm sorry, I know parents are a sensitive subject."

"It's fine," I say quickly.

I never mind when anyone brings up their parents, because at the end of the day, it's my fault I don't have any. Mine and Noel's. And for that reason, I'm fine with hearing about happy family relationships.

"She's supposed to let me know what I have to do tonight, so you'll probably hear me gripe one more time," Scar says with a sigh.

We pull up in front of the sorority and I run to my room to change clothes. When I open the door, I spot Mera lounging on her bed, scrolling through her phone.

I'm so glad Coll agreed to let her be my roommate.

She smiles. "Hey! How was work? Wait. Don't answer that. You're going to the library, right?"

"Yup. Scar is coming to help me study for Anatomy. She took it in high school and it's one of her favorite classes. While I know the basics, she can help me catch on with everything else faster."

"Awesome. Then you can tell me about everything that Noel is pulling on the way. Maybe while I'm there I can find some of those awesome romance books you keep talking about." She sits up quickly, walking over to her vanity mirror to check her hair. Recently, she's added hot pink highlights to her platinum blonde hair and it's made her look even more gorgeous than before.

I exchange my work clothes for some comfortable leggings and a baggy t-shirt. The baggy t-shirt is going to be a pain in the heat, but at least it's short sleeved.

Once I grab my school bag, we head down the stairs, passing by the girls doing shots and get right back in the car.

In the time it took us to come down, Peyton's gotten in the backseat.

Mera slides in the back with him while I take the passenger side once more.

"Didn't know you were coming Pey," Mera says excitedly. "You aren't taking any classes this summer."

I turn slightly to the left, watching as a dusting of pink hits his freckles. "Can't I just want to hang out with my friends?"

Turning away, I hide a smile in my hand.

Crushes.

I've almost forgotten what it's like to have one.

While Scar drives, I give them a quick recap of the day with Noel hanging around me all day. I don't tell them anything about the day before because I'm too embarrassed to.

Scar gets us a pretty prime spot in the library parking lot. It also helps that it's the summer and campus is emptier.

After signing in, we grab a table in the study area. There are plenty of empty tables. This one has six seats. Scar and I sit on one side while Peyton sits on the other, across from Scar. Mera immediately abandons us to find the fiction area of the library.

Since we're supposed to be quiet, we're using flashcards and I get to write down my answer to check if they're right.

When I get an answer wrong, she quietly tells me how to give myself little hints to make the answer pop into my brain.

In this case, learning all the bones in the human body.

We're about one hour in when I've got them all memorized and I'm able to point them out on my own body.

I whisper, "I'm going to go grab a drink from the vending machine outside."

She nods and I fumble in my bag for my wallet and pull out my card. As I turn to walk around the corner, I run smack into someone, barely stopping myself from falling on my ass.

"I'm so–" I whisper and then cross my arms when I lock eyes with him. "Never mind. I'm not sorry."

I walk around him quickly, hearing footsteps that indicate Noel is following me outside.

Why does he have to follow me everywhere?

I stop in place and turn around to face him. "What do you want? And how did you find me here?"

He glances around and shrugs. "Seems like a place like you'd come."

"Because I'm nerdy, I belong in the library?" I whisper.

"No," he responds, eyeing me, "what I meant is I know you want to get a head start on studying and this is the best place to do it."

I flatten my lips and sigh. He isn't wrong. "Fine yes. I'm getting a head start. So can you leave so I can study in peace?"

He smirks. "Okay, I'll leave you alone after I steal your attention for a second."

Closing the distance between us, he pulls me out of the aisle leading me to the far corner of the library. This corner has two tall bookcases in the way at angles. He backs me into one, cornering me with one hand above my head while keeping a hand on my waist.

"Noel, we're in a library," I whisper-yell. "This isn't the time for this."

He leans down, his lips brushing my ear slightly as he speaks. "It's always the time for this." His lips travel to my neck, peppering kisses until he reaches the collar of my shirt.

I close my eyes and try to think of the easiest way to get away from him. Kneeing him in the balls? He'd probably yell super loud and everyone would look this way. Throw up all over him and myself? My lunch is nearly digested by now though and also, ew. That'd be too extreme.

I don't have my phone so I can't call anyone.

Pulling back, he frowns and touches my shirt. "You're always wearing these outside of work. Do you not have anything else to wear?"

Sighing, I touch the bottom of my shirt. "I don't, but it doesn't matter anyway because I don't like how I look in V-neck shirts or anything low-cut. A lot of shirts tend to be clingy and then, well people see how ugly I look."

"Stop with that," he says with a frustrated groan as he rolls his eyes. He grabs my chin in his hand. "You're beautiful, and allow me to show you how beautiful your body is as it orgasms for me."

"What?" I ask, my mouth dropping.

Noel pulls my leggings away from my stomach and reaches inside my panties. I jump at the feeling of his long fingers moving toward my lady bits.

I hold his hard, shaking my head. "Don't. Not here."

My hands aren't enough to stop him as he finds my clit. "There it is," he whispers.

He massages a finger around it, and I jump at the familiar electricity that shoots through my body. Instantly, I'm taken back to those nights in Cancun when I touched myself.

No. There's no way he'll make me orgasm.

His finger glides over my clit, over and over, making me gasp and twitch.

I bite my lip to attempt to keep myself from making any embarrassing noises and look away from him.

"Sorry you have to be quiet, precious," he murmurs. Suddenly he changes tactics, traveling slightly lower and pushing a single finger inside me.

Oh God. Why does he have to have such a long finger? It's stretching me so much more than one of my own. I glance up to find him staring at me with heated eyes.

"You're so wet already. Does it feel good? Be honest for once, Gem."

I shake my head quickly as his thumb circles my clit and he thrusts a finger inside me, over and over. A gasp escapes my mouth and he places a hand over my mouth quickly.

"I don't need a nosy librarian coming over to ruin my

fun," he says with a smirk. "Just this once, I promise, you won't have to be quiet again."

Now I can't even scream even if I want to. I clutch my hand over his arm and pinch him as hard as I can.

"Go ahead," he whispers. "Pinch, scratch, bite even if you want to, but nothing is going to stop me."

The hand stays over my mouth as he tortuously adds a second finger, making come-hither motions with them. Something starts to rise out of me, and it's coming quickly.

I quake and shudder, scared at the pleasure I'm feeling. I don't want *him* to make me feel like this.

"Are you getting close?" he asks. "You're starting to tighten around my fingers."

He pulls them out and I let out a muffled gasp at the sudden emptiness. His fingers go to my clit, and he twists it, and pinches it ruthlessly. "I'm going to make you orgasm whether you want to or not, precious. Just let it happen."

His eyes search mine as I breathe heavily, letting out small moans as his fingers glide over my clit.

Each rub is going directly to my toes, making them twitch involuntarily. All of a sudden he pushes his middle finger inside me, making a waving motion and something explodes inside me. The biggest spark of lightning hits me so hard, I practically see stars.

No way. He shouldn't have been able to do this.

Why of all people did he have to cause me to have my first orgasm?

"Good girl, coming all over my finger." There's that satisfied smirk again on his face. I'm so angry I want to scream.

He pulls his hand out of my underwear and holds it in front of his face while he licks it clean. "What's the matter, Gem? You should be feeling nothing but bliss right now."

"No," I say in a low tone, stomping on his foot.

His face twists in pain. "Stop doing that," he hisses, stepping away.

When he moves back, I take that opportunity to walk away. With every step I take, I feel just how wet I am, making my cheeks heat up with humiliation.

No one can see and no one knows, but I do, and that makes me feel just as embarrassed.

In a library. He fingered me in a *library*.

Ugh, I feel so dirty.

I go back to the table, finding Mera reading a book and Peyton and Scarlett whispering back and forth.

They stop talking as I sit down. Scar looks behind and around me. "You were gone for a while. Did you already drink your drink?"

I plaster a small smile on my face. "Yep."

Scar picks up the cards and I whisper, "No it's okay. I think I've done enough studying for the day."

"Okay," Scar responds, handing me the cards. "Why don't we grab dinner then?"

Anything to get away from this library. "Sounds good to me." I shove the cards in my bag.

She glances at Peyton and Mera. "You guys want to?"

They nod and I grab my bag off the ground and put it over my shoulder. The four of us leave through the doors going out to the quad.

As we walk to the Dining Hall, I feel my phone vibrating and pull it out to find several messages from my aunt.

What does she have to say to me when she hasn't talked to me in months? Once they closed on the house, I figured she wouldn't message me again.

My phone vibrates again as more messages come in. I open the conversation between us to find picture after picture of her on vacation in popular spots. Not all of them are from the same places. Looks like Greece, Italy, Spain, England, France, and Iceland?

At the bottom there's a written message.

Cindy: Hope you're having as good of a summer as I am!

Nice of her to show off just how much she's profited off of me. If she cared even a little, she would've put some of the money into finding out what happened to my parents. Going to South America to try retracing their steps.

But she'd never do that because the only person she cares about is herself.

At the top, I click her number and hit block. I slide my phone back in my pocket, sighing happily. Now she can't contact me again.

I'm rid of her for good.

"Gemma, wait up!" A familiar voice yells behind us.

I stop in my tracks, as do my friends as I turn around as Brad jogs over, panting lightly. He smiles and straightens. "Hey, I know you're hanging with your friends, but is there any way you'd be interested in hanging out with mine, and me of course?"

Stepping slightly to the right, I watch as a crowd of students are slowly walking over from further away than the library.

Most likely, I don't know any of them. The only person I'd know is Brad and I can't exactly hog him. It'd be rude if I only talked to him alone.

It's too bad the invitation is for me and me alone.

After dealing with Noel, I'm not exactly in the best mood to make new friends. Some other time, definitely.

"Sorry, Brad. Not this time," I say with a regretful smile.

His smile fades slightly. "That's too bad. Soon though?"

"Soon," I assure him.

He moves away from me as his group of friends finally catch up. With a slight wave, he walks off, with his friends following him.

His friends look my way as they walk past me and a weird feeling causes goosebumps to pop up along my body. My reaction doesn't make sense until I see his last friend bringing up the rear. I'd know that orange head of hair anywhere.

Mera scoffs. "Bitch."

Ginger flips her off and continues walking.

He's friends with all of those students that went missing?

"Did you know he was friends with all of them?" Mera asks.

"No," I reply, staring at them turn off onto the path to the lake.

"None of those people were friends before going missing," Peyton points out.

"That's fucking strange," Scarlett muses. "But whatever, let's go eat."

We turn the corner for the Dining Hall and hooting and hollering fills the air.

"Do you really have to show those off when I'm about to eat, Noel? That's so gross," a girl says with a giggle.

A few other giggles follow hers.

I practically throw up when I watch Noel waving my teal underwear in the air.

Another girl, probably a member of his fan club, keeps widening her hands as if to show how big they are.

I glance away, feeling the heat of embarrassment coming on.

As if people don't laugh at me enough already, he has to do something like this.

The guys around him laugh and clap him on the shoulder.

"Please, tell me those aren't yours, Gemma," Mera says, horror in her tone.

Scarlett shakes her head. "Tell us what you want us to do, Gemma. Peyton and I can each hold down one of his arms while you grab the underwear while Mera keeps his asshole friends from interfering."

It's a nice gesture, one that makes me feel happy knowing that I have friends willing to help me. The only problem is, I don't want to get them involved with this.

"I'll get them back on my own," I tell their battle ready faces. "I'd rather you guys go in and get your food. I'll be okay."

And even if I'm not, I'd rather they not witness my embarrassment any more than they already have.

Scarlett pouts and Peyton says, "We'll be waiting for you inside."

Mera looks reluctant to leave so I smile. "I'll be fine."

She nods and dashes to catch up with Peyton and Scarlett who are almost to the doors.

I push my glasses up the bridge of my nose and stride over to the crowd surrounding him. His laughter dies down as he notices me pushing my way through the crowd.

"Looking for these?" Noel asks, holding up my undies with a smug look.

The girls make snide remarks under their breath thinking that I'm not able to hear them. The guys erupt into cruel laughter.

I stop in front of him, stretch up on my toes and reach for them. He has me by at least eight inches.

"I am. I'd like them back. After the horrible sex yesterday, I think that's the least you owe me." If he's going to lie about us having sex, I might as well too.

Everyone around us gasps as if it's the most unbelievable thing in the world. His eyes darken for a moment as he stares down at me before chuckling. "That's a good one. You weren't moaning like it was terrible though."

I refuse to have him have the last word. With a smile, I cross my arms. "That can be faked, can't it?"

The guys start jeering and I roll my eyes in annoyance as Noel grits his teeth angrily. He proceeds to grab my wrist, dragging me out of the circle swiftly. I feel their eyes on us until we turn the corner.

"Where are we going? Why can't you just give me back my underwear now that you've had your laugh?" I snap.

"Maybe if I'd actually gotten off earlier as you did, I would've been more open to just giving you your underwear back. That isn't the case now."

We come to a stop outside the bathrooms. He's angled more toward the men's room.

So that's what he wants? He wants me to get him off? "I'm not going in there," I voice, planting my feet firmly on the ground.

Not only do I refuse to help get him off after everything he's done today, but I won't have someone walk in on me doing it. Does he want to have sex inside a bathroom stall?

His grip tightens. "It won't take long if you behave. You'll get your underwear back and be on your way."

"So we're not having sex in there?"

A smirk forms on his face as he chuckles. "No. I'd need condoms for that. So come on."

Sighing I allow him to drag me into the bathroom. Luckily there won't be as many guys walking in since it's summer, it's later in the day, and these bathrooms aren't in a building but off by themselves.

He ushers me into the largest stall, locks the door and stands in front of it. Lifting a finger to his lips, he makes the shush motion.

What does he want to use? My hand? Please, not my mouth.

I cringe as he backs me into the wall. His hands go to my hips as he yanks my leggings down along with my underwear. Panic rises in me as he eyes me with a heated look.

His eyes are telling me he's about to do something really dirty.

Suddenly, everything feels so airy. I glance down to find my leggings completely off and on the bathroom tile and the underwear I was wearing, gone.

Peering around him, I find my new black underwear in the corner.

"What are you doing?" I ask exasperatedly.

He smirks and holds up my teal underwear. I don't look down as I hear him undoing his jeans.

But when he lowers my underwear to his hip area, I glance down automatically to see what he's doing with them. My stomach twists as I watch him lower them onto his semi.

"No," I whisper angrily looking up into his eyes. "Those are soiled forever now. Washed or not, I'll never wear those."

The sound of the bathroom door banging open makes me jump.

Someone is in the bathroom with us.

His eyes glitter as he grabs my chin and tilts my head to

the right. Hot breath hits my ear as he whispers, "You're going to wear them at least one more time, precious."

I utter a small gasp that's instantly covered by his lips as they come down on mine. I try to close my mouth before he can get his tongue inside, but I'm unsuccessful as he thrusts his tongue inside, mirroring him thrusting his dick into my underwear.

I try to pull away but his hand goes to the back of my head, keeping me in place as he ravages my mouth. Accidentally, I move my tongue slightly and his tongue quakes at the unexpected movement.

My body trembles as heat blooms between my legs. *No.*

A toilet flushes and at that exact moment, a guttural groan escapes his mouth, echoing into mine. My face feels way too warm all of a sudden.

Why?

There's no sound of the faucet running, only the opening and closing of the door.

Suddenly, he pulls away, his lips glistening and I gasp for air.

"That was close," he murmurs, his chest heaving slightly.

Did he finish then? In my underwear?

Noel bends down and my eyes widen as he grips my ankle, lifting it up slightly and putting it inside the hole of my teal underwear. My teal underwear that's currently soiled with his cum.

I kick him square in the shoulder as he does the same with my other ankle. "I am not wearing these!"

His jaw tics as he straightens. "The only way you're walking out of here is wearing panties full of my cum." He leans in whispering against my lips. "No one will know. It'll just be a little secret between you and me. You'll go back to your friends with my cum right there. A little reminder of me until it dries."

I hate this. I hate him. My stomach twists and bile rises up my throat.

I'll just forgo food. After swallowing it down quickly, I take a deep breath.

I don't even look as I bend down and pull them up. But I instantly feel the wetness of my underwear. Waves of satisfaction are coming off of him as he backs away. After pulling on my leggings and grabbing my black underwear from the corner, I stuff them into my pocket.

His body is still in the way of me leaving and he knows it. I stare up at him angrily, knowing more time is slipping by with his cum becoming acquainted with my lower parts.

"I hope you'll come to realize soon just how gorgeous you are, Gem. Not just anybody can make me come that hard that quickly." Noel's eyes move up and down my body.

I scoff. What a line and a good lie. "Let me leave."

He finally, thank God, steps aside. In a hurry, I unlock the door and rush out. I call Mera and tell her I'll be eating at the sorority instead. She wants to know what happened, but I just can't talk to anybody knowing that I'm walking around with Noel's cum in my underwear.

When I get back to our room, I shower and get right into bed. My teal underwear go right in the trash.

How much worse is this going to get? What will he force me to endure next? I don't want to go to class in the morning.

Over an hour later, I'm finally feeling better when someone knocks on my door.

"Gemma, are you in there?"

I slide out of bed and open the door to find Kori holding

a large drink with red palm trees around it and a white bag with the In n' Out logo on it.

"This was dropped off for you."

"Who dropped it off?" I ask, eyeing the bag suspiciously.

"Noel did." She hands it off to me and closes the door.

I stare down at the bag and drink. I set the drink down on my nightstand and peel open the bag. On top of the burger and fries is a white note, semi ruined by a patch of grease.

I pull it out of the bag and unfold it.

Don't forget to eat. More orgasms coming soon, precious. - N

I drop the note and cover my mouth. Did he watch me come straight to ZDB?

The drive-thru at In n' Out is notoriously long, especially around dinner time.

Why go through that trouble for me? I hope he isn't expecting me to bend over for him just because he gave me In n' Out.

The irony of the restaurant name isn't lost on me either.

With a small sigh, I pick up the fries and fork.

Any other restaurant and I probably would've given the food away. How did he know I can never turn down In n' Out?

CHAPTER EIGHT

Noel

Dad's voice is the first thing I hear bright and early. A Saturday. I haven't talked to him or my mom since the last time I saw them at their house.

Today, he seems to be in a better mood.

"Noel, you really pulled through at the end of spring semester and you're doing great in your summer class. To celebrate, I'd like to talk to you at the lab today. Something exciting is going on and I think it's time I let you in on it."

Today of all days? I had plans to drop by ZDB to see why Gem didn't come to work or class yesterday. It isn't like her to skip out on her responsibilities. As usual, she's ignoring my texts.

"I'll be at the lab this afternoon," I tell him to get him off the phone.

It'll give me at least a few hours with Gem.

He seems satisfied with my answer and hangs up.

After getting ready, I grab my phone to put it in my pocket when I notice the large number of texts on the lock screen.

All from my fan club.

Nancy is one of the less pushy members so I check her message first.

Nancy: OMG Noel, did you hear Jessica died last night? Four other girls in our dorm just got out of the hospital and told us.

Though Jessica had been annoying recently since I got together with Gem, it's still sad to hear of her passing.

There was a big party last night at some dude's house. I didn't bother finding out who since I had to pass on it in order to work on the stupid software. As far as I know, Callan, Ty, and Vincent didn't go either.

It's not uncommon to have someone end up at the hospital after a wild night of partying, but this many girls? And for Jessica to have died? She's never been a heavy drinker but she's never turned down C. It's another reason why I've never tried to go out with her.

Me: That's horrible. What happened to her?

Nancy: She was doing coke last night like she always does and then some guy came to the party and offered nearly everyone something he called Space Dust.

· · ·

My stomach turns. Space Dust again. I've been trying to find a supplier for weeks now. Something about it is nagging at me.

Me: What did the guy look like?

Nancy: Blond. Sorry I can't remember much else. He was very charming and I think that's why so many girls got some. Not to mention he gave it to us for free.

For *free*? What kind of dealer gives drugs away for free?

And that description isn't nearly enough to actually find the guy. With a sigh, I give her my thanks and put my phone in my pocket.

It's mostly quiet as I leave fraternity row, walking to ZDB. The sun is behind the clouds as they have been every morning this month while later it'll be in the low 90s, typical of a June day.

When I stop in front of ZDB, the door is open and a few girls are exiting.

They smile in my direction as I pass them going up the steps. I stop when I realize I don't know which room is Gem's.

Turning quickly before they can get too far, I point to the house and ask, "Do any of you know which room is Gemma's?"

One of them turns back to me. "208, but you probably won't get a response from her since she has a sign on her door that says do not disturb."

I smile back. "Thanks for letting me know."

Is she sick? She was at work on Thursday and she seemed like her usual self.

I go up the stairs in the foyer to the second floor and go down the hallway until I get to room 208.

Wasting no time, I rap my knuckles on the door. I pause for a few minutes before doing it again. The second time, the door flies open.

"Do you not see–" she starts and closes her mouth when she sees it's me. Her eyes are red and her hair is disheveled. Looking down, I notice she's wearing pajamas similar to the ones she wore in Cancun. She sniffs hard, wiping her nose. "What do you want, Noel? I'm busy today."

I intended to ask her why her phone always mysteriously leaves me on read, but something about the raw sadness in her eyes makes me put that aside for now. "You didn't come to work yesterday or class. It's not fun dissecting a pig on your own. Can I come in?"

Her mouth forms a thin line. "I'm not in the mood to have sex right now or do anything of that nature. I just want to be left alone."

In every relationship I've been in, I'm present for the physicality of it. The emotional part? Autopilot. I listen and nod while they talk without truly trying to understand. Nothing against them, but processing emotions has always been hard for me.

One thing's for sure, I've never seen Gem this upset and I want to know every reason why she is. I can either push my way into her room and force her to tell me or…

"Get dressed and come somewhere with me. I'll wait out here for you."

She narrows her eyes with suspicion. "Go with you, where?"

"I'm not sure yet," I answer honestly. "I'll let you make that decision. Better?"

"Not better," she says. Inching forward, she glances down the hallway each way. "I don't want to have sex today."

I raise a hand in the air. "I promise there will be no funny business...today."

She studies me closely, glancing from my hand to my face. Maybe she can see the honesty. Backing up, she closes the door abruptly.

I lean against the wall, waiting for her to come out.

Twenty minutes later, the door opens and the smell of freshness hits the air. As she exits the room, I notice her wet hair in a ponytail and her glasses in one hand and her purse in the other.

When she pulls the door closed, she glances up at me. "I'm ready."

Something about her face jars me, the same way it did on hazing night. My heart pounds as our eyes stay locked on each other. There's something familiar I can't place. If I stare long enough will it come to me?

Suddenly, panic flashes on her face and she puts her glasses on in such a hurry, her hands visibly tremble as she puts the temples over her ears.

"Can you take your glasses off?" I ask quietly. Why is she trying to hide her face from me?

Even when we stayed together in that room in Cancun, every morning her glasses were already on, even if she was fast asleep.

"No," she says quickly, going around me. "Let's go."

I'll let it go for now, in favor of finding out why she spent the day crying.

When we get outside, I lead her back to fraternity row's parking lot. Stopping at the trunk, I hold my key out to her as she starts for the passenger side. "You drive."

She shakes her head immediately. "No. I won't be responsible if I wreck this car."

Her eyes go over my Porsche with worry. "Don't worry about it. You wreck it, I'll buy another one. Just try not to? I'd hate it if something happened to you."

A hint of excitement grows in her eyes. "Okay," she slowly responds.

The unlocking beep sounds and I watch her bounce happily over to the driver's side. On the passenger side, I open the door, adjusting the seat before I slide in. Her purse is at my feet so I carefully maneuver my feet so I don't step on it.

"Before you start the car, can you tell me why?"

She sighs. "What does it matter to you? Why do you care?"

"I just want to know if part of it is my fault," I reply, staring at her.

Her eyes widen behind her glasses and she lowers her head, staring down at her hands.

"Yesterday it was eight years since my parents left and never came back. Every year I keep hoping that it won't hurt as much as it does. That the pain will dull and I'll feel better. But it's never happened because..." she wipes her eye under her glasses. "I don't have closure. I don't know what happened to them."

Relief rises within me knowing that it's nothing I did. "What happened that day? I can help you get answers if money is the problem."

"No. There isn't much to it. They left for a trip to South America and they never came back from it. I don't know any details other than that."

She clears her throat. "But thanks for offering monetary help."

"Did you ever go anywhere with them?"

She lifts her head, staring ahead at the road off campus. "No. We were supposed to go to San Francisco and San Diego once they came back."

I might come to regret this later. Whatever my dad has to show me can wait. If I text him now, he'll only stop me from going. "That's it then. Let's go." I settle back into my seat as she sputters.

"What do you mean let's go?"

I chuckle and clip my seatbelt in. "Drive us to San Francisco and when we come back down, drive straight to San Diego."

"That's a long time to be stuck in a car with you," she muses.

"That hurts, Gem," I say in mock sadness. "Come on, I'm pretty fun at car games."

She opens her mouth to argue and gets interrupted by her stomach rumbling.

"When was the last time you ate?"

"Thursday night," she mumbles.

I tsk at her and push the start button. "What we're not going to do, precious, is starve. We'll stop somewhere to eat on the way. Whatever you want, my treat of course."

She nods, a smile tugs at the corner of her lips as she backs out of the parking spot, leaving the parking lot.

I grab my phone out of my pocket when it rings and silence it. I'll talk to him later.

"Pass them, Gem. Come on. They cut you off, don't let them get away with that!" I exclaim.

I knew Gem wouldn't be as aggressive of a driver as me, but she's so passive it hurts.

"Oh my God. Just calm down. They probably cut me off by mistake."

I laugh and point to them. "So you missed how they flipped us off? You weren't even driving slow."

She snorts. "Now I'm really not going to pass them. You'll just flip them off when I do."

"You're fucking right I will," I respond, staring angrily at the truck.

"Well, I don't want to get shot today, so we're not doing that," she says, putting her blinker on and getting over.

"Gas again?" I ask.

"Yes. We really should've done this in a different car."

"But then it wouldn't be as fun," I reply, gesturing to the open top.

After we finished eating, I put the top down. It'll be cooler the closer we get to San Francisco.

After exiting the freeway she pulls into the gas station and I hop out. I throw away our food trash and fill up the tank. Glancing around, she murmurs, "I wonder what city we're in."

"Doesn't really matter. The middle of California looks the exact same. I pity the people who go to MGU. Nothing to do here except smell the cows and goats."

"Speaking of MGU. There's no update about Callan's cousin is there?" she asks curiously.

"As far as I know, no."

"That's so sad. Unlike Heath, her family doesn't know if she's dead or alive."

My stomach twists as I move around the back of the car, getting back inside. "Yeah."

She starts the car and takes off.

My intrusive thoughts start pushing to the front of my brain and I push them away in favor of staying present to make today a better day for her.

"You wouldn't happen to have heard anything about that Space Dust have you?" I ask, watching her turn onto the onramp.

Frowning, she glances at me for a moment before turning back to the road. "I didn't pick you for a druggie. Do you know how many people have been coming out to say how addicted they are and how badly it hurts to stop?"

"I'm not. Trust me, I have no intention of getting hooked on anything except for sex, that is."

"Of course," she mutters.

I continue, "But there's something about that stuff that's bothering me. If you ever come across some, can you buy it and show it to me before throwing it away?"

She lets out a short laugh. "You really believe someone would sell some to someone who looks like me? But fine. If I get some, I'll gladly just hand it over to you."

"I don't think there's a type," I reply honestly. "Some people are only looking for one thing. Profit."

Gem goes quiet as we zoom up the 5 freeway for a while. "Can I see my house when we get back?"

"Only if you show me your room. The mattress is still on your bed," I joke.

She gives me the side-eye. We stop for gas once more before getting off the freeway, changing to a highway.

"It must be nice to take spontaneous trips like this," she says, glancing off to the side at the aqueduct.

That's right. She has no idea how controlling my parents are. "My parents aren't as laid back as you probably think they are. They can be harsh if I don't give them what they want. Don't tell anyone but..." I stop, hesitating to continue.

The fear of saying words out loud that I've only kept in my head until now on the tip of my tongue. I don't know if my friends even realize how bad they can be.

They definitely don't know that every time my parents have a talk with me about how I'm a failure and I don't deserve anything. Each time I feel a tiny crack forming in my head. When they're done, it's like I put sealant over that crack, and then they talk to me again and the crack opens up and gets larger. The cycle repeats until...I guess one day I'll break. And that thought is scary.

Staying at the fraternity has saved me from being on the receiving end of many of their harsh words.

"No judgment here," she says quietly. "Emotional abuse is just as horrible as physical abuse, you know."

"Yeah. Which is why I'll do everything I can during the rest of our time together to make sure you never have to meet them."

"Right. Thank you for that," she says quickly with a nod.

As we move out of the hills, the path turns into a twisting one. The car is handling well, it's just the other drivers who are trying to fly down this hill unsafely in the increasing fog. One particular one is on our bumper. One hard stop and he'll rear end us hard.

I try to wave him around, but he flips us off in the mirror, making my jaw clench.

"This asshole is going to send us right off the highway," I grit.

The minutes tick by until we finally make it out of the hills to the country road that leads to the freeway. The asshole moves off to the left in the lane going the other way, and hops in front of us. At that exact moment, I watch a CHP car pull off from between a few trees.

Gem slows down, letting the officer get in between the

truck and us. She sighs happily while I whoop. "Karma, asshole."

The truck pulls off to the side with the CHP behind him while Gem drives on.

"I guess it's a good thing I wasn't the one driving. I would've been the one to get a ticket."

"I'll have to remember your need for speed," she responds with a small smile.

Leaning forward slightly, she looks at the dash and makes a frustrated sound. "We have to stop for gas again."

"Is that a surprise?" I ask, glancing over to her.

She wrinkles her nose in a cute way. "I just want to get there already."

"So impatient, precious," I murmur, brushing a finger over her cheek.

She slaps my hand away, frowning. "Don't ruin this. You've been behaving so far. You've actually been tolerable."

Something about those words causes a flutter in my stomach. "Glad to hear that."

I'm sure it's nothing though.

The parking lot near the Golden Gate Bridge is nearly empty and my Porsche is facing it.

Our last stop before leaving.

Dinner was the Shake Shack. Surprisingly, she never had it before. We walked through the streets, rode a cable car, and went to Fisherman's Wharf. The only thing we didn't have time for is to head out to Alcatraz Island.

"It sucks we couldn't go. I know I keep saying that, but I hate missing out on one thing."

"We could always spend the night somewhere."

"In separate rooms?" she asks, hopefulness in her voice.

"I'm not that generous," I respond with a smirk.

"Then maybe next–" she pauses, stopping herself.

I guess because there won't be a next time. Not with just us two.

For some reason, that thought is depressing. I've been places with other girls before. Vegas, Aspen, South Beach, and more. Never once did I feel the intense need to go back with them before leaving. But now, I can't imagine ever coming here without Gem.

"I'm sure everyone else would love to come," she suggests.

That's the best I can hope for, I guess. "Yeah, we'll have to do that."

I glance up at the dark sky. No stars. The city lights are too bright and there's too many cars going over the Golden Gate Bridge.

"My parents would have loved all of this. Thanks for taking me here. I'll remember this trip for a long time."

I gaze at her to find she's looking up at the sky as well. "Hey, this is only half of it, remember? San Diego. If we leave now we'll get there in the early morning."

"That's right. I'm going to be a zombie on the road. Don't let me fall asleep at the wheel."

"No," I reply firmly. "I'm driving back. You sleep."

She turns her head to look at me. "But then you might fall asleep at the wheel."

"Nah. You're more tired than I am. I got to sit back while you drove almost five hundred miles today."

She seems to consider that. "Okay. You drive us to a beach down there and I'll drive home. But if you feel too tired and you need company, wake me up."

"That's fair," I tell her and gesture outside the car. "Now come on, let's switch."

She opens the car door and gets out while I pull myself up in the seat and plop myself into the driver's seat. When she gets in, she shivers, moving her hands over arms. I hate that I don't have a jacket to give her.

I press the button to put the top up and start the car.

She turns on her side and gazes out the window as we leave the city.

"I probably would have stayed in my room crying all weekend if it weren't for you," she says softly. "I told Mera I needed to be alone so she's staying at Callan's."

"Yeah, and I know Callan doesn't mind. In fact, he's probably thanking you in his head right at this moment," I say with a laugh.

"You're probably right."

I fill up twice before getting on the 5 freeway.

"You really handle this car well," she observes, studying my hands on the wheel.

"I love cars. Fast ones, especially. I've driven lots of them and I like to collect the smaller versions. Someday, you should come to New York and see them."

I'm met with silence so I glance at her for a moment to find her slumped in her seat with her eyes closed. Her glasses are slipping off her face. I reach my right hand out to grab them, holding the wheel steady with my left hand.

Folding the earpieces quickly, I place them in the cupholder between us.

I fight with everything I have to not stare at her sleeping to figure out what this incessant feeling in my chest is. Why does her face stick out to me so much?

I can't see them now, but those chestnut eyes of hers, are calling out to something inside of me. Something I can't remember. Everything about her is screaming but it's like I'm not hearing the words properly or all the way.

She'd probably say I'm crazy if I told her. But then, why did she seem nervous when I saw her earlier without her glasses?

Could I have been imagining her nervousness?

———

I collapse against the seat, rubbing a hand over my face as I put the car in park.

My eyes feel dry and weary, and I feel like I could fall asleep at any moment, but it was worth it.

Raising a hand, I hover it next to her face. She hasn't woken up since falling asleep earlier. I let my hand move to her shoulder, gently shaking her.

Pulling my hand away, I wait and watch as her eyes blink open. First in confusion and sleepiness until she eyes me.

"Oh," she says softly. Her eyes move past me, looking around until they stop at the sand and water past the parking lot straight ahead.

It's just past six A.M. We're the only ones here.

"You really drove all the way down here while I slept like a baby."

"I did," I respond, slightly amused. Her soft snores filled the car, drowning out any music I tried to play. "Your snores echoed through the car. The longer it went on, the harder it was to stay awake, not gonna lie."

She winces and grabs her glasses, putting them on in a hurry. "Sorry." Stretching her hands above her head, she pulls the latch and gets out of the car. For a moment, she bends down, out of my sight, and then she places her shoes in the car. Without another word, she starts walking to the sand.

Even though my body is telling me to rest, I hurry out of the car, throwing my own shoes in the driver's seat and locking it.

By the time I get to the sand, she's already way ahead of me, almost to the ocean. I jog to catch up and get to the ocean at the same time she does. Both of our feet stick in the wet sand.

Though she can't see how the morning sun looks as it shines on the Pacific Ocean, Gem looks content. The ocean breeze is cold as it washes over us and she shivers slightly. Stepping a few steps to the right, I get behind her, putting my body flush with hers and my arms over her shoulders and around her chest.

"I'm fine," she says, moving her shoulders to try to escape my embrace. "You said you would behave."

"I can't let you be cold. Besides, *yesterday* I said I would behave. It's a new day." I grip her tits in my hand and squeeze.

She gasps and elbows me in the side. I release her and at that very moment, I hear a loud, "Good morning!"

Turning, I find an older man in exercise gear jogging on the sand.

"Good morning," I reply with a wave.

"Good morning," Gemma responds.

"Enjoy yourselves on the beach today. It's going to be a hot one," he yells as he's passing us.

A devious smile forms on my face. "Sorry sir, we won't be staying on the beach today. We have some business at home to take care of." I slap Gemma's ass and she looks at me in horror.

The man's eyes widen with understanding before he chuckles and yells, "Enjoy yourselves nonetheless."

As he jogs forward, I feel a punch to my arm.

Turning my attention to Gem, who looks red in the face. "Did you have to say that?"

I think for a moment before nodding. "Absolutely. I don't know why you're surprised." Closing the distance between us, I pull her against my body and lean down to her so our noses touch. "By the end of November, you'll feel exactly how embarrassed I was for eight months. If I could let every adult in the world know at once that you're getting fucked by Noel Hardington, I would. But sadly that's not possible, apparently I couldn't rent out the skywriting plane to go round the world."

She frowns and pushes me away from her. "You're an asshole. I'm not driving home now." Gem stomps away from the water, up the beach.

"Aw come on, Gem," I call out. "You said you would."

"That was before you ruined things like you always do," she yells. "Hurry up before I call Mera or Scarlett for a ride instead."

With a sigh, I run to catch up.

Like I always do, huh? She's expecting too much from me too.

When I get back to AAA, I'm completely fucking exhausted. And irritated with Gem. Which is why I'm not exactly enthused to see Callan, Vincent, and Tyrell talking animatedly about something in the foyer.

I just want sleep.

"What are you guys talking about?" I ask, closing the door behind me.

They stop immediately when they see me and Callan frowns. "Your dad came by. He told us to tell you as soon as we see you to go to their lab."

"Dude, I've never seen your dad that scary before. Reminds me of my mom," Vincent comments.

Tyrell doesn't say anything, staring at me with a mixed expression.

"Sorry you guys had to deal with him," I say slowly, looking between them. "Unfortunately," I start with a laugh, "I'm tired as fuck so I'm not going anywhere but to bed." I stride past them to the stairs and step on the first step.

"Before you go, at least tell us. Did you two finally fuck?" Vincent asks with a snicker.

Maybe if I wasn't slightly irritated with Gem, I would tell the truth. There's no one else in within earshot. I don't usually lie to my friends about my relationships. But on the way back, she told me that she'd be busy next weekend with Bradley and his friends. I still don't like that guy and I'm not sure what his intentions are with Gem. At the coffee shop, it seemed like he was interested in being more than friends, but at my house when she stormed off he didn't seem to care.

That could have been his shining moment to be alone with her and he didn't take it.

Maybe I'll get lucky again and run right into them.

But for now, I'll lie right through my teeth.

Turning back to them, I let a slow grin spread across my face. "Plenty of times. We fucked from here to San Francisco and from San Francisco to San Diego. Gas stations, bathrooms, you name it, we did it."

Tyrell walks away with a blank expression, down the hallway toward the kitchen.

"I knew it," Vincent says excitedly with a clap. "You're the man, Noel."

I think he just needs to get his own dick wet.

"Gemma was okay with all of that?" Callan asks, skepticism in his eyes.

"Absolutely," I respond cheerily and continue up the stairs.

Vincent will brag for me plenty to the other guys. He'll do that well.

When I get inside my room, I turn on my phone and sit at the edge of my bed. Sliding my shoes and socks off, I pull myself upright in bed, letting my head hit the pillow.

The moment my phone is fully on, notifications start popping up. Four hundred texts. Three hundred emails. And tons from social media.

I click on messages and find the majority to be from my dad and mom. But there's also a few from my fan club and Call, Ty, and Vin.

But one sticks out from Nancy. I open her conversation with me to, finding a message sent last night of a picture of a guy in a hoodie. He's wearing a black hoodie with a white symbol on the back. I feel like I've seen it before, but where?

Nancy: That's him. He's at the party tonight and giving out more.

Nancy: I'm going to talk to him and see if I can get some for you. I'll text you after I do.

I stare at the conversation, frowning when I realize that's the end of it.

· · ·

Me: Did you get any??

For as long as I'm able to with how tired I feel, I keep my phone in my hand, waiting anxiously for a response. It doesn't take long for exhaustion to creep up, and my bed is feeling comfortable. I'll check later when I wake up.

Before going to sleep, I go to my dad's messages and type a response without reading his rants.

Me: I'll talk to you next weekend.

Probably not the response he's hoping for, but right now I'm too tired to care.

I place my phone on the nightstand and put my hand under the pillow and pass right out.

No one knows where Nancy is and she isn't the only one that disappeared at that party.

I don't know about anyone else, but I know that guy has to have something to do with her disappearance if he was the last one to talk to her.

I haven't figured out who he is yet, despite having the picture of that hoodie.

When the weather is in the 90s, you'll be hard pressed to find someone wearing a hoodie.

I've asked around and no one has seen it on anyone. Did I imagine its familiarity?

Today was my day to relax. From school, from coding that program, from doing any work.

Somehow, I managed to postpone my meeting with Dad until the evening. I got to have a good day full of video games with my friends to override what I'm positive will be a night of more arguing and resentment.

There's nothing else between my parents and I any more .

I stride out of the elevator that lets me off on the ground floor. Instantly, the smell of chemicals hit my nose. Taking long sure steps, I walk down the sterile white hallway all the way to the end and stop at the door with a keypad.

The code isn't hard to remember. It's my birthday. This is their way of saying that this lab is where I belong. That all of this is meant for me.

Too bad I don't want it.

At this time of night, everyone who works down here has already left. I make a hard right and walk around all of the equipment until I reach my dad's office all the way at the very end.

With a quick knock, I wait with my hands behind my back for the door to open. There's a lot of rustling and noise behind the door until the door opens a crack, and then all the way.

Dad stands to the side, gesturing for me to come in. I walk past him and sit in front of his desk in the only chair besides his in his office.

Instead of sitting across from me, he stays standing next to me. I feel his hard gaze studying me. The air between us is suffocating. I clench my jaw and anxiously tap my finger against the arm of the chair.

Once. Twice.

"Are you going to tell me what I'm doing here?" I finally ask, breaking the silence.

"I'm waiting for an apology for standing me up last weekend, Noel."

"I'm sorry," I say immediately without really meaning it. "Now can you tell me? I have plans tonight."

His eyes narrow. "You don't give a shit about this company at all, do you?" His mouth forms a thin line as he stares me down.

The intensity of his gaze causes me to gulp. I glance away and put my hands together. "Of course, I care Dad."

"Liar," he responds. "But that's okay, because you can be reformed. This is only a phase. Once you see this, I think you'll be more than willing to understand just how important this company is to your future." He motions with his hand to his desk. "Go sit in my chair, pull open the drawer on the left."

To avoid further argument, I stand and walk past him to his chair. I don't sit. I just pull open the drawer and look.

The first thing I see is a clear baggie. Underneath it are papers. Does he want me to look at the latest numbers in revenue? More money won't make me change my mind about wanting anything to do with this company.

I put the baggie on top of the desk and start to grab the papers when he says, "Stop. The baggie, son. Open it up."

Glancing at him for a moment, I turn my attention back to the drawer and close it. My fingers find the sandwich sized baggie. Lifting it up, I notice how the contents are almost clear. I peel open the seal and stick my hand in to find little star shapes.

As I pick one up, I let it rest in the palm of my hand. The moment it settles, a scene flashes in my head of me grabbing one from underneath a microscope. And...me putting it in my mouth as if it were candy?

I've seen these before.

As I insert my hand back into the baggie for another one, I spot something chilling on my dad's desk. At the very edge of the papers spread out on his desk, there's a picture of someone. Someone very familiar.

I whip my head to look at him and hold up the starry object. "What is this? And why is his picture here?"

A wide smile forms on his face. "So you are taking an interest in this."

"What is it?" I repeat in a harsh tone.

He steps over to me slowly, his eyes getting a disturbing glint to them. He puts his fingers in the bag and brings one out himself.

"This is Space Dust."

My eyes widen as the world seems to stop turning. The only thing I can do is stare at it in his hands.

Deep down, I think I knew. How come I only remember that tiny bit of memory? I don't even know how old I was the first time I saw it.

"Your mother and I worked so hard on this. It's our best creation, next to you of course. Years and years of hard work and it's finally paying off."

I shake my head. "No. You can come up with something better. Something–"

"No," he shouts. "There is no other discussion, no persuasion. Space Dust is the future. It'll be the only drug that people need and we'll be the sole provider. And that kid who goes to your school is making sure we have plenty of customers."

"Bradley gives out your product for free. Are you aware of that?" I snap.

He stares at me for a moment with an amused expression before smirking. "Of course. Do you know how addiction works, son? I know you do. You're a smart kid. Keep them coming back for more, that's the key." He presses his finger into my chest. "You give them a taste and then they won't be able to get enough. Our profits have shot through the roof because of Space Dust."

"You need to stop selling it," I say. "Did you forget Grandpa who overdosed? Or how about Grams who still mourns him to this day? With a drug like this, people won't be able to keep themselves under control and you'll be condemning other people to the same fate as Grandma. The uncontrollable sadness that comes with losing someone you love dearly."

And to make matters worse, I know the FDA would never approve Space Dust. They're breaking the law and hoping they won't get caught.

The smile leaves his face and he sighs. "You know, I was hoping that you'd be more supportive than this. Your mother is going to be so disappointed with you. Bradley is doing everything he can to get our product out there and here you are trying to stop us."

Money really is his top priority. I start to say Bradley can go fuck himself when it all of a sudden it hits me exactly who he's supposed to be with this weekend. Is it today or tomorrow?

Shit. I should've asked but I was exhausted that day.

Gemma. Is he trying to make her a customer too?

Panic rises within me as I straighten, gazing at the door and back to my dad. I need to get the hell out of here right now and tell her. "Nothing you can say is going to convince me that this stuff is okay, Dad. I'm sorry. Now that we're done, can I go?"

He shakes his head slowly. "No." In a flash, his hand shoots out, punching me right in the gut. I clutch at my stomach with one arm, looking up at him incredulously when a hand shoots out and goes right into my mouth, pushing something into my throat.

"No," I rasp desperately trying to keep my throat still so I don't swallow. But his other hand goes to my throat, squeezing it hard and automatically making me swallow when I gasp for air when he lets go.

This can't be happening right now. He'd really go so far as to drug me?

As I stick my fingers down my throat to force myself to throw it up, he grabs my phone out of my pocket and before I can even breathe, he's out the door. I get to it right as it closes. "Let me out!" I scream, banging on it with one fist while I twist the knob with my other.

It only turns slightly. He's holding the fucking knob.

"When I come back, you'll understand the allure of Space Dust and I expect to hear exactly how superior you believe it to be to anything else. It won't be enough to make you fully hallucinate unless you decide to take more, the baggie is still on my desk. Honest opinions only Noel. Don't forget, I know when you lie."

A loud click echoes through the room. His electronic key. When engaged, it doesn't let anyone in or out.

I'm stuck here and Gem...Gem is...

Suddenly the room starts to spin. I place my hand on the door in front of me to steady myself. Blinking quickly, I shake my head to try and clear it but there's a buzzing. And it feels good.

With every second that passes, I feel light and airy. Like everything I've been holding in doesn't matter anymore.

Gem's face flashes in my head as I sink to the floor.

She needs me.

Wait. No.

She's smart enough to be fine without me. She'd never take this stuff.

She'll be fine.

A laugh bursts out from my mouth and I move away from the door to sprawl out on the floor.

The room spins as I start laughing uncontrollably at how much brighter things seem. Everything is closer now and the nervousness I feel from being in this office isn't even an issue.

That pressure on my chest is gone.

If I had a little more of this, I think I could say anything to my parents. No matter what they say it won't bother me.

Before I know it, I'm off the floor and staring at the baggie on my father's desk, full of Space Dust.

As I pull another star out of the bag and lift it to my lips, I suddenly remember the sting in my hand as it was slapped out of it by a girl. Her face is fuzzy, but her words echo through my head clearly.

"You shouldn't eat things if you don't know what they are."

Her voice almost sounds like Gem's.

I snort at the ridiculousness of that thought. Must be the drug making my mind run wild.

Tapping my hand on the desk erratically, I stare at the stars.

I want more and that thought is a scary one. Just how many people at my school are addicted to this stuff? It can't be many since it's the summer, but if this stuff is around during fall, who knows how many people will fall prey to Bradley?

Blinking hard, I rub my hand over my face. My brain is becoming cloudier.

But it doesn't feel bad. It feels good. Nothing else matters right now besides this good feeling. I hope it passes soon.

As I lean back in the chair, a tapping noise startles me. Glancing around the room, I look for the source of the sound, but just as it started, it stops suddenly.

With a groan, I lean back and stare at the ceiling. Now that stuff is making me hear things.

A bang makes me jump and I open my eyes to find my dad staring at me with an inscrutable expression on his face. My phone on his desk in front of me.

Did I fall asleep?

He crosses his arms. "Well? How did you like it?"

I inhale sharply and glance down at my phone before looking back at him. That heaviness in my chest is back and all I want to do is leave and find Gem.

Honesty is what will get me free. "It's effective and I fucking hate it. Grams would be ashamed of you"

A smile spreads across his face as he nods. "But Grandpa would be proud about how much money it's making. Anyway, I asked for feedback not judgement. You may go after one more thing."

He places his hand on the desk, leaning forward. "If I find out from Bradley that you're trying to stop him from distributing it across campus, I'll force you to take this stuff until you can't deny that you love it. And I'll have you expelled, along with that little girlfriend of yours. What's her name by the way?"

I freeze and grimace as rage ignites inside me. Gem hasn't done a thing to deserve that. That would devastate her completely. "You'd really try to make me an addict?"

"If that's what it takes," he says matter of factly.

Standing from the chair, I grab my phone and wrench the door open. I sprint out to the elevator while my phone powers on. When I get inside I stare down at my phone to find it's Sunday afternoon.

Of course there's no messages from Gem. I call her phone and it goes straight to voicemail.

"Answer the phone," I mutter to myself as the elevator dings and opens.

Five more times I call and it goes straight to voicemail.

Fuck.

I hit Callan's name in my recent calls and the phone clicks on the second ring. "Hello?"

"Callan!" I exclaim. "Is Mera with you?"

"No. She and Gemma just left to hang out with that guy."

"Bradley?" I ask, clenching my phone to my ear as I stare out the glass doors to the parking lot.

A sinking feeling forms in my gut.

"Yep. Fucker didn't invite me to hang out. Only Gemma and Mera. I found that strange. What do you think, Noel?"

I breathe a sigh of relief knowing that Mera is with her. I know they're both capable of taking care of themselves, but I need to see that Gem is okay with my own eyes.

An image pops in my head of Bradley forcing a few stars in Gem's mouth makes me see red.

"I think that guy is trouble."

"What do you mean?" he asks, his voice lowering.

"I'm headed back to campus right now," I tell him, pushing open a glass door. "I'll explain when I get there. Do you know where they are?"

"No. I didn't ask because I was sure she was safe with her bodyguards. Hold on, you're making me fucking worry Noel. I'll call her."

The phone call ends as I slide into my car. As I'm pulling out of the parking lot, my phone rings and I answer.

"She isn't picking up," he growls. "I'm going to the admin

office to pull up Bradley's address. She said she wasn't going far. He must live close by. Meet me outside the admin building."

Hanging up the phone, I speed around people to get back to campus. Bradley's smug face pops into my head and like a bolt of lightning, I remember now. That hoodie. He was wearing it that day at the coffee shop. I saw the back of it as I was walking in.

So he was interested in her, just not romantically. Only as a potential customer.

But I refuse to let him taint her. I'm sure Mera is safe with her bodyguards. Gemma is the easier target. If I stop him from giving it to her alone, he might not complain to my parents about it. Everyone else will unfortunately have to wait until I'm able to make a plan to bring Hardington Pharmaceuticals down from the inside.

CHAPTER NINE

Gemma

There's finally a breeze now that the sun is going down. The purples and pinks of the sunset are shining down on the lake. A few of his friends are laughing and swimming in it.

I gulp down the rest of the beer in my cup and turn to go back for more when I notice Mera's eyes are fixated on the lake.

"You've been staring at that lake all day. If you really wanted to swim in it, you should've brought your bikini," I tell her, pushing my glasses up my nose.

She shakes her head and clears her throat. "No. I was just remembering Halloween and..."

"And?" I question, urging her on.

"I'll just probably never swim in that lake." She smiles slightly. "But they seem to be having fun."

"Yeah," I reply, glancing around at his other friends milling around and talking or sitting on the grassy area near the trees.

Mera and I are sort of in between on the dirt with her bodyguards.

They're only standing a few feet away from us and I find it a lot awkward how blank their expressions are with everything we've been talking about these past few hours.

"Gemma!"

I turn around in the direction of Brad's voice. He's jogging over from the tree line. He's been hanging with us off and on, trying not to play favorites with his time. He thought some of his friends might approach us, but so far none have. Even Ginger has avoided us, only looking at Mera with contempt every so often.

Though I have noticed something strange. Once in a while I see them pull something out of their pockets and eat it. Is it candy?

Everyone seems to have some. Even the people who've been lazing around in the water come back to shore to get some from their clothes.

He comes to a stop next to me, exhaling with a smile. "I hope you're having a good time." Peeking around me, he gazes at Mera. "And you too, Your Highness. Mind if I steal Gemma for a bit?"

Mera smiles at the Your Highess bit and nods. "Of course."

Brad smiles widely and glances at me. "Come on, follow me. I have something I want to show you." I follow behind him as he steps through the dirt, walking around the part of the lake where his friends are to the other side.

The trees on the other side are a lot closer together,

making the area darker. There's more bushes and the air feels thicker the further we get to the other side.

It takes a while for us to get to the exact opposite spot of his friends. A weird fluttering in my stomach happens when I find him staring at me with an expression of delight.

"I'm so glad you joined us today, Gemma," he says softly. "Look. I brought you over here because I didn't want anyone to overhear me." He rubs a hand down the back of his head.

"Hear you say what?" I ask carefully.

"I think Noel is bad for you. I don't get what you see in that guy."

I blink at him a few times before chuckling. So he's worried about me? That's really nice of him. "You don't have to worry about me. I know all there is to know about him."

"That's good, but wouldn't you rather be with someone else? I have three friends that are super interested in you."

I turn around, looking out past the trees back to his friends. "I doubt that's true."

None of them have even looked my way all day, and I don't expect them to with how I look.

I gaze back at him. "I appreciate what you're trying to do, really, but it's okay Brad."

He steps over to me, closing the distance between us. "No. I think you need a little courage to get out of your shyness." Grabbing my hand at my side, he pulls it up and pulls something out of his pocket, placing it in my hand.

"Eat it," he says fervently, "and you'll feel like you're on Cloud Nine."

I stare down at the star-shaped object in my hand. It's clear and it almost looks like candy. And it looks familiar. Where have I seen it before?

"Go ahead," he urges.

All of a sudden, it clicks and I immediately let it fall to the ground.

Those were in Noel's parents' lab. I remember Noel almost eating one of them. So that was Space Dust back then and they created it.

This is what they were working on with my parents.

Why does Brad have something of theirs?

Does he work for Noel's parents?

"Where'd you get that?" I ask quietly, feeling my stomach drop.

He sighs heavily and bends down, picking it up. "That doesn't matter. What does matter is you should take it."

"What is it?" I ask, staring at him with a sinking suspicion.

With a grin, he rubs it on his shirt, attempting to get the dirt off. "Why are you so cautious Gemma? Don't you trust me?"

"Answer the question," I say, my voice rising.

"Space Dust," he says softly, holding it up to the small beams of light coming through the trees. "Or as I like to call it, the most magnificent drug there is."

I gaze at it in horror. "That's Space Dust?" The drug that Noel is looking for. He wanted to find the dealer and here's one, right in front of my eyes.

He holds it out. "Take it."

"I don't take drugs," I say firmly, taking a step back.

He laughs, putting a hand behind his back and rubbing his other one through his hair. "Wow. Okay. You know, I thought that you were more adventurous than this, Gemma." Taking a few steps closer, he grabs my arm in a flash in a grip that hurts. "Hold still."

I gasp when his other hand comes from around his back with a syringe in it and the needle jabs right into my skin.

He's trying to drug me. Panicking, I wrench my arm back,

and step on his foot at the same time. It hurts when the syringe comes with my arm and drops to the ground.

Wincing, he shouts in pain and I immediately run past him and into the trees.

I only get a few feet away when someone steps into my path. The instant we lock eyes, I know where I've seen him.

The trees around us rustle and from each direction, his two friends pop up and stand beside him, completely blocking the way now.

"Gemma, isn't it?"

Him and his friends harassed me in the Dining Hall last year. I didn't want to cause trouble and I didn't know what to do, so I sat there like a log and Mera swooped in and got them to leave me alone.

They've stayed away from me ever since, that is until now.

Frowning, I jump when I hear footsteps behind me.

"Gemma, if only you were more flexible."

I slide my hand in my pocket, brushing against my phone and try to initiate an emergency call when a rough hand grabs my arm, pulling my hand out of my pocket.

My gaze moves from his hand on my arm to the hazel eyes I used to think were so friendly. I feel so stupid.

For as smart as I pride myself on being, I let myself be fooled. Why would someone choose to be friends with a nobody like me? It's only sheer luck I have the friends I do have.

I believed Noel didn't like him for no reason, but I guess he's a better judge of character than I am.

"These were the friends you were talking about," I say in a low tone, looking from him to the three guys.

"That's right. If you had taken the drug nicely, I was going to force them to back off and only lightly suggest you try each of them out instead of wasting your time with Noel. Can't have them messing with a customer. But you chose wrong."

I clench my other hand into a fist at my side. "Did you approach me because you wanted a partner for the project, because you wanted to drug me, or because of them?"

A surprised look forms on his face and he seems to consider my question for a minute before answering, "All three."

He sticks the needle into my opposite arm, and a wave of heat washes over me as he pushes down the plunger of the syringe, injecting me with Space Dust.

I shudder as he laughs. "One minute you're just the smart fat girl in the corner and the next thing I know, my three friends are at the window of the classroom, urging me to be your friend so they can get another chance with you. They were patient because I asked them to be. Just like me, they hate hearing the word no. But their patience has run out."

When he pulls the needle out, my arm seems to pulse under the spot the needle went in. I glare up at him, "Just let me go."

He releases my arm without fight, and immediately the guy in front of me grabs me by the arm. I raise my other hand to slap him in the face when everything starts to get blurry and then clear. Blurry and clear.

I shake my head, trying to clear it when I feel another arm grab my wrist.

"Don't touch me!" I exclaim and lower my head quickly causing my head to buzz. Somehow I still manage to get my mouth around his arm and bite it with everything I have.

"Ow fuck," he yells, letting go quickly. I switch over to the one who initially grabbed me who slaps me before I can get my mouth over his arm. I fix him with a grimace, I think? My face feels funny. "She needs four more doses, Brad."

"Four?" He asks incredulously. "If she gets too much too soon, she'll die."

"Give her enough so she won't be able to move."

A wave of panic rises within me. "No," I mutter, scratching at his arm. "Don't do that."

He stares into my eyes for a moment, a sick excitement in them. His eyes travel down, studying my body. "We're going to have fun. And there's nothing you can do to stop us."

I lower my head, trying to think when all of a sudden, I feel that warm heat again in my arm, and then my other. Two more injections. My heart starts to pound erratically.

I'm scared.

I inhale and exhale, each breath catching in my chest. My head feels as light as a feather. It feels amazing. Even though I'm being assaulted by them, a smile forms on my face.

It's too good.

When I lift my head, it lulls to the side slightly. I stare up at them and all of a sudden, their faces start to morph.

"That's impossible," I slur.

My dad's eyebrows furrow. "What's impossible?"

My mom reaches out to grab my arm. "Let's go."

Their faces are clear as day, and their voices, it's been so long. Tears fill my eyes as I stare up at them. "It's been so long, why didn't you come back? You said you'd come back."

I hear murmuring behind me, but it's too far away. I don't care about anything but them.

Abruptly, my legs feel different, like they're too light or limp and they're the only ones holding me up.

"We'll take good care of you," they both say, staring at me.

"Okay," I murmur. Suddenly, everything goes dark.

The cool air on parts of me that shouldn't feel air forces my eyes open.

"You weren't supposed to pass out," a voice says angrily.

"Finally, she's awake!"

I gaze down at myself to find I'm completely naked on the ground with nothing beneath me.

I shouldn't be like this. And I should be upset.

But why do I feel so insanely bright inside? Like everything's just fine. I could just lay here and relax and not have to think about anything. I can focus on feeling good.

But weren't my parents here?

I whip my head around, looking for them but the only people I see are those three guys. And they're all staring intently at my naked body.

What time is it?

I sit up slightly and their leader immediately stands. "You shouldn't be able to move."

Glancing down at my body, I smile and wiggle my hands and feet. "I can move just fine."

All three of them move toward me when I hear a distant sound.

Yelling? Or is it singing? I want to sing too.

But what can I sing?

They freeze and worry comes over their expressions.

That's when I hear it.

"Gemma! Gemma are you here?"

Someone's looking for me. I stand up quickly and start to answer when a hand goes over my mouth. "Don't say a word."

The yell comes closer. Mera. It's Mera.

Their leader holding me looks at the other two. "Both of you, take care of whoever that is."

When they're gone, I open my mouth slightly, biting the inside of his fingers.

"Ouch," he shouts, shaking his hand to ease the sting of my bite.

Immediately, I run forward, dodging around the trees. "Mera, I'm over here!"

Should I be as happy as I feel?

We run right into each other.

Her eyes widen and she looks behind me. "Why are you naked? What's going on?" She glances behind herself. "Barnaby, Edmund, catch up!"

There's silence behind her and she looks back toward me and her eyes widen.

"What?" I ask, with a smile and turn around to find their leader right behind me. I feel the tiny prick of something against the side of my neck.

"If you know what's good for you, princess, you'll come quietly. Don't grab your phone. Don't touch anything. One more injection of this stuff and you can say goodbye to your friend."

"You," she spits. "Why can't you just leave Gemma alone?"

He gestures with her head to go back. "Right now. Come on."

Mera's eyes anxiously find mine.

"You don't look like yourself, Gemma."

Something about her words hit me and I realize it's true.

My mouth quivers and I cover it quickly, murmuring through my hand, "It's the Space Dust."

"You mean that stuff that killed that girl Jessica?"

I nod. As I gaze around, I admire how everything seems

to be so clear. Little stars keep popping up in places. "It's pretty," I murmur to myself.

Her mouth forms a thin line and she strides forward passing us. I move away from him, following her in the direction he wanted us to go, back to where I woke up. "Fine, I'll go, but I'll have you know you're probably going to die tonight."

"By your hand?" he asks with a snort.

"Not exactly, but I'd like to help. When Brad came back a few hours later without Gemma, I realized something was wrong and immediately started looking for her. Since this place is entirely too big to look with just me and my bodyguards, I called for help."

"The police?" he asks, real fear coming over his face.

She stops, ignoring his question. "Is this far enough?"

"No," he says, gesturing for her to keep moving.

We finally reach the same area, and I glance down at my clothes on the ground.

I should put them on. Maybe I'd feel even happier. No, the only thing that could make me feel better than this is another injection.

No.

But it'd feel good. Nothing seems like a big deal anymore. Noel has my house and I'm technically his ho. Not a big deal. I'm naked in front of strangers. Not a big deal. My friend betrayed me. Not a big deal.

Giggling soon turns into maniacal laughter.

"Sit down and shut up," the guy says, unbuttoning his pants.

I plop down as he says, happy as can be on my knees.

"You really do want to die, don't you," Mera says slowly, a smile tugging at her lips.

"The police won't kill me for having a little fun. And why

would they believe either of you that she doesn't want this? Just look at her, she's smiling."

I touch my face to find a wide smile.

"I didn't call the police," Mera says, inspecting her fingers. "I said I called for *help*. And they'll come, maybe even before my bodyguards do."

"Your little boyfriends? Is that it?" He bursts out laughing. "You really had me there."

Mera shrugs. "I wouldn't call them little. I'd say it's more like Lucifer and Asmodeous are coming for you and your *little* friends, wherever they are."

My stomach rolls as he moves closer, and with him, his pencil dick.

I burst out laughing. "What is that?" I ask, pointing to it.

"It's what he deserves for being a sleaze ball," Mera comments wryly. "Now, Gemma, I know you're high as a kite but do me a favor and bite it off?"

He looks at Mera with annoyance. "Maybe I'll have a taste of you as well."

"You wish you could," she responds, tossing her hair over her shoulder.

A sadistic smile forms on his face as he turns back to me. "And you. You won't be laughing when I force this cock into your pussy after you suck me off. Now *do it*. I've waited long enough."

His hand goes to my mouth as he moves my lip.

This isn't right.

I shake my head to clear it and he grabs my chin, forcing me to stop.

I glance up at him and his face starts to morph. I furrow my eyebrows as I stare at him, his muddy brown eyes are suddenly chocolate ones, full of lust and desire for me. His angular nose. The smirk on his face. His eyebrow lifts as if he's waiting. His huge dick sitting in wait in front of my eyes.

This is right.

"Open," Noel commands.

"Don't, Gemma," Mera says, urgency in her voice.

I tremble slightly, enjoying his gaze. But I want to please him. I open my mouth slightly.

The moment I do, a loud noise causes me to jump and he's suddenly not in front of me anymore.

I crook my head to the side to find Noel. No. That guy lying on the ground.

"Precious."

A hand tilts my chin up and another Noel stares down at me. Only the real one would call me precious.

His hand is trembling and his eyes are burning. "Are you hurt?"

"No," I respond cheerily.

Noel's nostrils flare and his chest expands. "Good."

His hand leaves my chin. In a flash, Noel reaches the guy getting to his feet and punches him right in the face, a sickening crack echoing through the air as the guy falls to the ground once more.

CHAPTER TEN

Noel

This guy. I know him. I've seen him and his buddies lurking around, slithering like snakes. Gem isn't the first girl he or his buddies have assaulted.

The rumor about their isolation and assault tendencies has slowly spread. A girl who used to be in my fan club told me.

"Brick isn't it?" I grit, landing another hit across his cheek. The impact causes blood to explode out of his broken nose. "She doesn't belong to you. You put your nasty fucking hands all over what's mine."

I punch his face, over and over again, delighting in hearing him gasp for air as he tries to push me off. Every noise in the background is irrelevant.

He stripped her naked. Not one ounce of panic lurked in her eyes when she saw me. Her pupils were dilated.

This fucker or the other one drugged her. He might be nowhere to be found right now, but I'll find him too and make him wish he never even looked in Gem's direction.

Dimly, I hear a sound behind me. But I don't care.

The only thing I care about is Brick's suffering. I'm not going to let up this soon. My head buzzes with rage as I go to land another punch. His eyes widen and he rasps, "Stop," holding his hands above his face.

A hand touches my shoulder and I automatically wrench my shoulder forward, away from their touch.

"Noel." I glance behind me to find Callan with a solemn expression. He glances down at Brick.

"He needs to pay more than this. It's not enough," I hiss, breathing heavily from exertion.

"I know. Wil just told me these are the guys that harassed Gemma last year. Somehow they found the balls to tell her that she'd be next on his list after they were done with Gemma." He locks eyes with me and his eyes darken. "Whether it's a touch or a threat, it doesn't matter. It's my turn with him now."

I stand up quickly, backing away.

I'd been wondering about that and now I finally have my answer. Good.

My body trembles and I wipe away the sweat on my brow.

Fuck.

It's getting worse.

Brick's eyes are both starting to swell closed. He inches back quickly, trying to get away. Callan stomps right on his stomach and kicks his side like a soccer ball.

I rub a hand over my face and breathe slowly.

Withdrawals.

I know I would've gotten out here faster if my body

would only stop shaking and sweating. The urge to throw up is getting worse with every second. The only reason I'm still standing is Gem.

Whipping around, I find Mera helping her get her clothes back on.

She's going to feel these exact same symptoms and it's going to be hell.

"Mera!" a voice booms.

"Over here," Mera calls.

Callan stands up, pulling Brick with him to a standing position. The guy looks completely wrecked, as he should be, but he's still noticeably breathing.

I turn toward the fast approaching footsteps to find Barnaby and Edmund, each carrying a crony over each shoulder.

"Apologies, princess, these two fools have been trying to inject us with these. One of them gave chase and we knocked them both out." Edmund holds up two injections of Space Dust.

"Is everyone alright?" Barnaby asks, gazing around at us.

"Except this guy," Callan says, gesturing to Brick.

Barnaby clears his throat. "You don't pull any punches do you, Mr. Goldsworthy."

"Noel doesn't either," Callan replies with a smirk.

Mera starts forward, back to campus. "I think we should get Gemma and these other idiots to the hospital."

Her bodyguards grunt in response and follow her with Gem at their side.

Callan and I drag Brick along who grunts every once in a while and mutters through his busted lips.

While Mera gets in the car with Callan, Brick, and Barnaby, Edmund gets in his car with the other two.

Gem glances at me with a puzzled look before I lead her to the passenger side of the car, urging her to get in.

I follow behind her bodyguard's cars to the hospital in my Porsche. My hands tremble against the wheel and I clench my jaw, focusing hard on keeping it steady.

Gem glances at me out of the corner of her eye repeatedly as we drive there. "Are you going to say something?"

"I told you that guy Bradley was a prick," I mutter.

As we pass by the coffee shop, I happen to glance over and see a familiar figure laughing on his way out.

Must be my lucky day.

Making a hard right, the tires squeal as I turn down the road on the right of the coffee shop. I barely make the turn, and pull right into the parking lot.

"What are we doing here?" Gemma asks, with a hint of awe in her voice. "I do love coffee."

"Not now, precious. Stay in the car." I eye the doors of the coffee shop, just in time to see Brad turn in our direction and run the opposite way, away from the shop.

I jump out of the car and run trying to catch up to him as he heads for the street. With five long strides, I catch up to him and tackle him straight to the ground.

"Get the fuck off of me!" he yells.

Moving off of him, I allow him to stand up and he faces me with a look of smugness. "Actually, you know what. Go ahead. Land one right here." He points to his jaw. "I'll be telling your parents tonight exactly how you treat the guy adding to your family's fortune."

I inhale deeply and stare furiously at him. He deserves to be as beat up as Brick.

I clench my fists at my sides. "At least tell me how this all started. How did you get mixed up in this?"

He smiles. "The dark web is a place that I happen to

frequent. I saw an opportunity and I took it almost three years ago."

Confusion fills me as I think about that timeline. "Three years?"

He laughs. "Well I had to go through some training with them first to know exactly what to say to people. Your parents are very good teachers in the ways of persuasion. But after that, I was able to start giving Space Dust out. Some of those people have already graduated and they're spreading the good word about it. Really only one person completely steered away from it in the beginning. Funny enough he was my very first test subject." His head tilts to the side slightly as he studies me. "You know, you're not looking good, friend. I think you need a star or two. Lucky for you, I have plenty."

I put my hand out and cover my mouth, nauseous from both the withdrawals and the Space Dust. "Keep that shit way from me."

Abruptly, his words echo in my head and I think about it through the fuzziness that threatens to consume me. That many people are addicted to this stuff on campus? "Then you still have a percent of failure."

He chuckles. "Sure, but that's because I spiked my first few test subjects. All of them were furious at first, but eventually they came around. Except for him."

My breath stills in my chest.

"Him who?" I rasp.

"A very annoying man of the campus. I kept looking around, trying to find my first subject and there he always was."

"Heath?" I exclaim, my eyes widening. My stomach turns and the bile quickly rises up my throat.

Even saying his name now feels like a betrayal. Hearing this...I..I can't...

I'm barely able to swallow it back down.

"Yeah. You know I heard he witnessed someone getting raped the very same night I drugged him. Nadine Silverstone, I think? It must be true that it ruined his experience because when I approached him about purchasing Space Dust the next day he almost killed me when I told him he already sampled it the night before."

I've heard enough. I need to get rid of this stuff and stop production.

Breathing deeply, I turn away, heading up the street back to my car.

"Enjoy the rest of your night, Noel," he yells.

I need to get back to Gem.

Hurrying back to my car, relief fills me when I see Gem still in the passenger seat.

"Thank you for staying put." I turn the car back on and make a sharp U-turn and head back up the street to the hospital.

"Mera called and asked why we turned off. I said I didn't know," she says simply.

It barely registers in my brain.

Callan is already pissed at Bradley, if I were to tell him that Bradley is responsible for the guilt that hung over Heath's head, he would kill him.

And how could I even think about telling him about it without confessing my own sin?

I rub a hand over my face, sighing heavily and shaking.

Our almost twenty year friendship would be over.

I'm damned if I do and damned if I don't.

Gem strides past me through the automatic doors, breathing deeply. "Finally. Those were the longest four days of my life. And the most expensive ones."

She glares. "It's not my intention to owe you more than I already do."

As we get in my car, she's quiet, staring out the window.

Both of us have fully recovered. In twelve hours I felt better, and early this morning, the final symptoms of withdrawals finally stopped effecting Gem. I stayed in her room after feeling 100% better. We had plenty of time to talk these past few days and despite her grumpiness about the withdrawals, we learned a lot about each other. She didn't seem to be that surprised when I told her my parents created Space Dust.

I've never had a girlfriend with an allergy before, but she's allergic to cranberries of all things.

Every day we'd get flower deliveries. Somehow, word spread among the campus about our trip to the hospital. No one seemed to know it was for drugs. Instead they ridiculously believe we came here because she's pregnant with my kid and having complications.

As if I'd ever get someone pregnant.

She's in a foul mood because of it.

Maybe that and the fact that I'm driving her back to ZDB and not Scarlett like she wanted.

Not to mention she wants Bradley to pay for what he did. I want him to pay too, but it's not possible right now with my parents' threat hanging over my head like a mushroom cloud. The only thing pacifying her is that Brick and his friends were arrested after they got out of the hospital.

The car is silent the whole way back until we pull up outside the sorority house.

"We have so much classwork to catch up on," she groans, getting out of the car.

As she turns to walk up the steps, I let the passenger window down. "Why don't we catch up together then?"

She whips around, pushing her glasses up her face. "I'll pass. But...I never did thank you for coming for me before any of those guys did anything. I feel so stupid. Fucking Bradley."

"Even smart people make mistakes," I remark.

It's true for her, but when it comes to me, I still have no excuse.

She nods. "Sometimes, I forget that." Turning back, she continues up the sidewalk to the porch. As I'm about to pull away from the curb, I watch her pause on the top step. I watch her lift her hand and point away.

Is she talking to someone?

She steps to the side and gestures down the porch.

The person she's talking to finally appears. A woman with a head of unruly hair and a designer outfit with a purse on her arm steps down the stairs slowly.

Immediately, I recognize her as Gem's aunt. The one time I met her, was when we were closing on the house. She had a giant smile on her face that day, anxious to get every last cent of the money from the deal.

Today, she looks the complete opposite. A pout on her mouth as she shouts at Gem. "It's not my fault!"

"It is fully your fault. This is an important lesson, Cindy. I can't and refuse to help you. You are going to have to learn to make it on your own without your cash cow."

She huffs and her eyes laze around until they lock on me. She smiles. "Well hello Noel." Straightening, she walks to the car, her head held high, pushing her chest out. When she reaches my car, she leans over, resting her arms on the window as she peers in. "I can help you, you know. Do whatever you want."

"Not interested," I reply without blinking.

"Are you really propositioning him?" Gem asks incredulously, her voice getting closer.

Her aunt rises, glancing back at her. "You might not be willing to help me, but maybe he will."

"I can't," I say quickly.

Her aunt frowns at me. "You can't or you won't?"

"I won't," I reply.

Gem stops next to her, smiling from me to her aunt. "There you go. Now leave."

Her aunt's lips quiver and she whirls around and stops down the sidewalk.

Gem stays standing by the car, watching her carefully until she turns the corner.

When she finally days, her shoulders relax and she murmurs, "That's going to be a problem."

"Because she'll be back?" I ask. "What exactly happened?"

She sighs. "She was dumb as usual. Some guy came on to her in Europe. I'm sure she was spouting off about all the money she has to anyone who would listen. Well that guy slept with her and robbed her."

I snort. "She kept money on her?"

"She always did, preferring to see cash in front of her face. I can't count the number of times I'd see her waving it around and counting it, over and over. Buying things when for a long time I wore clothes that wouldn't fit me. Not because I gained weight but because I grew taller. The school I went to told her that I needed new clothes and only after that did she buy some for me."

My stomach drops and I glance at the clothes she's

wearing now. A pair of teal sweatpants and a plain black t-shirt that Mera brought.

I wonder if she wears those clothes for comfort or because that's all she can afford.

Regardless of what she wears, she still looks sexy to me.

"Your day was probably ruined by your aunt, wasn't it?"

She raises an eyebrow. "No. Well, maybe a little, why?"

"Because I could make your day a whole lot better in a hotel room."

She opens her mouth to respond when she reaches into her pocket, pulling out her phone. "Someone from the admin office is calling me."

The admin office?

Guess that's none of my business. I put the car into drive when my phone vibrates in the cupholder.

I pick it up to find a number I don't know.

Another random girl who got my number from a friend?

I click answer and hold it up to my ear. "Hello?"

"Noel?" Gemma asks.

I glance up to find Gem putting her hand over the phone staring at me in confusion. We're on a three-way call only feet away from each other?

"Now that you're both on the phone, I'd like to introduce myself. My name is Randall Goldsworthy, I'm the interim Dean for SGU while my son recuperates." His voice is gruff, yet elegant. There's a smoothness to his tone that screams old money. This is Callan's grandfather.

Never in my life have I been face to face with this man, yet I know so much about him. If Callan hates his father, he hates his grandfather even more. This man shaped his father and his father's brothers into who they are today.

Priding himself on having three sons to take over each university in California.

"I apologize for the sudden call, however I felt the need to make sure that the rumor I heard is just a rumor. Something about drugs in the woods and the sexual assault of a woman. I have already talked to my grandson, Callan, and our royal visitor, Princess Wilhelmera. They've assured me that the three involved have been arrested. Is that correct?"

Gem's eyes and mine stay locked.

Callan knows the consequences if we tell on Bradley.

"That's correct," Gemma says.

"Good, good. I would hate for something to show up in the news about this. Please come to me if any situation arises and I'll take care of it."

"Of course, sir," I respond as enthusiastically as I can manage.

But he can't fool me. He doesn't care about whether anyone gets assaulted in the woods. He only cares about the image of these colleges. And more than that, he doesn't care about women in general.

Callan has told me over and over the only reason why his dad secured Southern Goldsworthy University is because he had a son before his two older brothers. His oldest brother had two daughters, no sons and his other brother had a daughter and then a son. His oldest uncle begged for the position in NGU and that is the only reason he wasn't relegated to the MGU.

I bet Callan hated his phone call.

"Have a good day then," Mr. Goldsworthy says, hanging up the phone.

The best karma for him would've been to have a daughter.

"No hotel," Gem says, crossing her arms. "We have too much work to catch up on."

"Soon, though," I tell her, picturing her body beneath mine.

Her face turns pink and she whirls around.

I grin to myself, and zoom off.

When I get back to AAA, Callan is waiting for me in my room with Ty and Vin.

"Welcome back buddy," Vin says, slapping my shoulder.

"My grandfather called you?" Callan asks, frowning.

"Yeah, but he didn't stay on the phone for long. What about you?" I ask, flopping down on the edge of my bed.

Callan's mouth flattens. "He had a lot to say actually, including that no matter what, I won't be allowed to marry Mera if I choose to in the future."

"What the fuck? Why bring that up all of a sudden?" I smirk and chuckle. "Is there something I don't know about? A slip up?"

"No," he says, quickly. "Marriage is the last thing on my mind right now. But now, it's all Mera can talk about after talking to my grandfather."

"So what's with the big objection then?"

Callan grunts. "I have to take over SGU once my father retires and I can't do that if Mera becomes Queen. I don't... have a brother to." He sighs. "Even if Heath was still alive, my grandfather is aware he isn't a real Goldsworthy."

"What about Collette? She's perfectly capable of running things. She runs ZDB just fine."

Callan shakes his head. "She's a woman and therefore inferior in his eyes. So he believes that I shouldn't waste my time and I should break up with her."

"Fucking ridiculous," I mutter.

I feel horrible knowing that Callan has to fight for his relationship with Mera. That he has to fight to be with the one he loves.

"He doesn't know that I can't breathe without her though," he says softly. "It's wonderful, yet terrifying."

Gem's face flashes in my head and I cover my mouth quickly.

No.

I'm only thinking of her because she's my current girlfriend. There's nothing more to it.

There can't be.

CHAPTER ELEVEN

Gemma

July, the second hottest month of the year in SoCal. It's almost 8 AM and it's already almost 90.

Last night I mentioned to Mera how our summer is already halfway over. She couldn't believe it. We went to Luella and Ashlynn's room and five minutes later, it was decided we'd go to the beach. We invited Collette along so she wouldn't be left out and Mera invited Scarlett and Peyton along.

That was going to be it until Mera told Callan she'd be busy and now here we are, all eleven of us headed to the beach in separate cars.

Noel pulls into the parking spot next to Callan and Scarlett parks next to us and Mera's bodyguards parking next to them.

All of us exit the cars in a hurry, anxious to get to the ticket window where the line is already long.

The parking lot on the pier is rapidly filling so we got here just in time.

Twenty minutes later, Noel and I step up to the window. "Two unlimited wristbands," he tells the lady behind the window.

I glance down at my wrist and circle it with my fingers. I hope the wristband fits. What do I do if it doesn't?

Noel holds it out to me and I grasp it in my hand. We step off to the side so Callan and Mera can get theirs.

"Aren't you going to put it on?" he asks.

I glance up at him and nod. "Yeah, I am."

I stare back down at it in my hand, studying the length of it. The width isn't the issue. He might laugh when he sees it doesn't fit, but oh well It's not like I haven't been laughed at before.

If it doesn't fit I'll have to keep it in my pocket. The ride attendants will surely look at me with pity.

Maybe it isn't too late to ask him if we could just get tickets instead?

Suddenly, it's lifted out of my hand.

Lifting my eyes I meet Noel's. "You're taking too long. Let me do it for you. Hold your wrist up."

Breathing lightly, I comply and watch as he lays the band on my wrist and wraps it around to the underside. To my utter shock, he tapes it in place, smoothing his finger over it.

"That wasn't so hard was it?" he asks, dropping his hands away.

Thank God it fits.

"Thank you," I say quickly, rubbing my wristband calmly.

I already figured today would be a nerve-wracking day

because of the beach later. I didn't expect to feel this way this early in the day.

"You can thank me by kissing me at the top of the Ferris wheel," he says with a smirk.

"I don't think so," I reply, stepping away from him to join Mera and Scarlett.

A minute later, we all head through the open park gate.

The few rides at the front already have people lined up and waiting to board. We walk past them, stopping at the area with all of the boardwalk games.

"Oh I'd love to win that bear," Mera muses, pointing up to the ceiling of the stall.

With this particular game, you have to land the rings on the glass bottles. What they don't tell you is the glass bottles are shaped in a way that it's almost impossible to get the rings to land on them.

I lean over, whispering to her. "Most of these games are rigged. You'll never win."

Her brows furrow as she whispers back, "They actually do that in America? That's super unfair. I want to at least try and see."

She digs in her purse and pulls out some bills, handing it to the attendant who gives her ten rings. Mera tosses them one by one at varying speeds and all of them miss their targets.

She sighs. "I guess you were right."

Callan grunts. "Let me try."

"Me too," Vincent says.

Collette sighs. "And watch none of them will land."

They both take turns throwing their rings so they don't collide with each other.

None of them land.

"What a bunch of bullshit," Callan murmurs.

I step away, glancing at the other games.

"That game is a lot better," Noel comments, pointing to the water shooting game.

There's a significant amount of people walking around now and by far that game has more people at it than any other.

"Come on," Noel says, grabbing my hand.

We stand behind the occupied seats, biding our time until the next round.

I stare down at my hand in Noel's. I should pull my hand away.

"What do you want me to win you?"

Glancing up, I lock eyes with him. I wish he'd stop looking at me like that.

A slow smile spreads across his face. "Are you going to answer?"

"Answer what?" I ask.

He chuckles and points to the roof of the wall where all the stuffed animals are hanging. "I'm going to win one and give it to you. Be ready when I win."

Oh, right.

The prizes.

There's no way he'll win. This game is easy enough that anyone can win as long as they start to shoot the water the moment the game begins.

He releases my hand, stepping up as the people from the last round leave.

Every seat fills up again with him seated right in the middle. The first person to fill the container all the way wins.

When the bell to begin dings, I hold my breath, watching his hands as he aims the gun at the hole first before starting to fill it.

When his gauge fills all the way and the bell dings once

more, he turns to me with a cocky grin. "You were saying, Gem."

I bite my lip and shake my head with a chuckle. "I underestimated you." He steps away from the chair and pulls me forward as the attendant comes over.

He holds a tiny bear and bunny out, neither of which are the giant stuffed animals hanging from the ceiling. These are the size of my hands.

"What about those?" I ask, pointing up.

He glances up and back down to us. "Oh. Those are for the people who do it really fast."

"Really?" Noel asks, annoyance in his tone.

Before he can say another word, I interject, "The bunny, please."

The attendant holds it over to me and I grab it, feeling its soft material brush against my fingers.

We move slightly away from the game so someone else can take his spot for the next round.

"That game is a ripoff too," he mutters angrily.

"This is fine," I say with a small smile, holding up the bunny. "Thank you."

It's not nearly what I wanted, but it's such a cute one nonetheless. I've never just gotten what I wanted so easily. It doesn't surprise me that this is any different.

He sighs and shrugs. "If you say so. I guess I'll just buy you a few similar ones online."

"No," I say quickly. "That's not necessary."

He ignores me, turning to face the other boardwalk games. Pointing over, he laughs boisterously. "They're still trying that fucking game."

I can't help but laugh as I watch Peyton slam his hands against the table and then hand some more money to the attendant.

"You know what, I'll probably fail too, but you never know, right?"

I glance at Noel to find him smiling down at me with a determined look.

"Odds are, you won't land any either," I reply, matter of factly.

He smiles from ear to ear. "Okay. I do enjoy a challenge. Time to prove you wrong once more."

Dashing over, he pulls his wallet out. "Me next!" he yells.

I clutch the bunny in my hand and look down at it and back to him. He turns slightly, talking to Callan and I stare at his jaw line.

My heart skips a beat and I dig my fingernails into my palm.

Noel is a jerk. An asshole who enjoys embarrassing me when all I want is to simply just stay in the background. The root of my deepest pain.

I need to remember that.

The four of us get in the first gondola. Callan, Mera, Noel, and I.

Our last ride of the day before we eat and go down to the beach.

Thankfully, this Ferris wheel isn't one of those you see in movies where it's tiny and open, only meant for two people. The kind where if one person swings forward the whole gondola does.

This one has a shade over the top with a circle shape and a bench on each side. The pole for the shade sits right smack in the middle.

I keep my bag with my towel on my lap while Mera sits hers next to her.

The smell of the salt on the ocean breeze is addicting. I breathe deeply and relax into the seat.

The gondola abruptly starts moving and I jump slightly at the sudden movement. A warm arm goes around my shoulders.

"You don't have to do that," I murmur to Noel.

He leans over to my ear, whispering so quietly I barely hear him. "Just be glad we aren't alone in here."

My mouth drops open as his eyes move down my body suggestively.

On a Ferris wheel?

The ride moves once more, getting us higher in the air.

I lean over, whispering heatedly, "You're insane."

Mera clears her throat. "You guys look like you have a lot to talk about. We can plug our ears you know–"

"It's not your ears that need plugging, but your eyes need to be covered."

Mera's jaw drops as she mouths "oh" and a small smile forms on Callan's face as he shakes his head.

I elbow Noel as the gondola moves again, feeling my face turn red.

"I like the way you think," Callan murmurs.

"We got on this for the views," Mera says, pointing out toward the numerous tall buildings in the distance. "Focus on that."

"I think both of us would rather focus on you two," Noel murmurs, his head coming down to my neck. His lips press against my neck and my mouth opens slightly as my breath hitches. He peppers kisses along my neck until settling on a particular spot, sucking my skin into his mouth.

I close my eyes because I can't bear to look at Mera and

Callan. I'm so embarrassed. But I have a feeling they aren't paying any attention to me by the sound of lips colliding wetly.

A moan almost slips out as Noel sucks harder on my neck. Why is he doing this when my neck is so sensitive? Any harder and he's going to leave a mark there. I push at his chest, but he ignores me, keeping his mouth attached to my neck. Squeezing my thighs together, I attempt to suppress the tingling feeling between them. When his mouth pops off, he laps at the area and places one last kiss against it. His hands go down to the hem of my shirt.

"Don't." I'm wearing my one-piece underneath and I'm not exactly ready to leave the security of my shirt.

"There's no time to waste," he says urgently. The heat from his eyes is blazing. With quick hands, he yanks my shirt up, forcing my arms out of it. The moment my arms come down, he stretches my shirt out.

"What are you doing?" I ask, only to have the shirt get closer, covering my eyes.

His fresh scent overwhelms me as I feel him reaching around me. "Noel, this isn't the place for this," I hiss.

He ties a soft knot behind my head and moves away from me.

The shirt isn't the best blindfold, but it's doing the job, obstructing my vision though it hangs down to my chin. My ears are only slightly covered.

The Ferris wheel moves again and I inhale sharply.

"Shhh," Noel says, putting a finger against my lips.

"Towel," I hear Callan say.

A towel?

My bag is moved off of my lap and a towel hits the area it occupied. The beach towel is spread out, hitting my bare thighs and covering my lap completely.

"Callan, what are you–?" Mera asks with a gasp.

Is Callan doing something to her too?

Is this really happening?

A hand tugs at my shorts, and then there's a hand, slipping inside against my one piece. It glides down until it reaches my crotch.

"Don't move, precious," Noel whispers into my ear. "You can't see, but we're really high up here now."

His hand parts my thighs and slips easily to my clit, rubbing around it.

His lips stay nestled against my ear. "Do you know how badly I want to fuck you right now?"

His hand slips down further as he teases my slit before slipping a finger inside. "Does this excite you? You're so wet."

"Noel, please stop," I beg in a whisper.

"When the Ferris wheel starts moving at a consistent pace, I'll take the blindfold off. Until then, be a good girl and let me enjoy you." His finger thrusts inside me and I grab his arm to try and stop him.

His thumb circles my clit as he adds another finger in. My mouth opens as I gasp, twitching at the glorious sensation.

Why does he force me to feel this pleasure?

"Noel," I whisper.

"Precious, make sure you clench around my cock as tight as you are my fingers."

The gondola jolts and I feel it starting to drop. In a flash, my shirt is gone and I glance to the right as the gondola passes the point where we got on.

There's a line of people waiting at the gate to gate on.

My eyes trail to Mera and Callan in front of me. Mera isn't wearing her shirt anymore either. It's in Callan's hands and he's whispering something into her ear that's making her turn redder than Scarlett's hair.

I glance at Noel to find him staring at me. He's not smiling and his gaze is the most intense I've seen it. "Don't worry, no one saw. Did you like it?"

I flatten my lips and contemplate whether I should even answer.

It felt good but why should I give him the satisfaction of hearing it from my mouth? I still hate that it's him of all people making me feel this way.

He lifts his fingers to his lips and licks them clean, one by one, ending with his thumb. "Well?"

The gondola slows to a stop and I'm the first one off of it when the attendant opens the door.

I exit through the gate and stop outside the ride, waiting for everyone else. Noel is the first to reach me.

"It's fine if you don't tell me," he says, sticking his hands into the pockets of his swim trunks. "I already know."

"You don't know anything," I snap, pulling my shirt back on.

I turn away from him, giving him my back. I'm thankful when Callan and Mera come out, with everyone else trailing behind. I stick to the edge of our group, feeling the heat of embarrassment on my cheeks.

This is almost over. Only four months and I'll be back to being in control of my body.

I cover myself in sunscreen so I don't burn. But it helps that I still have my shirt and shorts on.

Everyone else is making sandcastles, looking for seashells, or playing in the water, but I'm content laying on my towel.

There's really only one problem. The sun is blaring down

on us and I'm starting to sweat pretty bad. The ocean breeze is blowing, but it's only barely helping.

I put my sunglasses on and turn over so I'm face up. Wiping the sweat off my hairline, I sigh and reach for the bottle of water next to me.

My mouth is so dry.

Frowning, I touch the area over and over until I realize it's gone.

"Looking for this?"

I tilt my head up to find the bottle of water hanging above my head in Noel's hand.

Thrusting my hand out, I reach for it only to see him pull it back. "Nope. I'll give it to you if you come in the water with me."

I sit up from the towel, watching as water drips off his hair, traveling down his body in streams to his V lines. Trailing my eyes back up, I shake my head.

"Come on. In Cancun I barely got to see you without your shirt over your swimsuit and you didn't get in the water once."

Sighing, I take my sunglasses off and replace them with my regular glasses. "Are you really going to force me into the ocean?"

"No, but you should know that it's a lot of fun out there that you're missing out on. Who knows the next time we'll come out here as a group?"

I hate that he has a point.

"How many times do I have to tell you how sexy you are? And in a swimsuit? You're a fucking knockout, Gem. So they can see your stretch marks, who cares? Come on, you're strong. Ignore any rude stares and just have a good time with me."

Noel holds out my water bottle and I grab it, unscrew the top and gulp it down.

"I'm still not happy with you," I mutter, setting the empty bottle down on the towel.

"I know," he says, rubbing the back of his head. "But when are you ever happy with me? Anyway, I'll be out there."

He walks around the perimeter of my towel, through the sand to the ocean. Callan, Mera, Scarlett, Peyton, Tyrell and Vincent are far away from the shore, letting the waves hit their bodies. Luella is burying Ashlynn in the sand except for her head and Collette is building a sand castle next to them.

I could always just join them.

I glance up just in time to watch Noel reach them as a wave comes in, wrecking them. Moments later, they surface, laughing together.

My stomach flutters and I glance down at myself. I peel my shirt up slightly and touch my flabby stomach.

I deserve to have fun too. One step forward is all it takes.

Breathing deeply, I stand up and wrench my shirt off. My shoulders are finally able to breathe and it feels good.

I pull my shorts off and set them down on my towel along with my shirt. Before I lose my drive, I place my glasses on the towel and fast walk to the water. I focus squarely on the water in front of me, walking past Luella, Ashlynn, and Collette.

Abruptly a hand grabs my arm right as I reach the muddy part of the shore. My feet start to sink in as I follow the hand to its owner.

Collette?

She glances from me to the water. "I have to know since it's been four months. You haven't fallen for Noel, have you? You guys look pretty amicable today."

"No, not at all," I assure her. "Trust me, I hate him and I can't wait for these next four months to be over."

She smiles. "Good. Keep that mindset going. Don't let him sway you." Her eyes trail down my swimsuit. "And you look gorgeous, Gemma." Collette's purple glittery eyeshadow shines in the sun until she puts a hand over her eyes. "It does look fun out there."

"Yep. And that's why I'm going."

A man happens to pass behind Collette, looking at me with a hint of disgust.

Turning around, I wade into the water slowly. It's not as cold as I thought it would be and it feels refreshing against my sweaty skin.

I wade out further, swimming forward until I can't feel the sand anymore.

All of a sudden, someone's hands grip me by my waist and I squeal in surprise. I don't have to turn my head to know it's Noel.

One of his hands leave my waist and touch the side of my neck where the hickey is. "I'm proud you came out here, precious."

"Right, well you can let g–" I say right as I hear the rush of water followed by a wave that crashes into us.

We surface together and I gasp for air when I get to the surface. I should've expected that. He laughs and lets go of me. "I'll let you enjoy the rest of your day without me harassing you." He turns away from me, yelling for Vincent and Tyrell.

He splashes them and they splash back.

Mera swims over to me with Callan in tow. "I'm so glad you came out here, Gemma!" She grabs me in a hug and whispers in my ear. "We are never going to talk about what happened on that Ferris wheel, right?"

I nod quickly as she pulls away with a look of relief. "Good." Her wet hair whips around as she turns toward Callan, who hugs her as the next wave comes.

This time, I'm prepared for it and hold my breath. When I surface, my eyes unconsciously land on Noel.

He smiles widely, smoothing his wet hair back out of his face.

My stomach flutters as I watch him turn slightly, expecting him to look in my direction. But he doesn't. Instead, he looks slightly to the left of me at the shore, elbowing Vincent. I follow their line of sight to see Collette, Luella, and Ashlynn wading out.

I glance back toward him and our eyes meet for a moment. He's the first to look away and for some reason, my chest hurts now.

Grasping the doorknob, I twist it to the right and push the door open slightly.

Noel looks away from his computer.

"You wanted to see me?" I ask.

"Yeah, come in," he says, waving me over.

Closing the door behind me, I stroll over, stopping in front of his desk. "Yes?"

It's been almost a week since our day at the beach and we've been going along with things as usual. Our class will be over next week which means we'll have our final lab this week.

I'm at a B+ and I hate it. This is my last chance to help raise my grade before our final exam and lab test.

Noel hasn't said much these past few days and I don't

know why. It's not like him and I don't know why it bothers me, but it does.

I push my glasses up the bridge of my nose and he says, "Closer."

Moving around his desk, I stop at the very edge of it. "Is this better?"

"Closer," he insists.

"Noel, we're at work," I remind him.

My mind flashes back to when he handcuffed me to himself. I won't let something like that happen again.

As if he can read my mind he raises his hands. "No handcuffs. You can search me if you want to."

"Just tell me what I'm here for. I won't come any closer."

I still have work to do before I can go back to ZDB.

He rises from his chair, stalking over to me and grabbing my hand roughly. "I have a problem that only you can solve."

His hands grip my waist as he picks me up, setting me on top of his desk.

He brushes a finger over my bottom lip and cups my face. "Whatever you're going to say to get out of this, don't."

I move his hands off my face. "I have work to do and I'm sure you do too."

"I do, but my problem is, I'm starving." Noel's hands travel behind me, grabbing my hips and pulling me flush against him.

Instantly, I feel how hard he is in his slacks.

"I've never gone this long without having real sex, Gem. I need it."

I knew this moment was coming. The moment where his control finally snaps. But it can't be today, or here in this office.

Things are better when they're planned and every single

encounter with him hasn't been planned besides our nights in Cancun.

But just this one thing, I want to have control over.

But will he listen?

"Tomorrow, I'll do it," I tell him. "We can go to a hotel or whatever."

He curls his lip. "I've waited long enough. When I made that deal with you, I took you at your word that you'd have sex with me."

Frowning, I snap, "And I will! I just pictured it being in a bed instead of on an office desk."

He straightens, crossing his arms. "You realize at any moment I could decide to knock your house down. Demolish it to dust."

My heart clenches. "I know that."

He chuckles and sighs. "How do I know you won't suddenly have something to do tomorrow?"

"You'll just have to trust me," I reply with a shrug.

That word.

Trust.

How angry would Noel be if he gained his memories back and found out I've known this whole time who he is?

Over time, that worry has lessened. I halfway believe that those memories are gone forever. But at the back of my head, I know at any moment he could remember and all trust between us would be broken.

And then who knows what will happen to my house.

"Let's shake on it, then," he says with a smirk. "Tomorrow night, I'll pick you up and we'll go to a hotel, just like you want. I'll bring a full pack of condoms. You aren't allowed to leave until Monday morning."

"Monday morning?" I ask, flabbergasted. Just how many times does he intend on having sex with me? "I thought we'd only do it once." He plans on making me go from the hotel room straight to school for the lab exam?

"Once?" He shakes his head slowly, looking at me as if I'm completely naive. "After four months, no. Truthfully, I don't know how many times it'll be because I've never gone this long without it. *One week* was my old record. That should tell you how pent up I am."

"Fine," I murmur. "Let's shake on it."

"Great." He moves closer, dropping his hands to my stocking-covered thighs.

I've been wearing skirts all week since it's so hot in August.

Now, I'm regretting it.

I hold my hand out waiting for him to take it, but he only grins at my hand.

"I was thinking a different way," he murmurs, trailing his hand up my thigh. He places a hand on each thigh and parts them roughly.

"What are you doing?" I ask, staring down at his arm.

"Shaking on it," he responds innocently. His other hand touches my shoulder. "Lay back, precious."

I shake my head, a no hovering on the tip of my tongue.

"We're supposed to be shaking on it, precious. Be a good girl and lay back."

At the words good girl, I quiver and do exactly as he asks.

His other hand moves under my skirt and an audible tearing sound fills the air.

I tilt my head up, feeling the cool air touching my crotch. "Did you just tear my stockings?"

"I'll buy you new ones," he assures me. His finger trails along my underwear, from my clit to my slit, up and down. His finger dips inside me with my underwear in the way.

After a while, I realize it's a torturous movement. What a tease. This is frustrating. I can't let on that it is, though.

Abruptly, I feel him expose me to the air by pulling my underwear to the side. I expect to feel that same finger against my entrance, only to watch in shock as he crouches and lowers his head.

Feeling his tongue on me for the first time is nothing like I've ever felt before. From sucking on my clit to lapping at my wetness and eating me up like a starving man.

He did say he was starving didn't he?

A moan escapes my mouth and he freezes upon hearing it.

"More," he says with a groan. He drags me forward so my legs are draped over his shoulders. He feasts on me, gathering every bit of wetness that leaks from me. Both of his hands squeeze my thighs.

I can feel it building again, just like in the library, but it's faster.

"Do you know how sweet you taste, precious?"

He replaces his tongue with two fingers, thrusting them both inside me. I groan at the loss of it, only to feel the gloriousness of it again when he sucks on my clit at the same time. And that's all it takes for me to completely come apart, panting as lightning shoots to my toes making me spasm. His mouth stays on my clit all the while pulling his fingers out and eventually lapping at my wetness again, causing me to quiver with every touch of his tongue against my sensitive flesh.

His head comes up and he stares at me with lust-filled eyes. His gaze shifts away from me and his eyes widen in horror. "Oh, fuck."

He grabs my arm and pulls me off his desk in a flash. "What's wrong?"

"Quiet, Gem," he says, pushing me to the ground and gesturing me toward the open area underneath his desk.

Is someone coming? My heart pounds as I back myself in, facing the open area where his chair is.

The sound of the door opening makes me cover my mouth. Why didn't he lock the door?

"Mom, what are you doing here?"

My eyes bulge. His mother?

"Noel, you've been coming to work like everything is normal, and yet you've been ignoring our calls and texts. Why?"

Her voice sends a chill down my spine. She still sounds exactly the same. For a long time, his parents were in my nightmares, reminding me over and over that they weren't people to be messed with.

"I think you know why," he says stonily.

Lowering my hand, I breathe as quietly as possible.

"Space Dust? Really? We're doing this for you, Noel, in case you've forgotten. We've spent years and years on this. We can't just let it go."

Staring forward, I notice his pants are undone. Suddenly, an evil idea comes over me. Not just evil. A truly un-Gemma thing to do.

"Mom, the FDA will find out eventually. How could they not with how fast it's spreading?"

But he's caused me so much grief, embarrassing me in front of everyone. I can play this game and torture him too. I scoot forward slightly and pull his chair forward until my face is in his crotch. His dick is jutting forward. Eating me out made him hard?

He wags his finger at me under the desk and I push it away with my hand.

"That won't happen," she replies. "We have friends in powerful places, you know this."

I pull his underwear down and place my mouth right around his dick.

I have no idea what the hell I'm doing, but now he'll have to be careful and watch his reactions. He doesn't want his mom to meet me and I certainly don't want to meet her. So I'll be as quiet as possible while I do this and he'll have no control over any of it.

It's a risk but it'll be worth it to watch him lose control for a short time.

CHAPTER TWELVE

Noel

My cock is in her warm mouth.

Why is she doing this?

I grit my teeth as her tongue rolls around my head.

"Is something wrong, Noel?" Mom asks.

"Not at all. Listen, it's going to take some time for me to think about this. Right now, I can't fathom being the head of this company in the future if we're selling Space Dust."

Gem sucks me in her mouth, taking me halfway.

Holy fuck.

My fingers twitch as I ache to grab her head and thrust my cock all the way in until it hits the back of her throat.

But surely, my mom would hear her gag.

I can't.

"You'll be the CEO of this company whether you want to

be or not. That is your role, Noel. It always has been and always will be. I don't want to ever hear you suggest that you won't be," she seethes.

I gasp as she runs her tongue along the underside of my cock.

How is she so good at this?

"Noel?"

"I'm fine, I'm sorry," I say quickly. "Can we talk about this later?"

Gem swirls her tongue around my cock and sucks it in all the way, causing me to see stars.

I'm going to come so fucking hard if she continues this. I need to keep my cool.

"So you're going to come home then?" she asks, gazing at me with unbelieving eyes.

At this point I'll say fucking anything if she'll leave, even if it condemns me to spend more time in their presence.

"Yes!" I exclaim.

She smiles. "That's more like it. Be sure to let us know ahead of time so we'll be home at the same time." Whirling around, she exits the room, slamming the door behind her.

The moment I see she's a good distance away, I shove my chair back, and my cock pops out of her mouth.

"What the hell are you doing, Gem?"

She wipes her hand over her mouth. "Teaching you a lesson."

I glance down at my straining cock and back to her. "Teach me some more." I'm so close to coming.

She sighs. "No, I don't think so. Fun is over." Crawling forward, she moves to stand up but I trap her between my legs.

"Please, just finish me off and I'll take you home early."

"No," she says firmly. "Now let me go."

"Please," I beg.

She looks at me through her eyelashes. "Fine." She grips my cock in one hand and sucks on the head before moving down my shaft.

I groan low in my throat. "That's it, precious. Such a good girl. Suck me in deeper so I can come down your throat."

She bobs her head up and down, but she looks at me with stubborn eyes.

I can't wait any longer. I'll apologize for this later. I grab her head and thrust myself inside her mouth. It's so warm and tight. Exactly how her pussy is going to feel on Saturday.

With a loud groan, I come hard into her mouth, shooting my cum down her throat. She glares at me with tear-filled eyes. I let go immediately and she coughs, holding her throat. "I'm never doing that again, just so you know," she rasps, using my leg to pull herself off the floor.

I pull my underwear over my cock and button my pants. "Sorry, precious. I can't help that you're so good with your mouth."

She glares. "Just take me back to ZDB. I'll go grab my bag."

I move out of the way and watch her stomp angrily out of the room. Through the glass, I see her make a left into her work room.

I turn my attention to the computer, staring at the code on the screen and shut it down. Grabbing my wallet, I glance over everything before leaving and shove it in my pocket. On the way out, I lock the door and walk down the hallway, all the way to the entrance.

Luckily, Mom is nowhere in the vicinity.

Footsteps echo on the tile a few minutes later, and she charges out the glass doors. I unlock my car and she slides inside. When I get in, and start the car, she rolls down the window and turns whatever song is currently playing on the radio up.

To drown out my voice, I'm guessing.

But I'm fine with that because tomorrow I'll finally get what I've been craving for months.

The whole car ride she doesn't even look in my direction, and when I pull up outside ZDB, she gets out before I can even come to a full stop.

It's only after the door of the sorority closes and I'm about to pull off that I realize she left her bag under the glove compartment.

For a few more minutes, I wait outside in case she comes back out, but she doesn't.

Instead a few girls wave at me and start coming toward the car.

Nope, no. Not interested.

With a wave I peel away from the curb before they can reach me.

Oh well, I'll just give it to her tomorrow when I see her.

CHAPTER THIRTEEN

Gemma

I stare down at my bowl of oatmeal. It doesn't seem right that I have to be the one to stay with Aunt Cindy for weeks while my parents leave?

She hates me just as much as I hate her. I can tell by how she treats me.

But since my grandparents are dead, I don't have anyone else.

I only hope that they can get done early and be home fast.

This isn't their punishment is it?

I hope it's not.

Because if it is their punishment, then them leaving is all our fault.

A tear slips down my cheek and I wipe it away.

"Honey, we won't be gone for long, please try to cheer up," Dad says across the table.

I meet his eyes and shake my head, my lips quivering. "Why can't I go with you?"

He adjusts his round glasses and sighs. "You don't work for Hardington Pharmaceuticals, honey. We do. We have to go, I'm sorry. We promise we'll be back as quick as we can."

Mom grabs my hand, rubbing it soothingly. "My dear sweet Gemma, you know everything we do, we do for you. I know things have been rough recently, but things are going to change when we get back. I'm sorry you won't be able to see Noel until we get back, but you can go without seeing him for a few weeks, right?"

"Of course," I tell her with a nod.

A lie.

Noel has become my very best friend and I know he needs me just as much as I need him. If he gets put in the closet while I'm gone, who will be there to comfort him?

He'll be all alone.

I hate that there's nothing I can do.

Mom glances across the table at Dad. "How about this, when we get back we'll go on a trip to San Francisco and another trip to San Diego? We've never had the chance to take you many places since work has kept us busy, but I think it's time we change that. What do you think, honey?"

A trip with my parents? I smile and nod quickly, my sadness being drowned out by the excitement of our future trip. "That sounds fun. I only wish we could bring Noel."

Mom and Dad share a look across the table and Mom leans in with a sad expression. "I don't think his parents will allow that honey, I'm sorry. If there was a way to bring him along, you know we would. Noel is such a sweet kid. For now, promise me that you'll stay away from him and his parents. They're dangerous people."

"But why?"

Dad stands up abruptly, glancing at the watch on his wrist. "We don't have time to explain, honey. We have to get going. Keep working hard in your studies, okay? Cindy will be here in about an hour. Until she gets here, don't touch anything. Remember the rules, honey."

I nod and put a bright smile on. "I won't."

"And don't open the door for anyone except Cindy," Mom says, rising from her seat and rubbing my hair.

"I know. No strangers or salesman."

"That's my girl. You're so smart for your age, my beautiful Jewel." She kisses my forehead and joins my dad as they walk to the living room together.

I jump out of my chair and dash over to them as they reach the door. My mom is standing on one side and my dad opposite of her. Before they grab their bags, I grab each of them with an arm and pull them closer for a family hug.

They grab me with an arm each and wrap an arm around each other.

"We'll be back before you know it," Dad says softly.

They've never been on a trip more than a week before and their other trips have always gone by slowly. I'm afraid it'll be worse this time.

I let go of them reluctantly, watching as they grab their luggage. Dad opens the door and walks out. Mom is right behind him, turning around at the last moment with a smile. "We love you, Gemma."

"I love you too."

I close the door softly behind them.

Tears fill my eyes and I wipe them away quickly. No, it'll be fine. They'll be back soon. I shouldn't cry.

My eyes pop open as I bolt awake in bed, my chest heaving.

"Gemma."

I turn toward the voice to find Mera next to me.

"I'm sorry," she says quickly, "I didn't mean to disturb you, but you were sobbing in your sleep."

Startled, I realize my face is wet and lift my fingers to wipe the tears away.

I haven't dreamt about that day in a long time. I still remember it so clearly.

That day was the day my life changed forever. Two weeks turned into three weeks and three weeks turned into a month, and then a month turned into a year. At the year mark, that was when I knew that they were never coming back.

They had missed my birthday without a call and I was able to ignore that, but my parents would never tell me they'd be back soon and then be gone for a year without communication.

And here I am now, with no answers. The only possible thing that fits is that Noel and I did more damage than we thought we did.

We were stupid kids and my parents paid the price for it.

I cover my face with my hands and breathe deeply.

"Gemma? Are you okay?" Mera asks gently.

Sniffing, I lower my hands from my face. "I was dreaming about my parents. I hate that they've been gone for almost half my life now." So many years have gone by without Mom's laughter and Dad's jokes. From the time I was young, they nurtured my excitement about learning and encouraged me. Without them, I don't think I'd be where I am today.

"I'm sorry. I can't begin to imagine how painful that is. And you don't know what happened to them?"

"I don't." It's been weighing on me for so long. My guilt. I've never had a close enough friend that I confide in. No one would confess that their disappearance is partially my fault. Can I trust that Mera won't tell Callan so he doesn't tell

Noel? What will she think of me when she finds out that I've kept the truth from Noel?

In the past, every friend I had would always expect one thing or another from me. Whether it was to help them cheat on tests, to copy my homework, or even do their homework. And when I refused, they'd get back at me by bullying me about my weight.

Until I got here, I've never had close friends like these and Mera has been a great friend. She can keep a secret.

"We should go out for lunch with everyone," Mera suggests with a small smile. "What do you think?"

I glance at the nightstand to find it's two hours until noon.

"Sure, lunch sounds good. But, do you have time to hear a story?"

She nods, interest and curiosity in her eyes. "Talk away. That's what friends are for, right?"

I take a deep breath and think back to how it all began and open my mouth to tell her start to finish.

I hope he brings my bag. I can't believe I forgot it in his car yesterday.

Scarlett pulls up in front of Chateau Desire with Peyton, Mera, and I in tow.

"We'll get a table and wait for them to show up," Mera says getting out of the backseat with me.

Not everyone could come. Just us and Callan and Noel who are on their way.

Now that I've told Mera everything, I feel a lot better. Suffice to say, she was shocked when I finished. She didn't push me to tell Noel the truth or tell me I'm a terrible person for keeping it from him. She only listened and told me I'm smart enough to know what I'm doing.

I'm glad I told her.

She even promised she wouldn't tell Callan, without me even asking her to. It's a huge relief.

Mera leads the way, and at the hostess desk she asks for a table for six.

There's a moment of recognition when the hostess gets her name.

Despite the people many people waiting in the lobby for a table, she leads us straight to one. It makes me feel bad every time this happens, but people are afraid of displeasing Mera by making her wait for a table like everyone else.

Mera and I sit across from each other in the middle seats while Scarlett sits on Mera's right and Peyton on my left.

The hostess sets the menus down and immediately after, a waitress comes. She bows quickly to Mera. "What can I get you to drink, Your Highness?"

Mera smiles. "There's no need for formalities. Please, treat me the same as my friends. You can take their drink orders first."

The waitress' eyes widen and she turns to Scarlett, her pen hovering over her notepad at the ready.

Scarlett glances at the back of the menu. "Iced tea please."

The waitress writes it down quickly and gazes at me. "Strawberry lemonade."

She nods, scribbling it down.

While she gets Peyton and Mera's order, I pick up the menu and glance through it. All of it looks good, but I'm a creature of habit. If there's chicken strips and fries I'm getting them. When I reach the back, I glance over the drink menu once more.

Various alcoholic drinks, sodas, iced teas, and lemonades.

Maybe I shouldn't have gotten a soda instead. I rarely get strawberry lemonade because it looks so close to pink lemonade, and pink lemonade is something I can't have because sometimes it's made with cranberry juice.

I learned that the hard way when I went to a restaurant with my parents when I was younger.

But today, I feel like strawberry lemonade.

I set my menu down in front of me, already knowing what I want.

"You guys can get alcohol. I don't mind missing out," Scarlett says, setting her menu down.

Mera laughs. "No, I'm good. Peyton can get some."

He snorts. "Drinking alone isn't fun. I don't think Gemma wants any." He shifts his gaze to me with a smile. "Right, Gemma?"

I open my mouth to respond with no, when I remember exactly what I have to do later today. If I do drink anything I think it'd have to be later, right before it.

"I'm good," I respond with a small smile.

The waitress sets our drinks in front of us, followed by six straws. I lay the two extra ones on the side of the table where Callan and Noel are going to sit.

"I'll be back to get your order once the other members in your party show up," she says with a cheery smile before stepping over to the table next to us.

Picking my glass up, I move it closer and take the paper out of my straw and put it in. The strawberry lemonade is a light pink color with strawberries gathered upon the bottom. I prod the strawberries at the bottom of the glass causing a few seeds float out under the pressure. Lifting the straw slightly, I keep them away from the strawberries so I can have more of the lemonade itself.

I put my lips around the straw and suck it in.

A few large sips.

The lemonade hits my tongue and I marvel at how sweet it is. I've missed having strawberry lemonade. Strawberries are my favorite fruit.

"It's good isn't it?" I hear Mera ask.

Nodding, I go to take another sip when all of a sudden, I feel a tightness in my throat.

What's going on?

Gasping for air, I clutch at my throat and stare down at the lemonade.

No. That can't be. This is strawberry lemonade.

"Gemma! Gemma, what's wrong?"

"Gemma, breathe!"

I hear all three of my friends shouting my name as I collapse back into the chair, feeling my body tremble at the lock of oxygen.

"The lemonade," I gasp. "Cranberries. Epipen."

Then it hits me. I don't have it. Stupid, stupid. I keep two in my bag and right now, that bag is with Noel.

Suddenly there's silence in the restaurant and all I can hear is the sound of myself gasping.

In front of me, Mera's in tears on the phone.

"Where's your epipen?" Peyton asks beside me, looking under the table.

"Noel," I say as I fall out of my chair to the floor.

Everything is starting to fade away.

This is how I die?

Right as my eyes are about to close, Noel's face appears over mine. He's crying.

"Gemma, stay with me." I feel a tug and sharpness in my thigh and then I'm gone.

Beeping sounds are the first thing I hear. They seem so loud. I slowly open my eyes to to find a familiar white ceiling.

Oh God, I don't want to be at a hospital again.

I turn my head to the right to find Noel staring at me intensely in the chair by my bed. His elbows propped on his knees as he leans in.

"One minute later and you would've been gone from this world," he says. "And it would've been all my fault."

I shake my head quickly. It wouldn't be right for him to beat himself up about this. "No, it's my fault for not getting my bag back from you earlier. Every person with a severe allergy knows not to go anywhere without their epipen. I'm just so used to having it. But I don't understand why that happened. That was supposed to be strawberry lemonade."

He leans back in his chair, his jaw set. "That restaurant uses pink lemonade and strawberries to make their strawberry lemonade."

"Well, that's misleading," I say, grabbing my glasses from the table next to me and sliding them on. "I'm sorry for giving everyone a scare."

He runs his hand over his face. "Your whole face was blue, Gem. I'd say we were all beyond scared. Especially me. If you had died in that restaurant I would've burned it to the ground."

I still at his words, looking down at my hands. "You would have? But why?"

He stays quiet for a while. I don't look at him. I just wait for his response. Why would he have a reaction like that? The Noel I knew back then, sure, I'd understand. But this Noel, I don't get it.

"I'll go get the nurse so we can get you checked out." I glance up in time to watch the door close behind him.

That doesn't tell me anything, but oh well. What did I expect?

I'm nothing special. Just another girl for him to conquer and say that he's had.

Wait. Do I want to be special to him?

I bite my lip and shake that thought away, grabbing my phone. I have a slew of missed messages. Mera, Collette, and more. Collette's is the newest one so I click on hers first.

Collette: I saw the video. Are you really going to lie and tell me you don't feel anything for him? And him? I've never seen Noel cry before. What's going on with you two???

A video? There's a video of it?

I go to the internet and type in "allergic reaction restaurant girl" to find a few news articles about the incident. All of them, a video attached of my anaphylactic reaction. For my own sanity, I can't watch myself far on the floor like a log. Instead I start reading one article.

Noel Hardington's girlfriend, Gemma Brighton collapses at Chateau Desire after a severe allergic reaction. At this time it's unknown what caused it, but the victim has been taken to the hospital by ambulance after getting an epipen dose in her leg.

I set my phone down on my lap and sigh. The door opens and Noel returns with a nurse right behind him.

After she checks me over she says, "Gemma, we're so glad you're doing better. You're all set to be released. I'll go let the doctor know."

"Thank you," I reply as she exits the room.

I gaze over at Noel, his back to me in the corner of the room.

For some reason, I'm feeling waves of anger coming off of him. Is he mad because I asked him that question.

I'll just leave him be in his own head.

"We have a problem," he says, irritation evident in his voice.

"What is it?" I ask.

"We have to go somewhere when you get discharged?"

My stomach drops as he turns around, a grimace on his face with his fists clenched at his sides.

Why do I get the feeling I'm not going to like what he says next?

"We have to go to Hardington Pharmaceuticals. My parents are waiting on us."

My eyes widen as my hand shoots to cover my mouth. *No.*

He sighs and rubs a hand over his hair. "They saw those fucking articles and now, they want to meet you."

They know who I am. There's no doubt at it. And they'll tell Noel. And then…then he'll know who I am.

"I can't," I say firmly.

"There's no option but to go," he says. "If you don't, they'll have you expelled."

My jaw drops and I yell indignantly, "They can't fucking do that! They don't own this school."

"You're right. But my parents are close friends with Antoure Goldsworthy. If they want you expelled, they can make it happen."

I lower my head and stare down at the sheet covering my legs. Then this is it.

I won't hide then. I won't deny exactly who I am. But more than that, I'll get answers tonight. If they're confronting me, I'll confront *them* about what happened to my parents.

When we walk through the glass doors together, I'm not prepared to see his parents already waiting for us in the lobby.

I try to breathe evenly as I approach my parents and their former bosses.

Mr. Hardingotn looks like an older version of Noel with lighter brown eyes while his mother could be a former model with how long her legs are. Her eyes are the same shade as Noel's.

Mr. Hardington stares blankly at us while Mrs. Hardington smiles. A sharp contrast to each other, but even I know it has everything to do with the way they handle things.

Both of them just as firm, but Mrs. Hardington would rather smile while she inflicts punishments, as if seeing her smile would make Noel believe it was for his own good. Mr. Hardington was always more direct and he didn't care how harsh he seemed.

"Gemma," Mrs. Hardington says, clasping her hands together in front of her. "It's been such a long time. You wear glasses now, huh?"

My breath catches and I feel Noel stiffen next to me. "A long time? You know Gemma?"

Mrs. Hardington covers her mouth for a moment with a laugh. "Oh come now, Noel. You can't hide from us. *This* is the reason why you didn't want to introduce her isn't it? We've met tons of your girlfriends over the years by choice or accident, except this one."

"I don't know what you mean," Noel says slowly.

"What happened to my parents?" I explode, glancing from his mother to his father.

His dad frowns. "I don't know. What *did* happen to them? One day they just never came back to work."

"Your parents worked for mine?" Noel asks, his voice rising.

"That's genuine anger, dear," Mrs. Hardington says in a low tone, yet still loud enough for me to hear. "I don't think he knew."

"I want to know what happened to them," I seethe. "I've waited too long to know the truth."

His dad takes a step forward. "How about this, you break up with our son and never talk to him again. He doesn't need to be scammed by you just as your parents scammed us."

"She's not–" Noel starts.

I shake my head, barely holding my anger in. "They didn't scam you. My parents would never have done that. I'll give you what you want. Tell me what happened to my parents and I will stay away from Noel."

Mr. Hardington stares down at me. "You're in no place to make demands. That's not going to happen. Neither of us knows what happened to your parents. You're going to have to be satisfied with that. Now leave so we can talk as a family."

"No!" Noel shouts. "She's not going anywhere because I need to know too. Did you do something to her parents?"

Mr. Hardington glances over at his wife. "I can see this isn't working. Don't you?"

She nods. "We've strayed away from his punishments for too long."

Mr. Hardington turns back to Noel. "We'll give you some time to think all of this over."

"Think really hard, honey," Mrs. Hardington says with a smile.

Suddenly, I feel hot breath against my neck and the next thing I know, a sharp pain hits my neck and everything goes dark.

When I come to, everything is dark and...

I stretch an arm out and come into contact with a wall. A wall?

Sniffing the air, I note the smell of staleness.

Where am I?

I wonder, but deep inside, I know.

I'm back.

Back in the small dark closet with no light to be seen.

It must have been a long time since this closet has been in use.

This isn't good.

I can handle this as long as–

"Gem?" he groans. "What's going on?"

This can't be happening. I roll onto my knees and crawl over to the door. I bang on it hard. "Let us out!"

Please.

Before he panics again.

My heart clenches as I only hear silence on the other side.

"All this time, you knew me, didn't you? If your parents worked for mine, and my parents immediately recognized you. Fuck, they knew you before you wore glasses. I had to have known you like they said."

"Noel–" I start.

His voice rises. "So why don't I know? Why does everyone remember except for me?"

He yanks me away from the door, pulling me to him. "Explain it to me," he grits. "And while you're at it, why are we in a fucking closet? Why is my chest starting to tighten?"

"It doesn't matter anyway!" I yell, my rage finally boiling over. "You knowing won't change my hatred for you or myself for that matter. You're claustrophobic Noel, and the darkness of this closet makes it worse."

"So that's it," he whispers with a wry laugh. "You turned me down because you already knew me. You already hated me. I think I deserve to know what I did."

He releases me and I sigh heavily, moving back against the opposite wall.

"Fine. I'll make it as quick as possible. Just do me a favor and cover your eyes and breathe or else you'll panic like you did at your party."

As my eyes adjust to the dark, I watch him waver lifting and dropping his hand until he finally puts it over his eyes.

I clear my throat and begin.

"The first time I saw you, I was wearing a white shirt with teal polka dots and jeans. Doesn't that ring a bell somewhere in your head?"

"Polka dots…" he murmurs.

CHAPTER FOURTEEN

Noel

Twelve Years Ago

My driver drops me off in front of the building. I stare up at it, dreading the moment I walk through the doors. If they aren't waiting for me when I walk in, I'll have to go down to them.

Hitching my backpack over my shoulder, I crinkle the paper in my hand with my grade for yesterday's test. A B-. Not even a B+.

My stomach tightens and I feel the need to throw up as I grasp the handle for the door and pull it open.

Entering the lobby, I spot them standing near the desk of their secretaries. Neither of them are talking to them, but rather speaking to two other people and a girl right in the middle.

Slowly, I make my way over to them.

Dad notices me first, turning in my direction. "And there he is, my brilliant son Noel."

When I reach them, Mom urges me forward so I'm standing right in between her and Dad. "Noel, this is Mr. and Mrs. Brighton and their daughter, Gemma."

"Hello," I say politely, forcing a smile despite the fear I feel at showing them my paper.

I glance back up to Mom as she places a hand on my shoulder. "They'll be working directly with us so please, get to know Gemma well. She'll be picked up from school by your driver from now on right before you."

For the first time, I lay my eyes on the girl, Gemma. She stares at me without smiling and holds her hand out. "Nice to meet you."

I shake her hand and smile to make her feel more comfortable. "Nice to meet you too."

She pulls her hand away quickly, tilting her head up. "Can I go and play now?"

"Play?" I ask, looking at my parents.

Mom pats my head. "We cleared out a room, just for you and her, full of educational toys and videos for you two to play with and watch."

But they won't let me play once they see the results of my test.

"But Mom," I say shakily, holding it up. "I don't think I can."

Today, Gemma will have to play without me. I'll be spending my time in the closet instead.

She takes the paper from my hands, her smile fading

slightly. "I see." Her eyes shift to Mr. and Mrs. Brighton. "You'll have to excuse us. Follow me, Noel."

Fear grabs a tight hold of me as I follow them down the hall, stopping at a room. From the outside, it looks normal. But inside...

They open the door and stride over the closet and open the door.

"Don't be upset when it's your own fault. You didn't study hard enough, you don't get to play," Dad barks.

Mom sighs. "Someday, I hope you won't have to force us into doing this. That you'll actually do things to your full potential. You're the smartest kid at your school. No one should have a higher grade than you." She shoves me in and I fall to the carpeted floor inside. "It'll be four hours this time."

The door slams closed and tears fill my eyes as I'm faced with the small, dark closet.

"I'll try harder," I whisper to no one except myself, listening as the door outside closes.

Curling up in a ball, I close my eyes and fight the urge to cry, my eyes burning from holding it in.

"It's my own fault. I deserve this," I chant, over and over until I fall asleep.

I open the car door and slide in next to Gemma.

She glances at me in her silent way, saying hello. She's been picked up by my driver for almost a month now and she still refuses to talk to me.

And I want to know why.

"Hey, how come you don't want to talk?" I ask, putting my seat belt on.

She gazes at me a moment before glancing outside her window. "Because boys are mean."

"I'm not. So why can't we be friends? Come on, I'm a lot of fun. You can ask my friends Callan and Vincent."

She wrinkles her nose and sighs. "I guess it's only logical to give you one chance. Everyone deserves at least one."

A smile spreads across her face and she looks at me excitedly. "Today was the reading test. Everyone in California took it today. Did you?"

I nod quickly and show her my results. I'm at a 10th grade reading level. Six grades ahead.

"That's really great." She digs in her bag and shows me hers.

At the top, I see 12+ grade level. College level reading?

Her cheeks turn pink. "I love reading so that's probably why. We both did great. Our parents are going to be proud."

I nod. "You're right."

When we walk inside, both pairs of our parents are waiting.

"Let's see it, honey. How did you do?" Mom asks.

Both of my parents stay up to date on everything I do, even tests like these.

Dad looks over Mom's shoulder at my results. "Great job," Dad says, a smile on his face.

"Oh my God, Gemma. My little bookworm."

I glance over to find both of her parents giving her high fives.

"What did Gemma get?" my mom asks curiously.

Mrs. Brighton flashes her the paper. "College level, can you believe it?"

Mom smiles. "That's wonderful."

"Great job, Gemma," Dad says giving her a thumbs up.

Gemma smiles brightly and glances at me. "Are you ready to play now, Noel?"

"Yes I–" I start until I feel a hand on my shoulder.

"Please excuse Noel today," Dad says.

My stomach drops as he leads me down the hall.

Wait, why? Why am I going this way?

Panic fills me as they open up the familiar door and open the closet.

"Why?" I ask, panicking while I gaze into the dark hole of a closet. "You said as long as I got higher than middle school, I did great. That's what I did."

Mom grips my chin, turning my head so I look into her eyes. "Yes we did, but that was before we saw Gemma's score. Are you really going to let a girl who goes to public school do better than you?"

"You're smarter and you know it," Dad says firmly. "So you need to show it. Read more so your test score next year will be higher. Some time in the closet will do you good."

He pushes me in and I stumble inside. Anger and panic fill me as they close the door behind me.

"No," I yell. "I did what you told me to do that should have been fine." I bang on the door with both hands. "Let me out! Let me out now!"

The door outside closes and tears pour down my face.

When will this end?

I fit the last piece in on the 500 piece puzzle and sigh. Finally.

Gemma smiles at me. "Great job, Noel."

"Thanks," I reply.

I haven't figured out how to feel about being so friendly with someone my parents considered to be my rival.

Sometimes, I forget, but other times like this, I'm full of happiness at having put the last puzzle piece in instead of her.

She smooths her curly hair back behind her ear and gazed back down at the puzzle.

Her hand draws my attention to her temple. There's something pink in her hair.

"Hey Gemma, you got something here," I say, reaching forward to her ear.

She jumps as I touch the spot, encountering something incredibly sticky.

As I tug at it, she cringes. "That hurts. Just leave it alone for now. My parents will cut it out later."

"Is this gum?" I ask, feeling the sticky substance between my fingers.

"Yeah," she says softly. "Some kids put it in my hair after school ended. They've never gone this far before. I tried to get all of it out but some of it won't come out."

Frowning, I twirl a piece of her curly hair. "That's really mean. Your hair is really beautiful."

Her eyes widen. "Um thanks, but it's fine. I'm used to it. And don't tell my parents, okay? I don't want them to worry."

"Yeah I won't," I reply.

She grabs the box meant for the puzzle and starts to take it apart. Meanwhile, I can't take my eyes off of that spot of bubblegum.

The next day, I tell the teacher I'm sick and get sent to the nurse's office near the end of the day. Since it's so close to the end, they call my driver and he comes to pick me up.

"Young master, I'm afraid I won't have enough time to take you home before Gemma gets out of school."

"That's fine," I say quickly.

It's all going according to plan.

I can't tell her parents myself, but if I get involved then my parents will find out and then her parents will know.

We pull into the pickup line. Rolling the window down, I wait until I hear the bell ring. The minute it does, I hop out.

"Master Noel," our driver yells.

I don't have time to stop. I don't even know where I'm going. Running through the closest gate, I glance around, looking for the fifth grade classrooms.

The first hall is completely empty. The next one, the kids are definitely smaller, same with the next.

I dash toward the back of the school. A familiar head of curly brown hair makes me stop. A boy with bright red hair pushes her into the wall next to a classroom.

Over the roar of the other kids, I can't hear what he says. His other friends start laughing as he touches her hair where the bubblegum was yesterday.

No one stops, they just keep walking past. Glancing around, I look for a teacher or any adult before I approach them.

I don't see anyone.

He pulls out something from his pocket. A pink strip that he pops into his mouth.

So he's going to do it again?

I stomp over, parting through the crowd of kids until I reach her.

She looks at me with surprise.

"Hey Gemma," I say with a smile and turn to the guys who look at me with suspicion.

"Who are you?" one guy asks.

"I'm Gemma's best friend, and I think you should keep your gum to yourself."

They frown as if I'm a nuisance to them.

One of the guys pipe up, "We've never seen you before."

I cross my arms and respond, "You'll see plenty if you don't leave Gemma alone."

They look at each other for a moment and burst out laughing.

One of them grabs Gemma by the arm roughly. "Hold still."

She scratches at him and stomps on his foot.

"Ow!" He yells and looks toward his friend, pointing at her. "Hurry up and do it. I'm sick of her stomping on my foot."

His friend grabs the gum out of his mouth. As he reaches for her she slaps his arm away. She must not have done it yesterday because he a look of shock comes over his face as she moves away, getting behind me as he throws the gum.

His nasty gum lands right on my cheek.

I glare at him as I grab the gum off of my face. "That was a mistake. You should get a taste of your own medicine."

Closing the distance between us, I yank him toward me by his shirt and place his nasty bright pink gum on top of his head.

He shrieks and his friends laugh, holding their stomachs.

"This isn't funny," he yells, scraping at the gum.

"Careful. That'll leave a bald spot."

"There you are, Young Master." Our driver strides over, eyeing Gemma and then the three boys bullying her.

I glance around to find the hallways nearly empty now.

"Who are these kids?" my driver asks.

I turn my smile into a frown and lower my head, pointing to my hair. "They tried to put gum in my hair. I'm sorry I left the car, I was just anxious to see Gemma."

I peek up at our driver who narrows his eyes.

He glances at the three boys who run away with their tails between their legs.

"Gemma," our driver starts, "do you know who those boys are?"

"I do," she says in a small voice.

"Please do tell Mr. and Mrs. Hardington along with your parents when we get to HP. I'm sure they'll all want to hear about this incident. Now let's go. People are angry I'm holding up the line and going around me."

He puts his hands on our shoulders, leading us back to the car.

Feeling fully satisfied, I walk back to the car with them and slide in. After getting my seatbelt on, I feel a hand touch mine. "Thank you, Noel. In situations like that, sometimes I freeze and I'm not sure what to do."

I can't count the number of times I've watched someone try to talk down to Callan. Even the older boys. They'd get a fist right in the mouth.

But I'd hate for Gemma to punch someone only to get punched right back.

"Your parents can help you more than I can," I tell her.

She smiles and nods. "You're right."

As she glances out the window, it hits me that there's nothing that could ever make men not want to be her friend.

She's my first friend that's a girl. I can't really count Collette and she doesn't really like me anyway, always insisting I'm not funny. But Gemma is different.

She's nice and friendly and laughs at my jokes. I like that I don't win things so easily with her. In every game, we're always neck and neck. And if I win, she congratulates me instead of being angry about her loss.

I like that and I like her.

My hands tremble as Marva opens the closet door in front of me.

This time, my parents couldn't even do it themselves. They were so disappointed.

"I'm sorry Noel."

A B+ again. I was so close.

I hold my head down and walk inside. Getting on my knees, I sit on the ground in the middle of the closet, facing away from the door.

She didn't even tell me how many hours this time.

My chest starts to feel heavy. I try to breathe deeply, but it's not working.

Lately, this has been getting worse.

I scrape my fingernails against the carpeted floor and gasp.

Please, let this be over soon.

My head starts to pound and I crawl over to the wall, letting my back rest against it.

"Let me out," I say weakly. "Please."

Suddenly, the door opens. Wincing at the sudden bright light, I narrow my eyes and glance up to find Gemma standing at the open door.

My stomach drops and I shake my head.

My parents will be upset if she ruins my punishment.

"No you can't be here," I say shaking my hands.

She frowns. "Why are you in a closet? Is this where you go when your parents lead you away?"

My face is starting to feel warm. I don't like that she's seeing me like this.

"Please, leave," I tell her softly.

I close my eyes and pull my legs to my chest and put my arms around my legs.

When I hear the door close, I open them back up and sigh. I'll have to explain it to her later.

"This closet is really dark. No light streams through the bottom."

I jump, surprised when I hear her voice coming from in front of me.

"Gemma, you shouldn't be here."

"You said that," she says with an upset tone. "But I want to know why you're here. Every time you disappear I look for you. Now that I've finally found where you go on days like this, I want to know why you have to be in here."

My chest rises and falls rapidly.

"Hey, are you okay?" she asks.

"I want to get out," I say quietly. "But this is my punishment. When I don't get an A, if I don't score well or even..." I think back to that reading test we took months ago. "When you do better than me."

"Oh," she says quietly.

I lean my head back against the wall, focusing on breathing so I don't scare her and look stupid.

She stays quiet the entire rest of the time, and when the door opens, their secretary Marva looks surprised to see Gemma inside, but she doesn't say anything, letting us go on her way.

Every time after that, Gem joins me in the closet, and I get worse and worse. I'm unable to hide my tears and she hugs me every time.

But I'm afraid that the closet is starting to impact her too.

Today, I know I'm bound for the closet because our standardized test scores are in. I'm afraid to ask Gem what her scores are, so I don't, instead preparing myself to go in the closet.

Mom and Dad smile widely at me as we walk over to them and Gemma's parents.

"Let's see those scores," Mom says, opening her hand. I hand them to her and Dad looks over her shoulder.

"Over average, over average, way over average, and way over average. Good job, honey," Mom says, clapping her hands.

"I knew you had it in you, son," Dad says, clasping me on the shoulder.

They say this now, but my scores in the end don't matter as much as Gemma's.

I glance over to Gem and her parents. Gem's glancing away from them and her parents look at each other with weird looks on their faces.

"Well, how did Gemma do?" Mom asks.

Mrs. Brighton smiles slightly. "I think Gemma was nervous this go around. She scored average on everything."

Mom's smile lessens. "That's still great. Good job, Gemma!"

Gem looks at her with a strange expression and then stares at me.

No. Wait.

That can't be right.

Average in every subject?

I look at her in confusion until she smiles from ear to ear, dashing over to me. She grabs my hand. "Come on Noel, let's go play."

When we reach our playroom, she brings out Connect Four.

"I don't get it Jewel, how come you only scored average?"

Deep inside, I think I know. Tears fill up my eyes, making my eyesight blurry.

"I did it for you, because I'm tired of seeing you suffer," she says gently. "You're my best friend and I'd do anything to help you, okay? Now let's play."

Tears fall down my cheeks as I feel my stomach start to ache. I hate that she went so far for me.

What could I ever do for her in return?

The bathroom on this floor is out of order so I'll have to go to another floor.

Gem looks at me with scared eyes as I press the button for the ground floor. My parents won't be so mad if I use the bathroom on the floor they're in most of the time.

When we come to the big doors at the end of the white hall, I press my birthday in and they open.

Immediately the smell in the air makes me cough. Chemicals. I'm not supposed to touch them. I thumb toward the left side of the room. "Bathrooms are over there. Come on."

She follows me down to the end of the room. As we're passing, I spy something clear and slightly shiny under a microscope.

It looks like candy.

I put it up to my mouth to lick it and she slaps it out. "You shouldn't eat things if you don't know what they are."

I place it back where I found it, frowning at it. She's right. It's probably a medicine. If that's the case, it could make me sick if I don't need it.

Reaching the end of the room, I go into the bathroom and use it. Gem waits outside for me and when I get out, she looks mad.

"They haven't noticed me, but they're yelling a lot over there," she says, pointing over to our parents.

Crouching down, I gesture for her to follow me so we can find out what they're talking about. I hope they don't fire Gem's parents.

We stop at the end of a table, resting behind it. There's a lot of materials on the desk, there's no way they'll ever see us.

"You can't distribute this. So many people will be addicted. Please, we're begging you to reconsider." That's Gem's mom.

"We can do whatever we want. This formula belongs to Hardington Pharmaceuticals. You knew that when you signed the contract." And that's my dad.

"Millions of people are going to die when they can't get enough," Mrs. Brighton yells. "Don't you care about that? We altered your formula as a creative experiment, not for actual distribution."

People are going to die? Gem covers her mouth staring at me with a frightened look.

"And we're paying you well for it, are we not?" my mom asks. "Either you become fine with it, or you'll be fired. Give us the formula tonight."

No. That can't happen. If that happens I won't be able to see Gem again.

Crawling away, I gesture for Gem to join me. We get to the end of the room and hide behind the furthest desk.

I wait for their voices to stop before whispering, "What are we going to do?"

Gem bites her lip. "I don't know. That sounds really scary."

I go over what they said in my head. Formula. That's it. What can my parents do without their formula?

"That's it," I murmur. "We'll destroy it and that way they can't use it."

She gasps and smiles. "That's a great idea. But how do we know which formula it is and where to find it?"

I point to the back of the room where the computers are. Everyone who works in the lab here uses them. My parents wouldn't be able to prove Gem's parents did it. "It has to be over there. I don't hear them anymore. Let's go over there and take it. I'll hand it off to you and then I'll go in the computer and delete all the files since I won't know which one it is."

Luckily I have the password to all of their shared documents. My birthday.

Peeking over the desk, I make sure they aren't in the room anymore.

"Run with me," I tell her and run over.

I hope they don't hear our feet hitting the tile. We're not exactly being quiet.

Quickly, I grab all the papers on top of the desk. There's quite a few with things written on them so it's best if we take them all. I hand them over to Gem and click to wake the computer up.

There's no password on here. Now I'll go to the drive. It's a right click for delete.

I click on the computer icon and then the drive.

Holding my breath, I think it over. If they find out this was me, I'll be in trouble.

But if I don't do this, Gem's parents might be fired and millions of people could die.

I right click on each folder and click delete. After all five are done, I click empty on the trash bin icon.

"It's done," I murmur.

"Now hurry, Noel, before they come back," Gem says anxiously.

So we do, exiting the room and getting right in the elevator.

We go to the paper room and shred each one. They become tiny pieces of paper and now, they mean nothing.

The next day after lunch, I'm waiting for Gem in the playroom when my parents come in. They both have angry looks on their faces.

"Is something wrong?" I ask.

"Unfortunately, Gemma won't be coming here anymore. We wanted to let you know so you don't get your hopes up," Dad says with a sigh.

My chest tightens as I stand up. "Why? They didn't do anything."

Both of them look at each other and then turn to me. "Honey, they were not good people," Mom says sadly.

No. No. *No.*

"It was me," I blurt.

She frowns. "What are you talking about?"

"I deleted all your files and shredded your formula." As soon as the words leave my mouth, I close my eyes. "I'm sorry, I just didn't want to lose her."

A hard hand comes down on my shoulder. "This is a severe offense, Noel. We work hard for everything we have.

Those were important documents. All of them. You know your punishment, right?"

"I do, but please don't be mad at Gem or her parents, please re-hire them."

"That's not possible," Mom says.

They firmly push me out of the playroom and down the hall to the door. When they open it, I go inside willingly to the closet.

This time, I'll be going alone, and even more I'll never see Jewel again. I walk in and turn around to my parents who glare down at me. "We'll let you out when we feel like you've suffered enough."

The door slams closed and I collapse to the ground and sob. "Jewel," I cry. "I'm sorry. I'm so sorry."

I slam my fists into the ground and scream.

But of course, no one hears me except for me.

"Wake up, Noel. It's time for you to use the bathroom."

I don't move because I don't care.

The sound of the door opening is nothing now. It's not a good sound because it no longer means I'm free.

Hands pick me up off the floor, dragging me out of the closet.

How long has it been since I've been doing this routine?

It has to be longer than a week.

My parents must have taken me out of my summer school classes because I don't go anymore.

This closet has become my home.

I eat my meals in here, in the dark. I'm only allowed out to use the bathroom three times a day.

And the only thing I can think about is Jewel. Was she even real to begin with or did I dream her up?

I don't know.

My permanent watchers are two buff men. They rotate so only one watches me half the day and then the other takes over.

I don't like either of them.

They sit me on the toilet and wait for me to go, but I don't even though my bladder hurts.

When will things go back to the way they used to be?

Closing my eyes, I hang my head down.

I guess that will never happen, because Jewel isn't coming back.

Leaning back, I let myself rest against the toilet.

Someday, I'll have to find her.

The sound of silence in this restroom is a different kind than in the closet. This one is more peaceful and it causes me to pass right out.

With a gulp, I swallow down the pills.

"It's your last night here, don't cause any trouble," the woman at the end of my bed grunts.

Stretching my arms above my head, I sigh. "I won't, don't worry. I want to get out of here."

At the sound of the door closing, I look around my room.

The white ceiling, the white walls.

Why did my parents put me in here again?

I tap my fingers against the bed as I try to remember. For some reason, my head starts to pound.

Oh well, I guess it's not important. What matters is my head is back to the way it should be.

I'll finally be able to go back to school like a regular kid instead of doing these stupid assignments alone. And my friends Callan and Vincent will be happy to see me after so long.

After two years, I bet they haven't changed.

I pause.

Isn't there someone else? Someone I'm missing.

Over and over I think about it, but nothing comes to me.

Maybe I just imagined that there was someone else I want to see.

Anyone important to me would've sent me a letter and the only people who sent me some are Callan and Vincent.

"There's nobody else then," I murmur, even though that missing feeling still nags at me.

Present

"It's you, Jewel," I whisper as it all comes rushing back. "I can't fucking believe it. I forced myself to forget about you. One year of knowing you and then you were gone. Your memory was torture and I was tired of crying for you. It was a stupid plan, and I'm sorry your parents paid for it."

"You didn't do it alone," she corrects. "I hate myself too."

I breathe shakily. "It's no wonder you hated me. Your parents were incredibly kind. I'm sorry you got stuck with your Aunt Cindy."

After I got out of the mental hospital, they stopped putting me in this closet. They stopped being hard on me about my grades. Maybe they were afraid I'd break down again.

But obviously, me being together with Gem is a big problem. Big enough for us to be put back in here.

And now that I remember, I need to get out of here.

My hands tremble as I feel the carpet with my hands.

I can't believe they forced me to stay here for a whole month back then. It's no wonder I had to go away.

Two years and a month according to Callan and Vincent. I always asked them what I was doing before those two years in the mental hospital and they never could tell me because they had no idea. Now, I know.

Even after it's been so long, that fear is still here and it's getting harder to breathe.

"You're panicking again," she says in a low tone.

"How can I not?" I pant. "This place is even smaller now that we're both full-sized."

How am I going to handle being in here longer than a few minutes?

There's no fucking way. I can't.

CHAPTER FIFTEEN

Gemma

My heart pangs when I think about him forcing my memory away. What happened when he stopped seeing me?

"Just keep talking to me, keep your mind off of our surroundings," I tell him.

As my eyes adjust to the darkness, I watch him stretch his legs out to the right of mine.

"This place was my home for a month."

"A month?" I ask. I can't even fathom spending a whole day in here.

He nods. "And then I went to a mental hospital for two years. When I came out, I was good as new." Clutching at his chest, he pauses and laughs. "I can't believe you were right in front of me this past year and I had no idea. All because I decided to push you away."

TIFFANY RANSIER

"So you're not angry at me for not telling you who I was and helping you remember?" I ask quietly.

"I can't find it in me to be angry about that when I hurt your family like I did."

"The blame is on both of us, Noel."

He inhales sharply and rubs a hand over my face.

"Keep talking," I tell him.

But he doesn't. The only thing I hear is him desperately trying to breathe and the scraping of his fingers against the wall. It always did sound painful.

"We should probably talk about what's going to happen when they release us."

He laughs halfheartedly between gasps. "They're insane. Your parents never once scammed them. They expect me to believe that now that I have my memories back?"

I know he's right. I don't believe that lie for a second. I'm sure it's their shitty excuse to get us to break up. In the end, it doesn't matter though. "Look, why don't we just end this when we get out of here?"

He doesn't respond so I grab his leg. "Noel, are you listening to me?"

Silence is the only thing I get back.

"Stop being stubborn and just listen to me! I don't want to be expelled."

He doesn't reply, as if I said nothing at all.

I purse my lips and sigh.

As time drags on, I listen as he slowly loses control. Sobbing and scraping his fingers. They have to be bloody by now.

I can feel my own chest starting to tighten. It's getting to me too.

How much time has passed?

242

I wish I had my phone but it looks like they jacked both of ours before sticking us in this closet.

Right now, he's sprawled out on the floor with his hands covering his face.

"I don't completely hate you," I tell him, clearing my throat. "You've suffered over and over in here and I don't want you to suffer more."

It takes a lot for me to say it, so I expect something. Just some kind of acknowledgment, but he's too far gone. Too focused on this small, dark space. My heart pangs as I hear his uneven breathing. With a sigh, I move further into the closet toward him.

I pull his hand away from his eyes, noting how hard it's trembling and how sweaty it is. He stares up at me, his chest heaving.

I hold his hand up to my face and stare at his broken fingernails and the blood pouring from them.

They have to be incredibly sore.

As he pulls his arm away, placing it over his eyes, I think back to the last time we were in a closet together.

He started panicking and I kissed him. It was enough to grab his attention and make him concentrate on me instead of this closet.

Will it work if I do it again?

Slowly, I lower my head down and press my lips against his. His lips are sweaty and trembling. I press my tongue in between his slightly open lips, forcing it inside. One swipe, two sipes, three swipes, over his unmoving tongue.

My cheeks warm as I realize he's not responding and move off of him.

"Noel," I murmur. I place my hand on the center of his chest to get a sense for how he's breathing.

He's not breathing as harshly anymore.

Bending again, I press our lips together and pull back, giving him small tiny kisses and sharing our breath in-between them.

An ache in my back starts to pulse.

I back away to rub the annoying spot.

This isn't the best position. It'd be easier if he was laying against the wall instead of laying on the floor. I can't turn my body in this awkward angle anymore.

The only position that won't cause my back pain would be bending straight down. But I'd have to be on top of him for that. I'm already fat enough as it is, and he's already having trouble breathing.

I might make it worse.

But maybe, if I don't put my full weight on him, he'll be okay.

Holding my breath, I scoot down his body to his legs. I swing one of my legs over his body and settle myself over him with one leg on each side of his thighs.

I scoot up slightly, holding myself off of him and lower my lips to his again.

This is easier.

Before our lips touch, I murmur his name, "Noel, pay attention to only me. I'm right here with you."

His short breaths escape his mouth. I press both of my hands into his shoulders and his breathing changes slightly, catching in his throat.

In a snap decision, I lean away, grabbing his arm as I do. It's not as limp as it was before.

I stare down at his eyes to find them only slightly open. Grabbing his large hand, I feel heat rise to my cheeks.

Just a little more and he'll feel a lot better. This is working.

I place his hand on my breast and cup his hand to squeeze it.

"Noel, come on Noel," I whisper, biting my lip at the frustrating tingle I get from it.

He takes a deep breath for the first time in a long time.

"What are you doing?" he rasps.

"Distracting you, just like I did before. And it's working."

He tries to move his hand off, but he does it so weakly, I have no trouble keeping it in place.

"Keep listening to my voice," I urge him.

I rub his hand over my breast and hold my other hand out. "Give me your other hand."

"I don't think this is a good idea," he says in a low tone.

"Just give me your other hand," I order him, and he does.

I place it right on my other breast, rubbing his hand against my nipple.

A short bolt of lightning shoots through me, surprising me so much I accidentally adjust my legs, letting my weight settle on him and pressing me intimately into his crotch.

"Don't do that," he says shakily.

My face has to be cherry red by now. "I'm so sorry," I say quickly, lowering his hands off of me to the carpet.

I place my hands on the floor on each side of him as I lift my weight off of him. "There, I–"

Suddenly, I watch as he sits up on his elbows, watching me with hooded eyes.

"I liked it better the other way," he whispers.

His hands go to my ass in a flash and he uses his hands to urge my hips downward to meet his crotch. It really must be working.

If I stop now, he might regress.

With his hands on me, I lower myself onto his crotch and

settle there. Immediately, I feel he's completely hard underneath me.

"Even now," he says shakily, "look what you're doing to me, Jewel. But I can't imagine you being wet. Are you?"

My breath stills in my throat as his hands grip my ass.

"I don't know," I murmur. I roll my head back as I feel him pulsing beneath me. The sensation is driving me crazy. Why is it making me feel anxious?

"Maybe you should check," I say without thinking.

His sweaty hand comes around my body, stopping at my front and peeling my leggings away. His hand dips in my underwear and his fingers brush against my clit. "You are," he says in awe.

He moves his hand out of my underwear to my naked hip, kneading the flesh there.

"Gem," he murmurs.

"What?" I ask breathlessly, feeling his hand slide down my thigh.

"I appreciate what you're doing, but I'm going to die of blue balls. Please, get off now before this goes any further."

At the word further, my core clenches.

He takes his hand out of my pants, letting it fall to the side and drops his other hand off my hip.

"I have to keep your attention, Noel."

He lies back against the carpet again, his breaths coming out evenly. "I'll be fine."

For now he is, but I know the moment I get off of him, he'll go back.

And I think he's already suffered more than enough in here.

"I'm not going to stop," I say staring down at him.

There is one thing that would keep his attention for a long time. He won't be able to turn it down.

But the thought of doing that here is making me nervous. This closet which holds so many bad, rough memories.

It's not conventional at all.

But if it means he won't suffer then...

With a heavy sigh, my hands go to the bottom of my shirt. With a hard yank, I pull it off and toss it closer to the door. Letting my hands go behind my back, I unclip my bra and throw it with my shirt.

"What are you doing?" he asks. I touch his chest to check his breathing. He's still breathing okay. Even if he's not watching, he can still hear me stripping.

I stand up shakily. My legs feel like jello since it's been so long. I take my leggings off, pulling one leg out at a time, and tossing them away.

Without pausing, I grip my last barrier, my underwear, between my index and thumb and slid them off.

To show him I'm serious, I throw them in his direction. They land right on his neck.

His hands reach down, grasping them with both hands. "Put these back on."

I ignore him, getting down on my knees. With shaking hands, I unbutton his pants and tug his zipper down.

"You don't really want to do this, Gem."

I don't respond, pulling his pants down his legs and moving his feet out.

His pants join mine in the pile in the corner. When my hands touch his lower abdomen, he stiffens.

As I stare down at his covered dick, I bite my lip.

"Are you clean? And do you happen to have a condom?"

"I am and I don't, which is why I'm saying we shouldn't do this," he says, his voice becoming lower with every word.

Moving my hands to the edge of his underwear, I expose

him to the air. His dick stands at attention and he hisses as I grab it.

"Just promise you won't come inside me," I murmur, letting go of him. Scooting forward, I adjust myself until I'm directly on top of him. His tip is perfectly lined up with my entrance.

A wet sound fills the air as I rub myself along his length.

"Noel, promise me you won't. Come on, how long have you been waiting for this?" I egg him on.

I hate that my body is practically vibrating in anticipation, but it is.

Every other time we've done something, it's always been on his time. Never once have I initiated anything. Not until this moment. I'm doing this for him, but I can't deny that I'm nervous about this. I hate that I feel more at ease when he's guiding me through things and whispering dirty things to me.

But I do.

So I need to coax him into it.

"Fine, don't promise me. I'm still going to do it."

Pausing, I stop as his tip rests against my slit. Cringing, I try to lower myself on to it, but he slips away every time.

His body is quivering.

I can't lower myself. I need to go down in one go.

Raising myself slightly, I feel his dick once again nestled against my opening. I hold my breath and impale myself on it.

A strangled cry erupts from my mouth as he chokes, "Oh *fuck.*"

I feel as if I'm been split in half. It stings.

Tears slip down my face as I softly cry.

Gentle hands caress my hips. "I told you not to do this,

precious. You should've been warmed up to this more." His voice is light and soothing.

Sniffing, I wipe my face. "I know. But it's in now, so please, make it feel good." The stinging is slowly starting to fade.

He grips my hips hard. "I will, precious, I promise I will." He pulls me up slightly and thrusts his hips up.

A zing goes through me.

He repeats the moment several times, grinding his hips inside at a slow pace. I don't know, but it's frustrating.

"Harder," I murmur with a moan.

He pulls me down so fast I gasp, lying me flush against his body. His hips pump into me so hard, I let out an endless moan. Twitch after endless twitch goes to my toes and I'm quivering in his embrace. Sweat pops on my forehead as I pant hard.

"Do you feel how deep I am, precious? This is where I've needed to be these past four months." He grunts. "Fuck, your pussy is clenching me so hard."

Every second pushes my body further and further to a pleasure I can't even describe. It's so mind-blowing, I can't think of anything except for him. For once, my mind is quiet.

He's panting, his chest rising and falling underneath me, but only from exertion, not from panic.

He slows his hips down, thrusting into me slower, right when I could feel myself about to finish. I moan with frustration. "Why are you slowing down?"

"If I keep going at that pace, I'll come."

My heart clenches. That's right. Even if he comes outside of me, we can't go again. There might still be residual swimmers.

But if we stop completely, he'll regress.

What I really need to do is fuck him until he passes out.

There's no way he'll fall asleep so easily.

My stomach flutters as I realize there's no way to avoid it.

I stretch up to his ear. "Just come inside me then. Fuck me until we both pass out."

He stills. "I'm not doing that, Gem. Not when that means there's the possibility that you'll get pregnant. If you were on birth control, maybe."

I move my hips back, pushing him deep inside of me. "Just do it."

I wish I could know for sure that I won't get pregnant, but things have been so crazy, I can't remember the last time I had my period.

He groans as I pull away from him, rising up and slamming my hips down hard, over and over. I moan low in my throat, feeling my body heat up.

"You're riding me so good, Jewel," he praises.

I'm so close. Just a little more.

"Fuck, I can't hold it in," he grips my hip with one hand and thrusts into me at a furious pace.

Good. He's giving in. He forces me to my orgasm and I let out a cry as I reach the pinnacle, quaking and panting as lightning shoots through my body.

He groans, "Gemma, oh God." His hips slow and I feel a shot of warmth.

Panting, he pulls me forward to lay on his chest.

I'm still trying to catch my breath, but I can feel him pulsing inside of me.

"Let's go again. Slower this time," I murmur.

"Aren't you sore?" he asks quietly.

"I am, but I'll be okay. What did you say in the office yesterday? Once wouldn't satisfy you? And I'm sure with other girls you've never stopped after one time."

He tilts my chin up and we lock eyes. "Don't even bring up anyone else. No one else matters but you."

I feel him slowly ease out of me until I feel only the tip of him before he shoves himself deep inside.

My body zings again, still sensitive from my first orgasm.

"You want to fuck until we fall asleep," he murmurs, brushing a sweaty lock of my hair from my face. "I'll do just that or die trying."

And he does, helping me put my clothes on afterwards since I'm so sore, I can barely move.

After he puts his clothes on, I watch him fall asleep lying against the carpet. Once I'm sure he's fast asleep, I go to sleep myself, with my heart thundering in my chest and a few thoughts lingering.

How will I ever live without feeling that much pleasure again?

Deep inside, I know it's not just because of how well he did it, but because it's *him*.

I need to push him away as soon as I wake up. I can't feel this way about him.

I close my eyes and let sleep pull me under.

Jolting awake, I gasp and touch my chest. Glancing around, I note how dark it is, and then it hits me. I'm back here with Noel.

I hold my breath and listen to him snoring softly. But there's another sound. It's muted, like it's coming from outside.

How long do they plan on keeping us in here? Are they finally done?

It feels like it's been forever. How did he manage a whole month in here?

Staring up at the door, I crawl over to it, wincing at the soreness between my legs. I twist it to the left and right.

Of course it doesn't open.

I hold my ear to the door and listen, but I don't hear anything.

Sighing, I move my body to the wall, letting my back rest against it.

I wonder if our friends are wondering what happened to us.

The sound of a bang makes me jump.

What was that?

Noel groans at the back of the closet, signaling to me that he's awake. "What was that?" he asks, sleepiness in his voice.

"I don't know," I reply, looking up at the door.

The door knob twists to the side and light floods in.

CHAPTER SIXTEEN

Noel

I move my hand over my eyes as the closet illuminates with light from the room outside.

It's a shock to my eyes. Blinking quickly, I open them slightly and gaze up past Gem.

"You guys really are in here. I couldn't believe it when I heard it."

Callan's jaw sets as he pushes the door open fully.

Shame makes me turn away from him. It seems Callan now knows a tiny piece of what I've been through.

How did he know we were in here?

"What the hell is wrong with your parents?"

I gaze up to find Mera peeking inside the closet.

Callan holds out his hand in front of Gem and she takes it. After he pulls her up, he moves to the side so she can get out of the closet. When she's fully out of the way, he steps back in the door way, staring at me.

"Why do you have that look on your face? Come on, there's no time to waste." His voice is gravelly, as if he just woke up. "Come on, Noel. They're on their way and I know you don't want to see them. Do you?"

"No. I don't." They'll want to know my answer about Gem. If I leave now, it'll put it off for a little while at least.

He offers a hand and I scoot forward and grab it. My legs shake as I rise from the floor, straightening in the doorway.

Mera holds something out. My phone?

She points to the table behind them. "Yours and Gemma's phone was sitting there, along with your wallet and her glasses."

My eyes shift to Gem and she glances away from Mera, as if she feels eyes on her.

Her eyes widen behind her round-rimmed glasses and her face starts to flush.

"We should get going then," she says. "Wouldn't want to waste any time."

Turning, she leads the way to the door of the room. That's when I notice how the door is hanging on by its hinges.

I bring up the rear, chuckling at the door. "This your handiwork, buddy?"

"Unfortunately, dear old dad," he says sarcastically, "only had a key to the building, not the individual rooms. And of course, I knew the alarm code would be your birthday," he explains, rubbing a hand over the back of his head as he walks out. "I almost broke down the closet door, but Mera had the brilliant idea of using my credit card."

She smiles at us over his shoulder. "You're welcome."

The lobby is empty so it's definitely Sunday morning. Anyone who works on Sundays comes in late.

When we get outside, Gemma and I separate from them, getting in my Porsche. Callan follows us back to campus where we both drop off Mera and Gem in front of ZDB.

Gem hops out of the car as quick as she can without a second glance.

I wait outside all the way until the front door closes behind them. After a second, I zoom away over to fraternity row.

I pull into an empty parking space and Callan parks right next to me.

I'm about to get out of the car when he opens the passenger side door and slides in.

"What's up?" I ask cautiously.

"Noel, you know you and Vincent have been my best friends since we were just babies. I trust you with everything, so how come you never told me?"

Trust…he trusts me.

Guilt wells up inside me.

"About the closet?" I ask carefully, gazing at him.

His eyes are hard. "The closet and also my dad said something about how you might need to go back to the mental hospital if your parents try to continue their punishments. I overheard them talking to each other. Is that where you were when you disappeared for two years?"

I nod slowly. My parents brought me letters from Callan and Vincent. They always asked where I was but I'd never give them a straight answer, always promising to be back soon. When I came back, I dodged their questions and tried to forget I was even in there and for a long time it worked.

"It's not something I want to remember," I say in a low tone.

Callan's eyes soften. "Parents fucking suck, don't they?"

"They do," I agree. "Want to trade? Your dad doesn't lock you in a closet does he?"

He smiles wryly. "No, you got me there. Mine are just schemers trying to reach the top and be better than anyone else. Family be damned."

"Someday, I'll tell you all of it, but my body is starting to relax and all of a sudden, I feel completely exhausted."

Nodding, he reaches for the door handle.

Before he can open it, I exclaim, "Wait!"

He glances at me with a raised eyebrow.

"How long until you know whether a girl is pregnant or not?"

His eyebrows raise to his hairline. "You fucking serious? I thought you were a wrapper dude." He mocks me by smoothing his hair out past his forehead. "Wrap it, Callan. Always wear a condom or the next thing you know you'll have a mini Goldsworthy on the way."

I push him in the shoulder, laughing. "Hey. This is a first for me, okay? Now come on, you have to know. Tell me."

He snorts. "Find out for yourself. In the meantime, you should be thinking about having a mini Hardington on the way. Guess you should finally buy a house since you'll be a family man."

I laugh and shake my head, but sober up quickly. He does have a point though about buying a house. I'd been meaning to for a long time.

Even if it turns out Gem isn't pregnant, I still want to buy one, but I don't want to buy one without her input because in the long term, I'd like my home to be hers too.

But now, it seems that will never happen because my parents are determined to keep us apart. If it's me or the school, I'd rather she not give up her education for me.

I'll wait for my parents to call and I'll tell them what my decision is.

"But hey, if something ever comes up in the future, don't ride off into the flames without me."

"I won't," I lie.

He wouldn't be so willing to help me if he knew the truth. Right now, I don't deserve his friendship.

After I turn in my lab exam, I walk outside and wait by the door for Gem to come out.

I was hoping to talk to her before the exam, but both of us got to class just as the exam was about to start.

Every time the door opens, I straighten, thinking it's her, only to see someone else instead.

Glancing at the time on my phone, I realize there's only five more minutes left until this class is supposed to end. It's already been an hour and a half since I've been waiting.

Staring at the clock, I watch as the minutes tick by.

I don't remember her ever taking this long with exams before.

The moment that class is over, the door opens and she walks out, heading the opposite way without looking in my direction.

"Gem," I call out.

She whips her head around and strides over to me. Her cheeks are a lovely shade of pink and for some reason she's looking away from me and not meeting my eyes.

"Are you still thinking of that night in the closet?" I ask, smirking.

She looks incredulously at me, huffing cutely and

pushing her glasses up her nose. "I'm not. Anyway, what did you want?"

"Well," I say slowly, "I've been thinking and I believe the best course of action is to make it look like we broke up."

She coughs. "And why can't we actually break up?"

Her question stabs me right in the chest. It's hard to keep a smile on my face.

"Because I believe in keeping deals up until the end."

Her mouth flattens and she turns around. "Fine. As far as everyone knows, we're over."

I know it wasn't what she wanted to hear, but I want to treasure every moment with her while I still have her.

My parents were all too happy that Gem and I decided to break up. It sickens me.

Going to work without her has been rough. I kept expecting to see her pushing her cart around or see her in the room filing things.

So I need this trip to The Hamptons.

We used to go to our house there in the summer once a year. The last two years, I've gone with just Callan, Vincent, and Tyrell. This year, Mera, Collette and her friends are coming.

From what I know, Gem didn't want to join us at first. I guess something changed her mind.

We haven't spoken in person all week and the closest we've come to talking in private is short conversations over text.

It almost feels like we've actually broken up.

"Smile, dude, it's your birthday," Vin says, elbowing me.

"You're right," I respond with a small smile.

No matter where I am, I have a party on my birthday. This year it'll be in The Hamptons.

"You remember those girls from last summer?" I ask, remembering a red-head that came on to me pretty hard.

Vin's eyes brighten as he smirks. "Yes. Those four girls. One was into all four of us. Though Tyrell wouldn't give the girl into him the time of day. Oh, and that dark haired one was practically trying to yank Callan's shorts off every chance she got."

The conversation in the seats in front of us stops.

"Should I be worried about this dark-haired beauty?" Mera asks, turning to Callan.

"Princess, that was a long time ago," Callan replies, lifting himself up slightly to glare at us.

"Let's invite them again," I suggest, thinking I should have their numbers somewhere.

It'll be a good distraction in case my parents have people watching me.

I know they know about this trip.

Hours later, we've set the house up for the party, and guests are starting to arrive.

Callan, Vincent, and Tyrell disappeared off to get something they wanted for the party, leaving me to greet all the guests with the girls.

The door is perpetually open as guest after guest pours in. I didn't know all of these people so they must've heard I'm back.

For the life of me I can't remember everyone's names, so I just shake hands with them and pretend like I do.

That is until the four girls show up.

The red-haired one immediately sidles up to me with a suggestive grin. "You're all by your lonesome greeting everyone, I can stay with you."

"Thanks, Chanel," I say, smiling at her friends behind her. The dark-haired one, and two blondes.

The dark-haired one glances around. "Do you happen to know where Callan is? I want to give him my condolences about the death of his brother."

From out of nowhere, I feel a presence behind me.

Turning slightly, my eyes widen in horror when I notice it's Mera. She smiles widely, stepping over to me and immediately engaging in an eye battle with the dark-haired girl.

"Hi and welcome! Callan isn't here right now. Can I take a message?"

The dark-haired girl smiles. "I don't think so I'll just wait here by the door for him."

All fake niceness fades from Mera's face. I'm almost positive the dark-haired girl knows who Mera is, she just doesn't care. A lot of people don't because of how Mera denounced the United States. Mera glances up at me as if she wants me to say something. However, I refuse to get involved.

I cough hard and clear my throat. "Please no one crowd the doorway. There's plenty of snacks and drinks. Feel free to go wild. Blare that fucking music."

They all reluctantly leave except the red-head who hooks her arm through mine. "You haven't changed a bit, Noel. I can't wait to catch up. Sorry I didn't make it out to Cali like I said I would. Things have just been busy."

If I remember correctly, she goes to NYU.

"After seeing you again, maybe it wouldn't be such a bad idea to transfer to SGU."

"The more the merrier," I tell her politely.

She makes small talk with me as I greet the guests. When the amount of people lessens, I move away from the door with her at my side. The mansion is packed with people everywhere. All the doors upstairs are locked except for my room so everyone has to either be down here or outside.

Last year, everyone learned quickly that my room is off limits.

I toss back a beer and pretend to listen as Chanel drones on about how her dad is taking her on two more trips before college starts back up.

Suddenly, I hear a loud disturbance of many voices shouting at once. Turning in the direction of the noise, I spot Callan with Vincent and Tyrell in tow. Callan greets everyone he passes and a few girls get extremely close to crossing the line.

Vincent hugs each girl Callan neglects and behind him is Tyrell who has…a cake? He's rolling it in on a cart.

A giant one with a bunch of intricate details. A few race tracks on the sides and a big 19 on top.

Something like that had to take hours to make.

Callan finally reaches me at the kegs. "How do you like your surprise? I never know what to get you so this year, we all decided to get you this cake instead."

We only decided to come out here two days ago.

"Marianne was willing to do a last minute design," he says quickly.

Her bakery has the best sweets in New York by far. I've never celebrated my birthday here so this is a first for me.

"Thanks," I tell Callan and Vincent and Tyrell behind him.

"That cake looks so good," Chanel murmurs. "Can I have the first slice? Want to feed it to me?"

"No," Callan says quickly before I can respond. "We're going to sing happy birthday and then Noel is going to eat his slice."

I smile in his direction, thankful for his interjection.

Chuckling, I touch her arm. "But after that, sure, I'll feed you a slice."

Callan shouts. "Everybody listen up, get whoever's outside in so we can sing happy birthday to our host."

A few people scramble to get outside and after several minutes and it seems like everyone is in., they all sing an uneven happy birthday to me.

Somehow, my eyes find hers the moment the song is over. Our eyes meet and she stares blankly at me. After clapping a few times, she crosses her arms before looking away to Mera.

I get my slice of cake and eat it. As I finish mine, Chanel shoves her cake plate in my hands. Her eyes sparkle mischievously as she gazes up at me, opening her mouth slightly. "Come on, feed it to me, Noel."

I feel Gem's eyes on me across the room as I pick up the lemon cake and shove it into her mouth, removing my hand before her lips can touch it.

She looks slightly disappointed, using her own finger to get the residual frosting off of her mouth and licking it.

She wipes her finger on her dress. "Come on, let's dance."

Many people are still getting their slices of cake so there aren't too many people dancing.

The songs are fast so she has no excuse to grind up against me, but she does. An awkward smile stays plastered on my face as I look down at her.

"Having fun?" I ask.

She nods, fluttering her eyelashes. "Do you want to go somewhere more private?"

Months ago, I would have jumped at the opportunity. What a thrill to have a girl tell me that she wants to go somewhere private. Every single time it'd end up with my cock inside them.

The last time I saw Chanel, we didn't get to fuck because I got food poisoning. This is her asking for a second chance.

It really is too bad that part of my life is over.

"No, I'm fine here," I tell her.

She pouts but continues dancing with me. "You're here for a week though, aren't you?"

I nod and her smile returns. "That's great news."

No doubt she's thinking about fucking me another day, but my answer will remain the same. This is a show for any spies my parents have and nothing else.

It's tiring having to hang out with her when all I want to do is pull my girlfriend to the floor and dance with her.

I let my eyes casually wander around the room until I stop at the corner Gem was, only to find her gone.

Did she go outside?

I step backwards as if it's part of the dance to crane my head out, but there's too many people around.

"Noel," Chanel purrs, tugging at my shirt. "What are you doing?"

I move her hand away, frantically looking around. "Excuse me," I mutter.

Whatever she says after falls upon deaf ears as I walk around people until I get outside. Everyone is milling around the pool with drinks in their hands and their phones in the other.

None of them are Gem.

I edge back inside, whip around and walk away from the living room.

As I smile and nod at people as I walk by, I look for her. But she's nowhere to be found.

Did she go upstairs?

I take the flight of stairs two at a time and walk down the

hall and make a left, coming across the second largest room in the house.

No, I'm crazy. There's no way she'd be in here. She has to be out front.

Pushing open the door, I spot a familiar head of brown hair next to the wall with my car collection.

As if she's been caught, she sets the miniature car down in a hurry, and whirls around to look at me. "Shouldn't you be at the party?"

"Shouldn't you?" I counter.

"I just needed a break," she says simply.

Her lips twitch and I walk over to her at a slow pace, stopping just short of her. She stares up at me. "You're too close. Someone could come in here at any moment."

I smile down at her. "I know." Reaching behind her, I grab the car she was holding only a few seconds ago and back away.

Her shoulders droop slightly.

Was she expecting more?

I guess she doesn't know how much I'd love to give it to her. Lock the fucking door and drown out the party with the sound of our loud fucking.

But I can't.

I hold up the car. "Vintage Mustang. Do you like these?"

She nods and her eyes move over my whole collection. "When you told me about these I didn't believe you."

I laugh, palming the car in my hands. "I love cars just as much as you love reading."

Back then, she'd always talk about her favorite books and I'd listen and get hooked into every world she told me about.

Those were some of my favorite moments when we took breaks from playing.

"I do," she responds. "Unfortunately, my collection isn't as vast as yours is. But I guess we should leave before someone comes in."

She moves past me and I grab her arm. Her eyes follow my hand up to my eyes.

I pull her closer and clutch her body close to mine. Leaning down, I press a chaste kiss against her lips. It's torture to lift my lips off of hers, but somehow I manage.

All of a sudden, hands go to my cheeks and I'm pulled back down. She kisses my lips with hesitance and in a gentle way.

When she lowers her hands, she licks her lips and I feel myself tighten in my pants. Our eyes stay locked for a few moments more. An anticipation and hunger hangs in the air.

And then, I let her go.

"I'll be downstairs then," she says with a small smile, pushing her glasses up her nose.

When she's gone, I stick my hands in my pockets and whirl around to my collection of cars.

Even though she's gone, she doesn't leave my mind.

Does she feel this ache in my chest like I do when I'm not with her? Or am I the only one being tortured?

I wish I knew.

CHAPTER SEVENTEEN

Gemma

The day we get back home from New York is my birthday. Not exactly a day I enjoy. Before I came here, it was just a usual day at home with Cindy and her boyfriend at the time if it was on the weekend.

If it fell on a school day, the teacher would force the class to sing happy birthday to me up until high school and at that point it wasn't even acknowledged. And that's okay.

I just wanted to completely ignore the fact that this day exists.

But this year, I had my own party on the last day at Noel's house. It wasn't for anyone else but us, but still a magical day. In the late afternoon, we got back on the plane to fly back home after a whole week.

The Hamptons are definitely not for me. I stuck out like a sore thumb. At every boat party, or beach gathering, I'd feel incredibly awkward as people tried to talk to me about all the money they have and I wasn't able to reply back with something witty because I have no money and will never have any amount of money that compares to what they have.

It was still a great trip, though. Noel never tried to sneak off with me again. He spent most of the week on Chanel's arm. Part of me is glad because he's trying to make our breakup look as real as possible, but the other part of me wanted to rip her off of him. I wanted his attention for myself. His hands to only touch me. What an utter betrayal to my parents.

Our driver stops outside ZDB and we all pile out. It's still a little early in the evening.

"Do you guys want to go and get dinner somewhere?" Collette asks with a sigh as she hauls her suitcase out of the trunk.

"I'll pass," I tell her. I've gone out a lot this week and I don't have any money to go out for the next few months.

Mera, Luella, and Ashlynn all agree to go.

Luella looks disappointed at my response. "Come on, Gemma. It's your birthday. We'll treat you, don't worry."

Luella always seems to catch on fast when it's a money thing.

"You can order literally anything,"Ashlynn says with a small smile.

"Okay," I tell them.

They cheer and we all lug our bags in. Mera and I come to a stop outside our room when we notice a small package on the floor outside our door.

We don't usually get anything, but I guess Mera's parents sent her something to celebrate the start of our sophomore year of college in two weeks.

THE NERD AND THE BULLY

Mera leans down to grab it, lifting it up and studying the label.

She hands it to me. "This is for you."

Frowning, I accept the package and stare at the label.

Gemma Brighton.

Who could've sent me something?

I move the package through the air, feeling how light yet heavy it feels.

Mera unlocks the door and goes inside. I follow right behind her with my package in one hand and bag in the other.

Immediately, I flop down on my bed and set to work on opening the package.

My jaw drops when I see the familiar logo. An iPad?

And there's a gift note with it.

Happy birthday, Gem. Check your email when you get a chance.

Noel

I pull my phone out in a rush to check my emails. I have tons and tons after not checking them all week.

My eyes latch onto a few emails that mention eGift card in the subject.

"Oh my God," I murmur.

Dimly, I hear Mera ask, "What?"

I click all five emails to find five $1000 eGift cards for Barnes and Noble.

Five. Thousand. Dollars.

I can buy five thousand dollars worth of books.

Tears well up in my eyes as I drop my phone to my bed. This is too much. I can't even call to thank him because his parents are looking at his phone records.

Mera stops in front of me, staring at the iPad. "That's awesome. Noel got it for you?"

"He did along with five thousand dollars worth of Barnes and Noble gift cards," I say in awe.

She smiles. "Wow. That's sweet."

I nod, completely speechless. She moves away from me back to her side of the room.

How long has it been since I've been able to buy more than one book at a time?

Things like this make me feel…I don't know.

I press my hand into my chest.

I wish he'd stop making my heart feel funny. With every moment I spend with him, it gets harder to deny exactly how I feel about him. Ever since he got his memories back, he's acted a little differently.

When our agreement is over, how will I stand it when we go back to being strangers?

I'll thank him for this the next time I see him, and after that I have to start separating myself from him. Slowly but surely I will, and then when the agreement is over, my heart won't hurt and I'll go back to feeling less guilty about betraying my parents.

"Ready to go?" Mera asks.

Nodding, I grab my small bag, leaving my suitcase untouched next to my bed. When we get outside, Luella and Ashlynn are already waiting for us. The four of us wait on the porch for Collette to come.

While the three of them talk, my head spins as everything becomes so clear to me.

I think I'm in love with Noel Hardington.

Even saying it in my head makes me sick to my stomach.

He could never feel the same way and my parents...

He still holds partial responsibility for their death.

Thinking those words and feeling this way, it's wrong.

Somehow, I have to find a way to stop this.

Gazing out across the street, I bite my lip and sigh. My eyes immediately lock on an all white van across the street, a bright beacon in the dark evening.

I've never seen that before.

The door behind us opens and we all turn to look as Collette walks out.

"Sorry to keep you all waiting," Collette says with a smile. "I'm ready to go now, though."

All of us cross the street to walk to the parking lot. As soon as we cross, I get a feeling that someone's watching me. Glancing at the van out of the corner of my eye as we pass, I notice there's no one inside.

I guess I was just imagining things.

For some reason, all the way to the restaurant that van stays on my mind.

As soon as we're seated, we're given our drinks pretty fast. After the waitress leaves to give us a few minutes to look at the menu for our entree, Collette clears her throat.

"For the record, Gemma. Are you or are you not in love with Noel Hardington?"

I choke on the Sprite I sipped into my mouth prior to her question.

"No," I say quickly, as soon as I'm able.

She narrows her eyes. "Are you sure?"

"Yes, I'm sure," I lie.

She studies me for a long while before smiling. "Good. As you shouldn't. You've just seemed a little different lately around him. If that's the case, I think it's about time we find you someone new who can actually appreciate you."

"That's not necessary," I reply, slightly panicked.

Collette, Luella, and Ashlynn all believe my breakup with Noel is real and that he's just holding on to my house for November. Mera is the only one that knows it's fake.

"I think it's very necessary so I'll be on the lookout for you. Don't be surprised if I find someone quickly," she says with an excited smile.

Mera shares a look of pity with me across the table. She knows I have no choice but to go along with it. I hide my look of displeasure behind my menu.

Even before Noel, I've never had a boyfriend because I've always been uncomfortable with men. My Aunt Cindy had a lot of creepy boyfriends over the past eleven years. The way some of them would look at me was off.

Noel is my first and only as far as I'm concerned.

Somehow I'll have to pacify her and at the same time decline to spend any time alone with anyone she suggests to me.

Sometimes I wish she'd be more understanding, but this is just how Collette is.

CHAPTER EIGHTEEN

Noel

The software is finally done. They now have a secure place to store all of their formulas. I only started it in the hopes that it'd keep their attention off of me, but now it will also serve as my way of making it up to them for erasing all their files.

At the time, I didn't know my parents kept all of their hard copies in their office files. All of them have locks on them.

I'm sure my punishment would've been much more severe had they not had paper copies in their files.

Copies of everything except for Space Dust.

All of their late nights in the office over the years. I'm sure they spent tons of time rebuilding it and tweaking the formula to make it as addictive as possible.

When they accept this software, they won't know that this software is the start of their downfall.

They'll be so grateful they'll talk to me more and eventually, trust me enough with the details for Space Dust. I'll take it to the FDA and they'll have no choice but to do an investigation.

They only need to trust me enough.

And that starts today.

I quickly input my birthday into the pad and the doors unlock. Taking a right, I pass by a bunch of their workers, staring straight ahead at Dad's door. It's open. Mom's office is directly to the right, adjacent to his, and I'm sure hers is too.

When I get to the end of the room, I notice her door is open, but she isn't inside. I step into my Dad's office to find both of them hunched over his desk, staring at a few vials with their goggles on, whispering to each other.

They don't seem to notice my presence, so I clear my throat.

Both of them look up simultaneously and straighten.

"Noel, what are you doing down here?" Mom asks with a smile.

Dad's mouth flattens as he turns his attention back to the vials.

The room is suffocating as it usually is. It shouldn't be this tense when I'm with family, but every time I see them, I can't forget how many times they tossed me in that closet.

"I wanted to apologize," I say in a serious tone. "I ruined your file system back then."

Mom's smile grows. "So you remember that now and you're willing to apologize for it?"

"I am. I made something that I think will benefit Hardington Pharmaceuticals. I know you're re-using the same drive you used back then, but I have something better. A program where you can list all the medicines and drugs that we make along with all their formulas. There's room for multiple attachments, notes, and highlights."

Dad looks up. "You made something like that, son?"

"I did," I reply, putting my hands behind my back, trying my best to look humble.

He narrows his eyes. "And how much is it going to cost us to buy this software from you?"

Mom doesn't look as convinced. "We'll have to see how it works first, honey. We don't know if there are errors or–"

"There are no errors," I say firmly. "I've checked and re-checked all the coding. It's free. Again, this is my way of apologizing. I'll never do something like that to betray your trust again."

Mom and Dad exchange a look and glance back at me.

"Please, show us what you got then," Dad urges.

I lead them all the way back to my office to show them how it works on my computer.

Instantly, their whole demeanor changes.

"This is what we knew you were capable of," Mom says with a wide smile.

Dad nods and grunts. "I can't believe this. I didn't know you were good at coding. If there are any problems, we can ask you for help?"

"Of course, and if you ever want to add anything, I can always adjust the code and add it in."

A genuine smile forms on his face. "Good."

He stands up from where he was sitting behind my desk and offers me his hand. I grasp it firmly, shaking it.

Now to try to change the subject.

"I'll install it into the network today. But hey, why don't

we go back down to the lab so I can see what you guys are working on?'

Mom raises an eyebrow. "You really want to know?"

"I think it's time that I learn more about the company and spend more time in the lab with you guys instead of up here."

I cross my fingers behind my back and hold my breath.

Neither of them say a word as they stare at me. I keep a smile firmly planted on my face, but with every second that ticks by, I feel the tension in the room rising. They still don't trust me, but what can I expect when this is only the first day?

"I think it's a great idea," Mom finally says first.

"Yep. Let's head back down." Dad says.

I breathe out slowly, relief flooding every cell in my body as they walk around my desk and lead the way back to their offices.

They go out of their way to be friendly with me, making small talk on the way back. It's fucking annoying.

When we get back inside Dad's office, my parents get behind Dad's desk. Mom pulls open one of his drawers, pulling out a pair of blue gloves and handing them to me.

I put them on with mock excitement and look from them to the vials. "So what am I looking at?"

Mom chuckles. "Oh no, don't worry about the vials. We think it's time to take you into the real lab."

"The real lab?" I ask, feeling confused.

Last time I checked this is the lab. It's the only room on the ground level of the building.

Dad laughs. "Don't worry, son. It's hidden for a reason. Wouldn't want the wrong eyes to see it."

He turns around and reaches for a plaque with one of his many achievements on it. Pulling it off the wall, he presses what looks like the wall at first glance, but if you stare at it long enough, you'll see it's a circular button painted the same shade as the wall.

The empty space between his desk on one side and the stand open to reveal a dimly lit corridor, barely wide enough for only one person to pass through.

My blood runs cold as I stare at it.

That's been here the whole time?

"Come on," he says, waving me forward. "You first, son."

I move around the desk and walk past my mom to the doorway, entering it slowly. There's instantly a kind of cooling sensation that hits my skin the moment I get inside. It's a short path that opens up to a larger room.

It's larger than the regular lab and their offices combined.

This is their true lab. The other one is just for show.

I stare at the long tables in the middle in horror, stained with blood and other liquids. Along the sides of the room are cages upon cages. Most of them have people inside. Some of them are groaning, some are screaming, some are crying, and some are so silent, I'm afraid they're dead.

It's like something out of a horror movie.

My expression has to be one of shock because Mom touches my shoulder. "Don't worry. The cages are reinforced. We did have one escape not too long ago, but that was just a fluke."

Bile threatens to climb up my throat. All of a sudden, a specific moment pops into my brain. "What day was that?" I ask, covering my mouth.

Dad frowns. "I think it was the night I first told you about Space Dust."

So I didn't imagine it. I was high on that shit, but I still heard one bang. That was someone banging on the wall for help. Were they too weak to bang more than once?

Stepping over to the left, I start walking down the

walkway, staring at the people in cages. Some of them are adults. Some of them not.

My parents observe me the whole time, following me closely, perhaps to see what I'm going to do.

I stop in my tracks when I see a familiar body slumped into the corner of a cage.

Nancy?

Her eyes are blinking so I know she's alive, but she doesn't seem to register that anyone is in front of her cage.

I inhale sharply, fighting the urge to scream at them and ask them for keys.

If Nancy is here, I'm sure those other people who went to my school that disappeared from that party are here too.

"This is how you test out the drugs?" I ask quietly.

Dad responds with an unashamed, "Yes. We release them after a while."

"This is our second time kidnapping students from your school," Mom adds.

Suddenly, it becomes all too clear. Those students who disappeared during spring break…

This is where they were.

They never told anyone where they were. Is it because they're getting their fix?

"Honey, this girl needs her daily dose. Why don't we have Noel administer it?"

"What?" I ask, my head whipping around to face them.

I can't subject Nancy or anyone else to that.

Mom smiles. "Is there a problem with that?"

Her face is telling me that however I say it, my answer better be no.

"Not at all. I'm just surprised that you would ask me to do it."

She blinks a few times before shaking her head. "It's not a

big deal. You just push it in and that'll be it." Turning to my dad she gestures him forward. He pulls a few keys out of his coat pocket.

I don't watch him pull Nancy out. I can't.

How am I going to even handle injecting her with this stuff?

He hauls her on top of the table closest to us. I glance over at her still body. She's trembling slightly and her head is turned in our direction. Her mouth quivers as she watches my dad take a syringe out of his pocket.

He holds it out to me and she whimpers, "Noel?"

I close my eyes for a moment and take a deep breath.

If I do this, they'll trust me a little more.

In the process, I'll be hurting a friend with my own hand.

Whenever they decide to release Nancy, she won't want to be my friend again. I don't blame her for that.

Our friendship will have to be sacrificed.

I step over to her and use one of the alcohol wipes from the jar to wipe her arm. After dropping it on the table next to her, I hold her arm in place as I lower the needle next to it.

A tear leaves her eye as she watches me slide the needle in, pushing the Space Dust into her arm.

When I'm done, she turns her head away from me, with hopelessness flickering in her eyes.

Stepping back a step, I turn back to my parents. "All done."

"Bravo," Mom says. "While your dad gets her back in her cage, I want to show you something else."

I shudder to think what else they could possibly be doing.

She leads me to the back of the lab, past all the cages.

The cabinet is huge and there's jars and jars of substances.

"What are these?" I ask, staring up at them all the way to the ceiling.

"These are all of the drugs we've started on. Some of them are the same with a few small differences." She opens the cabinet and holds one up in a bright pink bottle with an A on it. "This one we just completed. The subjects on the other side of the room are the test subjects for this one."

"What is it?" I ask, staring at it uncomfortably.

She holds it out to me. When I don't take it, she thrusts it to my chest. "Take it, Noel. Your father and I took some and it's been great. I'm sure you and your next girlfriend will enjoy it too. I like to call it Ardor, if that gives you any indication on what is involved."

I didn't need to know about that. A sexual drug, most likely to heighten arousal and sexual desire.

I don't want this stuff. "You probably need it, don't you?"

She points across the room to a machine.

"We're making plenty of it as we speak, so go ahead and take that one, I insist."

Smiling back, I nod and say a quick, "Thanks."

She touches my shoulder. "I'll be back. Make yourself at home."

Her heels clack against the floor, steadily getting further away.

When I know she's fully gone, I drop the fake smile from my face and glance around the room in disgust and then down to the bottle.

I'll keep it for a little while and eventually I'll dump it down the sink and tell her I used it.

I need to fast track my plan so I can free these people and stop them from ever undergoing more testing.

How do they even live with themselves?

I hope they come back over here soon because I can't stand to be in this building a second longer.

CHAPTER NINETEEN

Gemma

S ophomore year didn't start out with a devastating bang like freshman year. This year, it starts out at a crawl.

I don't exactly know why since all of my classes are great. The professors are mostly okay.

I can't shake my feelings of restlessness.

It might have something to do with Noel and I only speaking in private once. I tried to thank him for his birthday gift, but he seemed distracted.

Since then, I only ever see him when we eat meals with our friends. We don't have any of the same classes.

The me from spring break would be thrilled, but now I just feel completely disappointed.

And I hate it.

I'd love to just stay cooped up in my room and read one

of the hundreds of books that I purchased from the gift cards he gave me. Instead, Mera is insisting I go out with everyone else to the club since it's Halloween.

She even brought me a costume. One of those school-girl outfits with a short skirt and a buttoned shirt. It came with fake glasses, but I'm going to keep my regular ones on so I can actually fucking see.

Moving my fingers along the fabric, I sigh.

Well, it's not much different from my pirate costume last year.

"Hurry and put it on, you're going to look great," Mera insists.

I scoff and pick it up, striding to the bathroom and passing Mera on the way.

She was Snow White last year and this year she's Cinderella. She looks absolutely gorgeous with her hair pinned up the way it is.

Closing the bathroom door, I peel my clothes off in a hurry and slide the costume on. It fits a little too snugly for me, but I have a feeling this is how it was meant to fit. The best part are the comfy white stockings.

Stepping over to the mirror, I immediately notice how this shirt not only feels tight, but it's making everything I have look bigger. My breasts, my hips, and my ass.

Ugh. Yeah, I hate this. I pull my hair back into a high ponytail and slip my glasses back on.

Mera did her own makeup again, and though I love it, I don't feel like having anything on tonight besides red lipstick.

As I exit the bathroom, Mera gasps. "You look hot in that. Noel is going to love it."

I shrug and go over to our vanity, pulling out a red lipstick from the drawer. He might love it. He might even spend the whole evening staring at me as I parade around in it, but I doubt he'll tell me, because he can't.

I should try and make the best out of this evening instead of being a grump about it. Everyone else is excited. Other people on campus are going to the club too, but ZDB is also holding their annual Halloween party like last year.

After spreading the lipstick evenly across my lips, I make sure none of it is out of place and put the top on. I stuff it back in the drawer and turn around to Mera.

"What kind of shoes should I wear?"

She points to my sneakers next to my bed. "Those should be good."

After pulling them on, I stand up. "Let's go down then."

She looks over herself once more in our vanity mirror and follows me out of our room.

This year there's no stupid makeup check because Collette is anxious to get to the club.

As we descend from the stairs, Mera comments, "My bodyguards are driving Callan and I, want to ride with us?"

"Sure," I respond.

Ten minutes later, I'm seated in the third row next to Noel.

They happened to leave out the fact that Noel was riding with us too.

He's wearing a regular button down shirt and pants with oval-shaped glasses.

"Who are you supposed to be?" I ask, looking him up and down.

He smirks and pulls his shirt open in the middle. There's a big yellow and red S in the middle.

"Ah," I say, settling into my seat.

I place my hands on my lap and glance out the window. It looks like it's about to rain.

All of a sudden, I feel a hand grab mine, startling me. I glance over at Noel to find him staring at me with heated eyes. "That's a lovely costume, Gem."

"Thank you," I say with a small smile and turn away.

"After the club, we should go somewhere. Just you and me."

I sigh and shake my head. "That's okay."

There's only one month left of this agreement. We can spend the rest of it as we have these past two months. Separate.

His hand trails up my thigh, slipping his finger inside my stockings.

I move his hand away and turn back to him, whispering, "Do you really want to take the chance that your parents' spies decided to follow us? I don't." My heart pangs in my chest as I continue. "How about we just ignore each other for the rest of the night and then go straight back to AAA and ZDB. We're only one mouth away from this agreement being over. Let's finish it without any more encounters."

His jaw sets and tics. His eyes search mine intently. "Sex," he mutters. "You mean without having sex."

"Yes," I reply.

He sits back in his seat and turns away from me. "Fine."

That word of resignation should be music to my ears, but it only hurts instead.

When we pull up to the club, we all take out our fake IDs and show them to the bouncer. The music inside is blaring and the smell of rain is in the air. He approves of each of us, letting us inside.

All of us disperse, well most of us. I feel someone directly behind me as I head to the bar.

When I sit down, I twist the bar stool to find it's Noel.

He flashes a smile at me. "My treat. Pick your poison?"

His stool is two over from mine so we're not sitting directly next to each other.

"Rum and coke," I reply.

He gestures for the bartender to come over and orders my drink and his shot of whiskey.

"Are you going to spend all night by the bar?" Noel asks as the bartender sets our orders in front of us.

I'm not really one to dance much and that's mostly what people do in a club. I always feel like a whale trying to swim when I dance.

When there's parties on campus, I usually stay out front on the porch by myself. I don't mind doing it since most of the time no one bothers me if I do. The equivalent to that would be sitting at one of the tables away from the dance floor.

"No, I'll probably go sit over there," I say, pointing to the tables. "What about you?"

He throws back his shot and clears his throat. "I'll be over here drinking for the rest of the night."

"So no hot red-heads?" slips out of my mouth before I can stop it.

He chuckles. "Were you jealous in New York, precious?"

Oh God, I need to keep a tighter lid on my mouth. "Not at all," I say as my cheeks flare with heat. Before I can say anything else that's stupid, I slide off the stool and rush over to the tables.

When I'm almost to an empty table, someone runs right into me, causing me to trip and fall.

"I'm so sorry," someone says anxiously.

A hand pops down in front of me as I gather my bearings.

I grab the outstretched hand, and glance up to find a guy dressed as Robin. His brown hair is short like Robin's is and his mask is painted on. He pulls me up easily and I smooth down my clothes and push my glasses up my nose. "Thank you, I didn't see you there."

"It was my fault," he says with a slow smile. "Are you supposed to be one of those hot nerds?"

"That's me," I respond wryly with a small laugh.

"Well, hey, I'm Cooper."

Cooper sounds friendly. But then, lately, I haven't exactly been a good judge of character.

"Gemma," I reply politely, glancing away from him searching for my exit.

The table I was going to sit at is still open.

"Want to dance?"

My eyes shift back to him in shock.

He seems to notice my expression because he laughs and sheepishly rubs the back of his head. "I just thought maybe we were meant to dance together since we ran into each other like this. Are you here with anyone?"

"Just my friends," I respond, gazing out at the dance floor.

None of them are anywhere close to where I'm standing.

A genius idea hits me.

There's no better way to enforce the fact that we're broken up if I don't go out and dance with someone else.

He still believes his family is keeping an eye on him.

So while I'm still wary of this guy, one dance shouldn't hurt anything. It should only help.

"Sure, I'll dance with you."

He offers his hand and I grasp it, letting him lead me to the dance floor. As he parts the way, I start to feel the air get thicker. Must be the sweat from the people dancing in their costumes.

I smother a laugh when I see a guy in a headless T-rex costume.

Cooper stops us, and pulls me close as the next song starts. It's a fast one with a lot of sexual undertones.

He opens his mouth and asks something, but I can't hear over the music. The music is so much louder over here.

"What?" I yell.

He smiles with understanding, leaning over slightly so I can hear him better. "You know you're gorgeous. Is there any chance we could see each other again after tonight?"

"Thank you." I accept his compliment easily. It still leaves me puzzled. Am I really? Not only Noel, but now this guy too thinks I am.

His hands slide up and down my waist. For some reason, it feels icky and wrong. "I'm sorry, I don't think so."

I fully expect him to get angry at me or protest, but he doesn't. Instead his hands stop moving and we just enjoy the rest of the dance.

It's actually more fun than I thought it'd be.

When the music ends, he lets go of my waist. "It was nice meeting you, Gemma."

"You too," I yell, my words dying in my throat as he grabs my hand, placing a chaste kiss on top.

As he leaves, I feel a shift in the air.

Almost as if someone's looking at me.

I swing my head around, trying to find the source of that feeling until it abruptly stops.

That's weird.

Squeezing through the crowd, I come out on the side with the bar.

My seat is still empty and Noel is still in his.

Was he the one watching me?

Strangest thing though, he has no shot glasses in front of him but two glasses each full of something different.

As I edge closer, I watch as he doesn't touch either of them.

I sit on my bar stool and ask, "Are both of those for you?"

He turns his head slightly to the left. An unreadable expression on his face.

"No. One is for you."

I glance down at the glasses and then back to him. "Well, what are they?"

"Whiskey sour and a Malibu sunset."

It's clear from the choices which one was meant for him and which for me. That Malibu sunset has rum in it. Maybe I should surprise him.

"I'll take the whiskey sour."

He slides it over and swishes the Malibu sunset in the glass before gulping it down.

"You didn't think I'd choose this, right?" I ask slyly.

He doesn't even look in my direction. Not even a chuckle.

Frowning, I sip at it, cringing at the taste until I finally decide to gulp it all down.

Setting the glass down carefully, I wipe at the edges of my mouth.

"That wasn't too bad. Did you enjoy the Malibu sunset?"

"It was good," he says flatly. He slides the glass around on the bar between his index and thumb finger.

Something definitely pissed him off. He's never acted this standoffish with me. He had to have been the one watching me.

"Did you see me dance with that guy?" I ask flatly.

"Maybe I did," he snaps.

I recoil and get off my stool and slide into the one next to him. "You did the exact same thing and I didn't snap at you. What's the big deal?"

He chuckles lowly. "The big deal is that you're mine,

Jewel. And that guy put his hands all over what's mine. He kissed your fucking hand. Only I should have the pleasure of putting my lips on your body."

He doesn't say it so openly, I glance around to make sure no one overheard him. If the music wasn't blaring, everyone in the vicinity would've heard.

"Noel, I only did it to help. And have you forgotten our agreement? This is only temporary."

He glares at me. "I remember our deal well. But you tell me no more sex and then you go and do *that*." He sighs. "You drive me crazy."

"Then why don't–" I stop when I feel a weird heat come over me. "It's hot in here."

"It's not," he replies.

A tingling starts between my legs and my mouth dries out. I wave the bartender over. "Can I please have a water?"

He nods and a few seconds later, sets a glass of water in front of me.

I suck it down and sigh. So good and refreshingly cool, but it's not enough.

"Must be a side effect."

Freezing, I turn to look at Noel. "What was that?"

He doesn't respond.

An ache starts to replace the tingle and I gasp. "What the fuck is going on?" I clutch my legs together and exclaim, "What did you do?"

He locks eyes with me. "It's called Ardor. I brought it with me tonight so I could show you what else my parents have been working on, but instead." He laughs. "Instead, I'm using it to prove something to you."

"You're unbelievable," I murmur, my eyes widening in horror. My body starts to buzz in anticipation.

Fuck. My body is screaming that it needs a dick right now. And the only one I want belongs to an asshole.

"How did you know I'd take the whiskey sour?" I ask quietly, wiping the sweat off my forehead.

He taps his fingers on the bar. "I didn't."

His eyes stare into mine. That's when I look at him real closely. The sweat on his forehead, the trembling in his arms. I cast my eyes downward and notice the tent in his pants.

"You put it in both drinks," I mutter, glancing back up to him.

He touches my arm and I gasp at the contact. "Come with me."

"No," I say with a shake of my head.

He leans in to my ear, his lips brushing against it. "Don't you want me to soothe the burn?"

I grit my teeth as I feel my lady bits getting wetter by the second.

I can't stay here like this for another few hours. My body needs something. It craves it. Denying it is only making it more painful.

"Fine," I snap, sliding off my chair. I let him handle getting the ride to the hotel. Everything is a blur until he throws me on the bed and starts pulling his costume off.

In a rush myself, I unbutton the skirt and slide it down with my underwear. I don't get the chance to get my shirt off before he's on me. He captures my mouth in a heated kiss, thrusting his tongue into mine with a groan.

I pant as I feel his body flush with mine, his lower half pressed intimately into mine.

My body feels so achy I can't take much more of it.

He moves off of me, laying on the bed. "Come here, precious." He taps his lips and I go to press mine into his when he stops me.

"Your other lips."

A wave of pleasure shoots through me at his suggestion. "You want me to sit on your face?"

His eyes are hazy with lust. "Yes. I only want to smell and taste you."

"I'm too heavy, Noel," I say, my core clenching.

"You aren't. Now *sit*," he orders.

I pull myself over him and adjust myself until he's right under me. Slowly, I lower myself down. "Good girl, precious. Let me saturate myself with your sweetness."

A strong hand reaches for my thigh and pulls me down. I feel his tongue enter me and lap at my wetness. "Oh my God, Noel."

My senses are so heightened with this drug. I shake at the intensity of it. His tongue thrusts inside me, over and over, trying to get every last drop of my wetness. Then he removes his tongue to lap at my clit. I feel his lips clasp around it and suck so hard, I finish immediately with a loud moan.

Tapping his hand, I moan, "Please, I need you inside me now."

Reluctantly, he lets me go and I move off of him, rolling to the left. I take my shirt off so I'm completely bare to him. He rolls on top of me, his hips situated so his dick is only inches away from being right where I need it most.

He stares down at me, his mouth slightly open as he pants slightly. "I don't have any condoms. We were lucky once, but we might not get lucky again."

"I don't care, just hurry," I urge him.

He presses his forehead to mine, causing our breath to mingle and breathing each other in. He parts my legs and enters me fully with one deep thrust.

We groan at the same time.

I let my head lull back into the pillow as he pulls out all the way and thrusts back in.

With a moan, I grab at his shoulders and pull him down, letting his six pack stay flush against my flabby stomach.

"Gem," he whispers, pumping into me so perfectly. "You feel so fucking good, I can't stand it. You were made just for me."

He moves his arms behind me, holding on to me as he fucks me hard. "You. Are. Mine. And mine alone."

I moisten my lips and pant, "But that's only for another month."

"No," he says, his voice lowering to a growl, "it's forever."

I gasp and clench around him with a loud moan, coming completely apart in his hands.

Does he mean that?

He grinds his hips into me and groans, "Oh fuck, I'm coming."

"Noel," I murmur, feeling ultra sensitive, "it's not enough. I need more."

He wipes the sweat off his forehead and pulls out of me.

"I need more too."

He helps me turn onto my stomach. "Hands on the headboard."

I place my hands there and open wide for him. He enters me slowly and I gasp, twitching as I feel every single inch again.

"I love you Gem."

My heart clenches as he drives himself into me, over and over again until I reach my finish.

I know I feel the same way, but the words stay lodged in my throat.

I moan and climax over and over, one leading into the next and becoming more and more sensitive each time.

Every time he empties himself into me, I feel more and more euphoric.

He sets me on his lap, and groans when he slides home. "Ride me, precious, just like you did in the closet."

I press my hands onto his six-pack and lift myself up

His fingers go to my clit, rubbing and squeezing it. I don't know how many it's been, but the feeling of pleasure never ends. Ardor is only a small fraction of it. He's the best drug I've ever had.

Nothing else matters but this.

All night long, we enjoy each other until I'm so tired, I fall asleep with him still inside me.

The sun hits my face and I wince at the harsh light.

Mera doesn't usually leave the blinds open.

I blink quickly when it hits me. I'm not at ZDB.

Staring down at the floor, I spot my costume and it all comes rushing back. I cover my mouth and stare over my shoulder at Noel, snoring peacefully.

He drugged me.

He actually drugged me.

My stomach twists as the night flashes through my head.

Those waves of endless pleasure were so mind-blowing I couldn't stop.

I can't believe he did this all because some guy danced with me and kissed my hand.

Carefully, I pull my clothes on, watching over my shoulder to make sure he stays asleep.

How can he say I love you after drugging me?

Tears of frustration well up in my eyes. Gasping quietly, I let the tears overflow. Crying because he drugged me. Crying because he confessed his feelings. Crying because I love him too. And crying because I can't be with him now.

And it hurts so bad, I can't breathe.

I use the bathroom quickly, crossing my fingers he doesn't hear me and wash my hands in a hurry and leave with my bag in tow.

Closing the hotel door, I pull my phone out. It's almost eleven and it looks like I have a bunch of missed messages.

I click Scarlett's name as I stop in front of the elevator, leaning forward to press the button.

A few voices startle me as the phone rings. Glancing off to the side, I check to make sure none of them belong to Noel.

As I step into the elevator, Scarlett answers, "Gemma?"

"Hey, sorry you couldn't come last night. We really missed you and Peyton at the club. Is there any way you can pick me up, please?" I ask, wiping the tears from under my glasses.

There's silence for a few seconds. I almost think she'll say no. "Girl, of course. Where are you?"

"The Hamilton," I say, exiting the elevator and walking out to the lobby.

She whistles. "Got it. I'll be there in fifteen."

Coming out of the lobby, I spy an empty bench where I sit and respond to messages. Most of them are from Collette.

Apparently everyone knows I left with Noel. I wonder if his parents know.

I guess it doesn't matter in the end, though, because now it's over for real.

Scrolling to his number in my contacts, I click block.

I know it'll only help for conversations over the phone, but it'll tell him that I'm being deadly serious about this. I don't expect him to release my house to me at the end of

November, but I'd rather never feel the tortuous touch of his body again.

I just hope I'm not pregnant after all of that.

A car honks and I tilt my head up, seeing Scarlett. Rising off the bench, I walk hurriedly over to her car and slide in the passenger side.

"You have sex hair," Scarlett comments.

I smooth my hair and cough. "I didn't get much of a chance to fix it. Thanks again for this ride."

She's never turned me down once and I can't thank her enough.

"Sure thing, but tell me, why isn't he giving you a ride? And why did you sound like you were crying over the phone? Give me the deets, girl."

Sighing, I glance out of the window, staring at the palm trees fluttering gin the wind. "Do you have time?"

"Always," she replies. "Can't be worse than your fake boyfriend's brother threatening you because he thinks you killed your fake boyfriend, can it?"

I snort. "No, I guess it's not," and then proceed to tell her everything that happened last night.

CHAPTER TWENTY

Noel

A noise echoes in my head.

Over and over until I open my eyes.

The noise continues and I rub a hand over my eyes.

It's not in my head.

At first glance at my surroundings, I know I'm in a hotel room. A Hamilton hotel room. There's just one thing missing.

I rub my hand over the sheets next to me.

When did she leave?

The knocking continues and I groan in frustration.

Dashing to the door, I open it slightly so they don't see I'm naked.

The man on the other side smiles slightly. "I apologize sir, but your checkout time was eleven. If you'd like the room for another night, we can extend your stay."

"That won't be necessary. I'll be at the front desk to check out in a few minutes."

Closing the door, I grab the regular pieces of my costume and pull it on, tossing the Superman part of it in my arm. Once I'm done, I close the door quickly and hurry to the front desk.

I need to talk to her.

I scramble to grab my phone out of my pocket and check it for messages. There's a ton, but none from Gem.

Wait. Of course there wouldn't be. She never texts me first.

After I call for a ride, I wait by the curb and fire off a text to Gem. An exclamation point immediately appears. A message in red appears underneath mine.

This message can not be delivered.

That's...never happened before.

Did she block me?

The car comes to the curb and I get in the back.

"Where to?" the driver asks.

"SGU," I reply and click her name, my heart pounding in my chest, hoping it isn't true.

But when my call doesn't go through and I hear the automatic voice say this phone is not in service, I know it's true.

I fucked up again.

I let my head fall back against the seat.

After the first time, I told myself I wouldn't do it again, yet here we are.

———

At every opportunity I get to talk to her, she's already trying to escape me. Any hopes I had to make it up to her slowly fade away. In the blink of an eye, it's Thanksgiving break. At the beginning of next week, I have to fulfill my end of the bargain and give her the house back. She'll be forced to see me then, and maybe we can clear things up between us.

Or maybe it all comes back to her not feeling the same way.

Tyrell and I both stay on campus for Thanksgiving break. Since he's the only friend I have around, I decide to ask for his advice.

When he wakes up on our first day of vacation, I'm already wide awake and drinking a beer.

He looks at me weirdly. "Isn't it a little early for that?"

"We're on vacation," I tell him, holding up the can, "and on vacation, we drink when we feel like it and right now, I really feel like it."

"I'd rather go back to sleep," he murmurs.

"Wait," I say, holding my hand up.

He peeks over at me.

"If you mess up with the person you love, how do you fix it?"

He sighs. "Why do you assume I know? Why don't you ask Callan? He actually has a girlfriend."

I set the beer down and cross my arms. "Come on, dude. Help me out. You're a sensitive guy. Tell me what to do."

He sighs. "Wait for her to come to you."

I wait for him to continue, but he doesn't.

"I'm too impatient for that. With how stubborn she is, she may never come back to me."

"Ask Callan then." He puts a pillow over his head.

Truthfully, I should've asked Callan earlier, but it was one of those times where I kept hoping that things would change.

I could always drive to his house and see him, but I'd ruin his time alone with Mera. It'll just have to wait.

On Thanksgiving day, I drive to my parents' home for dinner. When I pull up, I notice the third car in the driveway.

Whose car is that? They never said anything about expecting company.

I get up to the door and turn the knob, finding it's already open.

The sound of my mom's laughter echoes through the mansion, followed by the sound of another woman laughing.

Is that Callan's mom?

Walking through the foyer, I eventually reach the dining room.

Everyone seated looks expectantly at the doorway. Everyone being Callan, Collette, and his parents.

In all the years we've been friends, not once has Callan and his family been invited over for any holidays. This is strange and I don't know what it means.

My parents are each seated on one end while Mr. and Mrs. Goldsworthy are on one side of the table and Callan and Collette are seated on the other with one chair in between them. The only empty chair at the table.

"Thank you for coming, honey," Mom says sweetly.

Dad rings the bell. "Now we can eat."

As I pull the chair back and take my seat, all of the

servants come out, filling the table with food.

I cough and whisper to Callan. "Why the hell are you here?"

He clears his throat and whispers back. "I don't fucking know."

The maids turn the chandelier on above us, brightening the room.

Everyone starts to pass the dishes around making their plates. But I can't concentrate because I'm getting a weird vibe from this table.

I don't like it one bit.

As I take a bite of the dry ass turkey my parents had made, my dad says my name, "Noel."

I glance up, the turkey half in and half out of my mouth. "Yes?" I ask.

"Swallow your food, son," Dad says with annoyance in his tone.

After chewing the dry ass turkey, I gulp it down.

"Yes?" I ask again, clearly this time.

"We," he glances at the end of the table at my mother, "think it's time that you stop fucking every girl you see and focus on the woman who will be your future wife."

Excuse me? All of a sudden they're deciding to crack down?

I've been nothing but good to them these past few weeks.

"We've realized how much you've matured, and we think it's finally time. Once you graduate from SGU, you'll get married and start a family. Make an *heir* for this company."

I glance incredulously at the both of them. "Are you fucking kidding me?"

Mom clears her throat. "Language, Noel. We have guests today."

"I've known the Goldsworthys since I was a kid. I don't

think they're really guests."

She sighs and struggles to keep her fake smile plastered on her face.

Dad gestures to Collette. "Here she is."

I glance over to Collette and back to my dad. "Here she is *what?*"

"This is your future wife," he says, without a hint of a joke in his voice.

I wish there was.

I chuckle. "Okay Dad, you got me. Where's the hidden camera?"

My reaction is nothing compared to Collette's who shrieks. "You guys are kidding, right? Noel and *me?* I remember when he used to make mud pies and throw them at me."

"It was a lot of fun too," I reply with a laugh.

Callan smirks and glances at me. His father and mother glare at him.

Dad sets his fork down and presses his elbows into the table. "Noel, this is a serious matter. We let you have your fun, and now it's over. Simple as that."

I've been doing so well these last few months being on my best behavior and doing whatever they wanted. I'm still no closer to finding out what their password is for their computers.

But I won't allow them to control this portion of my life when I know the girl of my dreams is out there. I refuse to be subjected to living life without her.

"I won't be marrying Collette," I tell them, shoveling some mashed potatoes into my mouth.

Mom laughs, trying and failing at hiding her anger. "What do you mean, honey?"

Dad sighs as if he expected this exact scenario.

"I mean that I'm already in love with someone." I glance at Collette. "No offense."

"None taken," she responds as I turn back to my plate.

"Wait," she says in a high tone. "No way. No way, *no way*. Is it Gemma?"

Her beautiful heart shaped face pops into my head. Her rounded cheeks and captivating brown eyes behind her glasses. And her hair. When it's curly, it's the most beautiful texture in the world.

How could I not fall in love with someone as beautiful as her?

Mom sighs. "I can't believe we are back to this again. Honey, we told you that her family were scammers. How many times do we have to tell you before you actually listen to us?"

Collette murmurs, "What?" She elbows me. "What are they talking about?"

I shake my head as I start to lose my appetite.

It isn't my place to say if Gem hasn't already told her.

"I have been listening, and you know maybe if you told me the truth about what happened to her parents, I'd know for sure that I should trust your word," I lie.

Everyone except Collette goes silent.

"I'm so confused," she groans. "No one tells me anything."

Mrs. Goldsworthy stands up. "Maybe it'd be best if we leave."

Mom quickly exclaims, "No. We haven't even made the arrangements."

"There will be no arrangements," I boom. "It's Gemma Brighton or nothing for me."

Standing up quickly, I exit the room, and head for the door. I hear loud footsteps pounding against the tile as I open the French doors.

I walk out regardless. A hand touches my shoulder and I glance back, find Callan looking at me with worried eyes.

"I told you not to take it too far," he says in a low tone.

I pause and lower my head slightly. "I know."

"So how're you going to fix it? Wow. I can't believe it. Noel Hardington, the so-called man, in love."

I smile at that. "Just tell me what to do. How do I fix this?"

My question hangs in the air for a long while. "Well, you need to force her to hear you out. Once you get that chance, apologize until she forgives you. Give her the thing she wants the most."

I think for a long time, staring out at the circular driveway in front of me.

What does she want most?

Answers.

That's it.

"You're a genius, buddy," I say, giving Callan a quick hug before going back inside. While my parents are still talking, I go up the stairs to their room. The door is wide open, so I tiptoe inside and switch on the light on the wall.

I head straight for their nightstand drawers. They always like to keep things they use every day in reach.

When I open Dad's drawer, I spot his key ring I always see him use. I stuff it in my pocket and then close it quickly. Moving to Mom's drawer, her keys are more scattered. I don't even know if all of these are for Hardington Pharmaceuticals, but I take them all anyway.

I shove them all in my other pocket and dash down the stairs, stepping lightly so none of them creak.

Before walking out, I glance once more down the hallway toward the dining room.

All of them are still talking and laughing as if nothing happened.

Callan is still standing on the porch when I get outside, completely unmoved.

"Mind if I come along for the ride? The only reason I came tonight was because Collette begged me to."

"Come on, then." I rush over to my Porsche and hop in the driver's seat, anxious to get over there before they realize their keys are missing. I'll keep them even after I'm done using them and make copies.

He hops in the passenger side and I start the car and zoom around the line of parked cars. By going around people, I get to the building pretty fast.

"You unlock the door and I'll run and turn the alarm off," I tell him.

He grunts in response. I hand him my dad's keyring.

I don't bother parking in the parking lot. Pulling right in front of the building, I stop the car and get out.

Callan and I stroll over, keeping our faces straight in case anyone tries to stop us. No one should be at the office today though since it's Thanksgiving.

Callan sticks the key in and turns the lock. Immediately, the alarm starts to go off, a loud annoying beep. I run over and enter my birthday and the alarm chirps.

It's completely dark as we walk over to the elevator and press the button for the ground floor.

When the doors open, I rush out while Callan steps out, glancing around. "I can't believe I've never been down here."

"It's nothing special," I assure him.

Quickly, I press my birthday in for the keypad code for the fake lab room. We walk all the way to the end of the room where my parents' offices are.

I glance between them and sigh. Which one would be more likely to have information on Gemma's parents?

It'll take time and if we choose wrong, we might not make it out of here unscathed.

"We can both look once you figure out the keys to their file cabinets. You unlock all of them and then hand it off to me and I'll go look in your mom's files."

"Smart," I reply.

I stick a few keys into my dad's door knob until finally one works. I hand it off to Callan who unlocks my mom's office.

When I go inside, I suddenly remember how their test subjects are in their secret lab. I don't have to save them all.

"What are you waiting for, Noel?" Callan asks.

Sighing, I turn away shamefully from the wall and start unlocking file cabinets.

I'll come back for all those people soon.

After getting them all unlocked, I toss the keys to Callan.

"It's the smallest one," I tell him.

I start opening drawers and shining my phone light on the file names.

There are lots of medicines in one. Drugs in the other. This would be a great time to see if I could find Space Dust, but if it's not in the files with the other drugs, where could it be?

Opening another file cabinet, I find a bunch of files with names on them. Names of people.

This has to be it.

I go for the B and immediately find "Brighton."

Their file isn't as extensive as some of the other ones, though I can understand since the Brightons only worked for my parents for a year.

I glance through the other file cabinets to make sure I don't miss anything. Footsteps in the doorway cause me to straighten, but it's only Callan.

I hold up the file and smirks. "Nice."

Before leaving, I glance regretfully at the hidden lab door in the wall.

Sighing, I close the office door behind me and run with Callan at my heels.

Callan and I make it outside to my car without incident and I hand him the file as I peel away.

Gem is staying on campus so if I go to ZDB tomorrow, she should be there.

I'll give her this file and then hopefully she'll give me the chance to apologize.

After ringing the doorbell, I stand back and wait.

Ten minutes pass by and I ring it again.

I guess I was wrong.

Turning away, I start down the porch steps when I hear the door open.

I almost miss the last step because of my surprise.

Turning around, I find Gem in the doorway, stone-faced as she regards me. "What can I do for you?"

Holding the file up in the air, I walk back up the steps. "I have this for you. A file about your parents. Maybe it will help give you a clue about what happened to them."

Her eyes widen and she gladly accepts it, looking through it for a second before looking back at me. "What is this going to cost me?"

"Nothing," I reply quickly. "I found it because I know you want answers."

Her mouth tightens.

"And, I was hoping you'd hear me out."

She blinks slowly. "Okay."

I take a deep breath before beginning. "What I did was wrong. I made a snap decision and I drugged you. For that, I'm truly sorry. I promise it'll never happen again. I'll try to control myself better if you'd just give me another chance."

She glances at the file in her hands. "I don't think I can give you another chance, Noel. I'm sorry."

My heart drops and my hands start to shake. "Do you not love me?"

I watch her face carefully, searching for the truth.

"It doesn't matter," she says softly.

"But it does," I insist. "If you love me, we can make it work. Whatever stands in our way, we'll remove it."

She shakes her head. "I don't think so. I really appreciate this file and of course we'll still share mutual friends, but that's as far as I can go."

So that's it? Just like that?

It really is over.

"Is there someone else?" I ask, feeling my heart break.

"No, of course not."

"Then, why?" I ask. "Jewel, please, I'm begging you. Give me just one more chance."

She backs away. "I'm sorry. I'll talk to you next week about the house. Please don't talk to me until then."

The door slams right in my face.

I stare at it for a long time, waiting and hoping she'll come out. When I get tired of standing, I sit on the porch steps, my face in my hands. And when I get tired of that, I sit in my car and cry.

Until finally, the sun starts to go down. When it's dark, I watch the light outside of ZDB click on.

She's not coming out.

Slowly, I pull away from the curb and drive back to fraternity row.

CHAPTER TWENTY-ONE

Gemma

Whether he finally leaves in his car, I allow myself to breathe a sigh of relief. I felt guilty watching him just sit there all day. Reading the file didn't feel right until he left.

I have come to terms with the fact that I do love him, but I'm not entirely sure yet if I can give him another chance. I figure that until I get that part figured out It's probably better not to get his hopes up.

I need time to think.

Walking away from the window, I grab the file and flip it open.

That first page makes me instantly tear up. A picture of both of them graces the page. I cover my mouth as tears slip down my cheeks. They didn't take a ton of pictures of themselves. Mostly me with them, so to see two pictures that I don't have is a treat.

The next page is a picture of me along with a few notes about how smart I am. There's a few comments written in the margins that I'd be a shoo-in to work for Noel in the future.

Scoffing, I turn to the next page.

It goes on to talk about their achievements in college and their brilliance in the scientific area, specifically chemistry. There's a chart of all of the days they worked for them and which days they had off. There's a list of questions they must have asked Mr. and Mrs. Hardington. The list is in both of their handwriting, I'd recognize it anywhere.

My lip quivers as I notice every question is about how dangerous Space Dust is.

That stupid fucking drug.

There's studies they did. Observations. Tests.

The very last page of the file has a list of all of the transportation vehicles they had.

Mom's car, Dad's car, and also a plane.

I never knew they had a plane.

Dad's car sat at the airport until it was clear they were never coming back. Aunt Cindy sold it. Mom's car sat in the driveway for a long time and Cindy used it until it broke down completely.

They were only supposed to be gone on a work trip to South America, yet Noel's parents acted as if there was no trip at all. That they just never came back to work one day.

Did they go on their own trip instead using this plane?

Turning the page over, I spot the scribble of a name with "pilot?" next to it. My heart races as I smile down at the name.

Please, let this be the name of their pilot.

My phone beeps in my pocket and I pull it out to check who the message is from.

It's Luella, except the message is all jumbled.

I type back a few question marks.

Watching the phone, I see it change to read and wait for her response, but she never does.

What's up with that?

I call her phone and the phone rings and rings with no answer.

That's weird.

One more time, I call and just when I think the call will go straight to voicemail, she picks up.

"Hi, Gemma." Her voice is light like it usually is, but something seems off.

"Hi. Is everything okay?"

"Yes," she says, a smile in her voice, "everything is fine."

"Okay, see you at school on Monday," I respond.

She hangs up without saying anything back.

Frowning at the phone, I stare down at it, conflicted about what to do. If she was in trouble, she'd tell me. I just hope everything is okay with her.

I'll ask her in person on Monday. Tonight, I need to find that pilot.

Christmas songs are playing as I step into the hallway. I brush by other girls on my way out front. All of them, in good spirits for the upcoming season.

I can't enjoy it yet, not until I get my very own present, my house, back. It's been two weeks since Noel was supposed to sign it over. I gave him time, thinking he'd probably need some time to be okay with seeing me again after I rejected him.

I unblocked his number yet all of my calls and texts have gone unanswered. He hasn't been to the Dining Hall when I go, nor the library, or anywhere on campus.

I asked Callan if he's been to practice and he told me Noel has been temporarily red-shirted.

Why wouldn't he want to play in the basketball games when he lives and breathes being on the team?

I step outside and breathe in the cool air. It's another overcast day and it looks like it could rain at any moment.

Glancing across the street, I lock eyes with the white van. It's been sitting across the street almost nonstop now for the past week. I never see anyone behind the wheel or anyone inside, it just sits there. It's really starting to creep me the fuck out.

I wonder if anyone else has noticed it.

Before going to AAA, I head for the Dining Hall for breakfast. As I turn the corner out of sorority row, I feel someone knock into me from behind.

There's no way that was an accident.

Luckily I land with my hands against the pavement, but really?

A bunch of snickers behind me make me roll my eyes.

Definitely not an accident.

I push myself off the ground and get back up, finding the catty girls to be a group of ten or more. But I don't know any of them.

Wiping my hands on my pants, I clear my throat. "I don't even know you guys. What do you want with me?"

One girl steps up front, narrowing her eyes at me. "If it wasn't for you, we'd still have a chance."

A chance? Are they talking about Noel?

"I'm sorry, but he makes his own decisions about who he wants to go out with, not me." I turn away and they elbow me right in the middle of my back.

"Ouch," I mutter, feeling the tender spot. Turning around quickly, I glare. "Don't you have somewhere else to be?"

"No," the girl at the front says. "We don't have anything to do anymore because it's been shut down."

"What has?" I ask, barely caring enough to ask.

Because what could it possibly have to do with me?

"Our fan club," she says angrily. "He shut it down, for good!"

I stare at all of them utterly confused.

Why would he do that? Did he do that for me?

"Our club started freshman year in high school and now it's gone. He didn't give us a reason, but we all know it was you," the girl at the front says snidely. "You were the last one to be with him. He hasn't been with anyone else. But what I can't imagine is why he'd be all wrapped up with someone who looks like you?"

I shrug. "I don't know why either, but it is what it is." Whirling around, I run off before they can attack me again.

My mind runs wild as I try to pull air into my starved lungs.

Never once did he mention shutting it down before.

Not that this changes anything, but I need to talk to him to see where his mind is at. And I want my house back.

But first, breakfast.

I slow my pace long before I get to the Dining Hall. Saturdays are always less crowded here.

When I walk in, I look for an empty table first, hoping it'll still be empty when I have my food.

"Gemma!" someone yells.

I follow the voice to the right corner and spot Vincent waving at me. Tyrell is sitting opposite of him and he doesn't turn to look at me.

I don't know why he's waving so I wave and continue to the bakery line where I get a bagel and a breakfast sandwich with an orange juice.

When I turn to get out of line, I almost run right into Vincent. *Has he been right behind me the whole time?*

"Gemma," he says slowly. "Why don't you join us at our table so we can talk?"

When have I ever sat and ate alone with Vincent and Tyrell? What would they need to talk to me about?

With every second that passes, his light brown eyes grow annoyed and his jaw tightens.

"Fine," I relent, following him to their table.

I sit in the seat at the end of the table and unwrap my breakfast sandwich, holding it in my hands.

Now that I'm actually sitting with them, Vincent seems less uptight and Tyrell is ignoring me completely.

"What did you want to talk about?" I ask, getting straight to the point.

Vincent leans back in his chair, crossing his arms. "What'd you do to Noel? He's ignoring me and everyone else."

What did *I* do? Maybe, just maybe, things between us would've naturally happened if he didn't drug me.

Frowning, I take a bite of my sandwich and chew and swallow before answering. "Not that it's any of your business but–"

He puts a hand in the air. "Let me stop you there. You see, I need Noel. Without him, I'm stuck with Mr. Grumpy in Love, who is probably practicing knocking her up right now, and this quiet bastard." He looks pointedly at Tyrell and then back to me. "I need my partner in crime. So whatever you did, you need to fix it."

I flick my eyes to Tyrell who stares blankly at Vincent as if he's accepted that comment.

Vincent shrugs. "Sorry, buddy, you know it's true. Just talk, for God's sake. Who cares how it comes out?"

Tyrell glances at me with a flustered look. "I c-care." His hand forming a fist when he's done speaking. Sighing, his hand uncurls and he gazes at me. "Anyway, we're all worried about him. Listen, Noel didn't want me to tell anyone this, but it's been going on for long enough."

Vincent narrows his eyes. "Wait. Didn't want you to tell anyone what?"

That's right. Tyrell is Noel's roommate and probably the only person who Noel hasn't been able to fully ignore.

Tyrell rubs the back of his neck. "He's been doing the weirdest thing. He'll just spend almost all of his time in our bedroom closet. I think it's painful for him."

The sandwich drops from my hand and I cover my mouth in horror. He's torturing himself.

Vincent snorts. "Why wouldn't he want us to know about that?"

"I think that it was meant to be kept from Callan and I more than anybody," I say sadly, lowering my hand.

My heart pangs. "Is he in the closet right now?"

Tyrell shrugs. "I think he is. Unless he's showering or using the bathroom. He only eats dinner now and I bring it to him every night. Every time I open the closet, I see the blood streaks on the wall with gouge marks like he's been clawing at the walls for hours. He refuses to let me clean it up. Sometimes I hear muffled crying."

My heart clenches and I shove the rest of my breakfast

sandwich in my mouth and my bagel and orange juice in my bag.

Vincent stands up angrily, his chair scraping back and making everyone in our area turn to look at us. "If I had known he was suffering that bad I would've approached her earlier." His mouth flattens as he turns to me. "Let's go."

I'm already in the process of standing so I nod quickly and hurry after Vincent with Tyrell right behind me.

Several girls try to stop Vincent on our way to AAA, but he dodges them every time. How they even want to approach them with the grimace on his face? I have no idea.

When we get inside AAA, a lot of the guys are watching some on TV, crowded around it. As I go up the stairs, I realize how different our sorority is from this fraternity. Not one Christmas decoration in sight.

Vincent stops outside what I presume to be Noel and Tyrell's room.

Now that I'm here, what do I say? How do I stop him from torturing himself? I still don't know if I can trust him. How do I forget that his idea is what caused me to lose my parents?

When Vincent reaches for the day, I clear my throat and ask, "Can I? I'd really like to go in alone for at least ten minutes."

Vincent nods and I glance back at Tyrell who follows suit.

Entering quietly, I close the door behind me softly.

It's so quiet inside the room, you'd think there wasn't anyone inside. I step over to the closet and slide the door open. The clothes hanging from this part of the closet are spread pretty evenly out. There's such a small amount of space that it's easy to see the blood on the walls and the numerous scratches.

The sound of him stirring makes my breath catch. I close

the closet door on this side and stride to the other end and open the door.

His head lifts from the perch created by his arms resting on his knees. His eyes barely meet mine before his head turns away, stretching his legs out as he rests against the wall.

"You want your house back, right? I'll get the papers together and the notary." His voice sounds weak, like he's forcing it.

By the small glimpse I got of his face, I can tell he hasn't been sleeping well. And I know this is the worst possible torture he could put himself through.

I completely ignore everything he said and kneel down next to him. "Get out of the closet, Noel."

"I will. As soon as I can come to terms with the fact that I fucked myself over. When I can stop and realize I'm my own worst enemy. Drugging you was wrong and that moment plays on a constant rotation every single day in my head."

I place my hand on his shoulder, stopping his words and drawing his attention.

"It's not just the drugging, if I'm being truthful. It's…my parents wanting me to stay away from you and your family. It's that you and I are part of the reason for whatever happened to them. The drugging just added to it. No matter how much I love you–"

He inhales sharply and grabs my hand and I realize too late what I said. I glance down at his hand to find his nails are short once more. He's washed the blood off.

"Say it again," he says in a low tone, locking eyes with me.

"Noel," I reply softly.

He clutches my hand tightly. "I've had a lot of time to think and it all makes sense now. I pushed my bad memories away. Suppressed them somehow. But they never truly went away. With every girl I slept with, subconsciously, I was looking for you. Every time, it'd feel wrong and I never got why."

My eyes start to get teary and I try to remove my hand from his, to no avail.

"It only felt right with you, right from the beginning. Right from the moment I held you in my arms on hazing night. You're the one who's been within my heart from the beginning. I'm so sorry for everything I put you through. I know I don't deserve you, but…" he gulps "it'll be hell being without you."

"Noel, I can't," I murmur, tears begin to slide down my cheeks. My heart is pounding so fast, I can barely think.

"I love you, Gem. Please, say it once more. For one second, just think of yourself and your feelings."

"I do!" I blurt, wiping my face. "I love you, Noel."

A smile forms on his tired face and he lets go of my hand. "If you ever change your mind about us, I'll be waiting. There'll never be anybody else for me."

My lips quiver as I feel how totally empty I feel at the loss of his hand. These past few weeks have been hard and now I know why.

I crave him now.

His touch. His laugh. His presence.

My parents wouldn't want me to be unhappy because of them. They did like Noel at first. And while he might've had a part to play in their disappearance, how can I let myself keep holding onto this?

It's time, I think, to let them go. As much as it hurts, I'll never exactly know what happened to them. But Noel is right here to help me through it all.

"You don't have to wait," I declare, tugging him close by the front of his shirt.

His eyes widen as I capture his lips, putting every ounce of love and passion behind it. His mouth comes to life immediately, our tongues dancing together as we pull each other closer. I moan into the kiss and his arm goes around me.

I pull away when I've lost all the air in my lungs.

Both of our chests heave as we stare into each other's eyes.

He leans his forehead against mine. "For real this time?"

"For real," I agree. My heart soars as a sense of joy overwhelms me.

"Never again, precious, will I do anything to jeopardize this," he murmurs, and goes in for another kiss.

The door pops open and I jump back when I hear the words, "Time's up. It's my turn, Gemma."

I chuckle and stand up, moving over to Tyrell by the door. "Go ahead then."

Vincent dashes over and sits in the spot I vacated. "Noel, buddy. You look like hell. Wait, why are you pissed?"

"Because you interrupted," Noel hisses.

Tyrell looks on, a look of relief on his face.

"And Tyrell," Noel booms. "I assume it was you who's responsible for this?"

"Yeah." Tyrell and I watch as a hand gestures for Vincent to move.

Slowly, Noel exits the closet, closing the door behind him.

He walks over to us with a solemn look on his face. "Per our agreement, you told so as of this moment, we're no longer friends."

Tyrell's face drops and I gasp.

So that's the reason why Tyrell was so hesitant to tell us?

I open my mouth to tell Noel how wrong he is when he

starts grinning ear to ear. "Ty, lighten up. I'd never not be your friend."

He claps Tyrell on the shoulder and holds his hand out. Tyrell takes it and Noel pulls him into a hug. "Thanks, man. You helped me survive these past few weeks in there. Someday soon, I'll explain all of it."

Over his shoulder, I watch all the worry fade from Tyrell's face as he hugs him back.

"And you'll tell me too?" Vincent asks, raising an eyebrow. "You can thank me for getting your girlfriend here."

I clear my throat. "Actually, I was planning on coming here on my own. You guys just sped up the process."

Vincent approaches us and Noel moves away from Tyrell. "To answer your question, no. I have no plans in telling you, my best friend since childhood." Noel's face is stiff as a board and Vincent's brows furrow. Suddenly, their faces crease into smiles and Noel chuckles.

"Kidding, of course. It's not like I intended to keep it from you, I actually forgot about it myself for quite a while."

Now that this is settled, maybe I can get his help with that pilot.

I glance from Tyrell to Vincent. "You guys mind if I steal him for the rest of the day?"

Vincent smirks. "Oh sure, of course. Don't worry. Ty and I will leave so you can have the room. No need to do it in a car or anything."

Noel chuckles and I shake my head quickly as my face flares with heat. "No. That's not it." I glance at Noel. "Get your stuff and I'll meet you outside."

I rush out and wait outside on the porch for him, ignoring the stares I receive. Five minutes later, Noel stops next to me.

"Was that a cover for them or is there really something

you need help with?" he asks, his eyes traveling up and down my figure.

"There's no time for that now," I tell him, wicked images filling my head as I pull out my phone.

I show him the picture I took of the name of the man I believe to be their pilot.

"My parents told me they had a work trip for HP. Your parents say they just never came back to work. I don't trust anything your parents say, but to satisfy my own curiosity, I need to find this man. In the file you gave me, they wrote him down as my parent's pilot. I didn't even know they had a plane."

Noel nods. "So you just want someone to come with you just in case?"

Sighing, I lower my hand. "No. I actually can't find anything about him. Either he's never used the internet or he doesn't exist. His name is too unique for nothing to come up."

Noel pulls out his phone. "Let me see his name again."

I hold my phone closer and watch as he glances from my phone to his, typing in his name.

I thought maybe Noel knew someone who's good at finding people. If he's just doing another google search, I can already tell him nothing is going to come up.

When he stops glancing at my phone, I put it back inside my pocket.

He scrolls on his phone for a long time, keeping his eyes trained on it.

"Found him."

Flipping his phone around, he shows me the photo of an older graying man. But the name on the profile isn't his. Before I can open my mouth to ask, he says, "He must have changed his name. I was lucky to find one mention of his previous name when I did a search and this is the profile that came up when I clicked on his name in the post."

"Lucky find." I pull my phone back out and do a quick search. It doesn't take long for his name, phone number, and address to pop up. "Found him."

He lives in the High Desert. That's not too far away.

"I'll drive you, come on." Noel holds out his hand and I place my hand in his.

"You're cold," he says, pulling my hand up and breathing hot air on it.

I smile and say, "I'm fine."

He ignores me and shoves my hand in his jacket pocket with his. "Let's find out what he knows."

Two hours later, we get off the freeway and head down a road with nothing on each side of it but dirt. For what seems like forever, we drive down a few different roads that all look the same, until we finally see a house in the distance. The maps on my phone tell me that it's his house.

What if he doesn't live here anymore?

Noel and I get out of his car and walk through the dirt to the front door. He rings the doorbell and I anxiously look around. There aren't any cars in the driveway, but there might be in the garage.

Suddenly, the door pops open and we're face to face with the man from the profile photo. He looks between us suspiciously and barks, "What do you want?"

"Are you Martin Schletenberg?" I ask before he can close the door in our faces.

His face turns pale and he starts to close the door. Noel sticks his foot in the doorway, preventing the door from closing. "We just have a few questions. We mean no harm."

"I'm not him," Martin snaps, opening the door once more and glaring at us. "You have the wrong person and—" He stops speaking suddenly as he looks at me. "Gemma? Is that you?"

"Yes," I say slowly.

All of his anger leaves his face and he sighs. "Your picture was on the plane. Every chance they got they'd talk about you and show me pictures. They were so proud of you."

My heart pangs and I ask hurriedly, "So you were their pilot? Do you know what happened to them? Please, you have to know something."

"Did anyone follow you?" he asks, peeking around us and glancing around anxiously.

"No," Noel replies.

Martin leans in, whispering, "They made me change my name. Threatened my daughter and her family. If they found out I was talking to you, they'd probably kill me."

I glance at Noel and his eyes harden. "The Hardingtons?"

Martin nods and glances at me. "That day, I was supposed to take your parents to Maryland."

So they lied to me? My stomach twists. "Not South America?"

"No. They got to the airport and we were all set to go when they received a phone call. They told me there was an emergency, but they'd be back. They got in a taxi and left. Before leaving, they paid me to wait with their plane. Never saw them again."

Did the Hardingtons call them? "So you eventually just left the plane? What happened to it?"

"The Hardingtons came that night. Forced me out of the plane and into their car. They made me start the process of changing my name and told me never to speak about your parents again. I'm sorry, I don't know what happened to them."

I breathe deeply, letting it all soak in.

Truthfully, I knew Martin might not have the answers I'm looking for. But he gave me so much that the timeline of that day is becoming clearer. And to thank him, we shouldn't stick around here any longer, just in case.

"Thank you, I promise we won't come back again," I tell him with a small smile.

"Take care, Gemma." He glances at Noel. "And you too, Noel."

I flick my eyes to Noel whose mouth drops open in surprise. "You know who I am?"

Martin nods. "How could I not? You're the spitting image of him. And those are your mother's eyes. Her parents would always tell me that you were the best friend Gemma could ever have. I know you mean no harm and you aren't your parents, kid. Take care of each other." He glances between us and closes the door gently.

Noel whirls around and starts to walk to his car. I follow after him and slide in the passenger side, closing the door behind me.

"I guess this is it. I'll never know any more than this," I remark, staring out the window.

The only people who have the answer refuse to tell me.

"I'm sorry, precious," Noel says, touching my hand and rubbing his finger over it. "I wish I had all the answers."

"You helped plenty. Without that file, I never would've been able to find Martin."

Noel squeezes my hand. "There's something I need your help with tonight."

"What can I help you with?" I ask curiously.

"I'm sorry I didn't tell you before," he says regretfully. "There are some people that need our help."

He explains and with every passing second, I feel more horrified. "Of course, I'll help."

CHAPTER TWENTY-TWO

Noel

G emma and I go through the back entrance of the building, meant for the cleaning crew that arrive long after everyone else goes home. They're here tonight and already in the building so the door is unlocked.

My parents can't find out that we're here.

We'll stay in my office until later. This room and the ground floor are the only areas they aren't allowed to go. Once it's gotten late enough, I'll go out to the lobby and check and see if either of my parents' cars are parked in their reserved spaces in the parking lot.

As soon as I know for sure they're gone, we'll sneak all of their captives out. That's the main objective, but it's also the perfect opportunity to attempt to find the formula for Space Dust and grab a sample to take with me. I keep checking the program I made and they still haven't punched in the formula for it so they must still be keeping it in their old drive.

The only roadblock to cracking it is the password.

"What are you thinking so hard about?" Gemma whispers as we tiptoe down the hall.

We stop right outside the door to my office and I unlock it quickly, letting Gemma inside first and following behind her. I lock it firmly behind us and stare through the one-way glass.

"Just going over the plan," I murmur and pull my phone out to check the time.

It's only ten. We still have a lot of time to wait. I just hope tonight isn't one of those nights where they stay in the lab all night long. If they do, we're screwed and it'll have to wait until tomorrow.

Only thing is those people can't wait any longer.

"We have a lot of time to kill. What should we do?" Gemma asks leaning against the desk.

"Sleep."

She laughs. "If you sleep this whole building will hear you snoring."

"Well, I can always tell you every joke I know. What do you call two guys tied up and stuck in a window?"

She blinks. "I don't know, what?"

"Kurt and Rod."

She laughs a little and shakes her head. "Corny. I don't think I can stand to hear your jokes for at least the next three hours, sorry."

Closing the distance between us, I keep her pinned to the desk.

"There's another option," I murmur, caressing her cheek. "It'll keep both of us busy for a while. We won't even realize how much time has passed."

Her mouth opens slightly and she glances back at my desk. Is she remembering how I ate her out on top of it?

I turn her chin back to face me and stare down into her eyes. "Let's put this desk to good use, precious."

"Or we could talk?" she suggests.

Leaning down to her ear, I bite her earlobe and whisper, "I'd rather fuck you on top of this desk."

"Can you at least turn the lights off?" she asks breathlessly.

I pull away and frown. "Why?"

She looks around the room. "Because we've never done it with the lights on before. In the closet, we couldn't see each other well and in the hotel room the moonlight streamed in a few places, but again, it was mostly dark. I'd just feel better if the lights were off."

When she meets my eyes again, I sink onto my knees in front of her and undo the button of her pants. "I see that I have to remind you again how beautiful your body is."

After pulling them down, I yank her panties down and push my head between her thick thighs. I push them open slightly to expose her clit and latch on to it like a starving man.

She gasps as soon as my tongue brushes against it.

"You're the most beautiful person in the world, Gem." I grip the backside of her thighs and let my hands travel up to her ass. "Every inch of you was made for me."

I suck her clit into my mouth and feel her quivering underneath me. Her hand threads through my hair. She lets out the tiniest moan and it goes straight to my cock.

She pants as I suck harder. I glide my tongue down into her channel to have a taste of her and groan when it explodes over my tongue. She's so wet for me. The knowledge of it makes my cock so hard it hurts.

I free my cock and stand up. Her eyes are glazed over with want as I slide her glasses off. Crossing the room, I place them on the side table to prevent anything from happening to them. When I get back to her, her pants and panties are sitting in a pile next to her.

"From your cute feet to your thick thighs all the way to your wide hips and your waist, to these pretty tits," I grab both of them over her shirt, "to that gorgeous smile. You're all mine. Try and see yourself as I see you."

Her eyes get teary as I grip her legs and pull her up to sit on the desk.

Pressing a kiss to her forehead, I pull her arms up so they can go around my shoulders. She widens her legs and I edge forward until I feel her pussy against the tip of my cock.

"I don't have any condoms," I murmur.

"You never seem to have them," I tease. "We've been fine twice, one more time won't hurt."

But it's more than okay with me, because if we do this and she ends up pregnant, it'll be the best thing to happen to me. It's no longer a worry. In the future, I'm sure I'll wear condoms from now on, but if it were to happen, I know there'd be no greater thing in the world than to have Gem be the mother of my child.

"I'm okay with it. If you get pregnant a few years sooner, then it's what was meant to happen."

She shudders slightly as I slowly edge my way in. Groaning low in my throat, I let myself become completely immersed in her. Closing my eyes, I still for a moment and enjoy the feeling of her clenching around me, like a velvet fist.

"Are you going to move?" she asks softly, wiggling her hips.

I blink my eyes open to find her staring expectantly at me with want and desire. Fuck, I'm a lucky man.

Pulling out slightly, I thrust back in and a moan escapes her mouth.

"I'm sorry," I groan, pumping my hits fast. "I can't go slow today."

"It's okay," she pants. "It feels so good, Noel."

Her face twists with pleasure as I fuck her hard on the table. The sound of myself dipping inside her is music to my ears, coupled with her symphony of tiny moans.

While they might be unable to see us, if we're too loud they'll hear us and know someone is in here.

Her mouth opens slightly and I take that opportunity to claim her mouth. I thrust my tongue inside and she moans, the sound echoing into my mouth.

Her fingers grip my shoulders hard and I pump myself into her relentlessly. Heat races inside me like quicksilver racing up my spine as I feel myself getting closer.

With the way she's clenching around me, I can tell she's getting closer too.

Panting, I pull my mouth away from her and breathlessly say, "Be a good girl precious and come for me. Don't hold back. Your voice this time. I need to hear it."

She pants, nodding slightly as I fuck her hard, pushing her closer and closer to both of our limits. "I'm coming, Noel." A loud breathy moan fills the air and I feel her warm heat clench around me. Immediately, I let myself release inside her, filling her full of my cum.

Her whole body twitches and I groan at how her pussy twitches around me.

"You're so fucking good, Gem."

She smiles at me, pressing a kiss to my jaw. Both of us are a little sweaty now. I pick her up in my arms, intending to set her down on the floor when she looks at something behind me and shakes her head.

"What is it?" I whisper, turning my head to see a worker standing in front of my office.

She tilts her head, staring into the glass. Her eyes are so focused, it's almost as if she can see us though I know it's impossible.

Gem's legs wrap around my hips and I hold her tight to me.

The woman steps up to the door and knocks. "Is someone there? No one should be in there right now. Cynthia? You know we're not allowed to clean in there."

Gem glances worriedly at me and my eyes practically pop out of my head as I feel her tightening around my cock.

She's worried and not doing it on purpose, but holy fuck. I clench my jaw as I pull her flush against my chest. I lean down to her ear and whisper so quietly, I can barely even hear myself. "You're driving me insane, Gem. Don't move until I can set you back down safely."

In some spots, this floor likes to creak. With how close this lady is, she might be able to hear it. And then, we'll be in trouble.

Gem's eyebrows furrow for a moment before a look of realization comes over her face.

She nods in understanding.

Good.

Suddenly a mischievous smile forms on her face. Her hands tighten as I feel her lift her hips slightly and sink back into place.

I grit my teeth as a shock of electricity flows through me. I can't even cover my mouth.

She repeats the action and I shiver. I mouth "Why are you doing this?"

She mouths back "because it's fun."

As she repeats the action very slowly, I bite my lip hard. The lady is on her phone outside now.

Why can't she do us all a favor and go away?

As she bounces herself up and down my cock again, I feel my last thread of control snap. I grip her hips and force her up and down on my cock. She throws her head back, gripping on to me tightly as I fuck her hard. She meets every thrust, pushing herself down so eagerly I swallow back a moan.

Her want and need is just as high as mine. I'm getting so fucking close again.

I grind myself into her as I both watch and feel her orgasm again. Her hands shake as her mouth stays open in a silent cry. Thrusting all the way inside, I stay still as I pump another load of cum in her.

Relief floods through me as I watch the woman outside shrug and leave.

Thank God.

Gem unwraps her legs from behind me and I set her down, letting myself slide out of her. Her chest heaves and her cheeks flush as she clenches her thighs together. But it's no use. I watch as my cum trails down her legs and joins the few droplets that hit the floor earlier.

"How am I ever going to go back to using condoms after this?" I ask, with a smirk as she shakily grabs her panties.

"Gem, be a good girl and let me see for myself how I ruined you."

She turns a bright red. "No. You're...getting hard again."

I glance down at myself to find she's right, I'm already semi-hard again. "So I am. But that's what you do to me, Jewel."

Slowly, she turns around and widens her stance, bending

over my desk. I back away slightly and take in the sight of my pearly white cum glistening at her entrance.

Oh fuck.

"One more time, precious," I say, feeling myself harden completely for her. "I should take a picture and show you how sexy you look with my cum inside you. It made me fully hard."

She stays silent and I groan at the anticipation, until she finally whispers, "Okay."

I close the distance between us and thrust right into her. Covering her with my body, I grip her hands against the desk. "I love you, Gem."

She arches her body off the desk to minimize the creaking.

"I love you too, Noel," she says breathlessly as my hips meet hers.

Gemma is everything and more.

At 2 AM, the cleaning crew is long gone. I go out quietly to make sure my parents are gone. When I stare out the glass doors, I sigh gratefully when I see neither of their cars.

It's happening tonight, then.

They'll be free, I'll try to get in the computer and get the formula. If I'm successful, I'll go to the FDA and show them so they can begin an investigation and eventually stop them from creating any more Space Dust.

I rush back to Gem, finding her relaxed in my chair and her feet on the desk. "They're gone. Are you ready?"

When I left she was dozing off and now she looks a little sleepy.

I think I wore her out. I think she'd agree it was worth it though.

"Yes, I'm ready." She moves her feet off the desk and stands up, moving around the desk.

I close the door behind us and lock it. We head down the hall to the elevator and wait for it to show up. When we get in, I go around to the controls and press the button for the ground floor.

She stares at the doors as they close. "I hope the people in the cages are okay."

"They should be. They wouldn't have anyone to experiment on if they passed away."

She nods. "That's true, but I think your parents wouldn't hesitate to replace anyone who does die."

She isn't wrong. Sighing, I watch as the doors open. The white hallway is longer than it usually seems. Maybe because it's the last obstacle standing in my way.

When Gem and I stop at the doors at the end, I punch my birthday into the keypad and wait for it to click, except it doesn't.

Instead, there's an error sound that I've never heard before.

What the fuck?

I press the code in once more and the same sound comes out.

"What's going on?" Gemma asks.

"They changed the fucking code," I shout angrily. "They can't do that."

I should've done it earlier instead of waiting around.

"They used a date before, maybe the new code is another date," Gem muses.

I stare at the keypad. Maybe they used the day the company was founded?

I enter the code for it and the error sound comes out.

Well, I guess I'll cross that one off the list.

After going through their birthdays, their parents' birthdays, the day they graduated college, and the day they got their masters, I'm still at a loss. All of them seem like incredibly useless pieces of trivia.

"Have you tried their anniversary?"

I glance at Gemma and back to the keypad and type it in slowly. It clicks and I breathe a sigh of relief. Thank God.

Wait.

If they're use their anniversary code for this, maybe they're using it for their computers too.

"Come on." I hold the door open for Gem and allow her to step inside first.

It's been years since she's been in here. The last time she was, everything changed in our lives and because of that moment, we were separated for years.

I lead the way to their offices and open my father's door.

She glances around the room and I point over to the wall behind his desk. "This is it." I cross over to it and move the award out of the way to expose the button.

"I just want to warn you, It's not pretty," I say, glancing back at her. "Some of these people look haunted by what my parents have put them through."

Her lips flatten and she nods. I press the button and the wall opens. Walking inside the tunnel, that chemical smell floods my nose.

I'm halfway through the tunnel when I hear a disturbing sound. Someone is faintly humming. No one should be here. There aren't even any cars in the parking lot.

We have two choices. Either we continue forward or we go back. Do they have a guard that stays here when they're gone? But they have an alarm, so why would they need a guard?

No, it has to be one of their employees.

If they see me, they'll only want to call my parents. I'd have enough time to get them out of their cages, but I'd lose my chance to get the formula.

Still, my gut tells me that the right thing to do would be to continue forward.

But I won't make this decision alone.

I turn back to Gemma who looks back at me with resolve.

"Keep going," she whispers.

Facing forward, I keep going until the tunnel opens to the lab.

The moment I step out, I'm met with the back of the person humming. A familiar head of hair and that sweater.

I wish it could've been anyone else. He's fucking annoying. Pulling the keys out of my pocket, they jingle a little as I hand them back to Gemma. There's no way he'll allow us to free them.

If he did, he'd be fired, and he's making too much money off of this.

Bradley freezes and turns around slowly muttering, "No one should be here right now." He eyes the both of us. "What are you two doing here? It's past office hours. Leave."

I cross my arms. "Last time I checked, I partially own this fucking building, so you should leave, Bradley."

His eyes lower to the keys in Gemma's hand and the smirk vanishes from his face. "So that's what you're doing. Trying to play the hero and free the people in the cages." He walks toward us. "What if they don't want to be rescued? What if they're enjoying their daily dose of drugs and loving that they're contributing to helping us learn more about them?"

Gem sighs. "Is that how you rationalize it to your little pea brain? That these people enjoy being taken away from their lives because they're helping some company with their work and receiving no compensation whatsoever?" She shakes her head with disgust.

Bradley shrugs. "Makes plenty of sense to me."

I motion discreetly with my finger for her to go left.

"Well, it stops for these people tonight," she snaps and dashes to the left.

Bradley's jaw drops and he starts to follow her. "No fucking way I'm letting you do that."

I hasten my pace and step right in between them. "You are. You're going to allow her to open every cage and let them all go."

His mouth tightens and he hisses, "I'll be fired if I allow you to do that." Turning around quickly, he rushes over to a table and I follow him, grabbing his arm as he reaches for his phone.

"Noel, I'm halfway through and none of the keys are working," Gem yells.

"One of them has to work. Keep trying."

I tighten my grip around his wrist and he sighs and says in a low tone, "I'm going to enjoy this."

His fist delivers an uppercut to my jaw before I can blink.

The abruptness of it causes me to temporarily let go of him. The sound of the phone ringing on speaker makes my heart race and I deliver a punch right back, knocking him on his ass.

The phone is still ringing when I grab it so I hang up quickly and hit it against the edge of the table, making sure it cracks before I drop it to the ground and step on it.

Bradley gets up quickly, launching himself at me. I kick him right in the gut before he can reach me.

Out of the corner of my eye, I notice people racing into the tunnel.

They don't have a way to get home, but at least they'll be free. They'll eventually find their way back to their families.

But it's going to take a while for Gem to open every cage. There's at least fifty of them.

Bradley clutches his stomach. "Ow, fuck."

I stalk toward him to grab him off the floor when I hear a shout.

"I'm only trying to help," Gem says to one of them.

A shriek echoes through the air. "No!"

Bradley pulls a syringe out of his pocket and launches himself at me again, swinging it around wildly. I dodge him at every swing until I grab his arm and twist it. He grimaces as I keep bending it.

"Only so much longer before your arm snaps like a twig, Bradley. Drop the syringe."

He opens his hand and it drops to the ground.

"I don't want any more drugs," the voice screams.

Wait. I know that voice. Nancy? The last time I saw her I was injecting her with Space Dust.

My heart pangs and I turn around to face Bradley just in time to see him clock me in the face.

My lip busts open and I catch myself, stumbling backward. I swipe the blood pooling on my lip with my wrist and stalk toward him.

Fucker. I'm going to grab him and knock him out completely.

Full of rage and anger, I stalk toward him and he backs up until he takes off in a full on sprint. I run after him, passing by the cages on the other side that Gem hasn't gotten to yet. He's heading to the back of the lab where the cabinet of drugs are.

Before he's able to get there, I catch up to him, tackling him to the ground. I sit on his back and slam his fucking head into the ground several times. Each time there's less tension in his body.

I stop when he goes limp.

If only I knew he was truly knocked out. I hear the sound of footsteps coming from the left and glance up to find Gem with the keys in her hands. "I'm almost done with that side. Is everything okay?" She glances down at Bradley.

"Don't worry about me. I got this fucker. Keep doing what you're doing."

She nods. "Maybe when you get a minute you can talk to the girl that's refusing to leave her cage. I think she's one of the students that goes to our school. She's shaking and looks terrified."

Shame fills me all over again thinking about what I did to her. "Talking to me wouldn't help." Since we're being more open and honest, I should tell her exactly what happened. I gulp and squeeze my hand into a fist. "That girl, I know her. She's my friend Nancy. I don't think we're friends anymore. The last time I saw her, my parents forced me to inject her with some Space Dust."

She shakes her head. "That doesn't surprise me. Okay, I'll do whatever I can to convince her." After she walks away, I stare down at Bradley's limp body. Just looking at him annoys me.

I'm sure the person he called was either my mom or dad. And I know exactly how they work. They'll see the missed call and try to call back. When he doesn't answer, they'll try again. When he doesn't answer that time, they'll leave the house for the lab, unable to stop themselves from learning as quick as they can why Bradley didn't answer his phone. Their curiosity will get the better of them.

"You're the exact son my parents wanted and couldn't get," I mutter, staring at the back of his head.

And doing this is the biggest betrayal I could ever commit. Them changing the code was their warning to me. The correct thing to do to stay on their good side would've been to walk away.

Instead, I pushed forward.

There's no other way for me now.

Suddenly, I feel a prick to the side of my neck. My hand shoots up as I try to swipe it away, only to find a syringe there. I yank it out and turn around to find a guy with a crazed look in his eye.

"I hope you get as addicted as I do to this shit. Morning, noon, and night, whenever those times are, I think about it. It's *torture.*"

Gritting my teeth, I touch the injection site. Fuck! How much did he give me? "I'm trying to help you!"

Abruptly, I'm thrown off Bradley's back and in a flash he has me against the ground by the neck. He smiles down at me. "Sweet dreams, Noel. When you wake up, your dear parents will be here to *punish* you accordingly."

I gasp as his grip tightens and he bangs my head into the ground multiple times. At the same time, I flail my hands, reaching for him and kicking out at him as hard as I can. But things start to slowly fade away.

Each thud grows softer and softer until there's nothing but darkness.

CHAPTER TWENTY-THREE

Gemma

As I finally drag Nancy out of the cage, I hear a resounding thud and a groan.

"Noel?" I whisper when I don't receive a response I prop Nancy against the wall and run to the end of the aisle making as little noise as possible. Peeking over, I get there just as Bradley kneels on the ground in front of Noel.

"Not so tough now, are you?" he asks with a sinister laugh.

There's a man on Noel's other side. One of the men I just freed who glances at me with wide eyes and backs away slowly, before breaking into a run and leaving.

My heart clenches as Bradley rises from the floor and I get a clear look at Noel's face. His face is bruising in multiple places and his eyes are closed.

They knocked him out.

Did that man help because Noel injected him too or for a different reason?

Bradley laughs at Noel, clearly enjoying every minute.

Backing up, I frantically gaze around the tables close to me for something. Anything to get Bradley away from him so he can wake up.

I rifle through the drawer, only finding papers. Those won't fucking help me.

Panicking, my hands start to shake and I grip the drawer angrily. Something. I have to find something. As I close the drawer, I turn to go to the next table when I run right into Nancy. She scratches at her arm and I stare down at the needle marks decorating them.

"Noel is my friend," she says softly, "and I hate that guy. I can help you."

"No," I say immediately. "You've been through enough. You should walk out of here and go home."

She breathes deeply, shaking her head. "I can't until I know Noel is okay. Follow me." Whirling around she staggers down the aisle a few feet until she stops at a table, gesturing to the drawer. "That one has something you can use."

Yanking it open, I'm met with a bunch of syringes, all with the letter S on them. S as in what?

"Is it a drug or...?" I ask, looking at Nancy.

"Calms you down," she whispers, blinking erratically and wiping the sweat off her forehead.

And then it clicks. Sedative. That's what the S stands for.

"Thanks, Nancy. I'll figure out a way to get this in him."

If only I knew exactly how powerful one is. I grab another one and push it into my pocket in case the first one doesn't do very much.

Backtracking, I hurry to the back of the lab, keeping the first syringe concealed behind my arm. I watch as Bradley slaps the hell out of him, over and over. "Wake up, Noel so I can slap you around some more."

My stomach twists as I approach them.

He straightens in surprise, eyeing me. "Gemma, you might have been able to free everyone on that side, but I'm not letting that happen over here. I'm not opposed to knocking you out too."

I bite my lip and sigh. "I'm sad to hear you say that Bradley."

I try to stare at him with as much admiration as I can manage.

Tugging my top down slightly, I expose the tops of my breasts and thrust my chest out.

I feel so awkward doing this, but I can't show a moment's hesitation a moment's hesitation because this has to work.

His eyes shift downward just as I was hoping they would. "Wouldn't you rather *talk* instead?"

I edge closer to him until I stop at his side.

As much as it kills me not to kneel down and check on Noel, I can't show I have any interest at all in his well being.

I flutter my eyelashes. "Well?"

His hazel eyes meet mine. "I think I'm starting to see why Brick and his friends wanted you so bad."

"You do?" I ask innocently, touching his arm.

Inwardly, I cringe.

He leans his head down. "You know I've been so busy lately and it's been a while, how about you suck me off and maybe I'll think about letting you leave here unharmed?"

I smile at him. "Actually, I'd rather knock you the hell out." I flip the syringe over and jab it straight into his neck, pushing the liquid in quickly. His mouth opens in surprise and he's so shocked he doesn't even have a chance of not getting a full dose of this sedative.

His hand touches mine, forcing me to yank it out. I let it drop the floor and watch as he stares at it.

It's completely empty.

He glances up at me, his lip curling. "You bitch."

"That's right." In seconds, I watch him topple over, barely missing Noel.

Bradley murmurs something, slurring his words.

I guess there's still some fight left in him. Best to put him completely to sleep for now.

Squatting, I pull the second syringe from my pocket and inject it into his neck. His eyes roll into the back of his head and I stand up, satisfied, dropping the syringe to the ground and hurrying to Noel.

Picking his head off the ground, I search for any signs of blood by threading my fingers through his hair and feeling around. I don't feel anything wet, but I pull my hand back out to check anyway.

That's a very small piece of good news.

I touch his cheek and smooth his hair back. "Noel."

His chest rises and falls.

"Noel," I say insistently.

With every second that passes, a sense of dread fills me. What if he has sustained some internal damage from this? I should call 911.

Reaching into my pocket, I pull out my phone. As my fingers touch the screen, I feel a hand touch my arm.

"Oh, he's awake," Nancy murmurs behind me.

I jump when I remember she's still here, and gaze at his face to find his eyes open. "I heard you, Gem." His eyes shift to Bradley. "You did that?"

I nod and point back to Nancy. "Couldn't have done it without her help though."

His lips flatten and he grunts as he pulls himself to a sitting position. "I'm so sorry Nancy. I hope we can still be friends."

Her voice is jittery as she she says, "Yes."

He smiles gratefully and winces. "I don't feel right. That drug has me feeling funny already."

I rise off the floor. "Just let me finish the people on that side and then do this side and we can go."

A voice rings out. "Actually, you won't be going anywhere."

Horror and fear wash over Nancy's face and she immediately hides beneath the table in front of us.

Noel's jaw tics as he stands up next to me. His hands curl into fists as both of his parents come into sight, coming around the corner. They take their time walking slowly to us.

"We failed," I whisper to Noel.

"Not yet, Jewel. Not yet," he whispers back.

They stop in front of us and his dad's eyebrows furrow. "I can't say I'm surprised it's come to this. Even though I can't say I'm surprised, it's still very disappointing."

"What's disappointing is your complete disregard for others," I snap. "So for once, why don't you just do the right thing? Let us free these people and stop making Space Dust."

"No can do, honey," Mrs. Hardington says with a smile. "I'm afraid we've come too far to let things end this way."

His dad clears his throat. "There's only one way you're getting out of here, son."

Noel's hand clutches mine as he glances between them. "And that is?"

His mom glances at me with a hardened expression, the

smile on her face dissipating like it was never even there. She looks more intimidating with it gone. "With her dead as a doornail of course."

Noel's hand tightens and I can feel the rage rolling off of him in waves.

"That's not happening," he growls.

"It is," Mr. Hardington firmly states. "And you'll have a choice to make yourself. Since it's obviously going to take some reconditioning to get you back to the way you were before she came into your life again, we'll do one of two things. You can either go back in the closet for a few years or you can go back to the mental hospital. We won't make you do both this time."

"I'd say that's pretty generous," Mrs. Hardington says with a smile.

Fear and worry for him fill me. I squeeze his hand this time.

His parents stare him down, waiting for him to make a decision. I anxiously stare up at him as his mouth opens and closes.

He shakes his head. "I'm choosing neither."

Mrs. Hardington chuckles. "Okay, have it your way. You can pick later, after she's dead."

Noel pushes me behind him. "You aren't touching her."

His mom blinks and turns to his dad and they both burst out laughing.

"What's so funny?" I mutter.

They slowly stop laughing and Mrs. Hardington smirks. "We won't be killing you. *He* will." She points to Noel.

"You'd have me kill her even if she's pregnant with my child?" Noel asks.

It's not true, but if it's the only lie that will stop all this and allow me to live, I'll sell it as well as I can. "I'm already out of the first trimester. Soon I'll know what the gender is."

Mrs. Hardington glances from my stomach to my face. "Even if that's true, and I'm not saying it isn't, I don't care. And I wouldn't care even if you were carrying a boy. Another heir can be made, from the proper and true future Mrs. Hardington, Collette Goldsworthy."

I choke on my saliva, coughing hard and clutching my throat. "What?"

I glance at Noel who shakes his head. "So you aren't giving up on that."

So he already knew they wanted him and Collette together?

"She would never," I mumble.

"It doesn't matter if she would never. Her father has already agreed to it. It'll happen, we have an understanding."

"He doesn't own her," I retort. "Just like you two don't own Noel."

His mother takes a step closer. "We don't own him, no, but it's our responsibility to lead him down the correct path. That is exactly what we're doing." She holds the syringe out to Noel. "This is a concentrated dose of Space Dust. It'll kill her in a few minutes. She won't suffer, she'll just fall asleep and all your problems will be over."

Noel stares down at her palm and I hold my breath as he grabs the syringe, pushing the plunger down. He empties the contents onto the floor. "If you want to kill her, you'll have to kill me first."

Mrs. Hardington's eyes turn absolutely chilling as she turns to her husband. "Go ahead, honey."

His dad steps forward to grab Noel and Noel punches him right in the face. His dad grunts and returns it. Mrs. Hardington moves around them, stepping toward me.

There's another syringe in her hand. I back up slightly as she edges me closer to the back of the lab.

A sinister smile forms on her face when suddenly, a leg shoots out from under the table and she trips right over it, falling face first to the ground. She shrieks at the unexpected fall.

Nancy.

As the sound of Noel and his father trading blows echos throughout the room, Nancy's arm shoots out and she gives me a thumbs up before retreating back under the table fully.

Darting forward, I grab the syringe and sit myself on her back. She grunts and screeches as she attempts to move. Pulling up her pant leg, I hold the syringe above Mrs. Hardington's lower leg.

I hate that I have to pull it on Noel's mom. Somewhere inside, I know he still loves her because she's his mother despite the terrible things she's done. I just hope it works so I'm not forced to do something that I don't want to.

She squirms underneath me as I hold it above her skin. "Stop fighting if you want her to live."

Mr. Hardington's hands drop as he eyes me. He slams his fist against the table closest to us.

Pulling the keys out of my pocket, I toss them to Noel. "Go and get everyone else out."

He catches them. "Are you sure you're going to be okay?"

I nod. "I'm sure. As long as your dad makes no sudden movements. If he does the only thing I'll know for sure is that he doesn't truly care about his wife."

Noel gazes down at his mom for a moment before darting past me to the left side of the lab.

I stare down Mr. Harrington and keep my full weight on his wife. There's no way she's strong enough to wiggle out of this, so all I have to do is keep myself like this.

It takes a while, but eventually every single prisoner is released. The cages next to me are finally empty and wide open. When Noel gets back to us, he glances from his dad to me as if he's waiting for me to decide what to do next.

There's only one thing I can think of. Now that I have them here and they're both pinned, I feel tears welling up in my eyes. My parents' faces flash in my mind.

"Tell me what happened to my parents," I say softly.

Noel's eyes widen and he glances at his dad who stays completely still, not moving a muscle. I hold my breath and press the tip of the needle to her skin. "Talk!"

The tension between us rises as Mr. Hardington watches me raise my finger, hovering it above the syringe.

He holds his hand up. "Fine. We'll tell you."

I let the breath in my lungs release and pull the needle back to its position above her skin.

"Your parents helped us to create it. We had a small piece of the formula, but they perfected it to what it is today. Everything would've been fine if they could've kept their eyes on the prize," Mr. Hardington says. "We promised them tons of money if they'd stay on to help us with the distribution of Space Dust."

"But they didn't agree with our methods," Mrs. Hardington adds. "We told them we planned to get people on it and experiment on them. At the time, we experimented on two of our assistants. Both of them volunteered and easily got hooked on it. Their reactions are what scared your parents. Over time, they grew distant. And then one day, they tried to talk us out of producing it, period."

Yes. That was the day we overheard them talking.

"They had always kept the formula for it close to them, always keeping it out of our reach," Mr. Hardington says, his mouth tightening.

"Gem and I overheard you guys that day. That was the day I got rid of all of the papers on the desk they used and deleted all the files. I thought I fixed the problem," Noel says frowning.

Mr. Hardington locks eyes with him. "You thought you did. But in reality, us asking them for the formula was a test. A test they failed horribly."

My jaw drops as he continues.

"We thought if they slept on it, they'd bring it back to us nicely the next day and we could go as we were. But they chose not to. You see, you might have destroyed the original paper with the formula, but we'd already copied it down piece by piece without them knowing."

Noel looks incredulously at him and I feel my stomach twisting nervously.

"So what you're saying is you never lost the formula to begin with? From then to now, you always had it?"

His dad nods.

"So then why? Why didn't you start using it earlier than just three years ago?"

His dad looks past me at Bradley and grunts. "Bastard talks too much."

"It all goes back to your parents, really, Gemma. We had eyes on them and found out they planned a trip to meet someone in Maryland. It wasn't hard to figure out that they were meeting with a member of the FDA. It took us five years to figure out just who that was and eliminate them," Mrs. Hardington says in a nonchalant tone.

I cover my mouth. So Martin was right about them going to Maryland and not South America. Then what was the emergency call he mentioned that made them get off the plane?

"Then what happened to them?" I ask as my eyes start getting blurry with tears.

"I was lucky enough to meet your Aunt Cindy once. She gave me her number without hesitation. I finally had a use for it. I had Cindy call your mother and tell her that you had gone missing," Mrs. Hardington says.

Cindy. Everything around me seems to slow to a halt, including the air in my lungs.

They got off their plane for me.

"Nothing happened to me that day," I murmur. "I warmed up leftovers from the night before that evening and went to bed."

"We know," Mr. Hardington says coldly. "They kept calling us because they thought we kidnapped you. We pulled up at your house right after they did that evening. They didn't go inside, but we saw them leave your bedroom window. They looked relieved and that's when we grabbed them."

I dig my fingers into my palm, feeling an enormous wave of guilt hit me.

"What happened then?" I ask solemnly.

Mr. Hardington gestures to a cage. "We kept them here."

My eyes widen as I stare into one. "For how long?"

"Years," Mrs. Hardington responds. "We never experimented on them. We waited, hoping that they'd eventually change their minds and join us again. Their minds were brilliant. How could we ever live with ourselves if we eradicated minds like theirs?"

Mr. Hardington sighs. "Last summer–"

"Last summer?" I choke. Every year since that first year, I was so sure they were dead. That the Hardingtons had killed them, but all that time, they were *here*, suffering.

"Last summer," Mr. Hardington repeats. "Right before the

start of the school year, we found out your mother was sick. Thyroid cancer. She'd been hiding it well. If we had known, we would've gotten her treatment before it progressed. But it killed her within two days of us finding out. Your father was completely indifferent after that and two days later, we found him dead too. No evidence of suicide or any kind of blunt force trauma, he was just *gone*."

I hold my hand steady over her leg as tears flood my cheeks. I hold back the urge to sob. Both of them deserved so much better than to just die in cages as if they were animals. My poor dad had to watch her pass without being able to hold her and then had to suffer knowing she was somewhere he couldn't be.

I know his heart broke.

"I'm so sorry, Gem," Noel says gazing at me.

All of a sudden it hits me. Noel.

My lip quivers and I gasp, "Noel. I'm so sorry. All this time, I blamed you. I thought what we did that day is what sealed my parents' fate, but you truly had nothing to do with it. It was me all along. Just me."

"Gem, don't do that," Noel murmurs, running a hand through his hair. "You didn't know. It seemed like the logical conclusion. I would've felt the same way if I were you. And please, don't blame yourself. The real people responsible are standing right fucking here and they deserve to suffer for this. Keep that syringe right where it is."

He turns to his dad. "Starting now, your whole life is going to change. You're going to sign on the fucking dotted line. You and Mom."

Noel pulls his phone out and I watch as he turns to make a call. He speaks in such a low tone that I can't hear. When he turns back around, he shoves his phone in his pocket. "The notary is on her way. I know you have papers somewhere you planned to use in the future for when this company becomes mine. Now is the time to use them."

His dad looks at him with unbelieving eyes.

"The papers," Noel barks. "Now!"

Him and his dad leave the aisle and I wait patiently for them to come back.

I have nothing at all to say to Mrs. Hardington, so I stay quiet.

When they come back, they have a notary in tow.

The notary gives us a weird look as she crouches on the ground and gets a signature from Mrs. Hardington.

After going over a few more things, the notary takes the papers and leaves, letting us know that it's done and it'll be filed in a few hours.

Noel owns Hardington Pharmaceuticals.

Mr. Hardington glances between us. "What are you going to do with us now?"

Noel smirks. "I think you deserve a taste of your own medicine for a while."

"After all we've done for you," his mom snaps.

"Careful, Mom, before I send you to real jail."

"Fine," Mr. Hardington hisses. "Enjoy our hard-earned reputation. And I wish you all the luck telling Antoure you don't plan on moving forward with Space Dust."

"Antoure?" I ask in confusion.

Noel exclaims, "What does Callan's dad have to do with this?"

"You didn't read the fine print," Mrs. Hardington says. "Antoure owns 50% of this company. He was our original investor and as our best friend, we gave it to him. We wouldn't be around if it wasn't for him."

"I thought Grandpa helped you start up?" Noel replies.

"He did. He gave us half of what we needed. The other half came from Antoure," Mr. Hardington comments.

A flash of worry goes over Noel's face. It's quickly replaced by anger.

"I'll deal with Antoure Goldsworthy later. Right now, I'm dealing with the two of you. I hope you're both satisfied with the way this all turned out." Noel glances at me. "Gemma, use a small dose of that and then hand it to me."

"Are you sure?" I ask.

Mrs. Hardington screeches, "No. Don't."

Hearing her protest only makes me want to do it more, so I do. Just a little. I hold up the syringe and watch as he grabs it from me and injects his dad with a small bit.

"Drug addicts that need to go to a mental hospital to get in their right minds," Noel says with a small smile. "Who knows how long it could take?"

"Could be years," I murmur with a shrug.

The thought of them going away makes me feel a little glad, but it doesn't take away the hurt I feel knowing that my parents were so close for so long. And that of all people, Cindy knew they came back to check on me. She never once mentioned it. She was satisfied knowing that she was on easy street without them.

She'll pay for her role in this too as soon as I find her.

———

We took Bradley straight to the police station and told them he attacked us. They didn't care very much about what I had to say, but when they saw Noel's bruised face, they believed him pretty quickly. Noel is pressing assault charges on him.

It turns out a few people from the cages have gone to the police too and claimed that he assaulted them as well. None of the police officers brought up Hardington Pharmaceuticals, so I have to wonder exactly what they each told the police.

After getting his parents settled in at the same facility Noel stayed in, we leave and head straight for the Goldsworthy mansion. The people at the facility didn't say very much when Noel handed them a hefty sum of money to ensure their compliance.

Noel seems okay, but he's silent the whole way.

Callan gets out of his Lambo as we pull up behind him.

He yawns and stretches and Mera pops out of the passenger side.

"What are we doing here, Noel?" Callan asks. "Is this about the thing with my sister? I don't ever want to hear about that shit again."

"No," Noel says quickly.

"What thing with Collette?" Mera asks.

"So Callan knows about it too?" I exclaim.

"I was there when it happened," Callan responds with a shrug. "One of the most uncomfortable dinners in my fucking life. My best friend and my sister. The only thing worse than that would be my sister and Silverstone."

"Good thing neither will happen," Noel says with a small smile. "Now about why you're here. Did you know your dad owns half of HP?"

Callan scratches his head. "I didn't know that. Makes sense though. Our parents have been best friends since childhood. If my dad saw a way to make more money through other people, I know he'd take it. So what can I help with?" Callan glances from Noel to I. "Both of you look like you haven't slept all night long."

"We didn't," Noel says in a low tone. "I have my parents' shares of their company now. They don't own Hardington

Pharmaceuticals anymore. I need you to come with me and force your dad to give up his shares so I'll own it completely."

"How the fuck did that happen?" Callan asks in confusion.

"A lot of things fucking happened. It's nothing I want to talk about right now," Noel snaps.

I glance at him with worry. He's coming off Space Dust and I think it's making him a little testy.

"Sorry," he murmurs to Callan. "Let's go."

He moves around the car and hurries up the steps to the porch, stopping right outside the French doors.

Callan follows behind and steps around him. Pulling the keys out, he unlocks the door and moves aside, letting the four of us go in first.

When we get in, Callan walks straight through the foyer.

I gaze up in awe of the beauty of the mansion. This is where Callan grew up.

"Come on, Gem," Noel says. Shifting my gaze back down, I find Noel, Callan, and Mera waiting for me.

"Sorry." Hearing about mansions like these and seeing them are two different things.

Callan leads the way to the dining room where the table is set for two. His mom is seated at one end scrolling on her phone and his dad is on the other, eating his breakfast.

Both of them look up with surprise when we walk in.

"Callan," Mr. Goldsworthy says slowly, straightening, "you never come here this early."

He doesn't look like he was shot eight months ago. That's a sure sign that he'll be back at the helm of SGU soon.

"You're right. I need you to do me a favor," Callan replies, crossing the room to him. Noel is right behind him while Mera and I stay standing near the doorway.

"What do you want?" Mr. Goldsworthy asks, sounding annoyed with him.

Callan glances back at Noel and I hold my breath, hoping that this doesn't get uglier than it needs to be.

"I want your shares," Noel says firmly.

There's silence in the room and I can't see past Noel and Callan to see Mr. Goldsworthy's expression.

I glance at Mrs. Goldsworthy to see she isn't paying one iota of attention to us, scrolling through her phone with a smile.

"Why would you want my shares, Noel? I deserve those for helping that company get started."

"I appreciate that. Really, I do. But moving forward, I'm the only one who's going to have any say in what goes on in the company with my name on it. You having those shares was an agreement with my dad. Both of you decided to unleash Space Dust on the poor unsuspecting people in Southern California. That's not happening anymore."

Mr. Goldsworthy stands immediately. "What do you mean it isn't happening anymore? Just what did you do Noel?"

Callan grabs his dad's shoulder and forces him back down into his seat. "What he did was he took control. Now give him your fucking shares. Call the notary and sign them over to him."

"No," Mr. Goldsworthy responds.

I watch tensely as there's another silence.

Noel lowers his voice to a warning tone. "I've just been through hell the past twelve hours. I'm not leaving here without them." He glances at Callan and Callan nods.

"Give him his shares or I'll tell the whole world that Heath isn't your son," Callan says crossing his arms.

"You wouldn't!" Mr. Goldsworthy yells slamming his fist into the table.

Mrs. Goldsworthy stammers. "N-now wait Callan. You can't do that."

Callan's head whips to her direction. "Then tell this bastard to sign over his shares."

It's obvious to me that Mr. Goldsworthy is too prideful to let the world know that his wife cheated on him and gave birth to another man's baby. And Mrs. Goldsworthy doesn't want to look like a cheater.

"I'll call the notary," Mr. Goldsworthy mutters.

"Put your call on speaker," Callan orders.

Turning away, I breathe a sigh of relief. Mera looks as relieved as I do. She grabs me by the arm and pulls me out of the dining room to the living room only a few feet away.

Both of us sit on the pristine couch.

"So tell me, what happened last night?"

Lowering my head, I stare down at my hands. My glasses start to slide slightly and I push them back up my face.

Thinking about my parents still hurts and I still feel a massive amount of guilt.

But talking to Mera about it will help, just like I talked to her about Noel.

Slowly, I go over the events of last night. I distantly hear someone come to the door at some point while I'm telling her it all.

When I finish, I sigh as a stray tear escapes my eye.

"First of all, fuck your aunt. She can go to hell. Second of all…" Mera grabs me in a tight hug.

I hug her back for a long time. We eventually separate and I wipe my face. "The worst part of it is Noel's parents refuse to tell me where their bodies are."

Mera scowls. "Why? Are they afraid you'll report them to the police?"

"No. Noel promised them over and over that he wouldn't and I did too as long as they'd tell me where their bodies are. But they refused. Maybe they burned them to ashes."

A weird look comes over Mera's face.

While we wait, I get my phone out and unblock a number I never thought I would. I call her and after two rings, she answers.

"My favorite niece, have you had time to reconsider?" Cindy asks in a hopeful tone.

"Yes," I answer brightly.

I've had a lot of time to think about her. What she deserves after finding out the part she played in losing my parents. Something stuck out to me. A memory. Before sucking me dry, there was someone else.

"Please come to my sorority tonight at eight and we can talk about it."

She agrees and I hang up the phone, a smile tugging at my lips.

The blaring sound of my alarm forces me out of a deep slumber. Touching the side of my head, I feel it pounding slightly.

I was having a horribly vivid dream about my parents leaving me. Maybe that's why I have this headache.

Reaching over, I turn my alarm off and slide out of bed.

After Noel got the other shares from Mr. Goldsworthy, he dropped me off here so I could get some sleep. I should've been fully rested by this point, but every time I tried to sleep,

I could only think about how I'll truly never see my parents again.

Somewhere deep inside, I think I was holding out a tiny bit of hope that I'd somehow see them again. As much as I tried to deny it, that hope was still there. But now, it's been mercilessly snuffed out.

But tonight should help a lot.

There's this memory I had of Cindy talking to one of her boyfriends. One of the nastier ones that looked at me as if I wasn't a child. Cindy was drunk and going on and on about how she got a friend of hers to give her money all the time. How gullible her friend was for believing her.

Mina L. Jones.

Well, I found her after some digging and it turns out that Mina was shown a fake obituary for Cindy. All this time, she assumed Cindy was dead, which is why she never tried to find her again and get her money back.

That amount of money totaling to $50k.

What Cindy doesn't know is Mina is on her way right now.

Putting my shoes on quickly, I step outside to the porch and find Cindy across the street waiting for me. She's early.

She waves me over.

I glance to her right at the white van that's in the same spot again. It wasn't there earlier when Noel dropped me off.

Stopping in front of Cindy, on the sidewalk, I force a smile on my face.

"Hi Gemma, did you get your boyfriend to reconsider?"

I nod. "I did. I think you deserve quite a lot actually."

Her mouth drops open in surprise and excitement. "That's so generous of you! How much am I getting then? It's really important that—"

"Nothing," I interrupt her.

"What?" she asks, her mask she presented to the world dropping, hate and greed twisting her features.

I shake my head and sigh. "For years, you talked down to me. Made fun of me. Forced me to work like I was a servant in my own house. However, none of that compares to what you did to my parents and I...I know what you did."

Her eyes widen and she glances around worriedly. "I don't know what you're talking about."

"You do!" I shout pointing at her as tears well up in my eyes. "You deprived me of a life with my parents. You called Noel's parents and told them I was in trouble. Like the good parents they are, they dropped what they were doing to come and help me. And because they came back, they were both captured. And because they were captured, they died."

Cindy noticeably quakes.

"You'll never get another cent from me or anyone else. Mina says hi by the way, and you'll see her any minute," I tell her, crossing my arms.

"Oh fuck, Mina. How did you know about that?" Cindy yells. She runs her hands through her hair and looks down each end of the road. Muttering something under her breath, she shakes her head. "Tonight was my last chance, Gemma. I told them I was getting some money."

Glaring, I narrow my eyes. "Told who?"

Her mouth thins and she pulls her phone out and taps the screen.

"What are you doing?" I ask as I hear the roar of an engine.

I glance over to the right in time to watch the van zoom forward. As I watch the door slide open, I open my mouth to scream, but they grab me and pull me back into the van by my shirt.

My scream only lasts seconds as they cover my mouth with duct tape.

Gazing around the van, I'm horrified to see a group of three men in the back and one in the front driving.

The man closest to me curls his lip. "Your aunt sure was wrong about you helping her. We had a feeling she'd be wrong so we've been watching your every move, waiting and ready to take our payment."

Their payment? As in…me?

I shake my head and scream behind the duct tape. My hands shoot out to peel it off. One of the other men slides forward and keeps my hands together in a tight grip so I can't move them. Another one slides forward to grab my feet. The original one who grabbed me pushes a cloth against my nose, forcing me to breathe in the chemical.

Mera and Callan are at Callan's house. Luella, Ashlynn, and Collette took a trip to Vegas. And Noel said he'd stop by later. I have no idea when that will be.

No one is going to come and help me because they'll have no idea where I am.

As soon as I get wherever they take me, I have to find a way out of this.

After minutes go by, I start feeling more and more faint, until I feel everything fade away completely.

Cold water jolts me awake as I feel it hit me square in the face.

Glancing around, I find myself in the darkness. I can hear the sound of several men talking. Some of them laughing, but there's the sound of deep breathing coming from behind me.

A shiver of fear goes down my spine.

Something else feels different.

That's when I realize, it's my glasses. They're gone.

"Stay still," the man behind me mutters.

He pulls me by my pants, and forces me into a position where I'm on my stomach. His grimy fingers graze my hand as his hand goes to the bottom of my pants. He pulls my pants down quickly and a rush of air hits my backside.

No.

"Cindy really needed money bad so we gave her a loan in the hopes she'd pay us back," he says. "It's always a shame when they can't afford to pay us back."

Lifting my head up, I notice my eyes starting to adjust. This looks like a warehouse.

My blood runs cold when I see a group of men stationed in a corner with what looks to be a lot of things behind them. Are those girls?

Muffled noises fill the air and one of the men in the corner yells, "Shut up!"

The muffled noises stop.

I breathe deeply as I feel a hand pull down my panties.

"Don't worry, I always like to have a small taste before I ship girls like you off to their next destination."

I shake my head and wiggle my hands and feet, desperately trying to get the ropes off of them, but they're tied tight.

Suddenly, I feel the coldness of a blade against my butt. "If you move, I cut you. They won't mind if you're a little cut up either so don't think I won't."

Closing my eyes tightly, I hear the sound of pants being undone.

I don't know why I didn't see this coming. That Cindy

would go so far as to deal with lowlives like these for money. She doesn't even care that her own sister died.

The only person she cares about is herself, always has been.

Tears of anger flood my face and I scream behind the duct tape.

I hear the slap of his dick against my ass at the same time I feel it. His hand touches my ass, opening me up. Shivering, I clench my teeth together and try to prepare for his invasion.

I can get through this, I tell myself. Somehow, I'll figure a way out of this. As I let my head settle on the ground, I hear a shout.

And another.

What are they yelling about?

The man's hand clenches around my ass cheek as he shouts, "What's going on?"

Twisting my head around, I watch as the men in the corner leave their post and go out a door only a few feet away.

From outside, I hear the sound of gunshot after gunshot rip through the air. My heart pounds anxiously in my chest as I stare at that doorway.

"Are they coming back or what?" the man behind me mutters.

He gets his answer when a few seconds later, a shadow comes through. There's no light anywhere. Not from the outside and not from in here.

But I know that form as soon as I see it. And it makes my heart soar. How did they find me?

The shadowy figure glances over to the corner. All of the girls stay quiet. They're probably scared to death wondering who he is.

But I'm not scared.

Yelling through the muffled duct tape, I call his attention to me, all the way toward the back of the warehouse.

The man behind me quickly backs away, holding his hands in the air.

The shadowy figure wastes no time in running over quickly, a gun clutched to his side. As he gets closer, I come face to face with his familiar dark sneakers.

"Did he rape you, Gemma?" he asks, his voice shaky.

I shake my head quickly.

A click of his gun echoes through the air and he speaks slowly. "I bet you didn't think you were going to die tonight when you took her."

The man shouts, "You can have her! Go ahead! I'll let you leave."

Noel chuckles darkly. "You'll *let* me leave. No one is going to be able to stop me from leaving because all of your men are dead except for you."

"What?" the man exclaims.

The sound of a gunshot echoes through the air, followed by the sound of a thud. "And now you are too," he says in a deadly tone.

I lift my head up at the same time as he crouches down. The hardness in his eyes slowly dissipates. "I'm so sorry that it took me so long, Jewel."

Reaching down, he removes the duct tape for my mouth and I gasp at the sting of its removal.

The sound of police sirens in the distance make my stomach drop. "Noel." My voice comes out raspy. "You're going to be in a lot of trouble."

He shakes his head as he cuts through my rope with his pocketknife. "No, I won't. Or should I say, *we* won't." His hands pull my pants and underwear up before I can do it myself. His fingers go under my arm, helping me stand up off the ground. My legs feel shaky. How long have I been tied up for?

After he holsters his gun, he tilts his body to the side and picks me up into his arms in a bridal carry, exactly as he did the night of the hazing.

"Don't look," he murmurs as he carries me out, steeping around the bodies littering the ground.

When we get out, I finally see who "we" is. Noel sets me down next to his car as he hands the gun off to Barnaby while Callan hands his off to Edmund.

Mera rushes over to me, grabbing me in a hug. "I'm so glad you're safe. That was fucking scary."

My heart swells as I hug her back and look over her shoulder at Noel who looks at me with a hint of fear in his eyes.

The police sirens get closer until they finally reach us.

Mera whispers, "Remember, it was me who got taken and my bodyguards came to find me just in time."

She turns around and hobbles right over to the police car.

She'd really do this, for me?

Noel steps over to me and puts his arm around my shoulders, whispering, "Not in trouble."

As the police get her statement, Noel tells me how he saw Cindy running down the street and stopped her. He forced her into telling him that the men she got a loan from some shady men and when she couldn't pay them back with money we refused to give her, she offered me in its place. Once they took me, they'd call it even.

This is the place where they met and she received the money from them.

I got so very lucky that they hadn't switched locations yet. If they had, I would've been on my own desperately trying to form a getaway plan that might've never been possible. Men like them aren't rare. This happens all the time and they get away with it.

All of a sudden, everything seems so fucking overwhelming. I break down and sob, tears streaming down my face as Noel gathers me in his arms and pulls me to his chest.

He rubs my back soothingly as I let it all out.

From here, everything has to get better, doesn't it? The rainbow after a storm and all that. That's what I'm hoping for anyway.

CHAPTER TWENTY-FOUR

Noel

I almost lost her...again. Now that I have her, I don't want to let her out of my sight.

But I know I need to let her breathe.

We leave the police station after giving our statements and I open the car door for her to slide into.

They had more questions for us because we witnessed the whole thing. Mera and Callan were allowed to leave pretty quickly at the urging of Mera's parents.

Both of them were in on it too, happily playing along.

I'm so grateful that they allowed me to save her using their own guns, but I would've gone to save her even if I had none.

She sighs and leans her head against the seat. "I really wish I knew where Cindy was. If she was running to escape prosecution, I'm sure that Mina didn't get to her in time."

I press the start button and my Porsche roars to life.

I shrug. "You never know. Someday maybe, Mina will find her. Cindy can't go too far without a ton of money."

Gem nods, staring out the window. "Can we go somewhere, just you and me?"

Turning around, I back out of the parking spot and head for the exit. In my rearview mirror, I watch as Callan follows me.

Callan.

He offered to go with me, no hesitation whatsoever. That's what a good friend is.

And I don't deserve him.

"Right now?" I ask. It's a Monday and I know she'd be fine ditching her first morning class because she needs the rest, but to want to ditch her other class later today? That isn't like her.

"Don't you want to see everyone back at ZDB? Collette, Luella, and Ashlynn are waiting there for you." They told me they were ditching their morning classes so they could see Gemma as soon as she got back.

She smiles and sighs. "You're right. I should go see them so they can see I'm fine with their own eyes."

Her voice sounds exhausted. Hopefully, she can rest after everyone sees she's fine.

As we get closer to campus, my stomach twists as I watch Callan turn every corner behind me, staying close.

Starting today, Gem and I have a blank slate. A brand new start. We both agreed to it on the way to the police station. Everything in the past is the past where it belongs.

But how can I move forward when I'm still holding back a huge secret from her? One that she might hate me completely for. I need to get it off my chest before it's too late.

"Gem, I know our blank slate starts today, but there's something I should've told you before." My voice comes out more nervous than I intend for it to.

From the side, I watch as she glances away from the window. "What is it, Noel?"

"I did something," I croak. Flashes of that night go through my head and I clutch the wheel tightly in my hands. I come to a stop at a stop light and turn to look at her.

"It's my fault he's dead."

She furrows her brows. "It's your fault that *who* is dead? My dad? We've been over this Noel. You know that you had nothing to do with it now."

I swallow hard and shake my head, glancing at her out of the corner of my eye, afraid of what her reaction might be.

"Heath. It's my fault."

She covers her mouth and shakes her head. "No. You couldn't have done anything to Heath. Why would you? The four of them killed him. They confessed to it."

Turning away I clench my teeth together as the light turns green.

"It was stupid and I know if I tell Callan, he'll never forgive me," I say in a low tone.

"What did you do?" she exclaims.

I open my mouth and tell her everything I remember from that night.

When I finish, she mumbles, "Oh my God. You need to tell him."

We stop in front of the sorority and she hops out.

I lean my head against the steering wheel.

She might be reconsidering everything now and if she decides not to be with me because of this, it'll be on me. Why do I deserve to be happy anyway while Heath is dead somewhere?

A knock sounds on the window and I shoot up to find Callan. He gives me a questioning look.

Slowly, I unbuckle my seatbelt and get out.

"Something wrong?"

I shake my head as my head starts to spin.

Tell him. I need to tell him.

I glance toward the stairs of ZDB and watch as Gem gets encompassed in a four way hug that becomes five when Mera runs over to join it.

My heart clenches.

"Come on, buddy," Callan says, clapping me on the shoulder.

He steers me around the car and I mindlessly follow. We eventually reach the steps where I slowly glance up to look at Gem.

Her eyes are full of disappointment.

The girls separate and Gem smiles at them. "I love you guys, but I really need to get some sleep right now." She glances at Collette. "And one more thing. Please, no more trash talking Noel. I know you guys have had your issues in the past and he's Callan annoying friend, but he and I are going to be together for the rest of our lives so you'd better get used to it sooner rather than later."

Collette's jaw drops and Luella and Ashlynn gasp.

"Are you serious?" Collette asks, completely shocked. "You want to spend your life with *him*?"

"He's the only one I want," Gem says, glancing my way.

Her eyes soften and she sighs. "I love him, and no matter what happens, it's him and I come hell or high water. I'll stand by him just as he'll stand by me."

Her words might seem like a normal declaration to love, but it's more than that for me. It's her knowing what I did and still loving me despite it.

My stomach flutters.

No one else gets it, but they all smile happily at her, including Collette.

I haven't lost Gem after all.

Her knowing the truth is a small weight off my shoulders. However, the unrelenting weight still remains.

I glance at Callan and he allows me to see a rare smile spread across his face.

I know that after he hears what I have to say it might be the very last time I see it.

CHAPTER TWENTY-FIVE

Noel

1 Year and 4 Months Ago

For the first party of the year, it sure is a fucking wild one.

Everyone is ready to let loose after a week full of boring classes.

Maybe I can find a girl to hook up with tonight. One who doesn't look at me with disgust like Gemma.

Wait, no.

I'm fucking Noel Hardington. Last night, I told her I would ask her out once more.

And I will.

I'm sure she's thought about it again and seen the error of

her ways. So, of course. I'll ask her out, naturally she'll accept, and we'll go find a nice quiet spot to get closer to each other.

As I'm thinking about it, I watch a guy across the yard talking to one girl and her friend. When she looks away as her friend gets up, the guy dumps something into her drink.

What a slime ball. I'm sure it's Rohypnol. He shoves the bag in his pocket and looks around like he's completely innocent.

With a sigh, I throw back the rest of my beer.

No one else seems to have noticed except me so I guess the right thing to do would be to stop her from leaving with him.

Her hand reaches for her cup as she turns back around to him.

Moving around the pool quickly I reach them as she puts the cup to her lips.

I slap it right out of her hand, letting the drink fall to the ground.

She gasps and fixes me with a glare. "What'd you fucking do that for?"

Out of the corner of my eye, I watch the guy next to her look at me with panic in his eyes.

Pulling the guy up, I reach right into his pocket, much to his displeasure, and yank out the baggie. My suspicions are confirmed when I notice the giant R on the side of the bag.

I shake it in her face. "*This* is why. He tried to roofie you."

A look of shock hits her face as she eyes the tiny bag of Rohypnol.

She reaches her hand out and slaps him, the sound resounding throughout the back and making everyone stop and look.

"Asshole," she shouts and turns around to leave.

"Hey! I don't even get a thank you?" I exclaim.

The party resumes and the dude tries to snatch the baggie out of my hands.

"Nope," I tell him, stashing it in my pocket. "You won't be drugging anyone else tonight."

Whirling around, I leave him with a wave in his direction.

He grunts and I feel pretty satisfied with myself, putting my hands in my pockets as I leave the back of the house and head inside.

To the left, I glance at the alcohol lining the wall. A big shiny bottle of Absolut is sitting unopened. That sounds right up my alley. I open it up and take a few big gulps, my throat burning as I pull it away from my lips.

My head starts to buzz and my face warms. "That's it," I murmur to myself. This is exactly the buzz I needed.

I drink about half of it before heading for the living room where the majority of the party is.

As I get closer, I notice her in the hallway next to it near the door. It must be my lucky night, I don't have to hunt her down.

From the looks of it, she's talking to Princess Mera. She glances past her, staring at me with wide eyes as I approach the two of them.

Mera turns around to face me after noticing Gemma's deer in the headlights expression.

"Princess," I greet her politely, before flicking my eyes over to Gemma. "Nice to see you again, Gem."

Her mouth thins as she completely ignores me, turning her attention back to Mera. "I have to go, Mera."

Her eyes harden behind her glasses as she slips between Mera and I to the living room.

"Where are you going, nerd?" slips out of my mouth. Nerd? That doesn't feel right on my tongue. I turn and follow her into the living room. I hear footsteps behind me until they stop, running into me when I finally grab Gemma's wrist.

"Let me go," she says in such a low tone, only I can hear.

At this moment, the music from one song is ending and another is beginning so any talking can easily be heard.

"Just hear me out. Let's go out once. Anywhere you want, my treat," I tell her with a smirk.

Gemma squares her shoulders and fixes me with an annoyed expression. "Not interested."

"Just give me a chance, I'm a pretty cool guy," I insist. "I'm not asking for us to do something crazy like fuck on the first date if that's what you're afraid of."

Though a lot of girls would happily volunteer if given the chance.

Her jaw clenches again, as she closes her eyes for a second and pushes her glasses up her nose before opening them. "No. How many times do I need to say it for you to understand?" She yells it and it echoes throughout the whole house. The entire fucking party around us comes grinding to a halt to stare as the opening threads of a song start.

I can feel all their eyes on me. How could she reject me so openly like this?

Fury flows through me as I glare at her. My face feels warmer. Is this the heat of rejection that other guys feel? Gemma's face pales slightly as she stares at me and tries once more to wrench my hand off her wrist.

But I'm not letting her get away so easily.

"We're going to talk somewhere private," I say in a low warning tone.

"Let go of her. She said no." I roll my eyes as Mera interjects.

I turn to her angrily for disturbing us. She backs up slightly as if she's afraid.

"Hey, I thought this was a party."

It would be but someone fucking turned the music down all so they could listen to this fucking conversation that could've been held privately.

Glancing behind her, I watch as Heath enters the living room, looking around. He looks at Mera, smiling at her. "There you are."

Of course it's fucking Heath. Mr. Perfect who's the cause of all of Callan's suffering. Try as he might, he still hasn't been able to live up to him no matter what he does.

Mera walks over to him and Heath puts an arm around her shoulder as she whispers something to him.

He squeezes her shoulder before letting it go and walking over to Gemma and I, stepping partially between us.

Now he wants to get in my way too. I grit my teeth as frustration builds.

"Why don't you let her go, man? She's just one girl. There are plenty of other girls interested."

He's right. There are plenty, but none of them are Gemma and now that she's embarrassed me like this, I won't let her go easily. Not until she chooses to go out with me and restore my record of no strikeouts.

Gemma catches me by surprise, wrenching her arm away with one hard tug.

She scowls at me while rubbing her wrist. "I'm not interested in going out with anyone. If I was, I'd go out with..." her eyes go over Heath, "someone like Heath. Too bad he's taken."

I catch edge of Heath's smile.

Him? This guy over me? The golden boy of course.

"You're sweet, Gemma," he responds to her.

I glare at him. Look how proud he is to get more admiration.

Wave after wave of rage hits me like a tidal wave. But it doesn't feel normal. It feels amped up. It's not normal rage. What is it?

Whatever it is, it doesn't matter, because I think it's time I teach Heath a lesson.

Smiling, I glance at Gemma. *"My bad, Gem."*

The tension in the room lessens and someone turns the music up, pulling their attention away from us.

I just need to sit back and wait for the right moment to present itself.

I glance from Mera to Heath. "Sorry."

They don't say anything, staring at me with unmoved expressions. In one smooth move, I turn and peel the baggie open, keeping it hidden inside my hand as I dump it in and jostle the bottle quickly to make it look as if I was just drunkenly moving the bottle around for a moment.

This should teach him a lesson. I hand Heath the half-drunk bottle of Absolut. "Here, have the rest, I wiped the top off. No germs."

Heath looks disdainfully at it.

Come on, take it. To my surprise, Mera comes over and accepts the bottle from me, handing it off to Heath. "Thanks Noel."

I smile even though I know she doesn't mean it because pretty soon, Heath will be knocked out. He won't get to have a good time at this party.

Heath takes several swigs and I smile as I watch it slide down his throat.

"Have a nice night," I say brightly. After one more glance

at Gemma, I leave. I chuckle as I palm the empty baggie in my hands.

Maybe someday he'll learn to stop trying to be a hero and let me have what I want.

And believe me when I say I will have Gemma someday.

Present - Five Days After Gemma's Rescue

In a few days we'll be leaving for Kardenia again to spend Christmas with Mera's family.

I've put this off for five days to focus on our last week of classes before Christmas break, but I can't put it off any longer. Before we go, I have to get this off my chest.

Luckily, no one's around except for the four of us and Kane, who's been avoiding everyone every chance he sees us.

All the other guys have already left. Some of them, last night.

Gem is on her way over so she can be my support when I tell him.

I thread my hand through my hair.

He deserves to know I drugged him that night.

I open my backpack and rifle through it to grab the baggie. Why have I even held on to it for so long?

No, I know. To remind myself I'm not a good person.

I'm fucked up and I hurt my best friend's brother.

The three of them are waiting outside for me.

As I leave my room, I feel my heart race. I stop myself from thinking about it, and just go. Down the stairs to the front door and out.

The three of them glance at me.

Callan looks at me curiously. "Why do you look as pale as a sheet, man?"

At that exact moment, Gem rounds the corner. But she isn't alone.

Mera, Luella, Ashlynn, and Collette are with her.

"Sorry" Gem mouths.

I wanted as small an audience as possible for this, but I guess I won't get that.

If Collette hated me before, she'll want to kill me now.

I glance at Callan nervously. "There's something I have to tell you before we hit the road."

He nods. "Go on."

My stomach twists into knots. "So a while back, Bradley told me that he drugged Heath the night Heath witnessed Nadine's rape."

Callan grimaces. "That asshole drugged him with Space Dust? No wonder he didn't do anything to help her that night."

I nod weakly. "Yeah."

"Okay," he says slowly. "Is that it? I mean you could've told me but I understand that there was a lot was going on and as shitty as it is, drugging is common. I wish that I could've eased his guilt before he died, but I know even if he did know he was drugged, he would've still beaten himself up over it."

I nod, my throat starting to dry out. "There's something else."

Glancing up, I lock eyes with my best friend. Since we were in diapers, we've played together. Through thick and thin, we've stuck together. In his fights I've supported him. When I got out of the mental hospital, he made me feel normal again until I forgot about it all together.

"I…" I hesitate and glance over at the sidewalk where Gem is standing with her arms wrapped around herself. She nods her head and I sigh. And finally, I let the words I've been holding in for months out. "I drugged Heath that night."

Multiple gasps fill the air from the girls. I don't know who emits them. Nothing comes out of Vincent or Tyrell's mouth. But what does happen is Callan approaches me, getting right in my face.

"Noel, tell me that isn't true," he says in a low tone. "Tell me that you wouldn't do something so stupid. That the brain that your parents valued so much would never tell you to drug someone."

His eyes hold a fury I've never seen directed at myself before.

"How?" he screams in my face.

I dig my fingernails into my palms as hard as I can. "I'm so sorry. I was fucking jealous and angry and drunk. It's not an excuse, I know that. It was the wrong thing to do. I confiscated a half-full baggie that night with Rohypnol in it from this guy who tried to drug a girl. I was trying to ask Gem out and he got in my way so I poured the rest of the Rohypnol in the bottle and gave it to him."

"And I drank it," Mera muses. "Heath and I both did."

Callan turns to look at her when she talks and he turns back to me, fury in his eyes as he grabs me by the shirt. "Rohypnol causes memory loss, Noel. You're the fucking reason she couldn't remember that night. Without that drug, he might've been strong enough to fight back against the four of them!"

"I didn't know!" I shout. "I didn't know until you told me she couldn't remember what happened that night. I'm sorry!"

He clocks me in the jaw hard and I stumble back. As I

right myself, he drags me off the porch, letting me hit the steps.

I cringe, but I allow it to happen because there's no stopping it. If I ever have a chance of being forgiven, I have to accept this and not stop him.

The girls separate as he throws me to the ground and gets on top of me. His punches are relentless as his knuckles hit my face over and over. My lips and nose bust open and my whole face feels sore. But I still accept it.

From behind him, I hear someone crying. It has to be Gem. Everyone else probably hates my guts right now.

I stare up at him with partially swollen eyes as he punches me over and over his eyes burning with rage. Eventually, I stop feeling it completely and everything turns black.

Gemma

Both Tyrell and Vincent hold me back as Callan punches Noel until he goes completely limp, no longer twitching with every punch.

"You're gonna kill him, Callan," I cry.

Callan stands up, his knuckles bloody and his face positively feral.

"I think that beating was more than enough," Mera adds quietly.

I push both Tyrell and Vincent off of me and rush over to him on the ground. Placing my palm on his chest, I sigh with relief when I feel his chest rising and falling.

"As of right now," Callan says slowly, "we're not friends

anymore. Any friend of mine wouldn't hurt my brother no matter what. If you guys still want him to come to Kardenia with us, that's fine, but I'll have nothing to do with him."

Grabbing Noel's hand I gently caress it, hoping that my touch will help him wake up.

Suddenly, the door opens and I turn to look as Kane walks out.

He laughs as his eyes shift over all of us.

"Careful who you trust, Callan," Kane says with a smirk. "I told you, didn't I."

Callan stalks over to him. "So you knew that Noel did that to Heath?"

Wait. Kane knew this entire time and he didn't say a word? Of course. His hatred for Callan runs deep.

"You're fucking sick, Kane," Collette snaps. "He was your brother too."

All of the laughter leaves Kane's eyes. "No, Coll, I did not have a brother. I had a person I was biologically related to who thought nothing of me up until the day he was killed. That's the end of it."

Heath's been dead for almost a year and Kane still has so much bitterness toward him?

A smile appears on his face again as he turns back to Callan. "*I told you,*" Kane says with a chuckle, "I watch and I learn things." Kane's eyes flick over us and he smirks. "You guys really are a secretive bunch aren't you. So many secrets, you don't know who you can trust. Hey, why don't I join you guys in Kardenia again so I can keep watching this train wreck of a group you guys have?"

Suddenly, I feel Noel's hand move under mine. I bring his hand up to my face and move his hand so he cups my cheek. Noel's eyes find mine. His bloody mouth opens and closes and then, abruptly, I notice tears parting the bloody mess on his face.

"It's going to be okay, Noel," I whisper to him. "I'm right here and I'm not leaving you."

Everyone else talks in the background but I keep my focus on him. At some point, I'll have to help lift him off the ground when he's ready.

I don't think anyone else will, but that's okay. I'm strong enough to help him on my own.

As they talk in the background, I lean down and press a kiss to his cheek.

"I'm sorry," he croaks. "Sorry that you fell in love with someone like me."

"Don't," I tell him as tears trickle down his face to land on the sidewalk. "I love you. Only place we can go is upward from here."

"I love you too. Only upwards," Noel repeats.

EPILOGUE

Gemma

Two Years Later

With a long yawn, I walk into the bathroom completely naked as I approach the mirror. I stare down at the body I once hated. That I once thought was grotesque. But today, right now, I think I'm looking pretty damn good. I smooth my curly hair back away from my face.

The sound of the door opening makes me look away from myself in the mirror to the person behind me. I watch as Noel walks in, sweaty from the gym. His eyes flare with passion when he notices I'm naked.

"Were you waiting for me, precious?"

"We need a shower before we go to the airport," I tell him.

"Then let's shower," he murmurs, moving close to me and placing a hand on my hip as he bends down to press a kiss to my neck.

Heat starts to pool between my legs as he backs away and I watch in the mirror as he strips down to nothing.

He goes to our shower first, urging me with his eyes to follow him. I'll never get over how big this shower is. Ten people could easily fit in here.

I step into the shower, stopping next to the shower head next to his. We both turn them on at the exact same time, keeping the dial between hot and cold, with his a little colder and mine a little hotter. He watches me with heated eyes as I grab my body wash and squirt it all over my body.

"Want help?" he asks with a cheeky grin.

I nod, glancing down at his hard dick. He gets right behind me and starts spreading the body wash all over my body with one hand.

"You know you can use both hands," I tell him, glancing back at him with a smile.

He shakes his head. "No can do, Jewel. I have something I need to keep safe."

"What are you talking about?" I ask, furrowing my brows.

Turning around, I watch as he kneels in front of me.

"Oh my God," I murmur excitedly.

"I think it's way past time that I ask you this question, precious. You are the greatest treasure I could ever hope to have. Will you marry me?"

We've been through so much in such a short amount of time. He's taken over the company and running it correctly. The formula for Space Dust is gone and all supplies disposed of. My aunt died from an overdose of it only a few months ago, and I've sold my childhood home to a lovely couple with a young daughter.

This is the next step in my life.

I feel choked up as I stare into his hopeful brown eyes.

"Yes!" I hold my hand out and he takes my hand, kissing the top of it. He slides the ring onto my finger and rises.

Leaning down slightly, his hands drift to my ass. His hands continue downward as he spreads my thighs apart and lifts me into the air. I let my hands rest on his shoulders as he puts me against the wall of the shower.

The steam from the water starts to fill the air.

"Now that we're engaged, let's practice making a baby," he murmurs.

I shake my head, but I can't help but smile at that. "We aren't ready yet, are we? We haven't even graduated yet."

"It's still fun to practice though, isn't it?" he asks mischievously, sliding me down slightly until his dick remains poised against my entrance.

"Let out every single moan, precious. Be as loud as you want in our house," he says as he lets me down and slides his dick right into me.

I gasp at the feeling as my back arches against the wall. "Mmm, Noel. Only once."

"They won't leave without us, promise." he says with a smirk, pulling his hips back and thrusting himself inside me.

Tingles go through my whole body. I'll never get tired of this feeling.

I squeeze my fingers into his shoulders as he fucks me hard, showing me exactly how much I'm his and he's mine.

"I love you so fucking much, Gem."

"I love you too," I say with a moan, shamelessly pushing my hips down onto him.

After our steamy session in the shower, we race to the airport to make it in time. As we pull up, I smile at our friends who wave at us with knowing grins.

Shivering, I clutch my jacket tighter around myself. It's so cold today.

As I stick my hand inside, I feel something brush against my hand.

Like paper.

Did I stuff a receipt in here or something? I pull it out to find it's a note. Noel sets our bags down in front of us. "What's that?"

I unfold it and read it in my head.

Thank you for being a good friend to my sister. Keep this note to yourself, please.

What the hell is this?

I show it to Noel and he looks as utterly confused as I feel.

A good friend to their sister?

This handwriting is too neat, like it's been practiced to look this perfect.

There's only one person who could've written this note.

I glance over at Mera to find her and Callan close together.

I should tell her. She deserves to know if her sister is still alive after all this time. But this note says to keep it to myself.

"What are you going to do?" Noel asks quietly.

I stare at the note for a second more before shoving it right back in my pocket.

"If this note is real, and I believe it is, I'm going to do whatever I can to find her for Mera so she can get some clarity on how it all interconnects before she takes the crown."

Noel nods and glances over at them. "I understand and I'll help you, but don't get your hopes up if our search leads to another dead end. They've been trying to find Cate for years and they still haven't been able to."

"I won't," I reassure him.

I'm sure this wasn't the intended purpose for this note, but it's the only thing I can do.

Cate is out there somewhere and she's either staying away on purpose or she's in danger.

Luella

Present

I nervously watch as Gemma cries over Noel as he's sprawl out on the concrete. I hate that this is happening like this.

Callan and Noel were such good friends, I hope they find their way back to each other.

Sighing deeply, I turn away and walk to the edge of the porch, looking out at the empty street. I breathe in the cool air and smooth my blonde locks back as the breeze flows through them.

"What are you thinking about?"

I freeze and clench my hands together.

Don't turn around. Don't turn around.

"El."

I shut my eyes tightly and then whirl around to look into his icy blue ones. "Don't call me that. I don't know you. When will you get it through your skull?" I whisper harshly.

Tyrell's eyes harden. "I-I'm sorry. I just want you to remember."

"In my own time, I will, maybe," I say, glancing away and back to him.

Every look he gives me causes my heart to pound faster. I can't fucking breathe.

"Why can't you just give me a brand new chance, a new start until it comes back to you?"

I shake my head. "I don't want to. Now why don't you do us all a favor and leave me alone."

His eyes harden. "I've been nothing but nice to you and y-yet you t-treat m-me like…"

"Like what?" I burst.

He shakes his head and turns away. "N-nothing. S-s-sorry."

I breathe a sigh of relief as he goes back to Vincent.

As I look back at the street, I feel my phone ring in my pocket. My heart clenches as I dig it out. *Please be spam. Please be spam.*

But no, of course it's that stupid skull emoji I see. I've already let it ring a few rings too long.

After clicking the accept button, I raise the phone to my ear. "Yes?"

"Is that the correct way to answer your phone, Lu?"

I shiver and shake my head even though he can't see it. "No," I respond weakly.

"Then what is the correct response?" he asks.

I take a deep breath and breathe, "Hi Daddy."

"That's correct. Now, you're leaving soon so I need you to come and have dinner with me tonight. You're coming aren't you?"

I don't respond and he asks again more insistently. "Aren't you?"

"I am," I say quickly.

He grunts. "Good. I'll see you in a few hours. Love you."

"Love you too," I say and wait for him to hang up first. When the line beeps as he hangs up, I breathe a sigh of relief and stare down at my phone.

This will probably be the last trip I get to go on with my friends so I should enjoy it.

A tear slips down my cheek at the thought of never seeing any of them again.

Soon, it'll be a reality.

The story and mystery will continue in *The Poet and the Bully* on preorder now - https://www.tiffanyransier.com/the-poet-and-the-bully

If you'd like to discuss and chat about all things Goldsworthy U with other readers and I, please join us in the spoiler room - https://www.facebook.com/groups/goldsworthyuniversityspoilerroom

For news and updates, you can sign up to my newsletter - https://www.tiffanyransier.com/newsletter

CHARACTER GUIDE

Wilhelmera (Mera) Karden - Youngest princess of Kardenia, daughter to Edric and Annabeth Karden, younger sister to Mary Catherine, Callan's girlfriend (future fiancé)

Mary Catherine (Cate) Karden - Oldest princess of Kardenia, daughter to Edric and Annabeth Karden, older sister to Wilhelmera, currently missing

Edric Karden - King of Kardenia

Annabeth Karden - Queen of Kardenia, alumni of SGU, former treasurer of ZDB

Callan Goldsworthy - Youngest son of Antoure and Marguerite Goldsworthy, twin to Collette Goldsworthy, Mera's boyfriend (future fiancé)

Heath Goldsworthy - Oldest son of Legis Silverstone and Marguerite Goldsworthy; half older brother of Callan,

Collette, Nadine, and Kane; Mera's former fake boyfriend; dead

Collette (Coll) Goldsworthy - Only daughter of Antoure and Marguerite Goldsworthy, younger sister to Heath, twin sister of Callan

Nadine Silverstone - Only daughter of Legis Silverstone, older sister to Kane, younger sister to Heath, Kori's girlfriend

Kane Silverstone - Youngest son of Legis Silverstone, younger brother to Nadine and Heath

Scarlett - Mera's first roommate and best friend, Peyton's best friend

Peyton - Mera's other first roommate and best friend, Scarlett's best friend, accidentally placed in the female dorm

Luella Iverson - Shy childhood friend to Collette

Noel Hardington - Cocky playboy childhood friend to Callan, resident smart boy, Gemma's boyfriend (future fiancé)

Gemma Brighton- Newest addition to Collette's inner circle, resident smart girl, Noel's girlfriend (future fiancé)

Vincent - Pretty boy with a temper, Callan's childhood friend, stepbrother to Ashlynn

Ashlynn Browning - Outspoken, Collette's childhood friend, stepsister to Vincent

Tyrell Sonnenfeld - Callan's high school friend, quiet and reserved

Kori - Nadine's girlfriend

AUTHOR'S NOTE

Hi! Thanks for reaching the end. If you liked The Nerd and the Bully, please leave a review! It helps a ton. Gemma and Noel's background are very personal to me. I hope you'll continue to follow along with the story to find out more in Luella's book. All questions will be answered, I promise!

Tiffany

ALSO BY TIFFANY RANSIER

State Family

Alaska

Nebraska

Georgia

Goldsworthy University

The Princess and the Bully

The Nerd and the Bully (this book)

The Poet and the Bully

The Beauty and the Bully

The Ballerina and the Bully

ABOUT THE AUTHOR

Tiffany Ransier is a USA Today Bestselling multi-genre author. She loves writing twisty, heart-stopping novels. She has a love for diving in to different worlds and making theories about books and shows.

She lives in SoCal with her boyfriend James Ransier, another author. They are the parents of an adorable Siberian Husky/Shiba Inu mix named Peg.

When she's not writing or reading, she's swimming in her pool and obsessing over anime.

facebook.com/TiffanyRansier

twitter.com/authtiffransier

instagram.com/authortiffanyransier

goodreads.com/TiffanyRansier

bookbub.com/authors/tiffany-ransier

Made in the USA
Monee, IL
06 October 2022